Starving Hearts

A Novel

by
Lynn Ruth Miller

ISBN 0-615-11671-X
excentric press
Pacifica, CA

Published by:
excentrix press
441 Brighton Road
Pacifica, CA 94044
ISBN 0-615-11671-X

Second Edition - February 2001

Cover Design
Julia Gaskill, AVK

Cover Art
EMPTY TABLE
Lynn Ruth Miller

Dedicated to my mother
whose own unhappiness crushed us both.

This story is the product of the author's imagination.
Only the suffering is real.

IN APPRECIATION

I want to thank Robert Reed for his encouragement and all the hand holding he did to make this book a published reality. Without him, I would have had no idea how to begin this very long and rewarding process.

My thanks to Joan Pasch and Nancy Merchant who gave the book its final editing and made me feel that my story has something of value to say to the rest of the world..

Special thanks goes to Janis Alger whose faith in me and in the importance of this novel to others has taken the immense risk of publishing its first limited edition. It is this initial printing that will sell my story to a larger, national and international audience. Bouquets to Anny Cleven whose belief in the importance of the novel will pave its way to national recognition.

Comments about

STARVING HEARTS

a novel about eating disorders, verbal abuse and
Jewish life in the 'fifties
by
Lynn Ruth Miller

A page turner, *STARVING HEARTS* by Lynn Ruth Miller is the portrayal of a girl
growing up verbally abused, trying to cope in the only way she knows: good girls
clean their plate" and "pleasing daughters ask for seconds." I couldn't set this book
down.

Patrician Evans
Evans Interpersonal Communications Institute

I thought *STARVING HEARTS* was very effective -sometimes to the point of being
harrowing. The use of detail is very telling. It's not just that Susan is eating
everything in sight; it's that she's eating the kinds of food that were symbolic of
middle-class fifties prosperity - women's magazine cooking. People who are
nostalgic for the fifties don't remember what it was really like; how restricted the
social roles were; what a traitor you were if you didn't want the things your parents
could provide you that they couldn't afford as children.

Ann Singer
Librarian, Lerhaus Judaica

STARVING HEARTS by Lynn Ruth Miller leads the reader through a poignant,
personal journey through the hell that underlies and runs eating disorders. This
journey is filled with the aching despair that manifests in anorexic and bulimic
symptoms from which the main character suffers. This particular telling is
exquisitely layered, with brief moments of perspective and compassion lessening the
searing pain of the main character's anguish. . . The book offers the hope that the pit
of despair may prove the entry-way into the beginning of the recovery process.

Deborah Brenner-Liss, Ph.D.
Director, Association of Professionals Treating Eating Disorders

STARVING HEARTS was very painful for me to read, probably the most painful book
I have read in my life except the one about how the Japanese mothers killed their
babies when they were forced to by enemy soldiers. Every time I got up from the
computer I was shaking, and still was shaking even after an hour break. Some
involuntary screaming, some crying, a lot of kleenex. A quite different thing from
your average sad book where you use up kleenex but it's a purifying sadness. So
consider what I did a LABOR of love. Which is not to say it's not a great book. It's a
great book! This deserves to be a national book. You will be on Oprah, I kid you not.

It reads very well, and it feels to me like real life. I am very sorry to hear that your mother was far more abusive than Jean was. My mother, I would say, was sometimes like Jean in her better moments, and at times just as mean as Jean, but probably my mother was not mean such a large percentage of the time as Jean was. Once Mother told me about how she did nothing but scream and scream in horror when I was born because here she had given birth to a freak, and then later she said she was just kidding, and she had been loving to me when I was first brought to her. She thought this 'joke' very funny. (I could never figure out which version was the truth, but the screaming one was given in a more truthful manner.) So you can see she had a mean streak, and enjoyed making me feel rejected. -- Your mother must have been -- well, there's hardly a word for it, is there? But if your mother was worse, then yes, thank heavens you toned it down for the book. No one would have ever believed it. Some people won't believe it the way it is. But I have no trouble believing that a woman like Jean could exist (and be living a so-called 'normal' life). It feels dreadfully familiar.

Just a couple days ago I was talking with Nancy Merchant, and she was saying how much she liked your novel, and how good she thought it was. Not everyone manages to be good at both art and literature, you're amazing.

Joan Pasch
Poet

What a book! Great ending. I'd been wondering as the pile of unread pages dwindled how you were going to end it, or where you were going to end it, and ending it with a beginning was an excellent choice.(There will be a sequel, won't there be?) For some reason, your mother's *War With The Roses*, as it were, really resonated. The over arching theme of women's constricted options in the 50's really comes across, too. But also how that had been carried forward from the constricted options of previous generations, and how people unwittingly re-created family hells all for themselves, despite seeming free choice. What was also very good was how at different points heroes and villains within your family switched places, and even Debbie has her good moments (few!). Actually, I would have milked even the vicious dog running away for a few laughs! He couldn't take it either! And the funny thing about it all, or perhaps "ironic" is a better word, is that you're a superb food writer. I was very moved by the novel. So moved I was immobile, actually, another one of those ironies. We lack good published first-person feminist narratives of the Fifties. You'd be filling an important void. Oh, and your speech throwing Michael out of your life is in a league with Nora's more famous one in "The Doll House".

Michael McGuire; author, educator

"This book does a great job of describing some of the family dynamics that contribute to anorexia and bulimia. I certainly identified with it. It did a great job of describing my family. The parallels between your family and mine are mind blowing. I have noticed a difference between the eating disorder folks of our age and the young kids with anorexia and bulimia. I suspect the difference has something to do with growing up with parents who had to cope with the Depression and mothers who had more limited expectations and choices than those available to the moms of today. Thanks for letting me read the book. You have every right to be very proud of it."

Jean Rubel, Th.D., ANRED
Anorexia Nervosa & Related Eating Disorders, Inc.

STARVING HEARTS explores the complex relationship between food, love, body image and identity. It describes in great depth the painful cycle of eating disorders in which the obsession with food and the drive for thinness attempt to drown out the raging and destructive critical voices within."

Carol Normandi, co-author
IT'S NOT ABOUT FOOD

A moving and passionate account of solitude and a life at the edge of time and human affection. *STARVING HEARTS* is written from the heart of a woman always alone.

Marjorie Agosin, Wellesley College, Department of Spanish;
author of UNCERTAIN TRAVELERS; THE ALPHABET IN MY HANDS;
A CROSS AND A STAR, et al

STARVING HEARTS is a stunning portrait of the 1950's, the girls going for the MRS. Degree, feeling like failures if all college has prepared them for is a teaching degree. And the concept of the mother who only loves her daughter while the daughter eats, fixing all these amazing foods, while Susan alternates between anorexia and bulimia, it's a perfect vehicle. Good work!

Rochelle Ratner, Editor
BEARING LIFE & AMERICAN BOOK REVIEW

Although a serious and topical story, the author has brought her trademark humor to *STARVING HEARTS*, making it inspirational and enlightening.

Chris Hunter, Editor & Publisher
The Pacific Tribune

A moving, evocative narrative . . .

Phyllis Deutsch, Editor
University Press of New England

Out of one woman's pain has come a compelling and well-written novel that touches the soul. I am certain that it will find a devoted and large audience. A stunning accomplishment!

Marsha Lee Berkman, Editor
HERE I AM, The Jewish Publication Society

I just closed the cover on *"Starving Hearts"* and I want to congratulate you on having written a wonderful memoir. There are so many things to say about the book, what comes out to me as a reader, is that the entrapped women of the 1940's/1950's are so essentially voiceless. Quite frankly, it sounds like an absolutely horrible time to have been a woman in America, so limiting and constricting, so much pressure to conform to only one ideal of womanhood. You lived through it, you survived it, and you are able to tell the incredible tale. I don't think I've ever read any memoirs about women in the 1940's/1950's quite as insightful as yours.

Dr. Adam Strassberg,
Stanford University Hospital, Dept.. of Psychiatry

I've started reading STARVING HEARTS and think it is very good. It's certainly very good writing and the subject should be of great interest to women.

Sarah Anne Walz,
Marketing Manager, University of Iowa Press

I really enjoyed your book. Actually, it was like reading my own life story. *STARVING HEARTS* had great humor in parts even though it was a true story, your true story. The story is so much like my life that I had to laugh at certain parts.

Debby Hester
Special Education, Redwood City, CA

This novel is a blow by blow account the horrors of anorexia and bulimia.....The book serves as a wake up call to parents and reminds them to be mindful of the words, tone of voice and body stance that they use when talking with children and the possible deleterious effects on the children's perceptions of themselves and their world.

Esther Kletter
Book Reviewer & educator, Sunnyvale, CA

STARVING HEARTS raises issues on a topic of great relevance to society today. I found your discussion enlightening, particularly in the way you showed how dysfunctional family dynamics and using food as a reward/controlling mechanism can be a significant cause of eating disorders.

David Chard
Community Relations Manager
BARNES & NOBLE, Colma, CA.

STARVING HEARTS is a damn good book. It captures the color, jargon and flavor of the fifties. The author has successfully lured us into her world of cuisine, the diet/overeating cycle of anorexia and bulimia and the pain that creates it. The novel is a good read, inspirational and a gutsy overview of the fifties.

Anna Booth
Feature Writer, Teacher and Reviewer

Just finished reading your book *STARVING HEARTS* and I wanted to tell you how much I enjoyed it. It wasn't easy reading though as I knew it was based on fact. Brought me to tears on more than one occasion.

Linda Klein,
Reader and Critic, San Carlos, CA

STARVING HEARTS is a powerful book! A brave job - - thank you for getting it out there!

Aletha Nowitsky,
Ashland, Oregon

You certainly painted a very powerful picture of one family destroyed by anorexia and bulimia. It has helped me to appreciate what a devastating thing anorexia can be. I am sure many other people have found their understanding of the condition expanded by reading it.

Columba Corbett, Co.
Galway, Ireland

STARVING HEARTS is a stunning portrait of the 1950's, the girls going for the MRS. Degree, feeling like failures if all college has prepared them for is a teaching degree. ...it's a perfect vehicle. Good work!

Rochelle Ratner, editor of BEARING LIFE &
AMERICAN BOOK REVIEW

Susan Talberg is a woman we all know. She is our sister, our cousin, our best friend, our classmate. We see her as an attractive, happy, bright, well adjusted young woman. We think we know who she is, but only she knows what happens behind closed doors. She longs for love, comfort, caring and support, but hides her feelings well: her emptiness, her loneliness, her anger, her insecurity and fear. In STARVING HEARTS, Lynn Ruth Miller paints Susan in intricate detail. We long to reassure and help her, but must watch as she falls, until she is finally able to admit her loss of control and reach out for help. Those of us who have lived with obsessions, compulsions or addictions will recognize Susan's painful journey.

Marcia Cohn Spiegel is the co-author of The Jewish Woman's Awareness Guide and the founder of the Alcohol/Drug Action Program of Jewish Family Service, Los Angeles and L'Chaim: 12 Steps to Recovery

Prologue

Life never lets you win, does it, Susan? You are trapped forever in your mother's house. She plays with you like a cat teasing a wounded mouse and you cannot escape her. You are too weak. You are too stupid. You are worthless.

I am not hungry.

I have demolished the gigantic dinner my mother cooked. My stomach is distended and my body feels like it will explode. I loosen my belt, but the elastic waistline of my dress slices into my abdomen. My heart thunders against my ribs and I have great difficulty moving my body. I have finished cleaning the kitchen. The plates are in the dishwasher; the floor is swept; the sink is scoured. I take off my apron and hang it on a hook behind the door.

I open the refrigerator and pull out a large platter of roast beef. It smells like heaven to me. I take it to the counter and remove its plastic wrap. The meat is chilled and the gravy has congealed. Sliced onions and flecks of garlic are embedded in the brown clumps of fat on the plate.

I slice the beef and stuff it into my mouth. The fat is so thick it coats my fingers like Vaseline. The carving knife slips from my grasp. I wipe my hands on a paper towel and clutch the handle once more. I hack a second slab of meat from the roast and swallow it whole. Thick, yellow globules roll down my chin. My face glistens with cooked grease. My teeth tear into even more of the slick, fibrous mass of beef while I chop off another slice.

I stare at the roast but I don't see it. My shaking hands force the food into my mouth faster and faster. I swallow huge, lumpy chunks of meat. I peel the fat off the top of the roast and stuff it into my mouth. The pungent smell of cooked beef clings to my clothes. It fills my nose and I cannot breathe. I gulp down lumps of gristle laced with handfuls of fat. I gag. But I cannot stop eating. I don't taste meat; I taste hatred.

Chew and swallow, chew and swallow. Eat Susan. Eat so you won't think. Your marriage has crumbled and you have returned to hell.

My face is flushed; my jaws ache. My chest burns and I gasp for air.
God, my mouth is dry! I reach for the coffee pot.

Cold coffee. That's what I need. Cold coffee with thick, buttery cream and sweet, sticky sugar.

I try to pour the liquid from the pot sitting on the stove but the kettle slides through my fingers and falls to the floor. The coffee spreads over my toes and spatters my stockings. OH, MY GOD! It is staining my mother's linoleum!

I take a paper towel and try to mop it up but I cannot bend. My stomach is a giant beach ball; my dress, a prison. I drop the dishtowel to the floor and push it with my foot.

Hurry, Susan. Hurry. Eat your mother's potato kugel. Peel off the crust. Tear it with your slippery, grease caked fingers. Stuff it into your mouth. Chew faster, Susan. Chew. Are you proud of me, now, Mother? I have eaten every-thing you cooked. **There are NO leftovers!**

Gluey wads of potato pudding slip from my hand. They land at my feet and dirty my mother's immaculate linoleum. I squat to the ground, but I can't pick them up. I clutch at a chair to steady myself. It topples over and takes me with it. I land on my bottom and my head cracks against the table leg. I use both hands to gather the spattered mass of kugel that covers my mother's kitchen floor.

My stomach throbs; my vision blurs and the room spins around me. I close my eyes and I hear my mother speak: "I know you, Susan. You'd never make a decent wife. You're too willful. You're too stubborn. You're too selfish. You have only yourself to blame for this mess you're in. Only yourself."

I'm trying to make you happy, Mother. Look. I'm eating your chocolate pie. Sweet, sticky blobs of brown custard smear my fingers and push under my nails. A smudge is on my cheek; another on my arm. Whipped cream fell on my shoe. . . the suede Andrew Geller pump we bought when we shopped for my wedding trousseau. Remember?

Look, Mother. I'm scooping up your cauliflower soufflé with my hands. It spills through my fingers and slides down my chin. It stains my pretty party dress: the one from Saks that says Dry Clean Only.

The soft, white mass of eggs, onions and vegetable disappear down my gullet. It chases after the beef and the kugel. It lands on the pie and splashes into the coffee. My body feels like it will explode and I am glad. I deserve to die. I am useless.

Here's some cheesecake from last night. Oh, that feels good going down. So smooth; so cool, so sweet. I gulp my coffee. I push bread in my mouth. I cut another chunk of beef and I eat that too.

I pause. I sob and hug myself tight.

Look at yourself, Susan. You are despicable. Food is drizzling down your chin. Your eyes are glazed and your face is stained with pie and spots of cau-liflower. Your hands are so gummy, your fingers stick together.

What would Daddy say if he saw you doing this?

I bury my head in my arms and my grief overwhelms me.

Oh, God! What would he say?

I look at the butcher knife on the counter. I pick it up and grip it in my trembling hand. The blade is covered with grease and flecked with bits of meat. I hold out my arm and look at the blue, bulging veins throbbing in my wrist.

Now, Susan. Cut them now and it will be all over.

I raise the knife and then I pause. My tears overflow and they pour down my face.

I can't do it. I'm so weak I can't even manage the only act that will save me. I am a fool.

My stomach is going to split. If I don't stop eating, I will be fat as an elephant. I'll have arms like my mother. I'll waddle like Debbie. I will be as disgusting to everyone as I am to myself.

I stagger upstairs to the bathroom. I push my fingers down my throat and throw up. Then again. I take a suppository and wait.

Nothing.

I take two more.

There.

I flush the toilet and collapse into bed.

I fast for a week. I drink black coffee. I smoke and smoke and then I smoke some more. I cry. My throat is raw, my fingers tremble and my eyes are swollen shut. I want my marriage back but I don't want my husband. I am afraid of my husband. I hate my husband. I weep for the home I once had, the one I thought would be my refuge. I have nowhere to hide anymore.

I can see the villain who has destroyed me. I see her now in the bathroom mirror. I clench my fist and shatter that bloated face.

I nurse my bleeding hand and crawl into the kitchen to heat some coffee.

Oh, look. Cold chicken.

Part I: 1948 ~ 55

❧ Chapter 1 ❧

That was not the first time that I gorged myself with food I didn't want. My bizarre eating habits began when I was a child, and by the time I was a senior in college, need no longer governed my appetite. Food became a monster that crippled my life for eight horrible years. This book is the story of why I felt those mysterious hungers and my struggle to overcome them. I thought it was my stomach that cried for nourishment. I know now it was my empty heart.

Eating disorders were not in fashion in the fifties. I had no idea that others suffered as I did and I couldn't understand the compulsions inside me. I had never heard that people tried to starve themselves because they thought they didn't deserve nourishment. I still shudder when I remember how frightened I was. I couldn't understand what forced me to stuff myself with everything and anything edible or why I was tortured with fears of obesity. I thought I was hopelessly insane.

Even now, forty years later, I am haunted with the fear that something within me will snap, and once again I will become the irrational glutton I was in my twenties.

My family lived in Toledo, Ohio, a small, industrial city near the Michigan border. My father was a successful optometrist, and my mother had no need to work outside the home. My parents had traveled a long way up the economic scale from their childhood. They grew up during the Depression and knew hunger and deprivation I only read about. My mother wore the same dress to school every day until it hung in shreds and she never had enough to eat. My father fell in love with her when they were in the sixth grade, but I don't think she ever cared for anything but what he could give her. As soon as she finished high school, she and Daddy became engaged. They were wed on a Friday night at the height of the Depression. They went to Chicago for their honeymoon and my father was fitting glasses at nine that Monday morning. My mother reported to her job at the B.&O. Railroad. She worked there until the end of the Second World War.

The war brought my parents a new measure of economic security, and they were able to buy a three story mansion on an acre of land in a quiet, tree lined neighborhood far away from their childhood memories. It cost $9980 and my father paid off the mortgage in ten years. My mother hired a maid to help her clean her new home and a woman who came in once a week to do her ironing. She had an army of appliances to mix her cakes and wash her dishes. She had a disposal in her kitchen sink and she cleaned floors with a vacuum cleaner. Her mother scrubbed the linoleum on her hands and knees. My mother wouldn't dream of destroying her nylons that way.

After the war, Daddy opened his own optometrist's office and had enough money to indulge himself in miniature cameras and funny suits with big padded shoulders he called Zoot Suits. My mother no longer chose her dresses from the rack at Tiedtke's Ready to Wear. She shopped in Toledo's most exclusive dress shops and had her hair done every week by a charming man named David. People whispered that he was gay but my mother said it was impossible. "How could he be?" she asked. "He's Jewish."

Mother and Daddy could afford to vacation in Florida now, and they gave my sister and me ballet and piano lessons. Even so, my mother was careful to turn out the lights to save electricity and was incapable of throwing away an article of clothing or a morsel of food. She had survived on hand-me-downs and the butcher's scraps. She never forgot it.

My mother's parents came to this country at the turn of the century. When they moved to Toledo, they found a home on Baker Street where everyone spoke Yiddish, even the shopkeepers. I used to love to visit my bubbe and zayde. Their words were difficult to understand, but their love was not. I couldn't believe that the tiny little woman whose house smelled of roast chicken and gefilte fish was actually my mother's mother. She dressed in long cotton dresses covered with a big white apron and her hair was wound into a bun at the nape of her neck. When she smiled at me, her teeth were capped in gold and after she had kissed, hugged and fed me, she would pull me on her lap and teach me Yiddish melodies that made me smile and tap my feet. She called me her shayner meidele and even though I didn't have the faintest notion what that meant, I knew it was a good thing to be.

My mother was determined to be a typical American housewife like the ones she read about in Good Housekeeping magazine. She dressed in skirts that were just below her knees and wore high heeled shoes even while she was cleaning the house. She filled our home with popular music. She bought Perry Como's records and knew all the words to most of Bing Crosby's hits. She could sing along with Kate Smith and the Andrews Sisters, too, but she never sang about draydles and mazel in her American home. That was part of her past and she wanted to forget it.

I can still remember when I was in the first grade and I invited little Hymie

Schwartz to come over after school. He had started school in the middle of the year and I felt very sorry for him because no one could understand what he said. His words made perfect sense to me because he sounded like my cute little grandma. When I brought the little boy into our kitchen, my mother smiled and said, "Would you like some chopped liver and schmaltz, Hymie?"

The child nodded and I said, "Me, too, Mama?"

My mother scowled at me as if I had uttered an obscenity. "You know *we* don't eat greasy foods like that, young lady. That little boy is a refugee. *We* are American citizens."

My parents prided themselves on leaving the immigrant ghetto of their childhood but when they moved, they created their own comfortable, familiar community around them. Right after they bought our house, Aunt Evelyn and Uncle Max found a bungalow four doors away and two years later, Uncle Harry and Aunt Sarah moved into a white frame house a block away from us.

Aunt Evelyn was my mother's sister and Uncle Harry was her brother. Uncle Harry was a druggist and reminded me of a lovable clown. He told little jokes that made you laugh in spite of yourself. Every time he came to visit, he brought quarts and quarts of strange flavored ice cream. "This one is tutti-frutti with cranberry, Jean," he'd tell my mother. "Sealtest is promoting it for the holidays."

And Mother would thank him and put it in the freezer next to the coco-banana tropical ice (Hawaiian Special of the Month) and the strawberry-plum French creme Purity created for Bastille Day.

He and Aunt Sarah had twin girls who looked exactly alike and always dressed in identical clothes. I could never tell them apart so I called both of them Lois/Sally. They were my sister Debbie's age and she always knew which was which. "Lois has a brighter smile, Susie, and Sally is skinnier," she explained.

But they looked like carbon copies to me: tall, thin and brittle, with high, shrill giggles over things that were never very funny.

Before I started college, I wore Daddy's cast off shirts and rolled up jeans that sagged at the hips. My skirts swiveled around my waist and their zippers refused to stay where they belonged. I had long hair I rolled up in my father's old socks every night. It was supposed to comb out into a sleek, shining page boy but it never did. It had a disgusting texture: wispy and filled with cowlicks that made it look angry and alive and flew around my head like cobwebs caught in a fan.

Mother always told me I was a mess. "You look absolutely filthy, Susan," Mother would say. "Why didn't you wash your face before dinner?"

My eyes always filled with tears when she said things like that because I had scrubbed my skin until it burned.

"My God, Susan," my mother would say. "You are such a klutz! The way you lumber around, you look like a football player with a pantsful. Don't hunch up like that."

When I looked in the mirror, I knew she was right. I was a slob.

I certainly looked nothing like my mother. She was a cute little dumpling of a woman who loved to dress. Even her housecoats looked like fashion clips for Mrs. Casual. She was always meeting Aunt Evelyn after the beauty shop and the two of them would go shopping. That was her idea of the perfect afternoon.

She brought home wonderful things: laces and satins from Geralda's, or hats I never dreamed anyone could invent. And no matter how bizarre those hats were in their boxes, they looked marvelous on her. I remember one straw number with an open crown and a jaunty rainbow of feathers in front. Oh, how I loved that hat! But when I sat it on my flyaway hair, I looked like a farce from the twenties.

In my family, personal appearance was very important. My mother spent hours grooming herself before she went out and even when she came down to breakfast in her designer robe, her hair was combed and her face made up. My mother's fingernails were manicured every week, and I never saw her in a wrinkled dress. When Mama dressed to go out, she looked like a model for Cosmopolitan magazine. She was really beautiful, and I was sure that was the only possible reason my Daddy loved her. My mother was an angry woman and her targets were Daddy and me.

I do not remember one single time in my life when she hugged me or gave me a kiss. Sometimes, I would try to kiss her cheek to say hello the way my sister Debbie did, but my mother always pulled away from me. "Don't bother me, Susan," she would say. "Can't you see I'm cooking dinner?"

Every time I gave her a compliment, she'd say, "Don't try to butter me up, Susan. Your sweet words have no more substance than cotton candy. You're nothing but a hypocrite, young lady. I see right through you."

But she didn't see me at all. She never saw the tears that soaked my pillow after she attacked me. She only saw the mistakes I never intended to make.

She was just as harsh with my father, but for some reason, he didn't seem bothered by her cruel jabs. I was the one who flinched when she attacked him. "Can't you lift a finger to help around here?" she'd scream at Daddy when he came home from the office. "I put in just as hard a day as you do, Leonard. Just as hard. Why can't you hang up your coat and pick up your papers? You're not a boarder here, you know. It's your house, too."

Daddy would lean down to kiss her and she'd turn away. "I don't need your kisses, Leonard. I'm too busy," she'd say.

I guess that's what happens to most marriages. Love fades away and the couple barely tolerate each other. Well, that wouldn't happen to <u>my</u> marriage. I would pamper my sweet husband and we would always adore each other. I was determined to marry someone as wonderful as my Daddy and be gentle and kind to him. I would cook him lots of good dinners and let him relax with the paper as much as he wanted. I would never yell. I would never nag. I would just smile and kiss him a lot.

I never understood why Daddy and I were my mother's enemies. I was too young and too much her victim to realize she had unsatisfied hungers that drove her to punish us. Instead, my heart broke for my father and I forced myself to endure my mother for his sake. He said I made <u>his</u> life miserable when I argued with her because she took it out on him. And he was right. I heard her complaining about me all the time.

"The president of your fan club left her room in a mess again, today," she'd report to my exhausted father when he finally got home from the office. "And I'm the one who has to pick up after her." or "Miss Prima Donna was in the bathroom for two hours this afternoon! It was deliberate, Leonard, I <u>know</u> it was. She <u>knew</u> I had to get dressed to take Debbie to her lesson. <u>Two</u> hours, Leonard! She seems to think you and she are the only ones who matter in this house."

If I ever entertained a hope that my mother could love me, it vanished when I was fifteen. I was going downstairs after I finished studying for my world history test. I wanted to get some milk and chocolate doughnuts to calm the willies I always had before every exam. As I passed my parents' bedroom, I heard my mother screaming at Daddy, as usual. I stopped to listen and feel sorry for my father.

Then, I realized my mother <u>wasn't</u> screaming. She was sobbing. "How can you ask such a thing? All I ever hear from you is 'Susan needs this' and 'Susan wants that,'" she cried. "What about Debbie? What about me? You have no right to tell me how to run this house. You're never here. You stay out until God knows when doing God knows what while I do all your dirty work. I cook. I clean. I shop. I schlep those girls to lessons, go to their PTA meetings and cover for you while you make time with your patients or pick ups at the local bars. And what thanks do I get? None. Not from you and not from your number one supporter. She's always defying me, always whining, 'Daddy said I could' or 'Daddy won't let you treat me this way.'

"She makes me sick. She litters the house and monopolizes the phone. She doesn't lift a finger to help me out. Never. She thinks she's a princess and I'm her slave. She obviously takes after you, Leonard. Obviously. Sometimes I hate her just because she hates me so much. She thinks you're perfect but I know better. She doesn't do your laundry, Leonard. I do.

"Now, you want me to take time from my busy day to give her driving lessons so she can take my car away from me. Well, I won't do it. I'm not going to groom her to have another weapon to use against me. I'm tired, Leonard. Tired of your crap. Tired of hers. Now, leave me alone. If you want your precious daughter to drive around like Princess Elizabeth, send her to the Automobile Club. And don't expect me to let her use <u>my</u> car. Buy her one of her own."

Then I heard the rumble of my father's placating words underneath my mother's sobs. "Don't you touch me, Leonard," she said. "You get all you need from the chippies at your club."

"I love you, Jean," said my father. "Why do you insist on suspecting me this way? Why won't you let me hold you?"

I crept downstairs and I cried, too. I never realized how much she hated me, and I couldn't understand why she was so angry at Daddy. What was wrong with his laundry? What were his chippies? Daddy didn't work with wood, and those were the only chips I knew anything about.

She was absolutely right about my opinion of her. I hated her. How could I help it? She made me feel like a useless worm all the time. The only time she even smiled at me was when I ate the food she prepared.

My mother loved to cook, but she could never enjoy her food. She thought she was very fat and she made herself miserable about it. She always counted calories and tried to make up for the bread she couldn't resist at dinner by living on black coffee and grapefruit all day. She complained about her figure perpetually. I can still hear her: "My arms. My God! My arms. I can never get a jacket to fit my arms!"

For some weird reason, she enjoyed torturing herself by watching me pack in the food she cooked. "I'm on a brand new diet," she'd say as she loaded my plate with macaroni and cheese. "You eat three grapefruit a day and hard boiled eggs and you lose ten pounds the first week. Save room for the peach upside-down cake, Susan. I made it with lots of brown sugar and fresh peaches."

It didn't take me long to figure out that the only road to that woman's approval was through my stomach. My mother was so pleased with my appetite that she actually prepared things especially for me. "Susan is my best eater," I heard her tell my Aunt Evelyn. "It's a real pleasure to cook for her. Leonard just picks at his food and poor Debbie is so fat I can't <u>let</u> her do my meals justice. But not Susan."

I was always shocked when I realized she had really spent a whole morning in the kitchen making the spaghetti I loved even though no one else would touch it. I made a big fuss about how good it was and had three and four helpings of the stuff even if I was so full I couldn't move after I ate it. And then, she always made an angel food cake with pineapple custard for dessert. I ate at least two helpings of that, too. She never smiled at me while I sat and stuffed myself with her cooking. But she watched my every bite while she fingered her dry Melba toast. When I finished, she'd say, "More, Susan?"

The trouble was that I couldn't sit at my mother's dinner table all the time. The minute I stopped eating, my mother's attacks would begin again. "Where have you been, Susan?" she'd say no matter what time I got home from school. "Dawdling around with your friends? I want you to set the table right now," or "I want you to get some eggs at Milton's. Hurry to the store or I won't get the floating island done before your father comes home."

Whenever I asked my mother's permission to do anything, she said no. "You cannot go to the movies this afternoon. Why? Because I say so, Susan. That's why;" or "No, you cannot sleep at Roseanne's tonight. Don't you scream at me. I said no and that's final."

When I appealed to my father, he refused to help. "Your mother is in charge here, not me," he'd say and pat my head.

"Why do I have to do every single thing she says?" I'd ask him. "She's not *fair*."

"She's your mother, Susan," Daddy would say. "That's why."

Discussion closed.

My mother was a different person when she spoke to Debbie. "Sweet life," she'd say to my fat little sister. "Do your homework upstairs. We're having company, tonight;" or "Precious, will you walk Junior for me? He hasn't been out all day."

Mama made it no secret that she loved Debbie most of anyone in the family. "You're Mama's angel," she'd coo while she washed Debbie's face. "Mama's very best love!" and she'd pinch Debbie's cheeks and kiss her little rosebud mouth.

Debbie *was* darling. When she was a baby, people couldn't resist her. "Isn't she beautiful!" they'd say, and I'd try not to show the jealousy I felt. But inside, I boiled with resentment. Why did everyone ignore me the minute they saw my pudgy sister? It seemed to me she didn't do one thing to deserve their praise except look cute.

It didn't take me long to realize that I would always be the bottom of the heap at home. The only place I could succeed was at school. Obviously, my looks would get me nowhere, but if I worked at it, maybe I could dazzle the world with my brains and my personality. Everyone laughed at my jokes and envied my good grades, and I loved it. I felt like a success in school. It was the only place where I was proud of myself.

Margie Wiseman was my best friend all though school. Sometimes, Mother let me spend the night at Margie's house, and those evenings were my best memories. Margie wasn't afraid of her mother the way I was. She was actually *friends* with Mrs. Wiseman and so was I. Mrs. Wiseman stayed up with us all night talking about our problems. My mother would never do that. "Lights out at eleven, or no company ever again!" she'd shout when Margie was at my house.

And Margie and I would huddle under the covers and whisper, "That woman is a perfect bitch."

But we turned out those lights. My mother meant what she said.

Right before I began my freshman year at The University of Michigan, my mother and Aunt Evelyn took me shopping for school clothes. Whenever we three went out together, my mother relegated me to the back seat and ignored me for the rest of the afternoon. I never really minded because Aunt Evelyn always made a big fuss over me and besides, I felt a lot safer when my mother didn't notice me.

As soon as Aunt Evelyn got into the car, Mother said. "I can't tell you how much I appreciate your coming with us, Evelyn. It seems like ages since we've had an afternoon together."

Aunt Evelyn leaned over the back seat and kissed me. "Hi, sweetie," she said. "All excited about college?"

I started to answer, but my mother cut in. "I told Leonard this expedition was a complete waste of time, but he wouldn't listen to me," she said. "It is ridiculous to spend a fortune on clothes for Susan, Evelyn. She has absolutely no sense of style. She lives in jeans and Leonard's old shirts."

"I wouldn't have missed this shopping trip, Jean," said my aunt. "It will be marvelous fun to indulge Susie a little. She deserves it."

My mother sniffed, and the car lurched around the corner. "Susan is indulged quite enough in our house," she said. "Leonard fawns over her like she was a crown princess. I thought we'd go to LaSalle's. They have a nice back to school department and their prices are more reasonable than Steins or Lamson's."

Aunt Evelyn turned to smile at me. "Florence Wiseman says she's buying Margie some cocktail dresses and a formal. Michigan is known for the fancy parties the fraternities give there."

"Margie Wiseman is darling," said my mother. "And I don't blame Florence for wanting to dress her up. But Susan could put on a Dior original and still look like a slum leftover."

Aunt Evelyn reached for my hand. "Susan is certainly as cute as Margie Wiseman, and she has twice as many brains. I don't know about you, Jean, but I am delighted for Susie and very proud of her. The next four years will change her life."

My mother pulled into a parking lot and paid the attendant. "We won't be long," she told him and started walking toward the department store. My aunt waited for me to get out of the car and she took my hand in hers. "What's your favorite color, Susie?" she asked.

I smiled at my aunt and I thought my heart would explode with love for her. "Blue," I said. "But Mother says it makes my complexion look sallow."

Aunt Evelyn patted my hand. "Nonsense!" she said. "You've got gorgeous skin and when we get through with you, you'll have a wardrobe that does it justice. You're going to be the classiest coed on that campus. "

I shook my head. "I don't think I could ever be that, Aunt Evelyn," I said. "I'm too awkward."

My mother called out to us before Aunt Evelyn could answer that one. "What are you two chattering about? I only paid for an hour's parking at that lot."

Aunt Evelyn took my hand. "Oh, Jean!" she said. "You know how you hate to be rushed when you shop! I had counted on treating the two of you to lunch at Smith's when we finish. It's right around the corner."

For the next two hours, I didn't exist. I trailed after my mother and her sister as they selected the clothes I would wear for the next four years and I boiled with resentment. My mother never once asked if I liked the sweaters she chose or the skirts she bought. When we sat down for lunch, my mother shook her head. "Do you realize we spent over four hundred dollars on Susan's clothes, Evelyn? I just hope Leonard is satisfied."

She sniffed and picked up the menu. "My wedding dress only cost ten dollars and I earned that myself. Susan hasn't done one single thing to deserve such nice things. Not one."

Aunt Evelyn took my hand and squeezed it. "I just love that blue cocktail dress with the empire waist, don't you, Susie?" she said. "You look like a princess in it, honey. As soon as we get home, I want you to model it for Leonard."

My mother examined the menu. "I'll have the tossed salad and half a grapefruit," she said. "What do you want, Susan?"

Those were the first words she had spoken to me since I got into the back seat of the car that morning. "May I have chicken a la king?" I asked. "I just love it here and they always serve those yummy sweet rolls with it."

My mother shook her head. "You eat like that, and you won't be able to button one of those skirts we just bought." she said. "What are you having, Evelyn?"

Aunt Evelyn laughed. "Jean," she said. "You know Susie doesn't have a problem with her figure. She's built like a model. You're just jealous because *you* can't eat that way!"

My mother slammed down her menu and her face got very red. "Me? Jealous of *Susan* ? Oh for heaven's sake, Evelyn. You don't know what you're talking about. If I'd had her opportunities, I wouldn't be trapped in that house all day keeping house for a man who doesn't appreciate me. I could have been a famous singer or an important executive somewhere. Daddy didn't have the money to pamper me the way Leonard does our daughters. I had to contribute to the family income as soon as I graduated from high school, and I felt damn lucky he let me finish. Becky Karp had to quit as soon as she was sixteen."

Aunt Evelyn flushed. "I think you are so unfair, Jean. Leonard makes a fine living, and you always said you wanted to be rich. It's not every woman lucky enough to have a husband who idolizes her the way Leonard does you. Why do you talk about him the way you do?"

"Evelyn, you *know* what that man has done to me. Money is no substitute for fidelity. When I think what I've had to put up with. . ."

Aunt Evelyn shook her head and looked uneasily at me. I retreated behind the menu and she lowered her voice. "You don't <u>know</u> that Leonard has been cheating, Jean," she whispered. "Just because he's out late doesn't mean . . "

"You don't live with the man, Evelyn," snarled my mother. "And you should be damn thankful you don't. Here's the waitress. Have you decided?"

Aunt Evelyn nodded. "I'm having chicken a la king, too, Susie," she said. "And let's splurge on that brandied chocolate pie for dessert. Okay?"

I brightened and started to say something, but my mother interrupted. "I don't want Susan eating so much rich food, Evelyn. Her complexion has been very spotty lately."

Aunt Evelyn nodded to the waitress. "Reserve two servings of that pie, honey," she said.

Even Aunt Evelyn and the wonderful dessert we shared couldn't erase my outrage. I hadn't done one thing to make my mother ridicule me. I hadn't complained about all those skirts in horrid colors I would never wear or sweaters that were so tight I couldn't move once I put them on. It was my Aunt Evelyn who made her put them back on the shelf. "Molly Heffner was telling me that the latest rage on campus is cashmere," Aunt Evelyn said to Mother. "And it gets really cold at Michigan. If we buy these Pringles for Susie and a few good wool skirts that pick up their colors, she'll be able to mix and match."

My mother shook her head. "Evelyn, you are being absurd," she said. "That short sleeved sweater costs twenty-five dollars! And you want me to buy the cardigan that matches it, too! What are you thinking of?"

My Aunt Evelyn winked at me. "I'm thinking of your reputation, Jean," she said. "You will be mortified if Susan looks like a war orphan when that Heffner girl and Margie Weiss are dressed like models for *Mademoiselle*. I can just hear Molly when she sees Susie in one of those cheap machine knits you want her to wear."

My mother bought all three sweater sets and gorgeous long skirts to go with them but she was furious at my aunt and even angrier at me. I was certain I knew the reason she treated me the way she did. She despised me because my father loved me. She was furious that my father paid so much attention to me, and she struck back at him by bullying me. I reacted like a puppy who was constantly kicked. I cowered at her voice and longed for the courage to destroy her. I was petrified of her because I thought she had the power to destroy me.

I was so intimidated that afternoon that I didn't hear the anguish that coated my mother's words. If I had, I might have realized that her fury was nothing but a mixture of envy and disappointment with her existence. She was furious that life had been unfair to her, and struck back at me because she couldn't batter fate.

My mother wasn't around to remind me that I was a failure when I got to The University of Michigan, and I felt a lot better about myself. Margie Wiseman and I pledged Beta Gamma Chi together and we were roommates all four years. Margie was another Aunt Evelyn to me, and I was lucky to know her. She never failed to encourage me and give me hope. "You're darling!" she told me. "Your hair has marvelous specks of gold in it, and I know girls that would give their lives for your complexion."

Margie was a little taller than I was and her skin was unbelievable. It was so smooth it looked like cream velvet. She was a redhead, and her hair gleamed copper on a sunny day. She wore it loose and let it swing to her shoulders. She always looked immaculate, as if she had just stepped out of the shower, even when she walked into the sorority house after a full day of classes. And this vision was the one who kept telling me how darling I was. She really meant it too, and that made me feel ten feet tall.

Margie wasn't afraid to fail at things like I was. She didn't care that she flunked Latin in high school. She didn't even try to make up the grade. "Oh, so what?" she told me. "I'm just going to college until I get married. You don't need Latin to have babies, Susie."

In those days, women were groomed to lure a man into marriage. The secret was to tantalize him without giving away the only thing he wanted: your virginity. The girl who managed to remain intact was the one who won the house, the car and someone to pay the bills. The hussies who dared to love were stuck behind a cash register or a desk for the rest of their lives.

When I started college, I never dreamed I'd actually *graduate*. I went there to find someone who would marry me and get me out of my mother's house. I was typical of the girls in my high school class. Most of those who entered college majored in education or English and prayed they'd have their MRS degree before they were old enough to vote. *That* was their mission. Oh, some of us did enter the professions, but even those women hoped to combine their career with marriage and eventually, raise a family. The average college coed was on a husband hunt and so was I.

By the fall of my senior year, it looked like my worst fear was about to come true. I would be wearing a black cap and gown when I walked down the aisle instead of a white dress with a lace veil. And that was the biggest tragedy I could imagine. A lifetime in my mother's house was unthinkable. But so was living alone in a grim one room flat with nothing to do but go to work and come home to a solitary dinner and a book to keep me company.

I was very pessimistic about my prospects my senior year, and nothing Margie said helped. Even when I studied, my concentration disappeared every time I thought of what would happen to me after graduation, and I thought about it all the time. I had started the year filled with hope, but by October, I was back on my familiar merry-go-round, with plenty of casual dates but no one to give me that golden ring. I was trying to forget my social life and study for my history exam in our room at the Beta Gamma Chi Sorority House when Louise Heffner pushed the door open. "Busy?" she asked.

I took off my glasses and looked up. "What do you mean, busy?" I said. "I have three exams next week and I have to learn a zillion dates and battles, not to mention all those psychoses for Abnormal Psych."

Margie looked at me in mock disgust. "So what?" she said, and she flipped her Kiddy Lit book shut. "You'll get an A in both of them anyhow. You always do. Stop complaining."

"I am not complaining," I said. "I'm taking college seriously."

"Why?" asked Margie, and we both laughed.

When she said I didn't have to worry about my grades, I tried to believe her, but I was afraid to take the chance. I couldn't give up my only long suit in life. It was too risky. Before every exam, I stayed up all night drinking Nestle's cocoa sweetened with marshmallow fluff to keep me awake while I studied. I memorized. I drilled. I made up rhymes to remember history dates.

And I gathered A's like cherished gold nuggets. I was very proud of my grades. I sweated hard enough for them.

I knew I made all A's because I studied so hard, but I never let on. The girls who had boys telephoning them every night pretended they were dumb and I did, too. Whenever I took a test, I would always swear I failed it even though I knew I had answered all the questions right. No one liked "brains." They were "square."

Despite my twin obsessions about grades and my non-existent sex life, I still couldn't resist sitting around and talking about who was popular and why. It made me feel part of the group instead of the outsider I knew I really was. So when Louise came into our room, I closed the history book and grinned. "What's going on?" I asked.

"Nothing," said Louise.

She went over to the mirror and started picking at a blackhead on her nose. "Absolutely nothing, and it's Wednesday."

"So what if it's Wednesday?" asked Margie. "Stop that Louise. You'll make it all red and get a scab."

She got up and gave Louise some zinc oxide. "Put this on that thing to dry it up. It'll be gone by morning," she said.

Then she sat on the bed and started polishing her nails.

"Naturally, *you're* not worried that it's Wednesday," said Louise. "You're all set for the party. You have a date with Michael Rose. But Sandy and I haven't been asked and it's the first private the Delts are giving this year. It's going to be a treasure hunt. Are you going, Susie?"

"I guess so," I said. "Bobby said something about it, but I never know with him. He wasn't very definite."

Bobby Mosten had red hair and freckles and a bouncy walk like a boxer. He was the shortest guy in his fraternity, but he towered over me. I am just a shade over five feet tall.

I think his height affected Bobby's personality. He was always trying to be masculine and blasé, but it didn't work. The minute I saw his curly hair and his freckled nose I wanted to hug him. And that made him furious. He wanted me to react like he was Marlon Brando with a hard-on. You know, start breathing hard and rub up against him. I was afraid to do that. I didn't want to get sexy right in the middle of campus with the whole student body watching. Besides, he was too cute to disconnect my moral plugs.

Bobby never really asked me for a date. He would say something like, "The Carnation Ball is at the Union this Saturday night."

Silence.

"Yeah?" I'd say.

"It's going to be fun. The fraternity is having a cocktail party at the Tower before and afterwards we're meeting at The P-Bell for a beer."

More silence.

"Oh my God! Look at the time," Bobby would shout into the telephone. "I have to hurry to my ten o'clock."

Did he ask me to that dance? Did he ask me to that fraternity party? I never knew until the night before when he'd call and say, "Pick you up at six." (We were going to the cocktail party.)

Or "What color is your dress, Suzannah?" (We were going to the dance.)

I kept thinking of ways I could trap him into giving me his Delt pin. It wasn't that I loved him so much, but I was really desperate. June was only eight months away. I didn't have one single offer of marriage and that meant I was sentenced to my mother's concentration camp. If I couldn't get an engagement ring, a fraternity pin would have to do.

Margie held her hand up and spread out her fingers. She started blowing on the polish so it would dry. "Oh, Susie, don't be such a pessimist," she said. "Of course you're going to the party with Bobby. Michael told me Bobby asked if he could ride in his car to pick us up."

"Did he really, Margie? Why didn't you tell me?"

"What do you mean, why didn't I tell you?" asked Margie. "I thought you knew."

I wasn't surprised so much as relieved. I would have hated to sit home while everyone else was at the first fraternity party of the year. It would have been too humiliating.

The phone rang and someone shouted, "Susan! It's for you."

"Maybe it's Bobby," I said and ran out to the hall.

I went into the phone booth and sat down on the floor. "Hello-oh," I crooned.

I tried to sound breathless but not out of breath like Doris Day always did. She was my ideal, fresh and beautiful and just sexy enough. I breathed expectantly into the receiver.

"Hello, Susan. It's Mother."

Oh, my God. Mother. What a drag! I scowled into the telephone. "Hello, Mother," I said.

"Susan," she said. "Your father and I are driving up to Michigan this Saturday to visit you. We want to take Debbie to the football game. You'll come with us of course, and then we'll take you out for dinner. Ask Margie if she'll join us. Florence Wiseman is going to fill a big box for us to bring her."

I wanted to curl up in that phone booth and die right there. Count on my mother to pick the one weekend I didn't want to be treated to dinner. I was hoping Bobby would take me to the game and then we'd get some Chinese food or something before I got dressed for the party. We were all going to meet for cocktails at the Tower Hotel at seven, and I didn't want to miss that either.

Damn my mother! Damn her for always spoiling everything I wanted to do. When I left home to go to college, I thought I'd be free of her, but I wasn't. I'd forgotten about the power of the telephone. Here she was now, giving me orders to prepare for her next invasion and my stomach was churning just as if we were in the same room and she was shouting at me. "Why this Saturday, Mama?" I asked. "I have a big date that night and I'll be busy all day. Couldn't you make it next weekend?"

My mother didn't answer me and I could feel my hands begin to sweat so much I was afraid I would drop the receiver. I waited. At last I heard her voice. It crackled like ice. "No, Susan. It cannot be next weekend. This is the weekend Michigan plays Ohio State. Your father went to Ohio State, remember? Who is your date? We'll take him out for dinner, too."

And that, as usual, was that. You don't argue with a general; not if you want to survive.

I suppose I must have wanted to survive, but I'm not sure why. No matter what Margie said, I still felt like everyone else always had more fun and got all the lucky breaks while I slaved for grades and licked other people's toes to get their approval. I was afraid all the time. I was sure that once anyone got to know me, he'd see the same horrid flaws that my mother saw in me.

When I returned to our room I felt as if I had been flogged. I picked up my history book but the print clouded and I knew I was going to cry. "What did I tell you?" said Margie. "Bobby asked you to the party, didn't he?"

I shook my head and forced myself to control my voice. "That was my mother," I said. "She and Daddy are driving up this weekend with Fat Deb. They want to take you and Michael out to dinner with us."

Margie snapped her book shut and smiled at me as if I had just announced a bonanza. "Thank God!" she said. "When Michael takes me out for dinner, he's so cheap he always makes me share a plate of fried clams with him at Howard Johnson's. He won't even pay for two orders of french fries. Have you told Bobby?"

I shook my head. "Not yet," I said. "I think I'll wait until he asks me for the date."

I stood up and walked to the door. "I'm really thirsty," I said. "I'm going down to the kitchen to get some juice. Do you want some?"

Margie shook her head. "Michael said he'd call tonight," she said. "I don't want to miss him. You go ahead. "

I walked out the door with my books and papers. "Susie," called Margie. "If I'm sleeping when you come in, try to be real quiet. I have an eight o'clock tomorrow morning."

I nodded and shut the door. I went down the basement and into the kitchen. The place was empty and Kathy, our sorority cook, had left out platters of cookies and cakes to cheer us up while we slaved over our books. There were some cups of chocolate pudding with whipped cream, a pot of coffee and a large bowl of fresh fruit. I opened the icebox and reached for a platter of fried chicken.

That's the way to do it, Mother. The minute I find a decent guy to take me out, you come rushing in to destroy him.

I grabbed a chicken leg and stuffed it in my mouth. I pushed a few handfuls of lettuce after it and then yanked out a casserole of baked beans.

Bobby Mosten will take one look at you all polished and gorgeous and realize what a horrid mess I am, Mother. He will listen to you tell me my hair needs combing and my sweater has a spot on it and he will flush me out of his life like a bowel movement.

I scooped up the baked beans in my hands and forced them into my mouth. My face was covered with catsup and the brown gravy congealed under my fingernails. I took a spoon from the silverware rack and scooped out the poultry dressing. My jaws ached and my heart pounded against my ribs. I saw a large plate of pineapple and cottage cheese on the top shelf next to the jars of juice. I pulled out three slices and ate them as fast as I could. The cottage cheese and mayonnaise spattered my sleeve and plopped to the floor like soft snowballs. My throat felt sanded, it was so raw. My mouth was stuffed with food. It dripped down my arms and splatted across my shoes. My robe had trails of chicken gravy making rivulets across the front. A piece of pineapple had fallen into my pocket. My face felt sunburned and I panted like a thirsty dog.

When you've convinced him that I am despicable, Mother, it will be my sister's turn. Debbie can tell him what a selfish bitch I am because I don't let her wear my clothes and I don't help her with her homework. She will pout and look darling and tell the only guy that I have managed to interest that I am a selfish slob.

16

I closed the ravaged refrigerator and walked to the sink to wash my hands. I grabbed some paper towels and removed the crumbs and bits of food from the floor. I wiped the gravy stains from my robe. I smelled like a restaurant during rush hour. I put my face under the cold water but it still burned as if it were on fire. I shoved all the towels into the basket under the sink and wiped up the floor. I could feel the food rising in my throat and I swallowed hard. My eyes watered and my nose dripped. My chest ached as if it had been punched. I reached for those chocolate puddings and I heard footsteps. "Anyone down here?" shouted Sandy Thal.

I replaced the pudding, wiped my hands on my robe and cleared my throat. "Sandy?" I said. "God, I'm glad you're here. It was so lonely, I almost gave up the idea of staying. There's something spooky about this place when it's empty."

I hugged myself and shivered. "It gives me the creeps," I said.

Sandy Thal walked into the kitchen and looked at the platter of cakes. "Oh, goodie!" she said. "Kathy left us brownies and peanut butter squares. Come on, Susie, the hell with calories. You pour the coffee and I'll get us some plates. Oh look! I see some whipped cream. "

She brought the desserts to the long refectory table in the dining room. "Studying always makes me so hungry," she said.

"Me, too," I said.

She looked at me and frowned. "You look awfully flushed, Susie," she said. "Do you have a fever?"

I cut into a gigantic chocolate brownie covered with whipped cream and I smiled. "Where did you find maraschino cherries?" I asked.

ഔ ൽ

Bobby called on Thursday night. Before he had a chance to discuss the week end, I told him my news. "My parents want to treat us to steaks at the Allen Hotel Saturday night," I said. "Would you like that?"

"Like it?" said Bobby. "My God, Suzannah! I haven't had red meat since I left home! Your parents must be gods or something."

"Not exactly," I said. "Margie and Michael are coming, too. The only thing that worries me is that we might miss the party at The Tower."

"Hell, no, Suzannah. We'll just get there a little late. Your parents won't want to stay all night, will they?"

But he was wrong.

My parents picked Margie, Michael, Bobby and me up at the sorority house and drove us to the game. Daddy bought us those big pompoms to wave around, and Mother gave us blankets to keep us warm. Debbie squeezed between Bobby and me and she loved it. Michael and Margie huddled close together. Their cheeks were touching and they held hands.

Our team won, of course. Those morons from Ohio State didn't stand a chance against us. Bobby and Daddy argued all the rest of the night about which team was *really* best.

Then we all went out for dinner and it was such a good dinner, even Margie and Michael didn't mind staying late. The four of us had pink squirrels and they always loosen me up. My mother sipped a little of my father's whiskey sour and her cheeks were very flushed. She buttered a parkerhouse roll. "Can you pass me the bread basket, please?" asked Debbie.

My mother frowned. "Have some carrot sticks, sweet life," said my mother. "They're better for you."

Debbie's plump face got very red and her eyes followed my mother's buttered bread as it traveled to her mouth. "Why can't I . . ." said Debbie.

My mother's roll changed direction. It pointed at my outraged little sister. "Don't argue with me, Deborah Ann," said my mother.

She held out the relish plate. "No, thank you," said Debbie.

"I'll take one of those pickles," I said.

My mother finished her bread and reached for a corn muffin. "Don't these smell good?" she asked. "Will you try some, Bobby?"

"No, thank you, Mrs. Talberg," said Bobby. "I want to save room for my steak."

"I'll take one, Mother," I said. "They look delicious."

My mother smiled at me. "They *are*," she said. "Margie?"

Margie smiled. "Here comes the waitress," she said.

My mother put down the bread basket and nodded to the girl standing with her pencil poised. "My husband and I will share the club steak," she said. "Is that all right, Leonard?"

I ordered a one pound New York cut steak with mushroom caps and french fried onions and finished the whole thing. Margie ate part of a six ounce fillet and she was too full for dessert. Not me. I packed in that whole dinner and a huge piece of cheesecake, too. "I don't know how you do it, Susie," said Margie. "You eat like a horse and never gain an ounce."

My mother answered for me. "Susan starves herself for days on end after she eats like that," she said and her voice was sharp and bitter. "I wish I had that kind of self discipline. I can never resist bread, no matter how full I am."

She reached for one of the sweet rolls the waitress left on the table. "Are you using your butter, dear?" she asked my father.

My mother pulled my father's plate over to her. "Aren't you going to finish your hash browns, Leonard?" she said.

She poured catsup on the potatoes and began to eat them. "She smiled at us and blushed. "I just hate waste," she said. "Deborah Ann! No more cherry pie, Precious. **You've had enough.**"

I was so stuffed I loosened my belt. "If I had the self discipline to stop eating like an elephant, I wouldn't need to starve all week," I said.

"I know how you feel," said Michael. "We get such awful food all the time at school that when I get a chance to eat really great stuff, I can't resist."

Margie's Michael was such a treasure! He always said the right thing. He was very quiet, but when he talked, he said something really sensitive or very smart. Margie had been dating him for over two years, and he was beginning to bore her. I thought she was a fool. If Michael Rose had wanted me, he could have had me instantly. He was just the kind of guy I always imagined I would marry, even though he didn't look the least bit like Gregory Peck.

He was tall, thin and very intelligent looking. Maybe it was those horned rimmed glasses he wore; maybe it was his stooped shoulders. When I looked at him, I wanted to hug him to pieces. He had a hungry, lonesome look that made everyone mother him. That's what made Margie notice him in the first place. "He looks like he needs a warm sweater and a good joke," she said. "I wonder if he ever smiles?"

He smiled all right. His was a gentle smile showing beautiful, even teeth. It crinkled up his narrow eyes and made you feel warm and cuddly. That was what made him handsome.

I thought he was wonderful. His grades were right at the top, and he didn't have to sweat like I did to get them. He came over to the sorority house and helped Margie all the time with her English. He and I used to practice identifying symphonies for Music Appreciation after he finished tutoring my roommate.

Those hours with Michael were my stolen moments of bliss, because he was Margie's property, not mine. She found him first, sitting all alone at the Delta Omega Mu mixer the beginning of our sophomore year. The two saw each other every night after that, and Margie was wearing his fraternity pin in less than two months.

Margie and I talked about Michael all the time. "He seems so sweet," said Margie. "But sometimes I think he's only buttering up people because he wants to get something from them. He has absolutely no self-confidence."

Funny, how two people can see someone so differently. I thought of Michael as the strong, silent type. Margie talked about him like he was a helpless noodle. "I'll bet he's stronger than you think," I told her. "You have to be tough to get such good grades. There's lots of cutthroat competition out there."

"He's so smart, he doesn't notice it," said Margie. "He's always trying to hide what he really thinks. Sometimes, I feel like his mother instead of his girlfriend."

I didn't see what would be so terrible about mothering Michael Rose. Besides, I imagined you wouldn't get very far before he was in control in a masculine, storybook kind of way. "What's wrong with wanting to mother Michael?" I asked Margie.

"I don't know," said Margie. "But I'd rather mother my kids and be my husband's equal. I'm not comfortable with the Big Daddy/Little Woman thing. I feel demeaned."

She had a point.

❧ Chapter 2 ❧

When the waitress brought Daddy the check, he looked at his watch. "Do you know it's after nine?" he asked.

I couldn't believe it. We had missed the gathering at the Tower. And we'd be late for the house party, too. My disappointment must have shown on my face because Michael noticed it right away. "Don't worry, Susie," he said. "As soon as we leave here, we'll drive right to the fraternity house and pick up our lists. No one will know we got a late start."

"Lists?" I asked. "What lists?"

Margie got up and put on her coat. "Come on, Susie. Haven't you ever been on a treasure hunt? It's a contest. You look for things on a list, and the first couple to find everything wins a prize." she said.

"What's the prize?" I asked Bobby.

"I think you get a trophy," said Bobby. "I forgot to ask. Here, Mrs. Talberg. Let me help you with your coat."

He turned to me. "We probably won't win though, because we got a late start."

Somehow we got through all the confusion of thank you's and good-bye's to my family, and Michael drove us to the Delt house. Bobby and I took our list and got started right away. Every couple had to find different things, so we were on our own.

The first thing we had to do was to look for something that glitters under the big oak tree in the arboretum. "Bobby," I said. "There are thousands of oak trees in the arboretum. How are we going to find the one they mean?"

"That's the idea, Suzannah," said Bobby. "No one said this would be easy. We just have to go there and start looking."

He took my hand and swung it in rhythm as we walked and I felt very wanted for a change. When we got to the arboretum, we scurried around trying to read the plaques on all the trees to find the oaks. "I found one," shouted Bobby and I ran over to help him hunt.

We must have dug around that oak tree for twenty minutes and there wasn't one thing that bothered to glitter for us. Even if there was, it was too dark to see it. Finally, Bobby said, "Come on, Susie. Let's go look for another oak."

We found four more oaks but still hadn't discovered anything that glittered. I was really getting tired. "Let's stop here for a minute," I said. "I don't think

I can dig around one more tree. Besides, it's awfully late. How many things are there on the list?"

Bobby took my hand and we sat down. "There are at least nine more and they're all as impossible as this," he said. "The next one says, 'Find something soft and cuddly behind the Ad Building.'"

I giggled. "The only things soft and cuddly behind the Administration Building are the mice that foul up all our records."

"Let's call it a miss," said Bobby. "We'll rest here for a while and then go back to the house."

Well, you know how it is when you're sitting with a guy you think is adorable, and it's a cold fall night. The branches of the trees shivered in the crisp air and moonlight made Bobby's hair a halo of fire. The stars crackled above us and the Milky Way poured down in a sparkling flood. Everything felt gorgeous and unreal. Bobby had his arms around me and before I knew it, we were going at it hot and heavy. Finally, I pushed him away. "No," I said. "That's enough. If we keep this up, we may get in trouble."

"Oh, come on, Suzannah," said Bobby. "You can't go this far and then stop. It's not fair."

I shook my head. Everyone knew that sleeping with a guy was the worst thing you could possibly do. It made you cheap. I had heard about the way boys treated girls who were fast. They used them until they got bored and then dropped them to find another easy lay. I didn't want that to happen to me. The trouble was that I liked what we were doing as much as he did. I paused. "Well, one more kiss and then let's leave."

And that one kiss didn't stop. I can't blame it on being drunk because I hadn't had anything to drink since that pink squirrel before dinner. I can't blame what happened on anyone but myself because I loved every minute of it. The damp smell of the earth and the autumn leaves mingled with the warmth of our bodies and it was wonderful. I didn't want him to ever leave me.

I clung to him afterwards and sighed. I'd never felt so completely satisfied. I can't explain it, but after good sex your whole body sings. That's how I felt lying there on the dirt under an oak tree in the arboretum. Bobby's arms around me fit my body like my own skin.

Suddenly, I realized where we were and what time it was. I stood up fast. The spell was broken . . . almost. "Come on, Bobby. We'll have to go right back to the sorority house or I'll be late. It's only a 12:30 night."

"One more kiss," said Bobby.

I knew what *that* meant. I straightened my skirt and brushed off the pebbles. I kissed him on the cheek. "Okay," I said. "There's your kiss. We'll have to run all the way home. It's 12:15."

We dashed up the walk to the house just as Aunt Hattie was closing the door. "I'll call you," said Bobby and pushed me into the front hall.

I hurried past my housemother so she wouldn't notice my messed up clothes and my face. I swear Bobby ate up my mouth, it felt so bruised. I ran into our room and shut the door. Margie was brushing her hair. She turned around when I walked in, her brush poised in her hand.

"My God, what *happened* to you, Susan?" said Margie. "You look ravaged."

"Do I?" I grinned. "Well, I was, sort of."

I hugged myself and tried not to look like a Cheshire cat. "It was yummy," I said. "Bobby and I got lost in the Arboretum."

Margie looked at me with that all knowing look of hers. "Oh, Susan. You didn't do it, did you? Not with *him*? He's such a baby!"

In those days, nice girls were virgins when they got married. Well, so much for my being a nice girl. I could never say I was that anymore. All because I couldn't find anything that glittered under an oak tree.

I was still too confused with all the new sensations I felt to worry about what I'd done. But I was clever enough to know that I'd better erase Margie's suspicions fast. What would she think of me, getting screwed by a guy who always gave me a big run-around like Bobby did?

It was different with her and Michael. She'd been dating him over a year and he was committed to her. Even so, Margie never actually *told* me they went all the way. I couldn't imagine it. Michael respected her too much to do a thing like that.

So I looked my very best friend in the eye and did something I'd never done before. I lied like it was a lifelong habit. "Then we necked for a while," I said. "But I stopped him before things got out of hand. And here I am. Deliciously ruffled, but intact. . . completely intact. Let's go down to the kitchen. They had banana cake for dessert tonight. There might be some left."

๛ Chapter 3 ๙

I managed to obliterate Bobby and the arboretum with cake and chatter in the sorority kitchen. But only temporarily. That night when the lights were out and I was alone in my bed, I wasn't able to avoid my blue devils any longer. I pulled the covers tight around me to shield me from the icy fingers of night, but they couldn't blot out my terrible sin. My mouth was raw; my muscles ached. But the worst torment boiled in my guilty heart.

I forgot the warmth and closeness of Bobby's body filling mine. All I could feel was shame, red slashes of guilt that tore me apart and squeezed tears from my eyes. I'd really messed things up. I didn't want to *marry* Bobby Mosten; I just wanted the security of dating him until I found the right man for me. But now, if I married anyone else, that person would think I was some kind of prostitute or something. I shoved the blanket in my mouth to stifle sobs of lost hope; gone forever because of my intoxication with a boy under an oak tree.

Bobby Mosten didn't fit my picture of the perfect husband. He didn't look like my daddy and he didn't act like him. Bobby Mosten was a flip college kid. He laughed at cripples and scoffed at weakness. He wasn't kind. He wasn't good. And he wasn't a guy I wanted to cuddle for the rest of my life.

My father was.

Daddy was a gentle man, quiet and very plain. His face was square and solid. He wasn't much taller than Bobby was, but I always thought of him as a great big man. I guess you always imagine your heroes to be giants.

My daddy was solid gold. I trusted him and counted on him no matter what. Maybe it was his gray hair. He had it ever since I could remember and it made him look very wise. Or it could have been his wonderful voice. I snuggled up in the honey of his words like they were a velvet blanket. No matter how Mama's tongue lashed out at me and shattered my world, his "Now, now, kitten, everything's going to be fine" bandaged my ego and evaporated my tears.

The thing I remember most about my daddy is that he was always tired. He was so busy, he never had much time for us. He worked late every day, fitting people with glasses and liked to go back to his lab at night after dinner. "It's quiet there and I get so much done," he'd explain as he bolted Mama's roast chicken or pushed away her mint cream puffs with chocolate sauce.

Daddy acted like he really loved my mother. I'd heard him tell her so over and over again. He always tried to hold her hand and he kissed her whenever she'd let him, which wasn't very often. She usually turned away from him, and I thought that was cruel. "Not now, Leonard," she'd say. "I'm sewing"; or "I'm cooking dinner."

I'd never do a thing like that if I had a guy as darling as my daddy.

I was sure Daddy left the house to escape my mother. I had never seen her say one single loving word to him. The man paid for all those clothes she bought and her beauty shop appointments and not once did I hear her do anything but criticize him.

When the two of them went out at night, Mama took hours to get ready and when she finally came downstairs, she smelled of expensive perfume and those gorgeous powders she never let me use. Daddy glowed and seemed to stand taller when he saw her come downstairs on her three inch heels in some fancy dress she got at Lustig's. "What a glamorous cookie I married," he'd say.

And she wouldn't even smile. Can you imagine anyone being so insensitive? She'd snap out something sharp like, "Zip this up the rest of the way, Leonard. I couldn't reach," and turn her back to him.

Or else she'd say, "Do I measure up to your late night ladies, Leonard? Or don't they bother to dress?"

The only ladies Daddy saw late at night were old women who couldn't see through their spectacles. I didn't see how they could get my mother so fussed up.

I couldn't understand how Daddy could be so dumb that he didn't notice how nasty my mother was to him. I figured he either had a leather hide or he was some kind of masochist. I refused to believe he was devoted to my mother. That was like adoring the scorpion who stung you or the wolf that gnawed at your flesh. It really was.

But one day we had a talk and I understood him a little better. "My philosophy is not to fight about things that don't matter, Susan," he told me. "I let your mother run the house and take care of you and Debbie. But she doesn't run my life. I do. And your mother is smart enough not to interfere, usually. Oh, she complains a lot, but that's her nature. I just shut my ears when I think she's being unreasonable. I've learned that the worst thing I can do is answer her when she's upset. It just makes her even angrier and then she says a lot of things she doesn't really mean. I'm lucky to have such a good marriage, Susie. Your mother and I balance each other."

My Daddy was a very smart man. I loved those rare times when we were alone and he gave me advice. His understanding was so fine tuned that I didn't need to tell him what hurt. He knew and answered all my uncertainties before I even told him what they were. "Nothing is impossible, Susie. There's always a way to realize your dreams," he'd tell me.

I believed him. I refused to accept a D in Biology or even a pimple on my face. I couldn't live with my flaws just like he couldn't live with his. And we both had nervous stomachs that laced our high hopes with pain.

What would he say now, this perfect Daddy of mine? What if he knew that I lost my virginity under an oak tree to a guy I didn't really want just because I was so thirsty for love.

My father was scrupulously honest and very moral. He would say I should accept that Bobby Mosten was the only one I could marry with a clear conscience. If Bobby didn't propose, I was lost. I could either be an old maid or confess to the first guy that asked me to marry him that I had played around like some harlot.

Bobby Mosten was not the kind of I wanted to be stuck with for the rest of my life. Just like my father was glued to my screaming bitch of a mother. Oh NO! **This awful thing I've done must not destroy me.**

✂ Chapter 4 ✃

It was a long night, frantic with terrors. Finally, the bleak dawn light filtered into the open window. I stared at the sky with dry eyes, but my heart was drenched with tears. My sore, stretched muscles screamed their reminder of what I had lost. I kicked away sheets dampened with nightmares and struggled out of bed. The room was still dark and I could barely read the clock. I shivered and reached for a robe. I squinted at the iridescent clock next to my bed. It wasn't even seven o'clock on this chilled Sunday morning. I pulled on my jeans and a sweatshirt and tiptoed out of the room so I wouldn't wake Margie.

I walked downstairs into the empty kitchen. I rummaged around until I discovered some sweet rolls Kathy had made the night before for breakfast. I smeared a large cinnamon bun with apple butter and ate it. I piled butter on another roll with a jelly center. I washed it all down with two cups of coffee.

Now what will you do, Susan? Stay at home and take your mother's abuse for the rest of your life? What good are your brains, now, Susan? You aren't even smart enough to keep your pants on.

I discovered a tray of doughnuts right next to the jelly rolls. Chocolate covered ones! Glazed with strawberries! Covered with lemon whip! For one pristine moment, I forgot my torment. I inhaled the freshly baked aroma of those doughnuts and scooped them into my hands as if they were anxious lovers eager to caress me. I ate one and another and then another, but even as their frosting melted on my tongue, my mind steamed with anguish and regret.

*Imagine it, Susan! You will gobble your mother's food and help Fat Debbie dress for her thousands of dates **for the rest of your life**. You will never have a home; you will never have cute babies to love. You will not even be able to love yourself.*

I pushed myself away from the table, bloated and full. The coffee gurgled and sloshed in my stomach around a mountain of undigested pastry.

It's too late for you, now, Susan Talberg. You will HAVE to marry Bobby Mosten or no one. You will have to settle for less than your Daddy and forget about love.

I returned to the kitchen and opened the refrigerator. There was a casserole of stuffed peppers right in the center of the middle shelf. I grabbed a serving spoon from the counter and tossed the meatballs and green peppers into my mouth like billiard balls. I couldn't chew fast enough to get them down. My cheeks ballooned like a chipmunk's and still I scooped up the tomato sauce and rice gravy.

You can forget about love, Susan. All you'll get is lots of sex with an imma-ture boy who will bore you to death when you face him across the breakfast table. How's that for a life?

I shut the refrigerator door and washed the spoon. I cleaned up the mess I'd made in the kitchen with paper towels. I smelled like a Hungarian picnic in a bakery. I was repulsive.

ℂℂ ℂℂ

I could barely climb the stairs back to my room. My muscles were sore; my whole body was bursting with food, and my heart was dead. I managed to put on my coat and go outside to walk it all off.

I must have trudged for miles in the sharp fall air. It was noon when I got back to the house. Margie met me at the door. "Susie!" she said. "I was so worried about you! Michael called. He's picking us up in about a half hour. We're meeting Bobby at the Delt house for lunch."

"Did Bobby call?" I asked.

Oh, say he called, Margie. Say I was more than a quick lay on a moonlit night. Oh, please, Margie.

I looked at my roommate with my hope naked and quivering all over my face. Then I lowered my eyes. How could I want that little prick to call me? How *could* I?

Face it, Susan. He is your only chance to break away from your mother. It is Bobby Mosten or Jean Talberg and that's no choice at all.

"No, he didn't," said Margie. "Michael called for both of them. But your mother called. She wants you to call back tonight. I told her you'd be busy this afternoon."

Margie paused and took a good look at me. "Susie, you look like hell. What's the matter? Why are your eyes so red? Have you been crying?"

I fumbled for a bright smile. "No, the wind is cold, that's all. I wanted to walk off breakfast. I couldn't resist those sweet rolls Kathy baked for us. It's a good thing I did get some exercise or I'd never have room for lunch."

"Wear that salmon sweater set and your light blue skirt," said Margie. "You look so cute in that. And don't forget pearls, Susie."

This time my smile was real. Margie did what food and the nipping wind couldn't do. She got my mind off my tragedy and pushed it on to something far easier to handle: what to wear for a fraternity lunch.

Bobby and Michael came to the house just as I finished brushing my hair. I hurried downstairs and Bobby came right up to me and gave me a hug. Maybe he *wasn't* such an awful person. Maybe everything would be all right after all.

∽ Chapter 5 ∾

That night, I returned my mother's call. I braced myself for one of her verbal assaults and almost dropped the telephone when I heard the kindness in her voice. "Susan," she said. "You looked very nice, yesterday. That white sweater set was lovely. Your skirt was a little tight, though. Have you been gaining weight?"

A pat on the cheek and a stab in the back. That's my mother's technique and it always made me snap back. "No, I never gain weight, Mother," I said. "You're seeing things."

Silence. My mother cleared her throat and I could just see her frowning into the receiver. When she spoke, her voice was far colder than her words. "I called to apologize for keeping you from your party, Susan," she said. "Your father and I enjoyed all of you so much we let time get away from us. Were you too late for the treasure hunt?"

Oh, no, Mother. I wasn't too late for the hunt and I gave away the only treasure I had.

What would she say if I told her that?

I imagined her now holding the telephone to her ear with her shoulder while she polished her perfect nails, unchipped by housework and all that cooking she did. Her hair would look beauty shop fresh; she would be wearing a long, plush robe. She always did on Sundays. The breakfast dishes would still be on the table: pancakes, probably, the plates sticky with butter and syrup. *"Really, Susan," she would sneer. "You lost your virginity? How very careless of you. You never did have any self control."*

"We had plenty of time for the treasure hunt, Mother," I said into the telephone.

Then I softened. It would be so nice if we could be close like Margie and Mrs. Wiseman were. If she'd only stop attacking me, I was sure I could convince her to love me. I gripped the receiver and prayed I'd finally discover the pattern of words that would make us friends. "It was awfully nice of you to call, Mama," I said. "Bobby thought you were wonderful. He told me you reminded him of his mother."

"Yes," said my mother. "He's from Akron, isn't he? We have relatives in Akron. You might ask him if he knows the Talbergs there. They manufacture soft drinks."

I could hear her blowing on her nails to dry them. "I'll ask him," I said.

I'll ask him if I ever see him again.

Bobby had been the perfect gentleman at lunch. He kissed me goodbye as if he'd never done anything more. . . never touched me, never held me, never entered my body and filled me with love. It was a friendly, casual kiss. A "just buddies" farewell.

Now, my mother was beginning to make up a future for me. She'd probably call the Talbergs in Akron later on today to find out if Bobby's family was a "good" one. Or maybe she'd done that already because she said, "You know, Susan, Akron is pretty far for him to get home for Thanksgiving. We have that extra room here. Why don't you ask him if he'd like to spend his holiday with us? I always have a big Thanksgiving dinner, anyway. We could have Margie too if you like."

I smiled. Why was my mother being so nice? This was no time to start figuring out what she was up to. This was a chance to make sure I saw Bobby again. "That would be marvelous, Mother," I said. "I'll call and ask him tonight."

"You do that, Susan. And if you give me his address, I'll write him a formal invitation. I think it will be very nice to have him here. Your father enjoyed talking to him and I liked him, too. He's a real gentleman."

I called Bobby as soon as I hung up and asked him if he'd like to spend Thanksgiving vacation in Toledo with me. I thought for sure he'd hem and haw and think up some hollow excuse, but he said yes right away. "I like your parents a lot, Suzannah," he said. "It'll be fun. Besides, I've never been to Toledo. What's it like?"

How could I explain Toledo? It was my home town and I hated it. I blamed it for my own unhappiness. It was a prison to me; the place I had to be when I wanted to be anywhere else. I swore I would escape the minute I got out of high school.

But when I applied for college, I chose The University of Michigan, only ninety miles from Toledo. It was just far enough to be away from my mother and close enough to telephone.

I couldn't wait to let her know all the things I was doing that I would never dare try while I was at home. I was going to rub my freedom into her until she burned with rage.

The surprising thing was that I acted the same way at college as I did at home.

I obeyed every rule. I hated every authoritarian teacher I had, but I slaved for them and made appointments to have private conferences so they could tell me just how incapable I was. My mother had trained me well. I was taught to expect verbal torture. I thought it was as essential to life as breathing.

ಸಾ Chapter 6 ಅ

And so it was settled. Bobby would come to Toledo for Thanksgiving vacation and I'd have a second chance to get him to commit himself to something I didn't want to happen.

I saw him once or twice a week during that fall with another girl and I was shattered. I'd go over to the drugstore and buy a Hershey bar with almonds. I'd sit on the Union steps eating it while I imagined Bobby taking that other girl to the arboretum. They would cuddle close together under an oak tree and. . .

I reached in my purse and took out another Hershey bar. This one had lots more almonds than the first one. I lost myself in a chocolate moment, but once I swallowed, I saw Bobby Mosten leering at his latest interest and I ached for another Hershey bar.

Recreational sex was a risky business in those days. Our precautions weren't as foolproof as they are now. I'd heard stories of girls getting pregnant because the rubber broke or they miscalculated on the calendar and I was petrified. My lost virginity was *my* secret for now. If I got pregnant, it would be campus news, and unwed mothers were lower on the social scale than dust. Then, what would my daddy say?

I dreaded going to bed each night. I slept fitfully, afraid to drift into another macabre dream. I smoked so many cigarettes my throat was raw. I couldn't read a book or study for an exam. I lost ten pounds those three weeks. I stayed away from everyone and buried myself in my books. I was afraid that once I started talking to anyone, especially Margie, the truth would tumble out.

ᗞ Chapter 7 ᘓ

Once I was away from Mother, I went overboard trying to prove to myself that I dared to do things that would infuriate her. I loved practical jokes and earned a reputation for being ready to try anything at least once. Maybe that was why the B. G. pledges decided to kidnap me.

It was three a.m. on a bitter cold Wednesday night. I was huddled in the sorority basement in my baby blue drop-seat pajamas with the lace collar. I was trying to memorize a bunch of dates for my Psych midterm while I drank hot chocolate frosted with marshmallow fluff and nibbled at the cheese cake left over from dinner.

All of a sudden, I had a blindfold around my eyes and I heard a stifled giggle. "Shhhhh!" said a voice. "Or someone will hear us. Did you get her coat and boots?"

I started to protest, but a hand went over my mouth before I could make a sound.

"Be quiet and everything will be all right," hissed another voice.

I recognized that one. It was Joanie Held, the president of our pledge class.

"You hold her feet and I'll put on her boots," said another voice.

I could have struggled. I could have bit one of them or kicked the nearest shin, but I was too surprised to do anything at all. While I was trying to figure out what to do to save myself, someone put a scarf over my mouth and tied my hands behind my back with a nylon stocking. I felt like a fugitive in the latest episode on The Alfred Hitchcock Hour. Any second, I expected someone to whistle "The Third Man Theme."

It was so melodramatic, I started to giggle. By the time my captors propelled me out the basement door and into a car, I was limp with laughter. Then, someone untied the blindfold and the kerchief over my mouth. There in the back seat with me was Sybil Harris, my own "little sister," Joanie Held and three other pledges. "How could you do this to me, Sybil?" I said. "I'm supposed to watch over you and be your special friend."

I tried to look very serious and hurt but I was laughing so hard, I don't think I was very convincing. Sybil grinned. "It's all part of our initiation," she explained. "We had to kidnap *someone* and you're the only senior who wouldn't hate us all afterwards."

She reached in her purse and pulled out a long striped muffler in Michigan's colors: gray and gold. She tied it around my neck. "Not bad," she said. "It really sets off those baby blue jammies! Would you like a cigarette?"

I took the cigarette and smoked it for its heat as much as its comfort. "You crazy kids! It's freezing outside!" I said. "Just where do you intend to take me?"

"Wait and see," said Joanie. "Mary Anne thought of it and it's a stroke of genius! This is the perfect kidnapping because you'll laugh, too when we get you there."

"I will not," I said. "I'm all laughed out already."

Well, I have to admit they had a clever idea, but all the laughter in the world wouldn't erase my embarrassment. They tied me to a tree outside the Delt house. Then, they all sang "It's Howdy Doody Time" as loud as they could to wake Bobby up.

I wanted to evaporate. There I was in my frilly drop-seat pajamas, stadium boots and huge trench coat at four in the morning. If Bobby saw me, he'd think I planned the whole thing to embarrass him. I shivered and watched the girls drive away. I was really frightened. People died if they were outside in this kind of weather for a long time. No one in that fraternity house would be awake for at least three hours.

Then I heard a voice from the fraternity house. "My God, Susan! What the hell are you doing out there? It's ten below zero!"

It was Margie's Michael. I was saved. He'd untie me and maybe Bobby would never know. "Michael," I shouted. "Hurry down here and get me loose! I'll explain everything."

In a few minutes, a very tousled, very darling Michael Rose was cutting the ropes around my wrists and laughing at me. "Only you, Susie," he said. "Only you could get yourself all knotted up this way!"

"Very funny," I said. "Very funny. I'll be happy to laugh, too, if you can tell me how in hell's name I'm going to get home."

"I don't know," said Michael. "No one I could wake up has a car and the cabs aren't running this early. Why don't you sleep on the couch and stay for breakfast?"

"You're kidding!" I said. "Aunt Hattie would die if I spent the night at a fraternity house? She'd have me expelled at the very least!"

"Tell you what," said Michael. "Call her and let <u>her</u> figure out how to get you home. You sure can't walk. It's over five miles and so cold you'll freeze solid."

"Where's Bobby?" I asked.

"He's sound asleep," said Michael. "Come on. We'll call Aunt Hattie."

Aunt Hattie was the sweetest lady I had ever met besides Aunt Evelyn. Still, she was supposed to react like a mother and I knew all too well what my mother would have said if I called her at four in the morning. I dialed the house number and braced myself for an explosion. "Oh, Susie!" said Aunt Hattie. "Tied you to a tree? How funny! Honey, it's way too cold for you to be outside in your pajamas. You stay right where you are until seven when the cabs start running. I'll pay the cabby when he brings you home. You know, Susie, I am very proud of you. It's not everyone that can take a joke the way you can. Anyone else would have either been furious or in tears. "

So I stayed at the fraternity house and do you know what Michael and I did? We went into the kitchen and I made a big batch of French toast and coffee for the two of us. We sat around the table, eating like horses and talking about Margie and Bobby, like we were best friends. I was having such a marvelous time, I hated to see the hands of the clock land on seven. "Well," I said, "Thanks for keeping me company, Michael. You were definitely my knight in shining armor!"

I looked at the dark circles under his eyes and I was filled with guilt. "You poor thing!" I said and I gripped his arm. "You look like death warmed over. You're going to be a basket case for your classes this morning!"

"Speak for yourself, lady," he said and he grinned that cute little half smile of his. "The minute I put you in that taxi, I'm going right back to bed."

He gave me a big brotherly smooch on the cheek. "I don't have a class until one. Thanks for a great breakfast. You sure can cook, Susie."

I blushed. "And you sure can eat!" I said.

We heard a horn outside. "There's the cab," I said. "I loved our talk, Michael, I really did."

"We'll have to do it again," he said, and he walked me to the cab.

I waved goodbye and thought how lucky Margie was to have a guy like that. How could she think he was weak? He sure seemed strong to me . . . and very wise. I'll bet he'd never screw her and then leave her out in the cold. Lucky Margie . . . and she didn't even realize what a great guy she had.

Isn't that always the way?

❧ Chapter 8 ❧

Daddy drove up to Michigan to bring us home for Thanksgiving. I thought our Buick would explode, we put so much in it. I took home some of the clothes I didn't think I'd need and all the books I wanted to study over the holiday. I don't know when I thought I'd find time to work, but I wanted to keep my all A record. I figured I'd sneak in some reading after everyone else was asleep.

Margie had some extra clothes and things to take home, too. The back seat was so filled, Daddy could hardly see out the rear window. I sat in front with him. Margie and Bobby sat in back with Tom Hester. He was a Delt, too and when Bobby told him he was driving to Toledo with us for Thanksgiving, he asked if he could come along.

It was snowing and you couldn't see two feet in front of you. Daddy was a very careful driver, but still, it's scary slipping and sliding at twenty miles an hour down the highway the way we did. Margie, Tom and Bobby were telling jokes in the back seat and I felt very left out. I'm not witty like Margie. I always think of marvelous things I could have said when it's too late to say them.

I turned around and tried to join in the conversation but I couldn't think of anything to say. I was too nervous about having Bobby at our house. We were sleeping right down the hall from each other. What if he tried to make love to me again? In my own home? With my parents right across the hall? Unthinkable.

It took us almost four hours to get home. We dropped off Margie first. "We'll see you tomorrow for Thanksgiving, won't we?" I asked as we helped her gather together all her bundles.

"Sure you will, and I can't wait. Your mother is the best cook in the world, Susie. She invited my mom and dad, too, so the whole Wiseman family will be there."

"It'll be fun to have someone new instead of the same old uncles, aunts and cousins," I said. "Tom, you're welcome to come, too. I know Mother will have plenty of food."

Daddy nodded. "Why don't you see if you can, son?" he said. "Susie would love it. Wouldn't you, kitten?"

He put his arm around my shoulder and I glowed. I smiled at Tom as I nestled in the warmth of my father's alpaca coat.

"No, thank you," he said. "My mom is having the whole family over and I couldn't disappoint her."

"Well then, just come by for dessert," I said. "Your mom won't mind that."

Tom grinned and I could swear that grin was for Margie. Didn't he know Margie was taken? She belonged to Michael Rose. Tom Hester didn't stand a chance. "I'd like that," he said. "What time would be good?"

"We usually don't eat until seven so after nine will be about right," I said. "Then maybe we can go sledding in Ottawa Park."

"That sounds marvelous!" said Margie. "I'll bring warm clothes and my parka."

"It sounds great to me, too," said Tom.

This time, I knew he was talking to Margie. He had that smitten, puppy-like look in his eyes. He was hooked.

✑ Chapter 9 ✑

Mother had dinner waiting for us when we got home. "You must be starving!" she shouted when she met us at the door. She had to really scream to be heard. The dog was barking with blood lust in his eye. My mother caught him in her arms as he lunged for my jugular. "Now, now, Junior," she said to the struggling dog. "Be calm, Mama's Own. It's just Susan and her friend."

She clasped the snarling terrier to her and smiled at Bobby. Her hair was falling in her eyes and her scarf was askew. Her voice was almost drowned by the dog's shrieks. "He doesn't like men," she explained.

"You better watch out," said Debbie. "He rips everyone's trousers if he can get to them. The only one who's safe is Daddy."

"It's my ankle he's after," said my father. "This dog lusts for human flesh."

My mother kissed the dog. "You're unfair, Leonard. He's just very high strung."

I wondered what Bobby thought coming into our house. He left the cold outdoors for another kind of cold: my mother's glossy, show room environment. Our living room is huge and very formal. I never feel comfortable in it the way I do when I plunk myself on Margie's couch. The Wiseman house looks like people use the place. Ours is like a display ad in some fashion magazine. My mother and the maid are constantly plumping pillows or polishing floors. In our house, it was a crime to leave a book lying on a chair or an ashtray filled with cigarettes. If someone put a filled glass on a table without a coaster, my mother reacted as if he urinated on the floor.

Mother was as immaculate as our house. Even when she was holding a snarling dog and clutching a cooking spoon in her hand, she looked polished and cold, like alabaster. She wore an apron that was barely mussed and her red curls tumbled gracefully around her face, held in their deceptive dishabille by gallons of Spray Net. Her face was attractively flushed and she smiled at us like a gracious queen greeting her slaves. She had on three inch heels and one of her "casual" dresses, a denim number with the sleeves rolled up and a scarf tucked in the open collar.

I looked like a ravaged frump next to her. My thick Toledo coat was rumpled from the ride. My scarf had slipped from my head and my hair had lost whatever oomph it might have had. My nose dripped and I felt bulky, gray and exhausted.

The house reeked of roast beef, and I knew Mother had been cooking enough food for the fifth battalion. "You can unpack the car after you've eaten," she said. "Susan, take Bobby's coat and show him where the bathroom is. He might like to freshen up while we get everything on the table. You both look so tired. What happened to your lipstick, Susan? Did you eat it all off?"

"It won't take a minute to unload the car, Jean," said Daddy. "It's too cold to expect the children to have to go outside after dinner."

"I'll help you, Mr. Talberg," said Bobby. "You stay inside where it's warm, Suzannah."

We all pitched in, even Debbie. It wasn't easy because Bobby and Daddy had to dodge the dog and no one could kick him away with Mother right there. Debbie finally locked him in the bathroom where we could hear him screaming and clawing the door.

My mother was restless. She was afraid if she had to keep the dinner warm much longer her yam cups would dry out or the French fried brussel sprouts would congeal. "Hurry down and help me set the table, Susan," she called.

"Can't Debbie help?" I asked when I went into the kitchen.

Debbie was in the den watching television. The dog was on her lap. "No, she cannot help," said my mother. "She is controlling Junior for you so he doesn't tear your guest apart. Besides, Bobby is *your* company, not hers. Put out the serving pieces first, will you?"

Like most of my friends' families, we ate dinner in a formal dining room with a linen tablecloth, bone china plates and sterling silver flatware. My mother designed her table settings with an artist's touch and our meals were as beautiful to see as they were delicious to eat. This time she had arranged a low centerpiece of fall flowers, yellow and russet poms and white Fuji mums in a bed of greens and pine cones. She had a set of orange glazed candle holders she brought out for the occasion and her silver platters reflected their brilliance like dancing bits of fire. We all entered the dining room and gasped at the beauty of that table.

"Don't just stand there!" my mother said, and she smiled. "Sit down before everything gets cold!"

I will always remember our dining room as the scene of every emotional turmoil I ever had. I can't figure out how any of us managed to taste the food we shoved into our mouths. My mother would serve her list of grievances with the main course and I would try to defend myself. My digestive system reacted like a frightened pony. My stomach churned acid foam all over my mother's food and my intestines recoiled into knots of pain. Still, I ate. I wanted my mother to leave me alone and the only way I could manage that was to gobble up her cooking.

My father retreated behind his newspaper when Mother launched her attacks and my sister stamped her foot and pushed a lot of rich food into her mouth. The dog growled and nipped at our feet while he expelled billows of gas from the dropped food he devoured under the table.

This time, the atmosphere at dinner was pleasant and relaxed for everyone but me. My insides felt like congealed spaghetti and I was so nervous I almost bit a hole through the inside of my cheek. I kept my hands in my lap so no one would see them shake, and I looked around the table. Everyone else was smiling and laughing. Even the dog seemed at peace with the world. He nestled at my mother's feet and never once lunged at Bobby's trouser cuff or gnawed at my shoe.

Daddy and Bobby were good friends by now. They talked about the Michigan football team and about Bobby's future. Bobby wanted to be a lawyer, but his father had a huge shoe store in Akron. "I'm the only son," he explained. "I feel very guilty because I think Dad expects me to go into business with him. He's always saying how important it is for a businessman to have a good background in law. But I want to study international law. I don't want to sell shoes."

"Then tell him," said my father. "He'll understand and he'll be flattered too, because you confided in him. I know I would be. I always tell Susan that I'll help her do whatever she wants, whether I approve or not. She has to make her own decisions in life because only she can live with the results. Isn't that right, kitten?"

"Right," I said. "That's why you don't nag me to become a caddie so I can schlep your golf clubs all over the place."

"He doesn't want you to be a caddie because you're so weak you can't even lift a wet noodle," said Debbie. "My sister hates the outdoors. She sits around all day on the telephone talking about boys to Margie Wiseman."

I opened my mouth to shoot a nasty barb in her direction, but just then my mother began her usual platter passing ritual.

"Would you like some more meat, Bobby?" asked my mother. "There's plenty."

"No, thank you, Mrs. Talberg. I've had enough."

My mother's face fell. "How about some brussel sprouts, then? You seemed to like the sauce so much."

"It was marvelous," said Bobby. "But I want to save room for dessert."

"You don't want to miss my wife's dessert," said my father. "What is it this time, Jean?"

"I baked an almond nut cake," said my mother. "And I have some French vanilla ice cream to go with it. But doesn't anyone want more meat? What will I do with all this? We'll have all the turkey to finish tomorrow."

Her voice sounded like a forlorn wail of despair. I felt awful. She looked positively destroyed. . . and all because no one wanted a third helping of her special roast beef with the mustard topping.

"I'll have a little sliver, Ma. Just a little," I said.

My mother beamed. She took my plate and put on a huge slab of meat with the bone still on it. My mouth fell open. I had already put away two slices of that roast and I wanted to save some space for the pie to come. "Oh my God, Mother," I groaned. "Do you call that a sliver?"

"Just eat what you can, Susan," she said. "You're the one who always tells me how important it is to eat protein."

She stood up and smoothed her apron. "Debbie," she said. "Help me clear the table so I can serve dessert."

I pushed away my filled plate and forced myself to stand. I could feel the weight of the meal I'd demolished fall like a bowling ball to the pit of my stomach. I loosened my belt. Then I picked up Bobby's plate and my own and brought them into the kitchen.

When all three of us were at the sink, my mother was almost in tears. "No one ate a thing," she said. "And I've been cooking all week!"

"Don't be silly, Mother. We ate like depraved vultures," I said. "What shall I do with these scraps? Put them in the disposal?"

"No. I'll cut them up for Junior. At least I can count on *him* to eat my cooking. You put out the dishes for dessert."

❧ Chapter 10 ❧

Thanksgiving day was a polished diamond, gleaming cold without a flutter of wind. Before any of us could stagger out of bed, Mother was up cooking a gigantic breakfast. After three months of community cooking, both Bobby and I responded like starving lions. Mother pranced from stove to table in hostess-like ecstasy. "Have some more biscuits?" she asked Bobby.

"Better not," warned Debbie. "She has a gigantic feast ready for tonight."

"Now, Debbie, don't frighten Bobby that way," said my mother.

She hovered over a platter of sausages and eggs in a cheese sauce. "How about some more eggs?" she prodded. "Leonard?"

"Just coffee, honey," said my father.

Daddy never acted guilty when he refused Mother's food. I always felt guilty and cruel when I said no. And that was strange because my father *loved* my mother. I was the one who couldn't stand the woman.

My mother never threw out food. That was like dropping a sack of gold down a sewer. Food was too precious to her, especially after she had modeled it into a casserole or a roast. She was an artist; each meal her finished canvas. She'd die rather than destroy it. I could see my mother planning to mix all those cheese-encrusted eggs into a tuna casserole one day, add them to a vegetable sauce the next and feed the dog as much as he could hold as soon as we left the table. The biscuits would appear toasted one morning, grilled with salami at lunch and reheated with honey and butter with the leftover turkey by Sunday night at the latest.

She wouldn't have cooked such elaborate meals if I hadn't brought Bobby home. The grief in her eyes was all my fault. "I'll have some eggs, Mother," I said. "And one biscuit."

My mother smiled. "I'm not serving lunch," she said. "I want you all to have plenty of room for dinner."

⊷ Chapter II ⊶

Daddy drove us all around Toledo after breakfast. Then we took Bobby to the zoo and wandered around among the orangutans and the elephants. Bobby held my hand and Debbie held his other hand. It was very family and I loved the feeling. I was beginning to think maybe it wouldn't be so bad to marry Bobby. The problem was that I was pretty sure he wasn't thinking the same thing about me. Although he took me out a lot, he never talked about loving me or wanting me, even after that night in the arboretum. It was almost as if our union had been nothing but a bittersweet dream.

We got home just in time to get ready for dinner. In my house, you don't just sit down and gorge at a family feast. You dress up to pay homage to my mother's art. Bobby and I went upstairs together to wash and change. We shared the bathroom. He was shaving while I tried to do my hair. Now and then, he'd sneak a kiss or a squeeze, but he didn't fool me this time. I remembered all those girls I'd seen him hug on the Michigan campus. I remembered the fraternity parties I had missed and the hours I spent waiting for phone calls that didn't happen. Susan Talberg was only one more name in his bulging address book. He didn't love me any more than he loved Debbie. Let him pinch. I wasn't giving any.

Tom came over in time for pumpkin pie. Mother was delighted to see him. "Why Tom, how nice of you to stop by," she beamed. "We still have lots of turkey and stuffing. How about a having some before dessert?"

My mother hovered over us and watched us eat. She had barely touched any food since Bobby arrived, but when we all sat around the table toying with coffee, her resistance broke. "Aren't you going to finish that pie, Debbie?" she asked and pulled the plate closer to her. She nibbled at the crust and then piled some dishes together to take into the kitchen. "Does anyone want more coffee?" she asked.

There was a loud, painful chorus of no's and my mother nodded. "Susan, why don't you bring in the after dinner mints?"

I followed her into the kitchen. She was standing by the platter of turkey munching bits of dark meat. She wiped her hands on her apron and pointed to the three tiered silver tray filled with a rainbow of sweet mints. "That looks so pretty, Mama," I said. "You make everything just beautiful. How do you manage? No one else's mother could cook such a magnificent feast all alone. Mrs. Wiseman hires two maids when she has the family over and Mrs. Thal has all her dinners catered."

My mother looked at me, her expression so serious she could have been discussing religious salvation. "When you want something to be special, Susan, you have to do it yourself."

She motioned to the mountains of food sitting on the kitchen table and filling the counters. "I guess this wasn't extraordinary enough," she said. "No one even touched the sweet potato casserole."

She scooped up some cranberry relish and ate it. She covered the bowl and put it in the refrigerator. She began to scrape the uneaten food into the disposal. When she came to my father's plate, she paused and a curtain of misery masked her face. The dish was filled with untouched food. Daddy had barely taken a bite of his turkey. A congealed mound of curried green beans were pushed over to the side of the plate next to the chestnut stuffing. He had left a half eaten roll sitting on the rim of his dish. My mother picked it up and put a little whipped butter on it. She nibbled at the bread and then she started on Debbie's unfinished vegetables. Her eyes looked very red and her face was flushed. "When I was a little girl, we ate in the kitchen," she said. "We didn't even *have* a dining room. There were no such things as salad plates or fancy napkins. We owned five dishes and none of them matched. The glasses we used were emptied jelly jars. We ate soup made from beef bones my mother begged from the butcher and on Fridays when Daddy was paid, Mama boiled little bits of stringy beef for the five of us, or baked a chicken so small it fit into a saucepan. If we were lucky, we had cooked fruit for dessert."

She finished Debbie's sweet potatoes and picked out the olives and croutons from her salad. She looked at me and brushed a lock of hair from her eyes. Her face was very grave. She sounded like a history teacher describing The Great Depression, except she wasn't talking about a social tragedy. She was telling me about her own childhood. "I remember one year when we ate nothing but boiled potatoes. Sometimes, Mama could manage to buy one lemon to squeeze on all five potatoes and that made them taste a little better. That was the year no one got new clothes for school and my dress was so short it didn't cover my knees. I used to pull at my skirt and lean over so they wouldn't show.

"We ate like starving animals because that's what we were. I never saw my mama sit down at a table and eat a full meal. She finished what was left in the pot. I always swore that if I ever I had enough money, I'd serve my family like kings and queens."

Her eyes filled with tears and she stuffed another piece of turkey into her mouth. "I would have a white linen cloth instead of worn out oilcloth on the table and pretty flowers that smelled nice," she whispered.

She wasn't talking to me anymore. She was reminding a perverse fate of the immense effort she had made to improve her lot. Even though she could now buy the amenities she had been denied when she lived with her Yiddish speaking parents in their ghetto on Baker Street, she could not stop beating her fists at those doors that had been locked for her because she was an immigrant's child. "I never wanted to see my family so hungry that they didn't care what was on their plate. I never wanted to hear my children cry because they couldn't get enough to eat."

She took a roll from the bread basket and smeared it with jam. She looked at me and saw me once more. Her face hardened and she gestured toward the platter of candy. "Oh, what's the use, Susan?" she said. "Take the after dinner mints to your company. I have a headache. I'm going upstairs."

I looked at her and my heart shattered. She wasn't the mother I knew any more. She was a defeated little lady who couldn't erase the fears that had haunted her childhood. She knew what it was to eat dinner and still ache for food. She had never let that happen to me and I hated her for it. I had never realized before *why* food meant so much to her. She was still afraid there wouldn't be enough for tomorrow.

I put my arms around her but she pushed me away and my sympathy vanished. She didn't want it anyway. "You and Debbie clean the kitchen," she said. "I'm going to take a nap."

She turned and left the room. I wiped my eyes and returned to the dining room. "Time to clear the table," I announced. "Who's going to help?"

Margie stood up and smiled. "I will, Susie," she said. "The rest of you collapse in the living room and try to digest. We girls need a chance to talk."

It wasn't easy to wash that mountain of greasy dishes and put away so much uneaten food, but the two of us did it in record time. We hauled plates from the dining room into the kitchen and scraped, washed and dried until the kitchen looked like no one had been in it for a month. I vacuumed the dining room floor and we both took the leaves out of the table and stored them in the hall closet. I had worked as hard as a convict on a chain gang and I was still so full, I waddled.

Margie and I went upstairs to my room to change into warm clothes. "Don't you think Tom is interesting?" said Margie when we shut the door. "He's such a wholesome person. He doesn't have a line like so many of those guys in the Delt house do. Sometimes Michael makes me so sick with all his polished phrases and predictable reactions. This guy is different. He says what he *really* thinks."

"And just what marvelous revelation did he tell you today?" I asked. "My God, Margie. I can't button my jeans. Help me pull will you?"

Margie came over and started tugging. "Hold your breath, Susie. Your stomach is big as a balloon."

I held my breath. "That's because I ate too much," I moaned. "I couldn't bear the look on my mother's face when everyone else said they were full."

Margie tugged harder. "It's ridiculous to eat because of a look on your mother's face," she said. "People eat because they're hungry and stop when they've had enough."

She gave a mighty tug. "There!" she said, her face flushed with victory. "I got it."

I felt like I was wearing a tourniquet designed for an elf instead of a pair of blue jeans. "You're right," I gasped. "But I can't help myself. I feel sorry for my mother when she works so hard to make things nice for me. She never would have cooked all this fancy stuff if I hadn't brought Bobby home. You know how important it is to her for people to appreciate her meals."

"I think she makes rich, fattening things to torture herself," said Margie. "She's always on a diet. I've never seen her touch anything she puts on the table."

I remembered my mother standing at the sink trying to fill her empty heart with everyone's half finished food. I blinked away the tears that burned my eyes. "I guess she's ashamed of her appetite," I said. "She nibbles after we've finished dinner as if she didn't deserve to enjoy a full meal. I think it's very sad."

"It's a pity she doesn't take up some hobby like golf or pottery making," said Margie. "My mom has so many hobbies she doesn't have time to fix_din-ner, much less worry about who eats it."

I shook my head. "My mother isn't the type for anything athletic." I said. "Her only sport is beating hell out of a lot of eggs and flipping pancakes in a pan. What did Tom say? You haven't told me yet."

"He told me I was beautiful. Just like that," she said.

"When did he tell you that? When we were eating pie?" I asked.

"Better put on something loose to cover that belly of yours," laughed Margie. "That red sweat shirt looks big enough. He whispered it to me in the car."

"Who whispered what to you in the car," I gasped.

I couldn't breathe. My jeans were choking me to death.

"Tom," said Margie. "Who else am I talking about? He said, 'You look pretty.' And I looked just terrible. Remember?"

"I never remember your looking terrible, Margie. Come on. Put on some lipstick and let's go. It's getting late."

Oh, it was a wonderful night. I wish I could have packaged that crisp, crackly evening and kept it tucked away in my scrapbook of precious memories. Then I could have brought it out and loved it during the terrible times to come. We drove to Ottawa Park and slipped and slid up the hill, dragging our sleds behind us. The air was sharp and the smoke rings of our laughter floated to the sky. My eyelashes were icicles that twinkled in the moonlight. When we got to the top of the big hill, we swept down the hill like the wind hugging each other and careening between the trees. I clung to Bobby partly in fear and partly for warmth and partly to see if I could whip up a little love between us. I could see Margie hanging on to Tom, too and resting her head on his shoulder. Poor Michael Rose! The love of his life was sledding out of his future in a yellow toboggan while he was eating turkey in Columbus, Indiana.

We got home after midnight. Mother was waiting for us. "Invite Margie and Tom in for a while," she called from the front door. "I have hot cocoa and marshmallows for you."

We all trooped into the house. The dog barked with renewed vigor. He'd digested his Thanksgiving feast and was prime for a fresh kill. Mother scooped him into her arms and caressed him. He snarled softly in her arms. "Everything's on the dining room table," she said. "I put out some pie and some of the cake from last night, in case you were hungry."

Margie and I went into the bathroom to renew our lipstick and try to fluff up what was left of our hairdos. "Isn't he wonderful?" she asked.

She was leaning toward the mirror to put on a touch of mascara. I was brushing my hair in my eternal search for those gold sparkles Margie insisted were hiding there. "Tom? You mean Tom is wonderful?" I asked.

I forgot about my highlights and pointed my hairbrush at my best friend. "You listen to me, Margie Wiseman," I said. "You've got a perfectly wonderful guy who loves you and he's dreaming about you right now in Columbus, Indiana. How can you even *look* at someone else?"

"It's easy," laughed Margie. She took out her lipstick. "I'm doing it right now. And Susan, I like what I see."

"But you have Michael's lavaliere," I said.

I couldn't believe that anyone lucky enough to date someone as exciting as Michael, would risk his love by scouting around for something better. "Where's your sense of loyalty?" I asked.

Margie peered into the mirror and reached for the tweezers on the counter. She pulled out a stray hair from her eyebrow and turned to face me. "He is so handsome, I could die," she said. "Did you ever see shoulders like that? He looks just like Van Johnson, big, blond and solid."

"What's wrong with Michael?" I said. "I think he looks very intellectual."

"Michael is too skinny," said Margie. "Aren't Tom's freckles precious?"

She picked up her lipstick again and turned away from the mirror to face me. "Listen, Susie. I owe it to myself to find the greatest guy I can," she said. "I'm looking for a husband I can live with my whole life, not just a date to fraternity parties. This is our senior year and it's time to settle on the best prospect I can catch. I don't want to get stuck with some bore when I can be married to an exciting man who likes to do all the things I love to do. Besides, Tom Hester's family is the richest in town. If I married him, I'd never have to worry about a thing. And that's a big plus."

In those days, it was the husband's job to pay the bills and give his wife lots of babies. If he didn't make a good living, she had to work outside the home and still fulfill her obligations at home. She cooked, cleaned, mothered her children, entertained, and still reported to her job. She was expected to eagerly fulfill her sexual responsibility to her husband no matter how rigorous her schedule. "Honey, I'm too tired" was a line that men didn't think was funny.

But the women who had rich husbands lived the envied life. And that was what Margie was after. She wanted a guy who could afford to give her a maid and take her to The Riviera for her honeymoon. She was not being grasping and hard. She was voicing the unspoken wish of the single woman in the fifties.

"Michael is nothing," she said. "Michael's family is so poor, he has to be a bus boy at the fraternity to pay their fees. After he graduates, he'll have to start at the bottom of some firm or other. If I marry him, no one will give us a fat nest egg to get us started, and we'll have to live like paupers for a very long time. He wants to sell insurance and that means he has years ahead of him before he'll earn enough money so I can stop working and start having babies. Why should I suffer with him when I can have a comfortable, easy life with someone I like even better?"

"You mean you're letting Tom's money influence you?"

I was really upset, not just for Michael. I was upset because I never dreamed Margie could be so materialistic. I was far too idealistic to admit I wanted to marry money. And I was far too hungry for love to set up obstacles to finding it. It would be hard enough to trap someone who didn't see my millions of faults. I couldn't insist that he give me diamonds, too.

"Susie," said Margie. "I know it's not a very popular thing to admit, but life's a lot easier when you're wealthy. Tom hasn't said anything about marriage yet. But if he does, I'll consider it very seriously. I don't want to struggle for the next ten years. I want to have pretty clothes and travel. Don't you?"

I gave up on my hair and started working on my lipstick. "Sure I do, but I haven't found anyone who wants to marry me yet."

"You will," said Margie. "And Susie, believe me, it's not Bobby Mosten. He is a baby. He's a typical shortie trying to prove he's a Great Big Man and you are nothing but another conquest to him. You don't want that, do you?"

I shook my head. "There are some things you don't know, Margie. I have to marry Bobby or else I can't marry anyone."

Margie put her hands on my shoulders and shook me a little, just enough to let me know she cared about me. "You listen to me, Susan Talberg. Just because you let him go a little too far one night, doesn't mean you're stuck with him. You can always tell the next guy you rode horses a lot."

"You knew," I said. "How did you find out?"

"All I had to do was look at you that night, Susie. But don't feel bad. I'll bet not one of the girls in the sorority house is a virgin anymore."

"Not you either?"

"Not me either. And you don't see me getting hysterical about it, do you?"

"I guess not," I said.

"Now, let's hurry out there or those guys will think we fell in the toilet," said Margie.

ಉ ಲ

That night, after everyone left, Bobby and I sat in the den talking. "I have so many things I want to do after I graduate," he said. "I want a year in the Peace Corps and then I want to go to Harvard Law School. Someday I'll be a judge, Suzannah. Just you wait."

"That sounds really exciting," I said but I didn't mean it.

When he talked that way, he was telling me that he had no plans to settle down for years and years. I would get no offers from him, just a lot of sexy propositions. Sure enough, one thing led to another the way it always did with him, but this time I stopped him. I kept remembering what Margie said. This guy didn't want a commitment, and he had just confirmed her words. He wanted a quick lay. I took his hand which was wandering slowly up my leg and put it on his knee. "I don't want to start that here, Bobby," I said. "Not in my own house."

He looked very insulted. "What's the matter, Suzannah?" he asked. "Why are you playing iceberg with me?"

"How do you play iceberg?" asked Debbie.

I sat up and straightened my clothes. "Debbie. What are you doing down here?"

"I wanted some cocoa and marshmallows before I went to bed," said my little sister. "What's wrong with that?"

50

"Nothing's wrong at all," I said. "In fact, your timing was perfect. Bobby, why don't you keep her company? I'm really tired. I'll see you both in the morning."

🔊 Chapter 12 ❧

"Bobby hasn't called," I told Margie. "And neither has anyone else. What's wrong with me, Margie? Why can't I tempt men?"

We were sitting in our room pretending to study for exams. I was on my bed with all my history papers spread out in front of me trying to memorize a bunch of dates and battles. Margie was doing her nails, humming "Six Little Ducks That I Once Knew."

"Don't interrupt me," she said. "I'm practicing my Elementary School Music. 'Fat ones, skinny ones, there were, too.'"

I couldn't resist. I got up and fanned my hands behind me and sang, "But the one with the feathers upon his back. . . "

In walked Louise and Sandy. "He ruled the others with his quack, quack, quack," they roared. "You call this studying?"

Louise looked at me and stopped singing. "Susan, you look all dragged out. What's wrong?"

"Susan's got Bobby on the brain," said Margie. "She's been mooning around here reciting history facts in between complaints that he hasn't called. God knows why. He isn't worth her little finger."

"Maybe he's studying, too," said Sandy. "Maybe he'll call you after exams. Be patient, Susan."

"If he really wanted to talk to me, he could work in five minutes between Anthropology and Psych and you know it," I growled.

"Touchy, touchy," said Louise.

She took my hand. "Here we go round the mulberry bush . . . "

"You girls have the craziest way to study," I laughed. "Is this the only way you can pass your finals in kiddy cavorting or whatever the course is called?"

"No," panted Louise. "But it's the most fun."

Margie closed the nail polish bottle and grabbed Sandy's waist. I circled hers and Louise was the caboose. We formed a snake dance and wove down to the kitchen. That was the gathering place for the unprepared during exams. Kathy always left out plates of cookies and there was lots of ice cream in the freezer. We all ate to stay awake, or to calm our nerves or to feel the comfort of food going down our throats.

We sat down and promptly forgot our exams. I sampled four kinds of cookies and complained about my social life.

"Look, Susan," said Margie. "Face facts. Bobby Mosten isn't interested in you because he has other plans for his life. And I think you're lucky to escape him."

"I can't be as picky as you can," I said. "I don't have choices. Where is the hot fudge sauce? I want to make a sundae."

"You'll get pimples!" said Louise. "But what the hell, so will I."

She opened one of the cabinets in the kitchen and came up with hot fudge sauce and some peanuts. "Just what we need: energy and protein. Poof! There goes my diet!" she said. "Let's dig in."

"If you want to know why Bobby Mosten hasn't called, Susan," said Margie. "Analyze the kind of person he is. You're the one that got all A's in psychology. He has no sense of loyalty to anyone and besides he's an immature idiot."

"What's more," said Sandy. "He doesn't know a good thing when he sees it."

"I second that," said Louise. "Now, come on. Let's study." She grabbed my hand and put her other hand on her hip. "I'm a little teapot, short and stout," she sang.

"Here is my handle. Here is my spout," sang Margie.

"Who wants more ice cream?" I asked.

✂ Chapter 13 ✂

Poor Michael. Margie got the chicken pox and by the time the spots disappeared from her face, she had wiped Michael out of her life. Margie looked in the mirror one morning in February and her face was a mass of red, angry dots. She marched over to my bed and shook me vigorously. "Oh my God, Susan. Wake up! Quick! I have the chicken pox!"

I sat up in bed and stared at my roommate's gorgeous face covered with blotchy pimples between her little brown freckles. "Maybe it's something you ate," I said. "It might not be chicken pox."

"Oh yes it is," said Margie. "Mark Heffner in my practice teaching class was out with it last week and so was Patty McDonald."

I walked over to Health Service with her and the nurse there took one look at her polka dot complexion and put her into quarantine. I hurried back to the sorority house to get her some pajamas and books to keep her mind off the itching.

Every time I visited her, Tom Hester was sitting at her bedside. One day, just before Margie was ready to come home, I found her alone. "Okay," I said. "Confess. Have you switched lovers on me? And if you have, you're a fool. You'd better have a good reason for dumping a doll like Michael Rose."

I put an overnight case on her bed and started packing it. "We ought to be able to fit your books in here but you'll have to carry that plant.

"I'm in love, Susie," said Margie.

"I know you're in love, but I'm not sure who is the lucky guy," I said. "What's been going on in this hospital room besides a battle with chicken pox?"

"I'm serious, Susie. When Michael saw me here, all he did was laugh at my speckled complexion. You know what Tom did?"

I picked up a flannel robe with red stripes and little black footprints on it and stuffed it into the case. "He threw up," I said.

"Don't forget the booties that match," said Margie. "He kissed me and said, 'You're beautiful.'"

"And with those two little words he erased a relationship you've had for over a year with one of the nicest guys in the world," I said. "Oh, Margie. I can't believe it."

Margie handed me her nail polish and some make-up to pack. She got out of bed and began to dress. "I did some very serious thinking while I was in this hospital bed, Susan," she said. "Tom Hester loves me a lot more than Michael does. He thinks I'm perfect. Michael magnifies all my faults and nags me about them all the time."

"Besides," I said. "Michael's father is a kosher butcher from Columbus, Indiana, and Tom Hester's family owns just about all the salable real estate in Toledo. Is that it?"

"It's part of it, Susie. If I have a choice between struggling for every penny or starting out my marriage with all the things I've always wanted, I'd be a fool not to choose the more comfortable life, wouldn't I? Besides, if you think I'm materialistic, you should hear Michael talk. All he cares about is money and using people to get it. I think that's disgusting."

"You're the one who's being disgusting," I snapped. "You're trying to justify being cruel and unfair to Michael. He's been loyal and kind to you, Margie, and you're throwing him away for a big bank account."

"But I *love* Tom, Susie. I really do. And I need your help."

"What do you mean, you need my help? I don't have to help you love Tom. You did it all by yourself."

I was sad for Michael, and I was jealous, too. Here was Margie with two great men in love with her and I didn't even have one. It wasn't fair. But then, life *isn't* fair. Even Daddy told me that.

"What am I going to do about Michael?" asked Margie.

"You're going to tell him you're in love with someone else," I said. "And you'll give him back his lavaliere."

"I can't do it," said Margie.

"You should have thought about that before you decided to latch on to Money Bags Hester," I said. "Get your coat. We have to hurry. I don't want to be late for my three o'clock class."

"I thought you'd help me write Michael a letter," said Margie. "It's a lot better than telling him face to face, don't you think? Then, he'll have time to think about it. Besides, I can explain what happened more tactfully in a letter. You know how it is when you have to confront someone. Words never come out the way you plan."

"You mean chemistry gets in the way?"

"Maybe, but it's just that the conversation might get a little ugly and I don't want that, Susie. Michael has a disgusting temper. When he doesn't get his way, he won't *listen*."

Well, I wrote it for her. Margie could make me do just about anything if she was determined enough, and she was really determined this time. That night, we both sat down and composed a very tactful letter explaining Margie's new love. We assured Michael that he would always be an important part in Margie's memories and thanked him for understanding.

"I'm glad I won't be there when he reads it," I said. "You might as well slip the lavaliere into the envelope with the letter. That'll convince him you mean what you say. I wash my hands of it. He'll get your news just in time for Valentine's Day. Won't that be nice?"

Margie nodded. "I know it's bad timing, but it wouldn't be honest to drag this on when I'm so sure I'm going to marry someone else."

"Has Tom asked you yet?" I asked.

"No, not yet," Margie said. "But he said he had a very special Valentine gift for me and asked me my ring size. It would take a fool not to figure that out." "And you're no fool, are you, Margie?" I said. "You certainly move fast once you make up your mind, don't you?"

I couldn't keep the bitterness out of my voice. I resented her good fortune and I hated myself for not being delighted for her. After all, Margie Wiseman was my best friend. "I want you to be very happy, Margie," I said. "But this is a stinking thing you're doing. Someday, Tom Hester's money won't seem nearly as sweet as Michael Rose's gentleness. You'll see."

"Don't tell me about Michael Rose's gentleness," said Margie. "You don't know him the way I do. He's insecure and he's a big baby. You mistake his weakness for gentleness, Susan. Michael Rose is afraid to open his mouth to anyone he thinks is important. But just once let him get the upper hand and he is really cruel. He has no patience for anyone that he can't use."

I thought of Michael that morning I was kidnapped. He had plenty of time to listen to my problems, and I was totally unimportant in his world. He hadn't seemed like a wimp to me, either. He had taken charge of my dilemma and turned it into an adventure. I didn't think there was anything infantile about that. "Margie, you're so wrong," I said.

Margie put her hand on my arm. "Susie," she said. "People play roles with other people all the time. You have to really get familiar with someone to know what he's really like. Believe me, Michael's only interests are making money and making me. He needs constant sex to reassure himself that he's a man. I guess that's because he's so unsure of himself. He doesn't love himself enough to love anyone else. At least, Tom has guts. He's strong. And I want a strong guy, a guy who's not afraid to give."

"Don't try to bad mouth Michael just because you're finished with him, Margie," I said. "I know how wonderful he is and how deep and sincere his love is for you. I heard him talk about how marvelous you are when he rescued me from that tree outside the fraternity house, remember? Don't bother justifying your decision. Just copy our composition on your pretty perfumed stationery and write Tom into your life. I've got some studying to do, so there'll be a diploma in my future. I'm going to have to earn a living, damn it. I don't have any strong, wealthy men on the horizon."

"Touchy, touchy," said Margie and she gave me a hug. "Thank you, Susie. It's a marvelous letter. I couldn't have written it without you."

‰ Chapter 14 ‹₰

Michael got Margie's note on Wednesday. He called me that night. "Can I talk to you, Susie?" he asked.

I smiled. Maybe this was a good sign. Maybe Michael Rose would give me a second glance now that Margie dumped him. Every time I thought of our wonderful talk after he rescued me from the fraternity house tree, I felt warm all over.

We'd been so close when we shared that French toast and our secret confidences. I'd never had that kind of relaxed relationship with a boy. I was always too worried about saying the right thing or how I looked. But I was bedraggled and cold, huddled in my stadium boots and drop-seat pajamas with someone else's boyfriend. It was no use being self conscious. I was just me. And being "just me" felt exactly right when I was with Michael.

I didn't care if he was leftover material. Besides, I didn't believe a word Margie said about his being sex starved and money hungry. That was just sour grapes. I thought he was darling, and I'd take him any way I could get him. The minute I heard his voice on the phone, I was all sympathy. "Sure, Michael," I said. "Why don't we meet after my Art Appreciation class. It's over at four."

"At the League?" he said.

"Wonderful!" I said. "They have marvelous apple strudel there."

I really tried to get that casual "Margie" look when I dressed for class. I wanted to appear very nonchalant but put together the way my roommate always does. I put on my salmon sweater set and the brown pegged skirt. I slipped into my good penny loafers instead of my usual scuffed saddle shoes. I didn't want to drip jewelry, but I wanted to reek class, so I added a long strand of pearls and my sorority pin.

I didn't tell Margie that Michael called. I hadn't decided if I wanted her to know. Not yet. Not until I heard what he had to say.

Michael sat huddled like a dejected lump on the bottom step of the Women's League. His head was in his hands. He sagged a little and his mouth scrunched down to his chin. He looked so vulnerable, I wanted to wrap my arms around him. "Hi Michael," I said. "Have you been waiting long?"

He managed a weak smile and took my books. "I'm awfully glad you could make it, Susie. Come on. I'll get you some coffee and apple strudel. Want it a la mode?"

I nodded. "I'll get us a table," I said.

We hurried into the crowded, smoke filled cafeteria and I found a table that was relatively quiet. . . a secluded corner for Michael to bemoan his loss. Then, maybe I could move in and fill the empty place. It was probably too soon, but I planned to exercise all my charm and get him on the rebound.

I ran my fingers through my hair and pulled down my sweater so my little bosom wouldn't look so little. I pulled out a mirror from my purse. Thank God that pimple on my cheek had dried up. I wet my lips with my tongue and put my purse on the floor at my feet. I took off my coat and assumed a gentle, understanding expression. I was ready.

Michael brought a tray filled with apple strudel, ice cream and coffee. "I always get hungry when I'm sad," he explained. "So I got two for each of us."

He didn't even take the food off the tray before he looked at me with that hang-dog expression of his and said, "Guess what I got for Valentine's Day?"

I put my hand on his. "I know what you got, Michael, and maybe it wasn't as awful as you think."

Michael dug into his apple strudel with a zest that belied his emotional trauma. He stuffed the flaky pastry into his mouth. He waved his cream-laden fork at me. "Oh come on, Susie. Don't Pollyanna me. What could be worse than getting my lavaliere in the mail just when I'd decided to ask Margie to marry me?"

He gulped his coffee and waited. I took a deep breath. Now was the time to talk out of both sides of my mouth. I mustn't betray Margie; that would be disloyal. On the other hand, I wanted to fascinate Michael. It was a complicated strategy. I chose my words carefully.

"Worse could have been proposing and having her refuse," I said. "And even more ghastly would be her saying yes when she didn't really love you." I put my hand on his arm and looked deep into his eyes. This wasn't easy because Michael's eyes were glued to my apple strudel. "If you aren't going to eat your second one, I will," he said.

I abandoned his arm and reached for my dessert. "I *am* going to eat it," I assured him. "I just haven't finished the first one."

Michael stood up. "I'm going to get a Napoleon and some more coffee." he said. "Interested?"

I nodded and rehearsed my next campaign speech while he disappeared into the cafeteria line. When he came back, I took his hand in mine. "Listen, Michael," I said. "Forget your hurt. You just got a reprieve. You might have been stuck with someone who didn't give a damn about you, and never have found out until it was too late."

Michael pushed pieces of frosted cake around on his plate. Then, he looked up and smiled a real smile, the kind that comes from inside. "Oh, Susie! You're magnificent!" he said. "I never thought of it that way. What if Margie had said yes just because she felt too obligated to me to say no? Then, we would have had one of those horrible marriages where two people live side by side and can barely stand each other. I sure wouldn't want that."

I smiled like a good Jewish Mama should. I even patted his hand. "That's exactly what I mean," I said. "And Michael. This wasn't easy for Margie, either. You know, when you date someone for a year and a half, they become a part of you. Margie thought about this for a long time. She feels a lot worse about breaking off your relationship than you think she does. If you're not going to eat that other piece of strudel, I will." I said.

When we had demolished all the pastry and Michael had drunk several cups of coffee, he offered to walk me home. "You've been so understanding, Susie," he said. "The best medicine I could ever want. We'll have to get together again sometime soon. You can help me keep my head on straight. But right now, I wouldn't be good company for anyone."

No, no, NO. This couldn't be happening! My marvelous plan had back-fired. He had pushed me into the slot of understanding mother, and I'd be nothing but a confidante to him if I didn't redirect his thinking right away.

I was free Saturday night. If I played my cards right, I just might be able to console Michael at a movie or better yet, on Beer Mountain under the stars. February can be pretty cold and that meant . . . I looked hard at Michael and willed him to be enchanted. He looked down at his toes. I squeezed his hand. Silence.

I plunged on. Carefully. "You call me whenever you need to talk. I always have time for a good friend like you." I said.

He gave me a hug and I absorbed his wonderful scent. How could Margie throw away anyone so delectable? I kissed his cheek and wished I had the guts to give him a real kiss. "Thanks, Michael," I said. "Let's talk again."

I kept one ear tuned to the telephone all week and ran to the message board at least fifteen times a day. But Michael Rose didn't phone me. Bobby Mosten never called either. And Margie Wiseman got her ring for Valentine's day.

I didn't receive one single valentine that year. Oh, yes I did. Daddy sent me a bouquet of roses. Wasn't that wonderful?

❧ Chapter 15 ❧

I was too busy that spring to worry about Bobby or Michael. I was trying to find a teaching job anywhere except in Toledo.

It wasn't easy. Teachers were the cheapest commodity around, that year. No one needed any new ones, especially young, inexperienced women who could only teach the primary grades. And that was me.

I sent letters all over the country and, just in case, I applied to the Toledo Public School System. Most of my requests received no response, some elicited form letters, but the only one that had a specific job opening and wanted an interview was Toledo. Wouldn't you know it? The application even had a personal note attached that said, "We are very interested in reviewing your credentials, Miss Talberg."

I talked a lot about getting away from home, but when it came right down to taking the steps that led me away from familiar territory, I lost courage. I think I was afraid to let go of my home town. I told myself that teaching in Toledo was the best thing that could happen to me. I would be on familiar ground. Someplace new could only offer unimagined horrors to anyone as incompetent as I was.

In April, my mother called and told me I had to come home for Passover. "It's the one time of the year when the whole family gets together, Susan," she said. "You wouldn't want to miss it, would you?"

I most certainly did want to miss it. Passover is the Jewish holiday that marks the Jew's escape from Egypt. We celebrate the holiday for eight days and at sundown the night before it begins, there is an immense dinner made with special foods. Jewish people do not eat anything made with leavening like yeast breads and baking powder cakes during the holiday. We eat dry crackers called matzos for those eight days and magnificent sponge cakes made with dozens of eggs and matzo meal. Religious Jews change all the plates and silverware for Passover, and the orthodox rabbi in Toledo even wears a different set of false teeth.

We don't just sit down and eat. We have an elaborate service before, during and after the meal that tells about the Jewish exodus across the desert. My father and the uncles take turns reading from the Haggadah that tells the story of that journey and Aunt Sarah's twins argue about which one is going to ask the four questions. These questions are always asked by the youngest member of the family and there are long discussions about which one of two girls were born first.

The seder is always at our house so my mother can showcase her cooking skills. We stuff ourselves with buttered matzos, charoseth, a sweet relish made of apples, wine and nuts, greasy roast chicken and two or three kinds of sponge cake with fruit and whipped cream. At the end of the meal we are so full we forget that we won't be able to eat a decent sandwich or regular cake until the holiday is over eight days later.

I usually love Passover because of all the good food I can eat, and that marvelous sweet wine that makes everyone a little tipsy. This year, I would have to tell the whole family that I was returning to Toledo to teach if I was at the seder. All the Manichevitz wine in the world couldn't make that announcement fun.

"I can't come home, Mother," I said. "I have midterms the next week and I have to study."

"You can work in your room, Susan," said my mother. "I'm doing the whole thing myself this year and I need your help. Aunt Evelyn is going to be with Uncle Max's family, so I invited Cantor Alton and his wife. Sarah never helps with the cooking and you know your Aunt Marge."

Aunt Marge was Daddy's sister. She looked like a carbon copy of Debbie but in a much larger size. She was very social and very spoiled. Everyone said that the only thing Aunt Marge made for dinner was reservations. She never cooked at home and she obviously loved to eat. She was the biggest, most beautiful woman I'd ever seen.

She always dieted just like Mother did. But she'd go on kicks where she ate just one food for months at a time. Like steak. On one of her diets she ate steak for breakfast, lunch and dinner and nothing else. She said she lost thirty pounds, but she still looked like a blown up poster to me. It was Uncle Frank who got skinnier and skinnier every time I saw him.

Uncle Frank was an accountant and stared at tiny columns of numbers all day long. Maybe that's why he squinted as if his glasses weren't strong enough. Tax season would be over next week and that was the reason he and Aunt Marge would be out of town.

Uncle Frank always needed some kind of rest cure after the income tax deadline. He loved the mineral baths in Hot Springs. He said they were very relaxing. "They take the kinks out, Susie," he explained to me when I asked him why he wanted to go all the way to Arkansas just to soak in a lot of smelly hot water.

Every time he and Aunt Marge visited Hot Springs, he came back to Toledo smelling like sulfur and not squinting as much. Aunt Marge went on one of their diets and got lots of massages. When she returned, she always looked like she'd added forty pounds of muscle and a golden glow of excessive good health.

I think Mama resented her because she wouldn't eat anything my mother prepared when she and Uncle Frank came over for dinner. "I can't have anything but jello and skinned chicken on my new diet," she'd say. "I hope you have herb tea, Jean. I'm not allowed caffeine."

One time she came over and brought her own dinner in a plastic bag. "I have restricted myself to cottage cheese and chili peppers," she said. "I am determined to fit into my velvet sheath for the country club dance and this diet is supposed to simply melt away the fat. I *can* drink Ovaltine with it, though. Do you have any, Jean?"

My Aunt Marge swore she had lost and gained a thousand pounds in her life, and I believed her. She never looked one inch thinner after one of her marathon diets and she always looked very happy. My Uncle Frank adored her and so did I. She was very affectionate and caring with me and I think that's another reason my mother resented her. Aunt Marge protected me from Mother's commands. "Help clear the table, Susan," Mother would say after a family meal.

Aunt Marge would reach over and take my hand. "Let Debbie and the twins do that for a change, Jean. I want to hear what my oldest niece has been doing for fun. Tell me, Susie. Have you been outrageous?"

I was not going to encourage my mother's darts at my tubby aunt that April, and I was not going to endure Mama's triumph when I confessed to my family that I hadn't managed to escape her kingdom next year. I scowled at the telephone. "I am not your maid, Mother," I said. "I have more important things to do than help you cook a lot of greasy food to stuff our relatives like empty pillows."

"Your father is driving up to get you on Friday, Susan, " said my mother.

I went home. I packed my books and my resentment and hurled myself into the front seat of my father's car. He kissed my cheek and smiled. "Tell me about your plans for next year, honey," he said. "Have any of those places you applied realized how lucky they would be if they hired you?"

My daddy can erase my anger in one smile. "I've decided to teach in Toledo next year, Daddy," I told him.

I waited for my father to ask why I had changed my mind about working on the East coast. Or did I tell him I was going west? I only remembered telling both my parents where I *wasn't* teaching. And that's exactly the place I would be.

Daddy reached across the front seat and patted my hand. "I am so relieved,

Susie," he said. "I think you made a very wise decision. It's not easy these days to support yourself, and I don't want my daughter to have to worry about money. Time enough to feel the burdens of life after you're married."

"Mother never liked her burdens of life, did she, Daddy?" I said.

My father's eyes remained glued to the road. "Your mother is a happy woman, Susie," he said. "Little things bother her sometimes, but on the whole, I don't think she has any regrets."

"Oh yes she does," I said. "She regrets me."

Daddy turned and looked at me. "That's ridiculous, kitten," he said. "Your mother loves you."

Tell me another, Daddy. I am public enemy number one in our house and you know it. The hour's drive seemed like moments to me because I felt so relaxed and loved when I was with my father. He slowed the car and I braced myself to enter my enemy's camp. "We're home," he announced. "Jean is just thrilled that you're going to help her out, Susie."

I picked up my purse from the floor and snapped it shut. "I bet she is," I said.

I walked into that house as if I were going to prison. The dog hurtled himself against the screen door and I snarled louder than he. "LEAVE ME ALONE," I said.

My mother hurried to the door. She grabbed Junior and actually clamped his jaws shut. She smiled at me as if she really cared about me. "Oh, Susan," she said. "I am *so* glad you're here. I have one hundred things to make and the seder is tomorrow night. Debbie. Take this dog and put him in the den."

I wondered if she would have been as glad to see me if she hadn't needed a slave to clean up the mess she made in her kitchen. I turned to Daddy. "Can you help me with my suitcase?" I asked. "I filled it with books and it weighs a ton."

My mother took my hand. "I'm going to teach you to make a sponge cake, Susan," she said.

I straightened my shoulders and looked into her eyes. She wasn't fooling *me*. *She* would create that cake. I would wash the mixmaster. "I can't cook, Mother," I said.

My mother nodded. "I know it," she said. "And you'll need to know how if you ever have a home of your own."

She was right, damn her. I nodded . . . coldly. "Okay," I said. "When do we begin?"

"Are you too tired, now?" asked my mother. "I want to bake a lemon cake and a banana nut one and Harry just loves my wine cakes. "

"Three kinds of cake?" I said. "How many thousands do you plan to serve?"

My mother frowned and she looked very uncertain. "I want to have enough," she said. "The cantor is coming and he's never eaten here before "

I saw the troubled expression on her face and I remembered that moment last Thanksgiving when my mother's bruised soul stood naked before me.

When I was a child, my mama boiled little bits of stringy beef for the five of us . . . We ate like starving animals because that's what we were.

The picture of tiny Jean Talberg in her ragged dress doused my sarcasm and I blinked away my tears. I covered her hand with mine. "He'll love your dinner, Mama," I said. "He'd have to be made of iron not to make a pig of himself. . . . A kosher pig, of course."

I smiled at her. "I can't wait to learn how to make a seder! Don't expect me to be as good as you are, though. You are a genius in that kitchen."

My mother blushed. "Oh, you!" she said. "If you hurry, we can get that lemon cake in the oven before I start dinner."

I spent the next several hours beating thirteen eggs in my mother's kitchen. It was fascinating to see the way my mother planned a meal. She had her menu posted on the refrigerator door and a check list of the order she would do each thing. She was going to set the table tonight and she had already started the centerpiece and polished the silver. She had her cooking organized so that at the last minute, she had almost nothing to do but put casseroles in the stove and organize her entrees on serving trays.

"I made the charoseth last night," she told me when I came downstairs. "It needs to ferment a little. I did the matzo meal stuffing for the chickens, too and put it in the pantry. I thought I'd serve crabapple preserves with the chicken and candied carrots. I want this to be a special seder for the cantor. He must have had a million invitations and he accepted ours. I don't want to disappoint him."

"You won't," I assured her. "Should I start measuring the matzo meal?"

My mother shook her head. "I have all the ingredients ready," she said. "All we have to do is combine them. You start beating the eggs. They have to be *very* light. Here's an apron."

I beat and beat and beat those things until they were golden froth. Finally, my mother pronounced the mixture ready for the potato flour and flavoring. We poured the batter into an angelfood cake pan and put it in the oven.

My mother beamed at me. "You did very well, Susan," she said. "Now go upstairs and study while I do dinner."

"Don't you want me to help?" I asked. "I can set the table."

My mother shook her head. "Debbie can do that. You said you had exams, didn't you?" she said. "Tomorrow we're both going to have to work all day and you won't have a spare minute. I made lamb chops for you, tonight, Susan, and mint parfaits. Now go on, and I'll get started. The cake will be ready in an hour. Come down then and I'll show you how to cool it."

I went upstairs and took a relaxing bath. I managed to outline my notes for Psych 140 before the timer rang. "Susan!" called my mother. "Let's take out your cake."

"It's your cake, Mother," I said. "I just followed directions."

My mother shook her head. "Everything depends on the eggs, Susan. You beat them and *you* made that cake."

I removed my lemon sponge cake from the oven. "Now what?" I said.

"Test it to see if it's done," said my mother and she handed me a long stalk she had pulled from the kitchen broom. "Put it into the cake," she instructed. "If it comes out clean the cake is ready."

"Okay," I said. "What next?"

"You turn it over and rest it on that quart seltzer bottle," said my mother. "That way the air circulates around it and it cools evenly."

I paused. I looked at my beautiful creation and I experienced my first culinary thrill. I did that. . .myself . . . well, *almost* myself. "Won't it fall out?" I asked.

"Not if you beat those eggs enough," said my mother.

I turned the pan over on the soda bottle and held my breath. There was a sickening woosh and the whole damn thing fell on the kitchen table. I was dismayed. I looked at my mother and braced myself for her fury. "Oh, my God!" I said.

My mother patted my hand. "There isn't a cook in the world who doesn't have a setback or two. We will layer your collapsed cake with whipped cream and pineapple. It will look beautiful and no one will be able to resist it. You'll see. After dinner, we'll make a wine cake."

I blanched. "I'm afraid," I said.

"For God's sake, Susan," said my mother. "It's only thirteen eggs and a cup of wine!"

I couldn't believe my ears. *My* uptight mother telling *me* it was okay to destroy over a dozen eggs? I was definitely dreaming.

Mother continued. "It's just like falling off a horse, Susan. You have to get up and try again. You will make a delicious wine cake, I promise. But first, take off that apron and wash your hands. Dinner is ready."

She was right. The wine cake was a feather-light success. I beat the eggs while Mother salvaged the mess that was supposed to be my lemon sponge.

She layered it with whipped cream and crushed pineapple and decorated the top with pineapple rings and maraschino cherries. "I'll add the blueberries and strawberries tomorrow," she said.

She stepped back to see how it looked. It was gorgeous. No one would ever guess that this elegant confection had once been nothing but a moist avalanche of crumbs, lemon rind and soggy cake spattered across the kitchen table.

Mother and I slaved all the next day. Mother had made the gefilte fish before I arrived Friday. She ground the horseradish while she instructed me once again on cake baking. I did a banana cake in the morning and matzo meal popovers that afternoon. We stuffed three chickens and prepared the special foods used during the reading of the Haggadah. I watched my mother organize that meal the way an artist paints a canvas. The table was so long it spanned our entire living room. My mother had a special tablecloth and napkins she used for this dinner and she served everyone on glass plates because we didn't change dishes for Passover the way many families did. Mama's plates were lovely with borders of tinted glass fruit that glittered in the candlelight like precious jewels.

This year, Cantor Alton sang the service. He was a very small, fat man with a smile that made everyone feel loved. He always pinched my cheek when he saw me and said, "So, Susie! How's by you?"

His voice was a melodic tenor that I thought should have been singing arias from *Pagliacci* or *La Boheme*. My dearest wish was that he would someday lead the service at our temple because I would have more opportunities to hear him sing.

The cantor stood as tall as he could at the head of the table. He held up a tray with three matzos on it and sang "This is the bread of affliction that our fathers ate in the land of Egypt. All who are hungry, let them come and eat . . ."

The next four hours was an operatic experience for me as much as a religious one. When, at last it was time to eat, my mother and I served food I had helped prepare. I watched everyone's reaction to each dish with the same intensity my mother had always watched *me* eat, and when our guests smiled and held up their plates for more, I was exhilarated.

At the end of the meal, we brought out the cakes that I baked, and everyone gasped. My mother had sprinkled them with powdered sugar and they stood tall and shimmering in the flickering light of our crystal chandelier. When Mama cut into them, my heart stopped. What if the damn things collapsed and ruined this gorgeous meal?

My mother brandished her cake knife and asked everyone which dessert he preferred. The Cantor smiled and pointed to my salvaged lemon dessert. "Let me try that one, Jean," he said. "It's lovely to have something a little different for a seder dessert!"

I watched that man pick up his fork as if he were lifting a sword to smite me. He put a huge portion into his mouth and my mother and I stared as if mesmerized as the tiny little man chewed and swallowed his dessert. He looked at my mother, his face wreathed in happiness and filled his fork again. "My God, Jean!" he said. "This is a mechiah! Never have I tasted anything so light and sweet . . . So perfect after a heavy meal!"

My mother and I looked at each other. I grabbed an empty plate and ran into the kitchen. My mother got there before me. We looked at each other and we laughed until our throats were raw. "A new tradition!" my mother giggled. "We invented a Pesadic masterpiece!"

I doubled up with giggles. "If he could have seen that thing last night!" I sputtered.

I crossed my legs and the tears rolled down my cheeks. "My God, I can't stand it." I said. "Every time I look at that dessert, I see the two of us scraping it from the sides of the pan and patting it together as if it were clay. Oh Mama!"

My mother was sitting at the table fanning herself. She cleared her throat. "If we don't get in there, someone will think something's wrong," she said. "You take in the coffee and I'll bring the tea."

We straightened our faces and walked into the living room. Gert Alton was cutting herself another piece of my failure. "Jean!" she said. "I simply cannot believe how good this cake is. Would you share the recipe with me? Our sisterhood is putting together a holiday cookbook, and they would love to include something as delicious and original as this!"

My mother nodded like a queen accepting the accolade that was her due. "Thank you, Gert," she said and I could see her mouth twitching. "But I really can't take credit for this. It was my Susan that invented the whole thing."

I grabbed another plate and ran into the kitchen. It was too much.

∞ ∞

The next day, I returned to school. My mother walked me to the door. "I never could have done that dinner without you, Susan," she said. "Every time I think . . "

And we both dissolved in laughter.

I hugged my mother and this time she didn't push me away. "I had so much fun, Mama!" I said.

My mother looked at me and her face was very serious. "Thank you,

Susan," she said. "I had fun, too."

My eyes filled with tears and I turned my face so Mama wouldn't see. I ran out to the car and rolled down the window. I sniffled a little and waved good-by. My mother was holding the dog and she waved at me. She was smiling.

"What did I tell you, kitten," said Daddy. "Your mother loved having you home."

I settled myself in the seat and wondered what I had done right. "I loved coming home this time, Daddy," I said. "I really did."

I smiled at my father and tears rolled down my cheeks. I wiped them away and shook my head. Why was I crying when I'd had such fun being with my mother? Maybe I was sad because this was the first good time we'd ever had together. I didn't think we could ever enjoy one another that way and I was desperately afraid it would never happen again.

ഇ Chapter 16 ෬

Not one person in my family came to my graduation. My mother called me the night before. "Your father has been sick all week, Susan," she said. "I thought he'd be all right by now, but he still looks pale and I think the trip would be too much. The Wisemans said they'd be happy to drive you home. I'm sorry, Susan."

I graduated with honors and got to wear a special ribbon on my black gown, but none of it meant anything to me. My family had never taken my education seriously and their absence from the culmination of my studies proved their indifference. "Don't worry about grades," Daddy told me when he drove me down to Michigan that first year. "Just have a good time. That's what college is for."

My disappointment was especially bitter because I had expected to graduate with a ring on my left hand. The only thing I had achieved was a tiny red ribbon on my graduation robe and a job I didn't want. I hated my future and I dreaded returning home. My one bright hope was that Daddy would help me get an apartment that summer so I could have a place of my own. . . a private sanctuary where no one attacked me.

I didn't bring up the idea until we were home and I was all unpacked. I wanted to say it just right. I knew that if I sounded demanding or let my hatred of everything in that house stain my words, Mother would see to it that I was chained right to my old bedpost, the one she'd bound me to for twenty-one years. I didn't think I could stand it if that happened.

Mother had made all my favorites for dinner. "We couldn't take you out, tonight, Susan, because your father is still weak, " she said. "We'll have a little party for you this weekend. You can call up some of your friends. Maybe Margie and Tom can come over."

She cut up some beef and put it in a bowl for the dog. He sat slobbering at her feet. "My God, Ma. That's steak you're giving him. Why can't he eat kibble like every other dog?"

My mother picked up the dog and held him close. "I don't give *you* kibble, do I? Junior is part of this family, and I want him to be as healthy as you and Debbie are. Invite Louise Heffner, too, Susan. I understand she's as good as engaged to Mortie Best. He'll be back this weekend from Boston. His mother said he was top of his class at Harvard Business School. But Molly Best always thinks her kids are geniuses. Debbie says his brother Zale is a real schnook, and all I ever hear at Hadassah meetings is how her Zale is going to go to Georgetown to major in International Law."

"I never fooled you into thinking I'm a genius, did I Mother?" I said. "You've always seen me for just what I am."

"Don't dig into me, Susan," said my mother. "I made a very nice dinner for you. I wouldn't have bothered if I hadn't been proud of you."

"But you weren't proud enough to get in the car and watch me graduate, were you, Mother?" I said.

"Your father was ill, Susan," she said. "I couldn't leave him."

"He wasn't that sick," I said. "Maybe *he* needed to stay home, but you didn't."

Daddy looked up from the paper. "Stop bickering, you two. You better get used to each other. It looks like Susie will be living here for a while and I don't want you at each other's throats every minute. Is dinner almost ready? I'm hungry."

My mother gave me a triumphant smile. "Set the table, Susan," she said. "We'll plan your little party at dinner. Would you mind if we asked Aunt Evelyn and Uncle Max?"

Now I was sorry I had snapped at her. She was trying to be nice to me and I wasn't making it easy for her. I smiled. "I can't imagine a party without them, Mother," I said. "I think it's lovely of you to go to so much trouble when you've been nursing Daddy all week."

My mother blushed. "I enjoy it, Susan," she said. "I made turkey for you tonight with my own stuffing. I know how you love it. And guess what for dessert?"

"I know," I said. "I looked. That marvelous chocolate cake with mint frosting. You shouldn't have gone to all that trouble."

"It's a joy to cook for you, Susan," she said. "You know that."

We sat down to her graduation banquet that night and she watched me devour my favorite food as if I were a first run movie. She cut me a second helping of chocolate cake and reached for Daddy's slice of uneaten challah. She smeared it with butter and took a large bite. She was silent for a moment. Then she looked at me and shook her head. "Bread! I just can't resist it. And it all goes to my arms. My God, I'm getting fat!"

She pulled Debbie's dessert plate closer to her and filled a fork with a frosted corner that had escaped my sister. "Tomorrow, it's just grapefruit and black coffee. I swear it," she said.

She took another bite of the cake. "I used real rum instead of artificial flavoring this time. It makes a difference, don't you think?"

She nodded and sipped some coffee. "Susan, would you like some whipped cream for that cake?"

❧ ☙

After I finished my second piece of chocolate cake, I brought up my idea about living in a place of my own. "What would you think if I got an apartment nearer Belleview School?" I asked. "The school is clear on the other side of town and I'll have to get up at six o'clock to get there in time."

"I'd think you were ridiculous," said my mother. "Debbie, if you aren't going to eat the rest of your meat, cut it up for Junior, will you?"

"But you just gave him yesterday's steak and cornbread," said Debbie. "Will he have room for turkey, too?"

"Don't be silly," she said to Debbie. "Of course he has room. Are you sick, honey? You didn't finish your cake."

"You didn't give me a chance," said Debbie. "You took my plate away and started eating it yourself."

My mother pushed the plate back in front of my sister. "I am so sorry, Precious," she said. "Here. Let me cut you a fresh slice."

I wasn't going to let her drop my subject like that. "Why is it so ridiculous for me to want an apartment of my own?" I asked. "If I'd been teaching in another town, I would have had to find a place to live, wouldn't I?"

My mother picked up another slice of challah and started to nibble at it. She smeared it with butter and honey. "Don't start with me, Susan," she said.

She licked the stickiness off her fingers and pointed the bread at me. "This is your home. It doesn't make sense to go out and spend more money than you can afford to live someplace else. It's much better for a young lady your age to live at home when she's dating. If you were in your own apartment, your reputation would go poof!"

"What do you mean my reputation would go poof?"

I pulled some turkey from the carcass and chewed at it. "You've taught me what's right and wrong. I didn't have you breathing down my neck at Michigan, did I? And I didn't come out a Hester Prynne or a Flim Flam Floosie."

"She's right, Mommy," said Debbie. "Why, when Bobby Mosten slept here, she wouldn't let him touch her. I know. I walked in on them."

I was exasperated with Debbie for bringing that one up. I was angry with my mother for hinting at what was true: that I wasn't a "nice" girl anymore. I was furious with myself for letting both of them bother me the way they did. I cut myself another piece of cake. "Is there any ice cream? I feel like making this a la mode."

My mother's face softened. "In the freezer. Do you want me to get it?"

I got up. "No, I'll bring some in the dining room. Want any ice cream, Debbie?"

Debbie nodded. "Some of that peppermint stick sherbet would feel good," she said. "I think it would be fun if Susie had her own apartment. Ellen and I would come and visit. And maybe she could have a little kitty for a pet."

"You keep out of this, Deborah Ann," said my mother. She scooped up the sweet potato pie left in its serving dish and shoved it in her mouth. I could see the spoon shake as she brought it to her mouth and I was glad. She deserved to be upset. She was being horrible to me. "I can't see any point in Susan living away from her home," she said. "It would look just terrible. Everyone will think Susan doesn't like living here."

"And everyone would be right, Mother," I said.

I finished the cake and dug my spoon into the carton of ice cream. "I hate it here and we all know it. Daddy, won't you lend me a little money to get my own place? I'll pay you back with my first check. I promise."

For just a moment, I was flushed with pride. I finally stood up to my mother instead of crumbling into a mass of crumbs at her feet. I shoved a huge piece of cake and ice cream into my mouth.

My mother dunked some bread into a pool of ice cream on my sister's plate. Daddy looked up from the newspaper. "Susan, why don't you wait a little before you move out?" he asked. "Save your money and see how you like living here. I for one would feel much better if I met the men who took you places. After all, I want a little say about who will be my son-in-law. I don't want some schlub who doesn't deserve my daughter."

"Daddy, don't you trust me enough to pick my own dates?" I asked.

I refilled my coffee cup and cut a sliver of cake. "Besides, I may never get married. And I don't want to end up like the Wasserstrom sisters. They're both over forty and still living at home. Only now, they can't leave. They have to take care of their parents. They have no life of their own."

"Gert Wasserstrom devoted her life to her daughters," said my mother.

She picked up another slice of bread and picked at it crumb by crumb to make it last longer. "It's only fair that they should stay home and care for her after her stroke. You'd never do that for me."

She shrugged her shoulders and reached for the relish dish. "Well, Debbie would, wouldn't you, angel?" she said.

My mother licked the crumbs from her fingers and shoved a dill pickle into her mouth. She pulled over the turkey platter and scooped up some of the stuffing. "The only person you care about in this house is yourself, Susan. That's exactly what's wrong with you. You're selfish."

"Of course I'd take care of you, Mommy," said Debbie. "Is Susan talking about *my* Miss Wasserstrom? The one I had in third grade? She always told us how much she regretted not traveling when she was young. She said that now she could never leave the house because of her poor sick mother. We all felt very sorry for her when she told us that."

I washed down some cake with a hot gulp of coffee. "Why am I being selfish to want to live on my own? I think I'm being independent." I said. "Besides, I wouldn't be nearly as much trouble to you if you didn't have to worry about my meals and my laundry, and you know it."

"You'd be twice the expense," said my mother. "It's not just the rent your father would have to pay. You have to put in some decent furniture, too, you know. And that costs money."

She stood up. "The subject is closed. Help me clear the table, Susan."

She paused. "Unless you want more cake."

I looked at my father. "Daddy?" I said.

I could feel my eyes filling with tears. Damn it. I didn't want to make this a tragedy. I just wanted an apartment of my own. "Daddy. Will you help me find a place?"

Daddy put his hand on mine. "Wait, Susie. Don't make any decisions tonight. After you've been working a while, we'll talk about it again. All right?"

He stood up and folded the paper. "I'm going down to the lab, Jean. I want to have Mrs. Raven's glasses ready for her tomorrow. Poor thing just had her cataracts removed. She'll be thrilled when she can see clearly again."

"I'll bet she will," said my mother.

She took a spoon and scooped out the rest of the ice cream in the carton. "Will it be after midnight again, Leonard?"

"Now, Jean," said my father.

I stood up too. "Okay, Daddy. I'll wait. But I won't forget. I'll ask again."

Daddy kissed me. "That's using your head, baby. I'm proud of you."

I carried the platter of turkey into the kitchen. "Shall I put this in the ice box?" I asked.

"No, just leave it there," said my mother. "I'll cut it off the bone and put it in a casserole."

I picked off the browned leftover skin and ate it. My fingers were slippery with grease. Thick globules of turkey fat rolled down on my chin. "This sure tastes good," I said. "Here, I'll cut off the back and nibble on it for a while."

"My God, Susan," said Debbie. "You've eaten more than an elephant tonight. Mother would never let me do that. She says I'd be big as a house if I ate everything I wanted but you *never* get fat when you eat. I can't understand it."

"It's in the genes, honey," said my mother.

Her voice was bitter and cold. She looked at me as if I were an unwanted fly. "Susan is naturally thin. You take after my side of the family. We have to watch every bite we eat. Here, run this leftover cake over to Aunt Evelyn's. She and Uncle Max love my chocolate cake."

"Leave the corner with all the frosting for me," I said. "I might want some before I go to bed."

I put the turkey carcass in the garbage and wiped my hands on a paper towel. "Where's some waxed paper? I'll cover up the dressing."

"I'll get it," said my mother.

I picked up a spoon and began nibbling. "I think I'll explode," I said.

"I'm surprised you haven't already," said Debbie.

"Leave her alone," said my mother. "She hasn't had a decent meal since she was here for spring vacation. No wonder she's hungry."

She picked up the casserole of candied sweet potatoes. "Do you want any of this before I put it away, Susan?" she asked.

"Just a little," I said.

ᴓ Chapter 17 ᴒ

I spent a lot of time over at my Aunt Evelyn's that summer. Aunt Evelyn was my favorite person in the whole world. Aunt Evelyn and Uncle Max didn't have any children and I think I was sort of a substitute. She always made me feel wanted and very loved, like the time I dropped in on her on the first day of spring. Aunt Evelyn was standing at the kitchen counter trimming some daisies and carnations she had bought that afternoon. I never remember a time when my Aunt Evelyn didn't have flowers in her home.

"Oh, Susie," she said. "You're just in time to help me arrange a bouquet. No one can do a centerpiece like you can."

"Are you having company?" I asked.

She blushed. "No one special. But today is the beginning of spring. I do so love the season! All the crocuses and violets push their way through the frost to remind us that it's time to start thinking about gardens and sunshine."

I shook my head. "Not in Toledo, Aunt Evelyn," I said. "It's so cold here, the violets don't have a fighting chance until May."

Aunt Evelyn laughed. "Susie, you exaggerate. Why, only yesterday I saw a little white crocus in Crosby Park."

"That was a flower shaped icicle, Aunt Evelyn," I said and we both laughed.

"I made blintzes for Uncle Max and he just loves them," said Aunt Evelyn. "So I thought I'd make the whole dinner like a party. It's good for Uncle Max to come home to a surprise now and then, don't you think?"

Whenever I visited her, she always stopped whatever she was doing to talk to me. "I am really proud of you, honey! I must have boasted about you to a thousand people! Imagine! My very own niece graduating with honors from a prestigious school like Michigan! " she said that June after my lonely graduation. "But I always knew you had a wonderful mind."

She hugged me and I hugged her back. "Mother sure doesn't think so, Aunt Evelyn," I said.

Aunt Evelyn shook her head. "You can never tell what Jean thinks," she said. "She's got a lot of regrets you don't know about."

"Like what?" I said.

"Oh, just disappointments, Susie. I know it's hard to understand, honey, but a lot of times she's really angry with herself when she screams at you."

I couldn't believe Aunt Evelyn and Mama were really sisters. They were so different! Aunt Evelyn was a bubbly lady who thought life was a big joke. She was very small, even shorter than Mama and I. She had black curly hair, lots of freckles and the kind of face that got prettier the more you knew her. She wasn't glamorous like my mother, but her beauty seemed to radiate from inside her. I adored her.

Whenever I was over there, she was always cooking some special treat for my Uncle Max. Her kitchen smelled like an exotic restaurant, and she always let me taste the little delicacies she was creating. I ate Quiche Lorraine for the very first time standing over my Aunt Evelyn's sink.

She invented a creme de menthe parfait pie, I swear would have won first prize in the *Better Homes and Gardens* cookbook contest, if she'd enter it. But when I told her that, she just laughed. "Oh, Susie," she said and kissed my cheek. "You're so funny! How about another slice?"

The nice thing about Aunt Evelyn was that she didn't make me feel like an insensitive boor when I said no to her food. She just nodded and went on to other topics of conversation like my eternal problems with my mother.

"Why does she *hate* me so much?" I asked Aunt Evelyn.

Aunt Evelyn put her hand over mine. "Honey, Jean doesn't hate you at all. That's all in *your* mind, not hers. She hasn't stopped talking about that seder you two did together."

"That's because she needed me, Aunt Evelyn," I said. "She hasn't said one kind word to me since I got home. This afternoon, she yelled bloody murder because I was reading a book and didn't hear her come in the door. I was supposed to read her mind I guess and run out to help her with her packages. But she didn't even ask me, Aunt Evelyn. She just stormed into the den and shouted, 'Don't you have anything better to do with your life than get lost in a book? You get out to that car right this minute and bring in some of those packages. You're not a guest in this house, Susan. You have responsibilities, too.'"

I looked at my aunt and my eyes filled with tears. "All she had to do was ask me in a nice way and I would have helped her, Aunt Evelyn. But she started screaming at me before I even knew she needed help. What does she want from me?"

Aunt Evelyn sighed. "Susie, it's not you, your mother is angry with. It's her whole life. She can't accept that she's nothing more than a housewife. She had always thought she'd be a famous singer. She had a beautiful voice."

"She still does," I said. "You should hear how pretty it sounds when she sings around the house. She could still be a famous singer if she wanted to. Why doesn't she take voice lessons? Daddy wouldn't mind."

Aunt Evelyn cut me another piece of pie and shook her head. "Jean is too busy to do a thing like that," she said. "Running an efficient house takes a lot of time, Susie."

"You run an efficient house, Aunt Evelyn," I said. "And you've been taking night school courses for years to get your degree. You go to Great Books discussions and took a class in Oriental Flower Design last summer. And you still have time to invent marvelous things like this."

I spooned up my pie and smiled at my aunt. "Honestly, I just *know* you'd win a prize with this dessert!"

Aunt Evelyn blushed. "I'm not as picky about the house as Jean is," she said. "A little dust doesn't drive me up a wall. Your mother is a perfectionist. She likes everything just so. .. and that's hard to do with a lot of other people living in a house. I just have Uncle Max."

I got up from the table and hugged my sweet aunt. "You could have me, Aunt Evelyn. I would love to be your child and drive you crazy."

Aunt Evelyn kissed my cheek. "You could never drive me crazy, sweetie," she said. "Now sit down and enjoy your dessert."

I sat down and finished that wonderful pie. "Seriously, though," I said. "If Mother really wanted to sing or to do something more than be a housewife, she could make time to do it. I certainly don't expect to spend all <u>my</u> married life behind a stove or running a vacuum cleaner."

"Let me get out the old picture albums, Susan," said Aunt Evelyn. "Maybe you'd like to see what your mother was like when she was your age. She was so much fun! And popular? I used to sit on the bed for hours watching her dress for a party and then wait up to hear all about the boys who tried to get their names on her dance card. But your daddy always signed up way in advance for all the dances. 'He never gives anyone else a chance,' your mother used to say."

"Is that why she married Daddy?" I asked. "Because no one else could make a date with her?"

Aunt Evelyn brought in a huge scrapbook and opened it. She looked at me and bit her lip like she was thinking very hard. Then, she said, "I think Jean thought love was the magic ingredient for a happy marriage, Susie. She cared for Leonard very much in her way, and it was obvious that Leonard adored her. He spent more time at our house than he did at his own ever since he met your mother on the playground at school in the first grade. But marriage is a lot more than love, and I don't think she realized that."

I looked at her and thought of the way she and Uncle Max always held hands and gave each other kisses when they thought no one was looking. "I thought that love is what marriage is all about," I said. "You love Uncle Max, don't you?"

Aunt Evelyn nodded. "Of course I do, honey," she said. "But I also have a responsibility to him that is separate from my love. I keep house for him and give him his meals and he earns our living. That's his part of the bargain."

I was very confused when she said that. She was casting a shadow on all my pretty pictures of Big Daddy and The Little Woman sneaking quick kisses in a happy house filled with tiny tots. "You make it all sound so cut and dried," I said. "Like marriage was decided in court instead of in your heart."

Aunt Evelyn laughed. "Well, the marriage document is a legal one, Susie," she said. "But it's a lot easier to keep if you love the guy you've agreed to live with. A lot easier."

"Has Mother stopped loving Daddy, Aunt Evelyn?" I asked. "Is that why she screams at him all the time?"

"No, Susie," said my aunt. "Your mother loves Leonard. It's just the other parts of their life together that are difficult for her. When we were little, your mother managed to get anything she wanted, and she never had to do a thing to deserve it. She couldn't believe that happiness with Leonard involved more than just opening her arms to receive the good things in life."

Aunt Evelyn looked very serious. She nodded her head slowly. "I think she feels that life double-crossed her, honey," she said. "Marriage to your father wasn't what she'd expected it to be. She thought they would get dressed up every night and go to fancy parties, just like they did before they were married. She thought she'd have a maid to do the dishes and she would be a fine lady, but life didn't turn out quite that way. Leonard works long hours and he is not a rich man. He does very well, Susie, but he isn't wealthy and your mother was so sure he would be. Jean was never very good at watching her pennies."

"I can't see why that's such a terrible thing," I said. "We have plenty to eat and Helen comes in twice a week to help her clean. Mama can buy all the clothes she wants. Daddy loves to see her when she gets dressed up. Besides money doesn't really matter if you're in love."

Aunt Evelyn shook her head. "That's what they say in romance novels," she said. "But in the real world, life is a lot sweeter if you can afford some trimmings."

"That's what Margie says," I said. "But I know that if I loved my husband, I wouldn't care if he were rich or poor. I'd be too happy to even notice."

Aunt Evelyn sipped her coffee. "You'd notice when the bills came every month. Susie, reality can be a very bitter pill to swallow," she said. "Leonard was just beginning to make a good living when Jean got pregnant. When she had you she realized that all her pretty dreams would never happen. She was locked into her home with a child to take care of and there wasn't enough money to hire anyone to help her out. She never expected to work as hard as she did those first few years. I think that's what made her so bitter."

"She had a nurse help her when Debbie was born, Aunt Evelyn," I said. "And Helen came in every morning to clean for her. Why isn't she happy now?"

"Your father still doesn't have time to take Jean out as much as she'd like," said Aunt Evelyn. "When you're confined to the house all day long, you need to have a little fun, and Leonard is too tired when he comes home to entertain Jean. He can barely stay awake long enough to read the paper before he goes to bed. I think your mother feels cheated."

I shook my head. "I don't want to get married if it makes me angry and sour, Aunt Evelyn. And I don't want to be the kind of mother who never takes time to cuddle her kids or punishes them just because she's frustrated. That sounds like an awful way to be."

Aunt Evelyn stirred her coffee and watched the liquid swirl in circles in her cup. "It is, Susie. It is. That's why it's best to love your husband. It makes things much nicer. And no matter what you think, honey, your mother has a great deal of affection for your father . . . and she loves you too."

I pursed my lips and brushed pie crumbs into a little pile on the table. "I don't see why she has to take out her disappointments on me," I said.

Aunt Evelyn patted my hand. "That's human nature, Susie. Just human nature. Besides, I don't think Jean realizes how hard she is on you sometimes. She wants you to have all the things she never had. What she doesn't understand is that you don't want those things. You have other ideas . . modern ones that she doesn't really appreciate."

If I ever had enough money, I'd feed my family like kings and queens. I never want to hear my children cry because they can't get enough to eat.

My throat felt very tight and my eyes misted. "Do you think my mother has food and love all muddled together, Aunt Evelyn?" I asked. "Does she really think she can patch up her abusive treatment with a potato kugel or a lemon pie?"

Aunt Evelyn shook her head. "I don't really know what Jean thinks, honey," she said. "She has a funny way of solving her problems."

She turned a few more pages of the picture album and stopped at a snapshot of my grandma and my mother. The two of them were laughing together. I could see the special feeling they shared from the way they clung to each other. I blinked away unwanted tears. Why couldn't I make Mama look at me that way? What did I do wrong? "They were really good friends, weren't they,

Aunt Evelyn?" I said.

Aunt Evelyn nodded. "And Jean believed everything that Mama told her. It was our Mama who loved Leonard best. She told Jean that he was a wonderful boy and that if she chose him, she would be comfortable and happy for the rest of her life. 'It's always better if the man is the one who loves most,' she said."

"And does Daddy love Mama more than she does him?" I asked.

Aunt Evelyn touched her napkin to her mouth. She sipped her coffee and put the cup back in its saucer. She spoke slowly as if she were picking out each word. "Not *more* than your mother does," she said. "But in a different way. Anyway, Mama was so determined that Jean marry Leonard that she burned all of Frank Diamond's letters to her and Benny Hertz's too."

She turned another page and pointed to another snapshot of my mother. "Look, Susie, here's Jean all dressed up to go to a dance."

I looked at the picture and I couldn't believe how pretty my mother was. She had on one of those kicky straight up and down flapper dresses like you saw in old magazines. She looked just like Daisy from *The Great Gatsby*. . . all flowing and white. Her hair was short, but it had soft curls and she wore a garland in her hair. She had a sash around her hips and had on really high heels, even higher than the ones she always wore now.

"She must have knocked everyone flat," I said.

"She sure did," said Aunt Evelyn. "I used to be so envious of your mother! She got to go everywhere! I never had a date until I met Uncle Max."

I turned more pages of the book and stopped at one where my mother and Daddy were in the rumble seat of an old fashioned Ford with Aunt Peggy and Uncle Aaron in the front. Daddy had his arms around Mama and they were laughing.

"Look at that!" I said. "I wish they still laughed like that, now, Aunt Evelyn. All mother does is yell at Daddy, and he doesn't act like he even hears her. He buries himself in his newspaper or walks out of the house and goes back to the office. I don't think I've ever seen them smile at each other. I'd just hate it if my marriage turns out like that. I want a husband I can share private jokes with and snuggle like you do with Uncle Max."

Aunt Evelyn blushed. "Everyone has different ways of showing affection, Susie," she said.

She stood up and walked over to the stove. She refilled our coffee cups and then she sat down again. "Susie," she said and she paused.

She put a spoonful of sugar in her coffee and stirred for a while and then she tried again. "Susie," she said. "Your mother doesn't mean to be hard on you. She just has a lot of things on her mind that you don't understand."

"I don't think she's a very happy person, Aunt Evelyn," I said. "Why can't she laugh the way you do?"

I flipped the pages of the photograph album and there was Mama all decked out in a cloche hat and a fur coat. She was holding a little dog in her arms. "I didn't know you had a dog at grandma's," I said.

Aunt Evelyn peered at the picture. "That's Jack!" she said. "Jack was a little English Bull. Your mother went down to the Humane Society and got him with her first paycheck after she started working for the railroad. She just loved him! He barked and snarled at everyone but her!"

I grinned. "Just like Junior," I said.

Aunt Evelyn nodded and her eyes misted with memory. "And that's your mother's monkey fur coat. Oh, how she adored that coat, Susie. She saw it in LaSalle's window and she used to walk blocks out of her way after work just to see it. She told our mama all about it and she cried because she wanted it so much.

"We were very poor and she didn't think she'd ever be able to own such a fancy coat as that, no matter how hard she tried to save money for it. Her salary was so small, it would take years for her to put away enough for a downpayment. Besides, she always gave Mama all her paycheck except for lunch money. And when she got her first Christmas bonus, she went out and bought Mama her very first refrigerator. Up until that time, we had an old fashioned icebox."

"You mean the kind with blocks of ice in the bottom?"

Aunt Evelyn nodded. "Mama adored Jean. I think she was her favorite daughter although she never let on. Right before Chanuka that year, she broke open the pushke she kept on the window sill and dumped out all the coins she'd dropped into it to plant trees in Israel. That afternoon, I saw her leave the house with a sack of jewelry she never wore. She came back that night with a big box wrapped in blue paper and she put it on Jean's pillow."

I was fascinated. "What happened?" I asked. "Was Mama surprised?"

Aunt Evelyn smiled. "You should have seen her face when she opened that box, honey. She thought some fairy godmother had sent it to her. Mama never said a word. She just puttered around in the kitchen until Jean came running in and threw her arms around her."

"How did she figure out who gave her the coat?" I asked. "Did you tell her?"

Aunt Evelyn shook her head. "I didn't have to. Your mother knew that whenever good things happened to her, Mama was the reason. Nothing has ever been right for Jean since Mama died, Susie. Nothing."

My grandma died when I was eleven years old. I remembered the way my mother cried. She wore a black ribbon on her lapel for a whole year and every year, she lights a yartzheit candle for her and for my grandpa on Yom Kippur and on the anniversary of their deaths. But when she lights her mother's candle, tears run down her face and she can never finish the prayer without breaking down and sobbing. One time I saw her lean her head down on the counter and hug the candle as if it were really grandma. "Oh, Mama," she whispered. "Why didn't anything turn out right? I had such lovely dreams, Mama, and I tried so hard."

She rested her head on the counter and her whole body shook. I tiptoed out of the room because I knew how embarrassed she'd be if she knew I had seen her like that.

I felt awfully sad for both of us that day. I knew I would never be able to cry for her the way she did for *her* mother, and that was a terrible loss for us both.

Part II: 1955- 56

ஐ Chapter 18 ᯞ

Margie's wedding was in July and it took all my self control not to weep with envy. She had a mother who loved her. She had two men who desired her. I had nothing I wanted and I didn't understand why.

It never occurred to me that Margie made her own happiness. Daddy always told me that good luck is how you look at things but I didn't believe him. "Good luck is good luck," I told him. "And not much good ever happens to me. I know its my fault that I don't get what I want, but honestly, Daddy, the harder I try the worse things turn out."

Daddy shook his head. "No, Susie. When things happen, they just happen. You *make* them what they are. There is no such thing as good or bad luck, only good or bad attitudes."

It wasn't that I thought my father was a liar. It's just that I couldn't look at my events the way he or Margie looked at theirs. They coped with things as they happened. I worried about them before they occurred and when the reality wasn't the way I'd planned, I hated myself because I was convinced it was I who caused them to fail.

I wanted to be part of a couple like she was with Tom. I saw myself with a tall, faceless male beside me. We attended concerts and theater together. We played bridge. We shared private jokes and made continual love. I saw our children romping on our suburban lawn while he manned the barbecue and I dished out the salad. I saw it all, and I didn't give a damn who unlocked the gate to that kind of heaven. I wanted in.

I listened to Margie's wonderful plans for a future I ached to own and I tried to be thrilled for her. "You'll be my maid of honor, won't you, Susie?" she asked.

We were in a stationery store picking out invitations. "Do you like pure white or ivory?"

"For my dress or the invitations?" I asked. "Stick to one thing at a time, Margie."

"For the invitations. But will you be my maid of honor?"

"I'd love to," I said. "But won't you want someone in your family to stand up for you?"

Margie turned away from the book of invitation samples and gave me a hug. "I don't have any cousins I'm close to, and the only aunt I care about is Aunt Tess. She's too old to be in the wedding party. Besides, you're more than a sister to me, Susie. I won't feel married unless you're beside me. Would you like to wear light blue? It's your favorite color, and I don't want you to have to buy a dress you'll never wear again. What do you think?"

I smiled and I meant it. Margie was wonderful, and I was lucky to have such a loyal person who cared about me. "I'd love light blue," I said. "I can't wait to pick out the dress. But first, we better settle the invitations. If you use block printing, I'd take white, but if you use an old fashioned kind of script, I'd use ivory and print it in dark brown."

"You have such good taste, Susie," said Margie.

She looked at the saleslady. "Isn't Susie a marvel?" she asked.

I looked away from the love shining in her eyes. How could I resent my wonderful friend's good fortune? My shame was so intense I felt like I wore a neon sign across my chest that proclaimed HYPOCRITE. I blushed and forced myself to smile. "Margie, tell the lady what you want to order," I said. "I'm getting hungry. I'll treat you to a hot fudge sundae. Okay?"

so cr

I loved weddings and all the preparation that went with them: the parties, the planning, the happily-ever-after feeling for the bride. I had so much fun that summer, I almost forgot about what loomed ahead for me in the fall. Margie had a party or an afternoon shower almost every day. In between events, I helped her address wedding invitations, catalogue gifts and select patterns.

I gave Margie a kitchen shower at the end of June. I decorated everything in red and white. I composed poems for invitations and wrote them in red ink on white paper. I made the centerpiece out of kitchen utensils with red and white handles mixed in with red and white carnations. I even served strawberry shortcake because it fit into the color scheme. I had the party at my house and I hated to admit it, but my mother was magnificent about the whole thing. She must have spent a week baking the little shortcakes and freezing them. She got out all her best china and silver and polished her tea and coffee service while I made the place cards and decorated the table. She even put Junior in a kennel so he wouldn't bother my company.

When it was all over and everyone had left, she and I helped Margie pack up all her gifts. "Thank you so much, Mrs. Talberg," said Margie. "It was a wonderful party."

My mother started bringing in dishes from the dining room table. She smiled at Margie. "I'm glad you enjoyed it, Margie," she said. "But don't thank *me*. Thank Susan. She's been working on this shower for at least a month."

"I didn't do half as much as you did, Mother," I said. "All that cooking and baking! I don't know how you do it."

"It wasn't anything," said Mother. "The important thing is that you had a good time and Margie got some nice, practical gifts to get her started in her kitchen."

She put her arms around Margie and gave her a hug. I couldn't believe it. My mother was being decent to one of my friends! She wasn't sarcastic; her words held no nasty barbs; she was lovely, just the way I'd always dreamed she could be. "Believe me, Margie," she said. "Half the battle of being a good cook is to have the right cooking equipment. It doesn't take any special talent. Just good recipes and the right pots and pans."

"That's not true, Mother," I said. "I've tried baking cakes and making latkes and blintzes like you do and no matter how careful I am, nothing turns out as delicious as when you make it."

I shook inside as I spoke. One wrong word and this sweet, caring mother would disappear. I picked up a candied strawberry from the silver compote and ate it. I reached for another. I picked up the bowl and offered it to my mother. "You hardly had time to taste all the good food you made for us, Mama," I said.

She pushed the candy away. "I saved some fresh unsugared berries for Debbie and me," she said. "We can't eat the way you do, Susan."

She was still smiling, but some of the soft light in her eyes had gone out. I took a deep breath and tried to rekindle it once more. "Do you want me to pick up Junior now that the party is over, Mother?" I asked. "You deserve a rest. I'll help you clean up when I get back."

My mother gave me one of her rare looks of approval. "That's a good idea, Susan. You take Margie home and then pick up the dog. I have to start our dinner pretty soon."

I looked at my mother and I wanted to dare to embrace her. Why couldn't we ever talk like friends? I remembered all the times she'd pushed me away when I tried to hug her or kiss her cheek. I was far too afraid she'd rebuff me again to reach out and touch her now. I did manage a hesitant smile, but I folded my arms tight across my chest.

"I'm sorry your mother couldn't come this afternoon, Margie," Mother continued. "Tell her we missed her."

"Mother was really tired, Mrs. Talberg. I told her I'd excuse her from this shower because it was mostly my college friends," said Margie. "The Hesters are having us over for dinner tonight, and this is the only afternoon Mom had to relax at the beauty shop."

₭ ℙ

"Your poor mother is tied to her stove," said Margie when we got in the car. "She's been cooking and serving all day. Why can't you go out for dinner tonight, or just make your own meals from leftovers in the refrigerator?"

"Because Mother would never let us do that," I said. "She loves cooking because she loves eating. The sad thing is that she gains weight so fast. I'd hate to have to watch everything I ate the way she does. She weighs herself every single morning and if she gains one pound, her day is ruined."

"I don't think you're being fair, Susie," said Margie. "Her generation starved during the Depression. I'll bet happiness really <u>was</u> enough bread for dinner. We're lucky. We never had to worry about hunger the way our parents did. We can afford to be idealistic and look for love."

I never wanted to see my family so hungry that they didn't care what was on their plate. I never wanted to hear my children cry because they couldn't get enough to eat.

"You're so right," I said. "Isn't it sad how childhood scars warp adult attitudes? Every meal is a torture to my mother. She's petrified of getting fat even though Daddy loves her exactly the way she is."

"Susan," said Margie. "Every woman alive watches what she eats. No one can consume the food you do and stay as thin. I'll never figure it out. You had two helpings of strawberry shortcake this afternoon, and I'll bet you eat plenty for dinner tonight. And then, when we went to get your dress they had to special order a size six. My wedding dress is a twelve and I have to hold my breath to zip it up. I was so jealous, I could have spit snakes."

I grinned. This was some turnaround. Imagine Margie being jealous of me for anything. I had to admit my appetite was unusual. I sometimes thought I must have a very high metabolism. But actually, although I gorged at things I loved, I very often skipped meals entirely if I was too busy, and I absolutely refused to eat anything I didn't like. At the sorority house, I never got enough to eat because I hate goopy casseroles where you can't identify what's in them. They all taste like a mixture of flour, drippings and lima beans, and the very smell of them made me ill.

It was different now that I ate at home. Mother cooked all the things I loved, and I wasn't skipping very many meals. As a matter of fact, I was eating a lot of extra ones. I always tasted everything at Margie's parties and before I went to bed, I indulged in a snack that was the size of a normal dinner for most people.

By the day of the wedding, I had trouble buttoning my dress. I wasn't worried though because everyone said I was too skinny. Besides, I was having a marvelous time.

At the wedding, I met Ben Weiss. He was Tom's cousin. I'd never seen him around because he was about five years older than I was. He was tall and gorgeous and said he loved music and children. We danced every dance. "I'm glad you'll be teaching in town," he said. "You know, I didn't want to come to this wedding, and I'm sure glad my parents talked me into it. If I hadn't, I never would have met you."

I held my breath. Maybe he would be The One. Maybe I could find someone to love who would take me out of that house and let me be a wife and a mother. Maybe. . . I gave Ben a brilliant smile. "I'm glad you changed your mind," I said. "Are you?"

I snuggled close to him. "Oh, look," I said. "Margie's about to cut the cake. Let's go watch."

"I'd rather stay out here with you," said Ben

Obviously, I would have preferred being alone with him, too, but I remembered Michael Rose and how my hard-sell approach had failed. This time, I was going to do things right. Not too anxious; not too casual. I took a deep breath to calm my voice. "Let's go watch and then we can dance the rest of the night, okay?" I said, and to my relief, he followed me into the main hall.

❧ ❧

Ben called me the night after the wedding and made a date for Saturday night. "There's a marvelous movie at the Fine Arts," he said. "Have you ever seen 'Mr. Hulot's Holiday?' It's a classic. This will be the fourth time I've watched that man try to pour tea when the wind is blowing. Anyway, afterwards, we can have some espresso at La Chez Parisienne. How does that sound?"

"Sounds wonderful," I said. "What time does this magic evening begin?"

"How does seven sound?" said Ben.

At seven o'clock I was still putting the finishing touches on my face when I heard the dog shriek with rage. I shut my eyes and imagined the scene downstairs. Mother would rush to pick up the dog who would be snarling and squirming in her arms. Daddy would answer the door and try to make himself heard. And then they would all sit down in our antiseptic living room where no one but a statue could feel at home.

Mr. Davies at Bennet's had decorated it for us and he must have thought we entertained royalty or something. There were formal groupings of tall, uncomfortable velvet chairs or brocade sofas. One was around the piano, another by the fireplace that mother filled with artificial plants. "A fire just gets everything all smoky," said Mother when I asked her why she never burned logs in it. "I don't want to dirty this furniture, Susan. It was very expensive."

The room was a huge, brilliant cavern. You actually squinted from the glare when you walked into it. Everything shined, the furniture glowed, the candelabra sparkled.

Mother would usher Ben to the kidney-shaped couch by the bay window. She would sit across from him, holding our snarling dog, while she gave him the third degree. Nothing he said would suit her. I was sure of that because she had frozen every date I brought home out of my life with her brittle interrogations. I just couldn't let her do it again. I hurried as fast as I could to get downstairs and rescue my newest hope for salvation.

When I entered the living room, things were even worse than I imagined. Debbie was there, talking a mile a minute about her figure skating class. Daddy was fingering his newspaper and smothering a yawn. Why wasn't he helping? Usually, it was my father who kept these agonizing social catastrophes from happening. He must not like Ben, either. But why?

Mother said nothing. She just held the growling dog tightly. Junior's teeth were bared and his saliva dripped on my mother's sleeve. Evidently, Ben Weiss hadn't made a hit with anyone but Debbie. Her face glowed as she talked to him.

"I've been in your candy store so many times," said my sister. "It's our favorite place to hang out after school."

She heard me come into the room and looked up. "There you are, Susan," she said. "Did you know Ben owns Confectionaire Candies on Summit Street? That's the place you always go to when you want Bavarian Creams."

"I didn't know that," I said. "I thought you sold real estate."

"I do," said Ben. "But I also own the candy store. There's lots about me you don't know. I have a dog, too. A great big standard-sized poodle named Bon Bon."

"Does he charge at strangers like Junior does?" said Debbie.

Ben laughed. "No, he only assaults roast beef bones."

"Just like Susan," said Debbie. "You should see *her* attack a roast beef bone. Like a cannibal."

I wanted to curl up into a little ball and slide under my mother's plush carpet. Did she have to discuss my elephantine appetite? "I don't attack roast beef bones," I said. "But I do attack little sisters who make me late for the movies."

I smiled at Ben. "We'd better get started. The show begins in half an hour."

Mother stood up. "Come home early, Susan," she said. "I have to get up at dawn tomorrow."

"You don't have to wait up for me, Mother," I said.

"I know I don't," she said. "But I can't sleep until I know everyone's home and tucked in for the night."

She was doing it again. She was erasing Ben Weiss from my future and the rest of my family was helping her along. Debbie was smothering him with nonstop conversation about his chocolate covered creams. Daddy was yawning in his newspaper. I could feel the glow I had about my date with Ben Weiss flicker and threaten to go out before we even crossed my threshold. I groped for something . . . anything I could do to restore Ben's interest. "My, you look nice," I said to him. "That's a marvelous tie."

He smiled and linked my arm with his. "You look pretty wonderful, too, Susan. Let's hurry so we aren't late for the show."

ஐ Chapter 19 ஐ

It was a funny movie. We laughed all through it and we didn't stop. We were sipping espresso and eating chocolate eclairs. We took a walk in the clear night air, Ben's arm around my shoulder. The warm July air wrapped us in a velvet blanket; the Milky Way washed the sky with prisms of light. Ben kissed me. "You're delicious," I said.

"Better than Bavarian Creams?" he asked.

I opened my lips for an encore. "Much."

Then I remembered Bobby. My eyes snapped open and I pulled away. "Look at the time," I said. "Mother will be waiting. We'd better start home."

Ben took my shoulders. "What do you mean, start home?" he said. "We're just getting to know each other."

He kissed me again. If I didn't act fast this would be Bobby Mosten all over again. Only this time, it would happen under a lamp post on Adams Street with all of Toledo looking on. "Listen, Ben. People talk in this town," I said. "And my mother watches my morals like you do property values. If I want to go out with you again, I better get home fast."

"What kind of baby are you?" Ben asked.

I didn't blame him. I'd obviously loved his kisses. I was twenty-one years old and beginning a teaching career. He couldn't possibly know I had a screaming bitch of a mother who would make my life miserable if she suspected I so much as held hands with a man she didn't like. He didn't know that the one guy I slept with dropped me like an exploding light bulb.

He didn't realize the shadows I battled every day. And he didn't care. Why should he? I took his hand. "Try to understand," I said. "I'm not leading you on. I'd love to stay out with you all night. But this is our first date and I live at home. Let's save something for next time."

Well, it worked. He took me home, kissed me at the door and asked me out for dinner the next Saturday night. I kissed him back and could feel myself melt. This one would be ecstasy in bed. I kissed him once more, and tasted sweet anticipation of all the good things that could follow. "See you next Saturday," I said.

He reached for me to kiss me again. I could feel my resolve melting away. And then the dog came snarling down the stairs and lunged for his pants. That ended the evening.

I grabbed Junior and pushed Ben out the door to save his overcoat. "Good night," I shouted over the dog's outraged yelps. "I had a wonderful time."

I tried to smile and subdue the squirming animal locked in my arms. Ben waved goodbye and I wept. I wept for all the things I'd wanted to say, but didn't dare. I grieved for the trump cards that never came my way. I clenched my teeth until I got myself under control and then my rage burned away my tears like a sunlamp. I was not going to give up so easily. I was an adult. I could fight back.

I stormed upstairs into my parents' room. "Why did you let him loose?" I said to my mother.

"You'd been down there long enough, Susan," she said. "I have to get up early to get your father's breakfast. Have you no consideration?"

"Tomorrow is Sunday, Mother. You don't have to get up." I snarled. "Why can't you tell the truth for once? Your best entertainment is to make me miserable."

She stood immobile as an iceberg in her gorgeous designer robe. Her hair looked as if she had combed it to go out, not like it was brushed before she went to bed. Her face didn't have a blemish or a wrinkle. She wasn't a mother. She was an alabaster statue. Nothing touched her. Nothing.

Next to her, I felt so vulnerable, so human. My lipstick was eaten away. My hair was a tangled mess. I sweated, I cried, I cared. My eyes filled with tears once more. "I finally get a decent guy interested in me and you turn that man eating dog of yours on him."

I buried my face in my hands and fought to control my fury. "Oh, what's the use?" I sobbed.

"Will you two stop nipping at each other?" said my father. "I have an early golf game, tomorrow."

I turned to my mother. My eyes were red and my voice accelerated into a shriek of pain. "Why didn't you like him? Why couldn't you be decent to him? I'll never get out of this disgusting place if you treat every guy I bring home this way. My God, if you didn't tear him to bits, you made sure the dog tore his pants off. And I'm stuck. Just like the Wasserstrom sisters. Stuck forever in your nightmare of a house."

My mother's expression didn't change. She observed me like a scientist watching a frantic rat trapped in its maze. "That's enough of your dirty mouth, Susan," she said. "No, I don't like Ben Weiss. He's got a reputation a mile long. Everyone says he was the one who got the Goldberg girl pregnant. He's the kind who would schtup anything in skirts. I don't want my daughter's name associated with him. I'm warning you for your own good, Susan."

"Daddy. Daddy, *say* something," I cried.

"There *is* talk about him, Susie," said my father.

Then he turned to my mother. "But after all, Jean, Susan's a big girl and she can take care of herself. Can't you, kitten?"

"Oh, can she?" said my mother. "It didn't sound like she was taking very good care of herself a few minutes ago. If I hadn't sent that dog downstairs, your daughter would have been sprawling on the living room couch with that sleazy candy vendor. Believe me, Leonard. I know."

"No one could sprawl on that couch," I hissed. "No one could even *sit* on it for six minutes without needing emergency care. I'm going out for dinner with Ben Weiss next Saturday night, whether you like it or not, Mother. *I* don't think he's sleazy. I think he's marvelous."

"You are not going anywhere with that man," said my mother. "I will not allow it."

She turned away and walked over to her bed. "You just try to stop me, Mother," I said to her back. "Just try it."

I ran out the door and stormed downstairs. "Where are you going?" called my mother.

"I have to hang up my coat," I said.

As I hurtled down the stairs, I heard my mother say to my father, "Don't you start, Leonard. I'm trying to save *her* from my mistake. But it's no use, is it? She wants a man just like her father, and it looks like she's determined to get one."

I didn't have time to absorb that piece of news before she was shouting at me again.

"Be sure to lock up before you come upstairs," she said. "And Susan, there's some lemon pie in the icebox. I saved it for you."

∞ Chapter 20 ∞

As long as I lived in my mother's house, I would be at her mercy. My only escape was a home of my own, away from her illogical furies.

But I had to buy a car before I could even think about an apartment. The way things were now, I needed my mother's permission if I wanted to drive anywhere, and I hated it. My mother could think of one hundred ridiculous excuses for saying no to me. The last time I asked her why I couldn't use her Chevy to drive to the dentist, she said, "I was thinking about washing it this afternoon, Susan."

"I'll wash it for you as soon as I get back," I promised.

My mother looked at me as if I were a derelict asking for a handout. "I've heard *that* before," she said and walked out of the room.

I had crashed into her iron wall again. I sighed and took the bus to my appointment.

My mother ignored me when I came downstairs the next morning, and I ignored her. She was a hateful tyrant and the sight of her made me furious. I ignored the juice she had squeezed for me.

I pushed away her homemade coffeecake and shoved the platter of blueberry pancakes to one side.

I made my own instant coffee and opened a box of Hostess doughnuts. I bit into one of the powdered ones and glared at my mother. "Delicious," I said.

I called Margie as soon as I finished breakfast. She had just returned from her honeymoon in the Bahamas. I suspect the last thing she wanted to do was chat with her ex-roommate about her mother and men. But Margie, being Margie, never let on that she wasn't vitally interested in anything I had on my mind. "We're just getting up," she said. "Why don't you come over for brunch? We can talk while we do the dishes."

"I can't," I said. "Mother is barely speaking to me. She'll never let me drive over."

"Don't even discuss it with your mother, Susie," she said. "Tom will come and pick you up. I can drive you home and that'll give us more time to talk."

I redid my face and my hair and hurried downstairs. I put on my coat and announced, "I'm going out for a while."

"Where are you going, Susan?" Mother asked. "Will you be home for dinner?"

Tom's horn sounded outside. "I don't know," I said.

I walked out of my mother's house and slammed the door . . .hard. The dog shrieked and ripped the screen. I got in Tom's car and we drove away.

ഇ Chapter 21 രൃ

Margie's apartment was darling. The minute I walked in the door, I relaxed. The whole place was cool and peaceful, a gentle pastiche of ivory and blue. The kitchen was a red and white wonderland. "And it's all thanks to you, Susie," Margie said. "Look how cheerful everything looks. I decorated the whole thing with gifts I got at your party."

Tom was so delighted with his wife and his home he strutted around like a satisfied rooster. "Wait 'til you taste Margie's cooking! You won't believe how gourmet everything is!" he crooned. "You'd think she won a bunch of recipe contests and actually she's never really cooked before."

"I'm just having poached eggs on English muffins," said Margie. "What's so special about that?"

"You are," said Tom and kissed her.

Time out while the newlyweds chirped and cuddled. I tactfully looked away. My eyes wandered over the ceiling. They trailed around the plants in the kitchen. They darted back to the loving couple. Whoops, still at it. I shifted from one foot to the other. I cleared my throat. Still?

Margie finally came up for air. She patted Tom on the cheek. She radiated love. "You go read the paper, honey," she said. "Susie and I will get everything ready."

While we got the dishes on the table, I told Margie all about last night. I didn't leave out a thing, not even the lemon pie. "Well," said Margie. "Are you going to break the date?"

"No, I am not going to break my date," I said.

My voice reverberated in that small kitchen as if I were the main speaker at a football rally. I could feel my courage grow as I chanted my defiant proclamation. I AM NOT GOING TO BREAK MY DATE! Was I stating a fact or trying to convince myself that I could win a battle with my enemy?

I looked Margie in the eye as if *she* were the one who doubted my words. "I'm going to get a brand new dress and look absolutely smashing. . . if that is possible."

I paused for breath. I felt uncertain and very shaky. I had just declared war but I wasn't sure the battle was worth a fight. I arranged Canadian bacon on a platter and carefully avoided my best friend's knowing eyes. "Margie, is it true that Ben got Marilyn Goldberg pregnant?" I asked.

"Well, someone did," said Margie. "Don't you remember that year she decided to visit an aunt in Maine? That's when she had the baby."

I put the plate down and stared. "How did *you* know about it?" I asked.

"Mother told me," said Margie. "But Susan, that doesn't mean he'll knock you up, too. Just don't fall for his line. He always starts by having you come up to his place to meet the dog. Once you do that, only your own will power stands between you and mad, passionate love."

"I wouldn't mind a little mad, passionate love," I said. "Or the novel experience of meeting a well-trained dog. All I've had since I got home is an angry mother and that barking maniac she calls a pet. What did Marilyn do with her baby?"

"She put it up for adoption," said Margie. "It was your Uncle Max who placed it in a good home. Lots of lawyers do that for their clients. Everyone knows your uncle has all the right connections. Didn't you?"

"No one in my family tells me anything," I said. "Do you want me to put the eggs on the table now?"

Margie nodded. "Will you, Susie? I'll get Tom."

More murmuring and gurgling in the other room. The eggs cooled. The bacon congealed. This was not the place to visit on a Sunday morning.

Eventually we sat down at Margie's kitchen table and began the meal. Everything tasted like brunch at The Ritz to me. I was actually tasting food, instead of clashing wills with my mother. After we cleaned the kitchen, Margie popped some popcorn and we played Monopoly all afternoon. About five, Margie drove me home. "Susie, I'm not doing anything but returning wedding gifts tomorrow. Would you like me to pick you up and we'll shop for a good-looking dress for you?"

No one, and I mean no one, could pick out clothes for me like Margie. I always felt like June Allison when she chose my outfits, very fresh and delicious. One look at me in a gown Margie Wiseman selected, and Ben didn't stand a chance. I would captivate him.

"I'll see if Louise can meet us at Smith's for lunch," Margie continued. "They have the most wonderful chef's salad: lots of chicken and cheese and ham."

"I love those little sweet rolls they put in the bread basket," I said. "And I'd kill for their deviled crab and coconut cream pie."

"That's too fattening for me," said Margie. "Lucky you. You can gorge on all that stuff and you don't get so much as a pimple. All I have to do is look in a bakery window and I get ballooning hips and angry red blotches!"

There was Margie, envious of me again when I'd give ten years of my life to have only one of her magnificent married moments. I smiled at the irony of it all. We pulled into my drive. "What time, tomorrow?" I asked.

"How's ten o'clock?" asked Margie. "Then I can get some of the gifts returned and we'll still have a couple hours to shop. I'll tell Louise to meet us at 1:30. Okay?"

℘ Chapter 22 ℘

It's fun to shop with Margie. We laugh a lot and make fun of the man-
nequins we see in the windows. We play "I wish I could afford. . . ." when we
stare at the jewelry counters. We take all the free samples in the promotion
displays and come away from the perfume counters smelling like an
overblown flower garden. Our fingertips twinkle in ten different lacquers; we
have lipstick measles on our arms in every imaginable shade of orange, pink
and red.

But this time, shopping was a disaster. Not one thing I tried on fit. The size
eights wouldn't button around my middle. I even had to hold my breath for
the size tens. What happened to the sylph like size six who waltzed down
Margie's aisle not two months ago?

A wave of fury choked me tighter than the skirt I was trying to force over
my bulbous tummy. Mother! *She* did this to me. She was determined to make
me suffer at every meal the way she did. She deliberately tempted me with a
relentless barrage of fattening dishes because she was jealous of my ability to
enjoy food. My God! She was a demon! She decided to punish me for my
only pleasure, and she had won. For the first time in my life, food stuck to my
hips and bloated my stomach.

Louise met us at Smith's and I ordered pineapple and cottage cheese.
"What's gotten into you?" asked Louise. "You always make me jealous when
you pack away cream soups and ice cream parfaits."

"Susie can't button a size ten," said Margie. "We finally had to settle on an
ivory silk chemise. I think it's gorgeous. Simple, flowing lines and a marvelous color with her dark hair. But Susie won't believe me."

She turned to me and put her hand on my arm. "Susie. You're not a naturally fat person. Even now, it's just your middle that's bloated. The rest of you
is slender as ever."

She took my hand. "See?" she said. "Your arms are skinny! And so are
your legs. If you just cut out desserts for a little while, and touch your toes
twenty times every day, you'll be back to a size six. This is NOT a tragedy,
Susan. It doesn't even rate a worry."

"I am fat," I said. "I'm fat, like Debbie is fat. I'm fat like my mother is fat.
And I can't stand it. No cream, thank you. I'm going to learn to drink black
coffee."

"Your mother isn't fat, and you're not fat," said Margie. "And you can have cream in your coffee for God's sake. You always overdo things, Susie. Moderation. That's all you need to do. Eat in moderation."

But moderation was too mild for me. The only thing I hated more than living at home was the specter of obesity. All my life, I heard my mother scream that her arms were huge, her hips were too big, her stomach sagged. All my life, I saw her hate herself for enjoying a meal and then punish herself for the rest of the week on grapefruit and black coffee. I didn't want that to happen to me.

Well. I wasn't weak like she was. I was strong. Food wasn't going to make me ugly so no one would marry me. Not me.

"I am declaring war on food," I announced to my two friends. "Hurry and finish your lunch. I want to buy a calorie book."

❧ Chapter 23 ❧

Margie dropped me off at the house at about four-thirty. I trudged up the front steps with my new dress and my firm resolve to lose weight. Mother was preparing dinner.

Whenever I came home, my first stop was the refrigerator even before the coat closet. I walked into the kitchen. Mother didn't even look up from her chopping board. She sliced onions and chopped garlic as she talked. "Where have you been, Susan?" she snapped. "I needed you to run to the store for me."

"I was shopping with Margie," I said.

I left the room to hang up my coat. She came into the hall wiping her hands on her apron. "Shopping? What for?"

I squared my shoulders. Courage, Susan. This is your life and you are the one who is leading it. My stomach started to churn and that infinitesimal pineapple and cottage cheese lunch rose in my throat. I swallowed and braced myself for what was sure to come. "I bought a new dress for Saturday night," I said.

I held my breath.

"You mean you really think I'll permit you to go out with that man?" said my mother. "Don't you *listen*, Susan? I said you cannot go out with him again."

"I am twenty-one years old, Mother. You don't rule me anymore," I said.

I didn't raise my voice. I kept my face down so she couldn't see the hot flush of defiance color my cheeks. I grabbed my dress box and started up the stairs. I could feel tension crack my voice and fill my eyes with nervous tears.

"As long as you live in this house, I'll decide who is suitable to come here," she shouted to my back.

I didn't turn around. I would not give her the satisfaction of seeing the tears oozing out of my eyes. "Then I'll have Ben meet me someplace else," I said. "I wouldn't want him to defile your living room."

"Who is going to pay for that dress, Susan?" called my mother. "If you charged it to my account, you might as well return it. I won't pay the bill."

I looked down the stairwell at her. Her face didn't look human to me. It belonged to a demon. I could no longer control my rage. "You can't <u>do</u> this to me," I screamed. "I won't let you! Daddy won't let you, either."

My mother's smile was ice. "We'll discuss it at dinner, young lady. Hurry downstairs. You have to pick up the bread I ordered at Goodman's. And I want you to help set the table."

"But it's only four-thirty and Goodman's is just around the block. Besides, we don't eat until six. Why should I come down now?"

"Because I want you to," said my mother. "That's why."

I opened the door to my bedroom. This time, I was going to score even if I didn't win. I was not returning to the battlefield in her kitchen until six. Debbie could waddle over to the bakery. Not me.

I went into my room and tried on my new dress. Margie was right. It looked beautiful, but I didn't. I was a picture of a furious child, my mouth pursed with rage and my eyebrows an angry line across my brow. My color was gone except for two vivid spots on my cheeks. My eyes were red, and even as I stared in the mirror my fists were clenched and ready to strike. I took a deep breath and turned from the mirror. I took off the new dress and looked at my bloated body. That pot belly was unmistakable. I got on the scale. The last time I'd weighed myself was in the doctor's office months ago. Then, I weighed 93 pounds. The doctor thought that was a little thin but I didn't. "I would rather be on the slender side," I told him. "I don't ever want to have to diet the way my mother and my sister do. I love food too much."

Well, I wasn't too thin, now. The scale said 108. How had those fifteen pounds crept up on me? I always wore loose clothes and most of my skirts had been too big anyway. In those days, we all wore sloppy joe sweaters that came down to our hips. I loved flowing skirts and always bought large sizes so they would be long enough. I guess that's why I didn't notice when the pounds added on. Now, I realized that my skirts never slipped around my waist the way they used to do. In fact, I always had to unbutton them after I ate.

I looked down at the scale. "This is the last time you're going to surprise me," I said to its silent accusing number. "From now on, I'm watching every single thing that goes into my mouth. The only place you'll go with me is down."

I got off the scale and returned to my room. I settled down on the bed and opened my book. "Susan!" called my mother. "Hurry. I'm waiting."

I took a deep breath and read on. I stared at the page but not one word penetrated my brain. Five minutes later, I heard her once more. "Susan! I am not going to ask you again. Come down here NOW."

I could just see her accosting Daddy with her latest grievance about me the minute he came home. If she did, I wouldn't stand a chance of convincing him to pay for my dress. I sighed and closed the book. She won again.

I trudged downstairs and began cutting vegetables for the salad while

Mother played games with a big pot of spaghetti sauce. "I'm having French bread with garlic, Susan," she said. "And a very special angel food cake for dessert. Run over to Goodman's and get some rye bread for sandwiches later tonight. And hurry. I want you to butter the Pepperidge Farm loaves and smear them with garlic as soon as you get back."

No wonder I had expanded. This was one of my favorite meals and my mother's angel food cake was like an addiction with me. Mother thought that by morning it would all disappear. That was why she made such a huge cake for just the four of us. Well, she was in for a big surprise. "Who do you think is going to eat all this?" I asked. "You've made enough for an army and both you and Debbie are on diets. Daddy and I couldn't possibly make a dent in so much food."

"Once you taste it, you'll do all right," said my mother. "Since you've been home, I never have enough left over from one meal to the next. I decided to make plenty so I wouldn't have to cook again tomorrow. I can use the sauce in a casserole or make Spanish rice with it."

"Do you always have to make such fattening things?" I asked. "No wonder Debbie has a weight problem. You serve her buttered bread and noodle-rich dinners finished with gooey desserts. How do you expect her to get thin?"

"I can't help it," said my mother. "You and your father like sweets. Debbie is just going to have to learn self control."

"And so will I," I said. "I'm on a diet."

That got a reaction.

"A diet. Whatever for?"

"I have gained fifteen pounds on your cooking," I said. "And that's too much. I'm not going to let this get out of hand the way you and Debbie do. I have fifteen pounds to lose and I'm going to do it as fast as I can. I bought a calorie book today."

"What do you mean, you have to lose fifteen pounds? You're way too skinny and you know it," she said. "Aunt Evelyn was just saying how much better you've been looking since you got home. You finally have color in your cheeks, and you don't look so gaunt."

I permitted myself a small smile of victory. "I don't care about Aunt Evelyn. I don't care about your leftovers," I said. "I'm on a diet. I can't eat anything you've made for dinner. I will poach myself an egg."

The front door opened and Daddy came home. I was so happy to see him, I ran to give him a hug. The dog came charging after me nipping at my ankles and snarling his usual greeting to my father. "Hey, kitten," said Daddy. "What's up? Give me a minute to hang up my coat."

"Can I talk to you, Daddy?" I asked. "I have something private to discuss."

"Sure you can, honey," said Daddy. "But can't it wait a little? I'm awfully tired. Where's Debbie?"

"She'll be home any minute," said my mother. "She had chorus today after school. You know, Leonard, she has such a pretty voice. Maybe we should give her singing lessons."

Daddy patted my hand. "After supper, Susie. We'll talk."

"Dinner will be ready in about fifteen minutes." said Mother. "Please set the table, Susan."

I set the table. Debbie came home and we all sat down. I brought in one poached egg on half a piece of diet toast. Daddy looked at me. "What's wrong, honey? Sick?" "No," I said. "I'm on a diet."

"Diet?" said Daddy. "Why do you need to diet? You're finally getting a few curves worth pinching and now you want to go on a diet!"

My mother nodded happily. "That's what I told her, Leonard," she said. "But she never listens to me."

And that brought her around to her next grievance. "Leonard," she continued as she heaped his plate with spaghetti. "Susan defied us both this afternoon and I am very hurt. Here, have some French bread, honey. And a little salad. I put Roquefort cheese on it."

Daddy looked at me and saw my misery floating like fog over one tiny poached egg lying in the middle of my mother's oversized dinner plate. The torture of abstinence colored my face gray and fogged my eyes with unshed tears. My heart was thundering so hard, I was sure he could see my blouse flutter. I chewed my bit of toast and it tasted like soggy cardboard. I waited.

"She had the nerve to charge a ridiculously expensive dress to our account without even asking us. She is *really* planning to risk her reputation on that cheap Romeo of hers Saturday night. Save room for dessert, darling. It's one of your favorites."

My father took his plate and set it down. He never defied my mother in front of us, but sometimes, he said just the right thing to get her to leave me alone. This time, he stepped right in and fought my battle. I couldn't believe it. I loved him so much I didn't care if I never ate anything but poached eggs again.

"Listen, Jean. If Susan wants to go out with Ben Weiss, I see no reason why she shouldn't. We've brought her up to know right from wrong. She managed to survive college, didn't she?"

"That's beside the point," said my mother.

She grabbed a piece of French bread as if it were a weapon. She pointed it at my father. "That boy is cheap and you know it, Leonard," she said. "He's scum, pure and simple. What will everyone say if they find out we let our daughter go out with him? I'll be the talk of the Sisterhood!"

She took a bite of bread and waited.

"We'll discuss it later, Jean," said my father. "I can't argue with you and still do justice to your cooking. You know that."

My mother scooped a tiny helping of spaghetti on her plate. She ate it quickly. The determined expression on her face reminded me of a gorilla devouring his victim. She swallowed the tomato-covered noodles in one gulp and then she attacked the sweet and sour cabbage. She chewed the bits of fruit and crusted breadcrumbs mixed with the cabbage and shoved another forkful into her mouth. She downed the portion whole and wiped the corners of her mouth with her napkin. "I used peaches in it this time, Leonard," she said. "How do you like it?"

"I haven't tasted it yet, Jean," said Daddy. "I'm still working on this wonderful spaghetti."

My mother served herself another helping of the vegetable casserole. She didn't look at me, but her anger was a tangible thing. It actually flamed and I looked down at my skin to see she had blistered it.

We ate in silence. I finished my egg and rubbed my empty stomach. I watched my mother. Her face was limned with anger. She speared her food as if it were running away from her. She shoved each bit in her mouth as if she were punishing it. She stuffed a chunk of garlic bread between her teeth and reached for more spaghetti. Her manicured fingers clamped around the spoon like a red-tipped vise and she thrust food into her snapping mouth. I could see the veins bulging in her neck as she masticated ground beef, garlic and noodles and gulped it down. She wiped her reddened lips with a grease-stained cloth. "Are you through with that asparagus, Leonard?" she asked.

Debbie loved this meal as much as I did. While the three of us tangled with each other, my fat sister had eaten half the spaghetti on the platter and most of the bread. She finished two helpings of the cabbage and all the asparagus Hollandaise. I watched her with the same interest a keeper watches the hungry animals he has just fed devour their meal. I wanted what she was eating with the same intensity I ached for the attention she got from my mother. I craved the food she was devouring so badly I could hardly breathe. My eyes narrowed. What right had she to enjoy that dinner when I was so hungry for it? Debbie wiped up the tomato gravy from her plate with a piece of bread. She burped. "What's for dessert, Mama?" she asked.

"A lovely surprise, sweetheart," said my mother.

She pushed back her plate and went into the kitchen. She returned with the most magnificent angel food cake I had ever seen. It looked glorious, all fluffy with yellow custard, decorated with pineapple rings and maraschino cherries. I poured some coffee and watched as everyone dug in. My abstinence reminded my mother that she hadn't finished tearing me to shreds. "What about that dress, Leonard?" she hissed. "Are you going to let your daughter use your charge account whenever she pleases that way? The least Susan could do is ask permission before she decides to buy a new wardrobe."

She cut a small sliver of cake and put it on her plate. She spooned the pineapple custard sauce over it and dropped several maraschino cherries and marshmallows across the top. I wiped my mouth with a napkin so knotted and wrinkled it felt like a wet dishrag.

"How much did the dress cost, Susie?" asked my father, and he smiled at me.

I could feel my muscles relax. My teeth stopped grinding against each other and my heart resumed its normal pace. My wonderful daddy smiled at me! "It cost fifty dollars but it's beautiful," I said. "Wait 'til you see it, Daddy. Margie helped me pick it out."

My mother took another helping of cake and swept it into her mouth. She scooped up the pineapple custard and filled her spoon. She paused and pointed it at me as if daring me to inhale its pungent sweetness. "You have a closet full of gorgeous clothes," she said. "Why do you need something else?"

The custard shimmered and danced its way into my mother's mouth. I was hypnotized and I could not look away. "Here, Debbie," she said to my sister. "You can have another small piece of dessert. It won't hurt you. We'll have to take the rest over to Aunt Evelyn. I don't want it sitting around here if Susan won't eat it."

"Is there any sherbet?" asked Debbie. "I just love this stuff with Uncle Harry's coco-banana nut sherbet."

"Now, Jean. You know how you love a new dress when you're going someplace special," said Daddy. "Tell you what, kitten. Let's consider it a welcome home gift from me. I'm very proud of my college graduate. Now, hurry upstairs and try on the new dress. I want to see how tempting you're going to be for Ben this Saturday night."

I smiled. I glowed love at him from the tips of my toes. I hurried upstairs and put on the dress. I combed my hair and tried to cover up my red, puffy eyes with make-up. "You look like a queen!" said Daddy.

""I just love that dress," said Debbie. "Why don't you ever let me choose my own clothes like Susan does?"

"I will when you're thin enough to wear nice things," said my mother.

She pulled my father's half-finished dessert over to her and dug into it. "Besides," she continued, her mouth full of Daddy's cake, "Lane Bryant is the only place that can outfit you now, and they don't handle the name brands you see in *Mademoiselle.*"

My sister slammed her fork down on her empty plate. "Susan always gets her own way with everything," she said. "I want some more sherbet, please."

I took Daddy's hand. "Are you going back down to the lab, tonight?" I asked.

"I have to get a prescription for Mrs. Jackson ready," he said. "I was just waiting to see how gorgeous you looked."

I turned and pirouetted in my new dress. "Help me clear the table, Deborah Ann," said my mother.

"I haven't finished dessert," said Debbie. "Besides, I have to study my English. I got a D on the last test, remember?"

"All right, sweet life," said my mother. "I can finish up here."

She demolished the rest of my father's untouched cake. "I just hate waste," she said.

I left the dining room and started upstairs. "Susan!" called my mother. "You come here this minute to do these dishes. You're not a visitor here, you know."

Chapter 24

That night I had the first dream. I was in a very large room filled with table after table piled high with food. The odors intoxicated me. My mouth watered; my stomach ached. I was transfixed by a chocolate eclair blanketed with thick, glossy frosting. It oozed a creamy custard that glistened with sugar and cinnamon. I had to have that eclair. I would die if I didn't consume it.

I reached for it. It receded. I reached again. It eluded me once more. I heard a loud voice echoing, "FAT! FAT! You're fat and ugly! That's what you are!"

I looked at myself in a mirror. I was huge. Flaps of flesh hung from my chin and jawbone. My arms were so thick the seams of my sleeves were split. My ankles folded over my shoes and my legs looked like tumescent oil drums.

"But I haven't eaten anything," I screamed. "Why am I fat? I haven't eaten anything."

I woke up soaked in perspiration. I sat up in bed and looked at my arms and legs. They were their usual shape, their ordinary size. I stumbled out of bed and got on the scale. One hundred and eight pounds.

I hadn't gained. I hadn't lost.

Fifteen pounds. I'll never do it. Fifteen pounds! It sounded like a mountain of flesh.

I staggered back to bed but I couldn't sleep. I tossed and tussled with my nightmare and watched the night turn dark before the rising sun gilded the horizon. I couldn't bear to begin the day. Breakfast for me would be a tiny boiled egg and black coffee. Goodbye to sausages and omelets. Farewell to sweet rolls and pancakes, dripping butter, oozing syrup. I could never eat those things again.

Never.

I closed my eyes and tried to forget food, but I couldn't. When eight o'clock finally came, I got dressed and inhaled the hickory smoke of broiled bacon, the salty, butter rich essence of fried eggs and biscuits. I ached with hunger.

But I kept to my diet. I did better than that. Each day, I trimmed the amount of calories I ate a little more until, by the end of the week I was down to eight hundred a day. I was cranky. I was tired. And I was furious. Other people ate desserts. Other people put butter on their potato, enjoyed a piece of soft, flaky bread and wore the same size clothes year after year. But I couldn't do what other people did.

Never, ever again.

❧ Chapter 25 ❧

Ben called me Friday night to make definite plans for our date. Mother answered the telephone. I could hear the steel edge to her voice. "I'm fine, Ben. Thank you," she said. "Just a minute. Susan is right here."

I was too hungry and tired to care if I sounded tempting. I took the telephone receiver from my mother. She sat down and picked up the paper. I tried to keep our conversation brief. I didn't want to give my mother any ammunition. Not when I was so vulnerable to her attacks.

"How's seven o'clock?" asked Ben. "I thought we'd go to the Commodore and stay for dancing. Would you like that?"

Like it? I would love it. If I had enough strength to move. Well, tomorrow night I'd break the diet. *Just for one night,* I told myself. *You've been so good all week.*

The thought of food cheered me. I began planning what I would order in the back of my mind while the front of my mind flirted with Ben. "Wonderful!" I said.

I blinked away the charcoal broiled filet mignon wrapped in shining, fat riddled bacon that shimmered before my eyes.

"I love dancing," I said.

I shook my head to erase the image of a sour cream covered potato with sparkling green chives peeping through rivulets of butter and cream.

"I know you do," said Ben. "I found you on the dance floor at Margie's wedding. Remember?"

I closed my eyes so I couldn't see the tremendous strawberry shortcake that floated over the telephone. My mouth watered at the thought of those ripe, tart berries; my stomach churned as I imagined flakes of shortbread melting on my tongue. I swallowed hard. "Sure I remember. Sure," I said.

I looked at my mother. She pulled a banana out of the large bowl of fruit on the coffee table. She pulled back the peeling and ate. Her eyes were riveted to my face like magnets as she chewed. She knew. I could hide nothing from her evil eyes. She knew all about the procession of pies and puddings that haunted me as I sipped black coffee and spooned sour grapefruit into my mouth because they haunted her as well.

I slept late Saturday. I managed to prolong a half piece of dry diet toast with gallons of black coffee. I smoked half a pack of cigarettes and exhaled angry blue clouds as my mother started dinner. It was roast chicken. The smell drove deep into my nostrils until I wept with wanting. I watched her prepare the dressing: mushrooms, onions and wild rice. The onions danced in hot butter and their perfume inflamed me. My stomach growled. I gulped my coffee. I lit another cigarette. She was making a lemon chiffon pie, too. She had the eggs out on the counter and was working on the crust.

Mother ignored me as I watched her cook. She hadn't spoken about Ben or my date since I refused to break it. *Thank God for Daddy,* I thought. *He must have said something to keep her quiet.*

I crushed out my cigarette and stood up. Mother was grating the lemons and their citrus smell painted pictures of the glorious confection to come. I left the room.

I devoted the afternoon to getting dressed. I spent hours washing my hair, doing my nails and shaving my legs. I ironed my new dress and rubbed perfume in the collar and cuffs. I even manicured my toenails. Anything to fill the time until Ben came to the door. I didn't want to eat anything, not if I was going to order the huge dinner I'd planned.

I drowned out my mother's kitchen smells with peach bath salts and floral bubble bath. I tried to soak the hunger and fatigue out of my body in water hot enough to boil eggs. I got out of the bath so limp I didn't know how I would manage to stand up when Ben came to the door. My mind was filled with visions of food: the dinner I was missing downstairs and the one I would have tonight at the hotel.

Tonight, I would splurge.

Just tonight.

೫ Chapter 26 ೬

Ben arrived promptly at seven. The dog dashed to the door. He clawed the screen and snarled ominously. "Just a minute," called my mother.

I listened at the head of the stairs. It seemed hours before she quieted the dog and opened the door. "Sit down, Ben," I heard her say. "I'll call Susan."

Debbie came upstairs. "You look nice, Susie," she said. "I wish I had a dress like that."

"Well, you can borrow it if you ever manage to get a date," I said. "It'll even fit *you*. I'm big as a house."

"Oh, could I, Susie?" she said. "It's so loose and flowing. I just know I can wear it."

She frowned. "No one ever asks me out," said Debbie. "I'm the only girl in the sophomore class who has never had a date. And even if someone called, Mama would never let me accept. She treats me just like a baby, and I'm fifteen years old."

I looked at my angry sister. Her round cheeks were puffed with fury. She was pouting and tears made her eyes look like glass prisms. My eyes narrowed and I didn't bother to hide my scorn. What did *she* have to cry about? Mother stuffed her with all the good things in life and never gave me so much as a kind word. I looked away. It wasn't Debbie's fault that my mother lavished her with love. I had no right to resent my little sister for accepting what was given to her.

But I was hungry and my tolerance level didn't exist. I wanted to get to the Commodore as fast as I could. I could taste that steak, now. I smelled the French fried onion rings. I barely controlled the saliva that filled my mouth. My empty stomach throbbed. The dog yelped, and I remembered poor Ben stuck downstairs with that granite woman and her blood hungry pet. I hurried downstairs.

"You're gorgeous," said Ben when I walked into the living room.

"What a glamour puss!" said Daddy.

Mother held Junior, but every few seconds a yelp erupted from him like periodic bloops from a percolator. She nodded to me, and her eyes narrowed. "Susan, you'll have to get more sleep," she said. "Those dark circles under your eyes look awful."

"I'll get my coat," I said.

ഇ Chapter 27 ര

Ben was darling all evening. I didn't care if he was trying to charm me with the same line he'd used on every eager maiden in Toledo. All I cared about was dinner.

We had daiquiris first and we danced. Ben held me close and I tingled. I was beginning to want him even more than I wanted that food we'd ordered.

I remembered the Bobby Mosten fiasco and my hormones froze. *If you give in to this man, you'll never see him again,* I told myself and switched my thoughts to rich cheese sauces and creamy gravies. Much safer.

Dinner was on the table when we finished dancing. I had ordered the king-sized New York cut steak, French fried onions and baked potato with everything on it. While we drank our daiquiris, I ate every roll but one in the bread basket.

Ben had that one.

I savored each morsel of food slowly. I hated to see this dinner end. My face gleamed with exertion. My eyes sparkled with happiness. My stomach felt like it would burst.

I had strawberry shortcake for dessert.

I was so loaded with food, I could barely move.

It was midnight and the band stopped playing. Ben kissed my ear. "Come home with me for a drink," he said. "Bon Bon wants to meet you."

Somehow, my moral resolve penetrated my bloated euphoria. This was the line Margie warned me about. This was the way he schtupped the Goldman girl and he wasn't going to get me that easily. I shook my head. "Mother always waits up for me," I said. "It's past midnight and I have to get home. Maybe next time we can leave earlier."

My body was boiling with my need for this man who held me now. My breathing was uncontrollable. But my will was stronger than my desires, and I won. Or did I? Ben took me home. He kissed me at the door; a brotherly peck on the nose, and I died inside.

"I had a marvelous time, Ben," I shouted above the scratching, snarling dog on the other side of the door. "Let's do it again."

"I'll call soon, Susan," said Ben.

I'd heard that before. Oh yes, I'd heard that too many times before.

I waded through a blur of bouncing, yelping dog into the house. I walked to the closet, took off my coat and leaned my head against the wall. And I cried. A salty torrent of tears poured down my face, making wet jagged stripes on the wall. *Meet Susan Talberg, world. The all-time loser.*

I didn't bother to say good night to Mother and Daddy. I wasn't going to give my mother the satisfaction of knowing that, once again, she had her way.

I went to bed. I dreamed I stood fat and alone on a huge glacier in the middle of the sea. I shivered and looked longingly at the shore. Hundreds of thin, beautiful women were eating succulent roasts and sugary sweets as they danced with tall, wonderful Bens and short, darling Bobbies. Hundreds of them eating. Hundreds of them getting laid.

I stood fat and alone on my glacier.

❧ Chapter 28 ❧

The next week I limited myself to 400 calories a day to make up for all that rich food I'd stuffed into myself on Saturday night. I weighed my food and trimmed my portions ounce by ounce. When I was tempted to cheat. . . and I was tempted all the time. . . I closed my eyes and saw my hips expanding, my arms sagging in loose folds of fat.

The smells of dinner made me wild with hunger. Mother made greasy pot roasts, thick, rich kugels and pungent cheese sauces every night. Every dessert had chocolate in it. I refused to sit at the table with everyone. It was more than I could bear. I stayed away from home and its intoxicating odors all day.

After I helped Mother set the table and get dinner ready, I called Margie or I walked over to Aunt Evelyn's to visit until I knew my own family's meal was over. I tried to dull my appetite with cigarettes. I chain smoked until my fingers were blistered and yellowed with nicotine. My throat was raw, and I coughed until I gasped for breath.

When I came home, I made myself a huge salad with a head of lettuce and no dressing. I washed it down with gallons of coffee and packs of cigarettes. I took a book up to bed, but I couldn't concentrate. I couldn't sleep, either. My mouth was dry; my head had an anvil trapped inside. I was always tired, always angry, at Mother, at food, at the torment of not being able to eat anything I loved.

Food was my enemy now. I fought it with a viciousness fueled by a macabre desire to consume everything in my mother's icebox, all the entrees at a restaurant, every bakery window display.

I began reading cookbooks. I told myself I was looking for low calorie dishes. But I wasn't. I hungered for the pastries they described. I ached for the custards, the cookies and the cakes. I wept with desire for a hot fudge sundae. I could taste the sticky, warm sweetness, feel the coolness of the cream as it slid down my throat.

Oh, dear God, how can I live through these endless days without food?
I can't, I told myself.

I shut my eyes and pictured a tremendous balloon of a woman with my bloated face. I straightened my shoulders and tightened my lips into a determined line. *Oh, yes you can*, I told myself. You MUST. Do you want to have fat arms like your mother or have to buy dumpy clothes at Lane Bryant's? No, NO, NO! I staggered upstairs to bed, *The Joy of Cooking* tucked under my arm.

When, at last, I slept, I dreamed of chocolate cakes mocking me, their hideous laughter muffled by thick curtains of coffee mint frosting. Huge, belligerent apple pies attacked me. They smothered me in their thick brown crusts screaming, "Eat me. Eat me. Eat me."

I awoke, saliva running down my chin, tears soaking my pillow.

🔊 Chapter 29 ☙

I didn't eat anything the next day and I lived on black coffee, lettuce and cigarettes the rest of the week. By that Sunday, my stomach was a hollow drum; every cell in my body screamed for nourishment.

I lost two pounds.

School began that Monday. Suddenly, my life was cluttered with teacher's meetings. Every day, I faced thirty-five seven year olds and tried to sort out which little body went with what name. Every day, children milled around me like scraps of colored paper sandwiched between sterile, never ending commutes to my mother's house in the car my father bought me.

He did buy me a car, and I was thrilled. I guess that's why I loved my daddy so much. He always gave me the important things, no matter what Mother said. "I need a tax deduction, kitten," he said. "Let's get you a little car."

I burst into a torrent of tears. Poor Daddy. The last thing he intended was to make me cry. He gave me his handkerchief and looked all confused. "Don't you *want* a car?" he asked.

I nodded and blew my nose. "Sure, I do," I sobbed.

"Then why are you crying, honey?"

How could I explain? My life had been a macabre soap opera since Margie's wedding. I hated teaching. I had imagined myself as a jolly Mother Goose romping through lessons with a bunch of cheerful, bubbling cherubs. That wasn't the way it was.

My classroom was a huge, chilly prison that smelled of chalkdust and yesterday's packed lunches. The children burst into the room, shouting and tussling. I had to scream like an army sergeant to gain control. Still, they shuffled their feet, threw spitballs and stifled secret giggles until the dismissal bell rang.

I left my classroom, weak, tired and disillusioned, only to face my other hell: Mother.

Living at home was even worse than I thought it would be. I had no privacy. Debbie made running comments on my telephone conversations and so did my mother. I called Margie after I'd starved myself all week and Ben didn't call. "Let's meet at Crosby Park," I said.

"It's going to rain," said Debbie.

"No it's not," said my mother. "Only a thirty per cent chance. But she'll

117

have to pick you up, Susan. I need the car."

She and Debbie had everything worked out before Margie had said a word. They sat back, complacent in their unanimous verdict: Susan can't do what she wants. Hooray!

But they were wrong.

Margie did pick me up and it didn't rain. We walked together in Crosby Park while I immersed us both in dark, soggy clouds of self pity and disgust. "Nothing works with me, Margie," I complained. "Nothing."

Margie handed me a Kleenex and put her arms around me. She knew how much I wanted to get married, and I think if she could have sliced Tom in half, she would have shared him with me. She was a real friend, the kind some people are never lucky enough to have, but I was too filled with my own sense of tragedy to appreciate her.

"The trouble with you, Susie," said Margie, "is that you try to *make* things work. Just *live* and everything will work out. I didn't look for Tom and he didn't look for me. We just happened. You're too damned uptight about getting married. Believe me, if Ben doesn't want you, you don't want him. It takes two loving people to make a marriage. Two. Not one."

She was right and I knew it. I had told Michael Rose the same thing when he received Margie's fatal valentine. It didn't console him and it didn't console me, either. Michael had wanted Margie back, and I? I wanted anyone to love me. Anyone at all.

"I must be abnormal," I said. "I hardly eat a thing and I'm big as a house. I got on the scale this morning and I haven't lost one single pound. Not one."

"How often do you weigh yourself, Susie?" she asked. "Dr. Fingerhut put my mother on a diet last year and he told her never to weigh herself more than once a week. You're supposed to do it at the same time, too: first thing in the morning, after you've gone to the john."

"I know," I said. "But I weigh myself all day long. I can't help it. I can't wait to see the scale go down. I'm so hungry, I read my mother's recipe books while I drink black coffee and eat sour grapefruit. I'm not like other people, Margie. I'll bet I don't get 400 calories a day and I still can't make that scale budge."

"Well, what did you weigh this morning?" asked Margie.

"One hundred and six," I said.

"Susie, that's very good," said Margie. "You only started dieting three weeks ago. Dr. Fingerhut told Mother she couldn't expect to keep off more than one pound a week and you can't count the first week because you spoiled all your hard work when you went out with Ben."

"All I can think about is how fat I am," I said. "It's like an obsession that winds itself around me tighter and tighter every day. I dream about food at night, I fantasize about it all day and I eat less and less. I'm beginning to believe that all I have to do is *think* food and I gain weight."

"Don't be ridiculous," said Margie. "You are not fat, Susan; you just have a little pot belly. Exercise can solve that. Exercise, not food. But you won't believe me."

I wouldn't believe her, not about letting romance happen, not about my being thin enough. All I saw was my barren reality. I was trapped at home with no rewards, no food to soothe me and no place to run from a job I didn't want in the first place.

There I was, wallowing in my thick, black fog, when the sun fought its way through. Daddy decided to buy me a car.

That's why I cried.

ঙ Chapter 30 ଔ

It was a tiny Renault and I loved it. I named it Pierre and tied a bright blue ribbon on its radio antenna. The freedom it gave me made me drunk with joy. I could drive to Margie's. I could go to a movie. I could get out of that house. But I could never drive away from myself.

In spite of the food binges, I managed to trim down to one hundred and three pounds by February of that year. I felt like recycled dog food. I couldn't keep off the scale. I got up in the morning, went to the bathroom and took off all my clothes. I stood on the scale. I got off and readjusted the pointer to *exactly* zero. I stepped back on the scale. I jiggled it and moved it into a better light. When I was absolutely convinced that the pointer was not going to descend one more millimeter, I stepped off the scale and got dressed. As soon as I came home from work, I stripped and got on the scale. I repeated the ritual whenever I had my clothes off, before I took a bath, when I was getting dressed to go out and before I went to bed.

I multiplied the calories I ate each day and I devoted myself to shaving off pounds. . . nothing else. Everyone was singing Elvis Presley songs and talking about his tight blue jeans, but I didn't know he existed. Estes Kefauver was campaigning for president in a coonskin cap and I wasn't sure whether he was a Democrat or a Republican. I hadn't read the newspaper or even absorbed a decent book since I got on the scale and saw three numbers instead of two.

I monitored everything that entered my mouth. I made weekly menus and juggled my calories to get the largest portions for the smallest amount of food value. I spent hours cross referencing calorie guides and recipes. I weighed my food and trimmed every bit of visible fat off any meat I would allow myself, and that was one three ounce portion a week. I skinned chicken breasts and stewed one quarter of the meat in water for my meal. I filled up on greens punctuated with a tiny slice of carrot and one quarter of a tomato. I was afraid of celery because it had so much sodium it would make me retain water, and water weighed pounds. I ate radishes and mushrooms because they had almost no calories at all, but my salads tasted like sawdust. There aren't enough herbs in the world to give dry lettuce zip.

I took long walks, and did frantic aerobics three times a day for longer and longer periods of time. I smoked two packs of Marlboros a day to dull my hunger. I was determined to win the diet game. . . something Mother had never been able to do.

My mother fought my efforts with her most effective weapon: the food she cooked. She continued to prepare foods rich in butter and dripping with sauce. She baked three-layer cakes and topped her pies with whipped cream and shaved chocolate that she refused to touch. She always left them on top of the bread box and their aroma filled the kitchen with perfume so sweet it brought tears to my eyes. "They won't get crushed," she said. "And besides, someone might want a snack later on."

That someone was obviously me.

She was determined to crack my will power. And it didn't take long before she succeeded. I'd start with just a nibble. A scoop of meringue. A sliver of meat. That first taste was pure happiness. But I wouldn't stop there. "Tomorrow, it'll be black coffee and _that's all_," I'd say.

Then, I would take bite after bite, faster and faster, more and more. The bites expanded into huge mouthfuls, the portions so gigantic, my mouth puffed like a squirrel's and saliva ran down my chin. I swallowed food until it took me to a place completely isolated from the universe. Nothing seemed real as I stood at that kitchen counter chewing my mother's cooking, not even the food I was eating.

I'd stuff until nothing hurt but my stomach and I'd stagger upstairs. I'd try to vomit and I usually could. I'd take several suppositories to be sure I got everything out. Then I'd take a bath so hot my skin blistered to punish myself. I wanted to boil away the food I had packed into my fat, ugly body. I'd stagger into bed with a heating pad to soothe my sore, abused stomach and I'd dream.

I'd see my mother, her arms folded and her face victorious. _Now everyone can see how worthless you are Susan,_ she would say in that cold voice I had heard all my life. _I have always said you were useless and now you are fat and ugly as well. And it is all your fault, you know. You are a glutton. You have no self control._

In spite of my lapses, I lost five pounds by Valentine's Day. But I didn't have a valentine.

Not one prospect. I'd dated a few real droops, but if Mother and our carnivorous dog didn't drive them away, my own distaste did. I saw Ben a few times. I dropped into his candy store to buy presents for friends. At least, that's what I told him. But I really went there to remind him that I existed.

It was torture to enter that store. The smell of the candy intoxicated me even more than Ben did. And all my visits, all my suffering and humiliation brought me nothing from him but breezy hellos and "Excuse me, Susie. I have some telephone calls to return."

It was obvious that Ben knew all about my existence and had no intention of participating in it. Even when he didn't disappear right away to make those mythical calls, our conversation was far too dull to crack the cold impersonal veneer of our "how are you's."

I faced Valentine's Day hungry and alone. I sat down at my desk and shut the door against the delectable cooking smells Mother was mixing in her cauldron of temptation. Tears filled my eyes and I wasn't sure why.

I was sick of dieting and afraid to stop. I was lonely all the time. Sometimes, if I felt too barren to face going into my mother's house, I drove over to Margie's apartment.

I knew my calls and visits often inconvenienced Margie, but still I haunted her. She was all I had; the only one I could count on. One time, I dropped in to cry on her shoulder while she was fixing dinner for her in-laws. She came to the door, her face smudged with flour, her apron spotted with grease and stains. "Susie!" she said. "I'm so happy to see you."

What else could she say? Even I could figure out that the last thing my friend needed was unexpected company five minutes before she had to be Mrs. Domestic Tranquility for Mr. and Mrs. Hester. Just the same, Margie kissed me as if my visit answered all her hidden longings. "I can't understand how my mother could cook for so many people and have everything ready at the right time," she said. "I just got the apple pie out of the oven and I still have to roast the chicken. We won't be eating until midnight."

I hadn't planned on comforting *her*. I thought her world always sailed along on a sea of silk. But her dilemma was something I knew about. I couldn't have been Jean Talberg's daughter if I didn't know my way around a kitchen. I hadn't done much real cooking other than at that seder a year ago, but I had watched my mother create the food I loved so much while I set the table or cleaned her pots and pans.

"Don't be ridiculous," I said. "It'll take about an hour and a half to do that chicken and you'll be serving drinks first, won't you? Then serve the salad and rolls as your first course. By that time, the chicken will be ready. Why don't you make a caesar salad? You can mix it at the table. Do you have any croutons?"

I took off my coat and wrapped a dishtowel around my middle. "I'll get these dirty dishes cleaned up while you put the chicken in the oven and get your vegetables ready. Peel some potatoes to roast around the chicken. The fat will make them nice and crispy."

"Oh Susie!" smiled Margie. "You're a lifesaver! Want to taste my pie before you start the dishes? I made a little one with the leftover apples and crust."

Did I want to taste that pie? Hell, I wanted to devour the whole thing all the rolls Margie had on the counter, even the pretzels and chips she'd put on the coffee table. I clenched my teeth and swallowed. "No, thank you," I said. "I'm on a diet, remember? But I would love some black coffee if it's handy. Don't start a pot just for me, though. You've got too much to do."

I washed Margie's dishes, set her table and arranged flowers for her centerpiece. We talked about cooking. We talked about Tom. We talked about what Margie should wear that night. We talked about Tom. We discussed how to make eggs Benedict. "I tried it last Sunday morning for brunch, and the sauce curdled. It was awful. I just threw it out and gave Tom poached eggs with grated cheese on top," said Margie.

"I bet you let the water boil in the double boiler," I said. "I saw a never-fail recipe in Mother's Betty Crocker cookbook. You put the butter and lemon juice in the blender with hard boiled egg yolks or something. I'll copy it for you."

"What were you doing reading a cookbook?" asked Margie. "Are you planning a secret party?"

I thought of my nighttime reading material and I blushed. "I was looking up some fancy brunch dishes for one of the other teachers at Belleview," I said. "Why would I give a party?"

Just as I started to unload my troubles, Tom walked in the door, and I knew what I had to do if I wanted to be a good friend. I had to leave Margie to her dinner, pack up my worn out grief and take it right back home. I kissed Margie and Tom and walked out the door.

"Would you like to stay for dinner, Susie?" asked Margie.

I shook my head. I knew she didn't mean that. Besides, her dinner was too fattening for me. I was safer alone in my room with a dry salad. I tried to light a cigarette, but my hands shook with hunger, or was it defeat? I knew I had no one to turn to but myself; and I wasn't strong enough to help me.

ᔄ Chapter 31 ᔅ

When I finished the 300 calories I allowed myself for dinner, I decided to send out some valentines. Maybe I'd get one back.

And then, maybe. . .

I bought some gold foil and red construction paper at the drugstore and came home filled with creative ideas that had nothing to do with food. I was very proud because I was doing something positive to help myself. *Wallowing in self pity will get you nowhere,* I told myself.

I sent a card to Bobby Mosten and included a breezy, brittle note telling him I adored teaching. I was busy but I often thought of him. How was he?

So much for that.

Then I sent a valentine to Ben with another buoyant note. I told him I hoped he survived the huge crowds that filled his store to buy candy for their sweethearts. I had received three boxes from his place alone. I ended my note with "I'd love to hear from you one of these days. You owe me a visit to meet Bon Bon."

If he didn't get that hint, he didn't want to.

I still had one card left. I couldn't think of anyone to send it to so I went down a mental list of all the dates I'd had in the last several months. There wasn't one name that didn't make me gag.

That was when I got my bright idea.

I sent a valentine to Michael Rose. I hauled out my old address book and there it was: his parent's address. Was he still living at home? I didn't know. I never saw him or talked to him after we'd had our magic conversation at the League in Michigan. I knew he graduated with his degree in Business Administration last year, but I had no idea where he was working. And I sure couldn't ask Margie.

I wrote Michael a very newsy letter telling him about my students and my life as a career girl. I never mentioned Margie. I never mentioned my own blue devils. I only said I'd love to hear how and what he was doing. I addressed the envelope to his home in Columbus, Indiana and put "please forward" on the envelope just in case.

Then, I put on my coat and walked my three love seeds to the mailbox. Who knows? Maybe one of them would sprout.

ᔕᦉ Chapter 32 ᥴᧉ

At the end of March, Toledo had one of its famous spring snowstorms. The main roads were bumpy mounds of ice pocked with tons of salt. The snowplows never got the side streets cleared at all. They were treacherous winding alleys of ice and slush.

Belleview School was on a tiny cul de sac off a suburban lane. My little Renault slipped and catapulted from one glacial ice pack to another. It skidded into snow drifts and refused to move until some kind motorist pushed us back into the ruts made by larger and heavier cars.

I arrived at school an hour late as tired as if it were the end of the day instead of the beginning. It snowed all day. . . no recess, no relief, just restless, impatient children picking at my composure and fraying my rattled nerves. By the time I dismissed my class, my car was just another snow drift in the parking lot.

The school janitor helped dig it out and I began driving home. I moved inch by inch over cascading mountains of snow sliding from one side of the road to the other. I couldn't see a thing. I faced hours of driving ahead and then what? A lot of tasteless lettuce at the end of the road.

Why did I struggle to be glamorous and thin when no one in Toledo ever asked me out? Why was I fighting snow and creeping traffic to reach a house I detested and live a life I loathed? Why didn't I give up, just let the car skid into one of the others creeping along the clogged streets?

"I know I can make things work if I try harder. I know it," I told myself and I wiped the steamed window with my headscarf.

But I wasn't all that sure I wanted to try.

It was seven o'clock when I pulled into our driveway. Daddy was standing at the big bay window watching for me. As soon as I careened to a halt, he hurried outside to help me bring my things into the house. "I should have come to get you, kitten," he said. "I never realized how bad the side roads were. They keep downtown pretty clear. I got home in half an hour."

I kissed him. "It's okay, Daddy. It was slow, that's all. This morning was much worse. Cars were skidding all over the place."

"Susan, I kept dinner hot for you," said my mother.

"I can't eat your dinners, Mother," I said. "They're too fattening."

I hung up my coat. "Any mail?"

I asked the same question every day and got the same answer: "Nothing for you today, Susan. Were you expecting a letter?"

Today, the answer was different. "You got a letter today, Susie," said Debbie. "I put it on your dresser."

I was too tired to hope it was a sprout from one of those love seeds I'd planted over a month ago. I figured it was a bill or an invitation to join some book club or other. Mother came into the hall wiping her hands on her apron. "Susan, I broiled you some chicken and made green beans for you without butter or almonds. That's not fattening. If you don't want it, I'll take it out of the oven. I thought you'd like something hot on a cold day like this."

I smiled. Things were looking sweeter. Chicken would feel like scraps of happiness caressing my throat. The day's tortures stopped bleeding just a little. "That was awfully nice of you, Mother. Chicken sounds wonderful. I'll go read my letter and wash up."

I felt the slow warmth of someone caring about me flow through me. Maybe my mother *wasn't* such an animal. And Daddy was a prince. I could never stop believing that.

I looked at the envelope on my dresser and suddenly, it was spring. The daffodils were blooming, and the scent of dogwood filled the air. Life was Technicolor once again, a rainbow of dreams that really happen.

I had a letter from Michael Rose.

March 22, 1956

Dear Susie!

I couldn't believe my eyes when I saw your letter sitting on the hall table. It seems like ages since I saw you last; over a year ago, anyhow.

I was afraid to call you after we had that marvelous talk at the League. I was too interested and you were Margie's roommate. And Tom was my fraternity brother. It made things much too uncomfortable for me to pursue you. I'm sorry now that I didn't.

I have a nice job selling group life insurance plans for Prudential. It involves some travel. That's why I haven't answered your note sooner. I was out of town all of February and didn't get your letter until today when I got home. Your timing was great because I have to do northern Ohio next and I'll be right near Toledo the first week in April. How would you like a visit? I'll be driving from Louisville to Columbus and I could spend a night or two in a hotel in Toledo.

I'd love to see you, Susie, and take up where we left off. We wouldn't have to worry about Margie or Tom. We could just concentrate on nurturing the wonderful friendship we started too long ago.

> *Love,*
> *Michael*

It worked! It really worked!

One of my love seeds took root and now it was pushing tender green shoots of hope into my life. I danced downstairs filled with the lilting rhythm of success. I sat down to the first hot dinner I'd had since I started my diet in September.

My mother sat down across from me and smiled. "How nice of you to sit with me, Mother," I said.

"Well, you eat alone so much of the time, Susan. I thought you might like company." She paused. "I noticed the return address on your letter, Susan. Was that the same Michael Rose that used to date Margie?"

So that was it. I should have known my mother would never want to sit and chat with me. She was curious, that's all.

I didn't want to expose my brand new little love sprout to the destructive beam of my mother's eyes. She'd wilt it before it ever took root. I took a deep breath and tried to sound very casual. "That's the one," I said. "He just wrote to find out how I was."

My mother's eyes narrowed. "I remember how attentive he was to Margie when we took all of you out for dinner that time. Whatever happened there?"

She paused and reached for a parkerhouse roll. She buttered it and looked at me once more. "He certainly was a good eater, wasn't he?" she said. "He ate a steak as big as yours and still had room for Margie's hash brown potatoes and his own."

I nodded. "He's driving through Toledo first week in April and he wants to visit," I said. "He asked me to recommend a hotel. Do you think he'd like the Commodore?

I lit a match and reached for a cigarette. My hand trembled so violently, the match went out.

"Why doesn't he stay here?" asked my mother. "We have that extra room and he wouldn't be any trouble."

"You wouldn't mind, Mother? You really wouldn't mind?"

The sky was bright blue. The chicken was ambrosia. My mother cared about me. And my valentine was coming to call.

Welcome, heaven! I've been waiting for you for such a long time.

Part III: 1956

✍ Chapter 33 ❧

That night, I wrote Michael and invited him to come to Toledo, but I didn't mention Mother's suggestion that he stay at our house. I was afraid. Good things never happened to me in my mother's arena and I wanted lots of nice dreams to come true when Michael Rose re-entered my life.

He telephoned the day my letter arrived. "I'd love to visit you, Susie," he said. "I can drive down next weekend if you're free. Do you know a good hotel that's near your house?"

"I'll make reservations for you at the Park Lane," I said. "That's a very comfortable place and it's near our house."

"Great!" said Michael. "I can't believe I'll be seeing you again in five little days!"

I gulped. So soon! I could never organize myself to charm Michael Rose in five little days. Impossible.

Michael had sounded exactly the way I remembered him and I couldn't wait to see him. I hung up the telephone and hugged it as if it were the voice I had just heard. Then I took off my shoes and got on the scale. I subtracted what I thought my clothes would weigh. One hundred and three pounds. I was still too fat. I'd have to accelerate my diet if I wanted to get rid of my pot belly before Michael came to Toledo.

I needed to do some emergency shopping because I didn't have a thing to wear. My "Ben" dress would be fine if we went dancing, but what if Michael wanted to do something casual, like walk in the park? I didn't have a decent pair of slacks that buttoned around my middle. Besides, there were two nights in a weekend, possibly three if he stayed over Sunday night. I couldn't wear my Ben dress all three nights.

I was petrified that I'd do or say some stupid thing and spoil the weekend. What if he lost interest when he saw me? What would we talk about after we had worn out the topic of his disappointment with Margie? What if he scrambled into bed with me and then forgot me like Bobby Mosten did? What if he didn't kiss me at all?

I went downstairs to watch "Westinghouse Theater." They always did marvelous plays on that program. If I got absorbed in the story, I might stop worrying about Michael's reactions. Daddy was sitting in his usual chair reading the paper. I walked over to him and sat on his lap. Daddy folded his newspaper and smiled. "What's up, kitten?" he asked.

"I just got a telephone call from one of my best friends from Michigan, Daddy," I said. "He was in Bobby's fraternity and we used to talk a lot even though we never really dated. I invited him to visit me next weekend. I told him I'd get him a room at the Park Lane."

Daddy shook his head. "Don't be silly, Susie," he said. "He'll stay right here with us. Mother will be thrilled."

I shook my head. It was far too risky to have Michael in constant contact with my mother. She would destroy my romantic dreams in moments with a few well-aimed remarks. "That would be too much trouble for her," I said. "You know how she hates extra work."

Daddy smiled. "Nonsense," he said. "We both liked Michael very much when we met him at Michigan. It would be our pleasure to entertain him here."

Maybe it wasn't such a bad idea invite Michael to stay with us. He would have to see what my family was like if anything could happen between us. Besides, I wanted to know what my father thought of Michael Rose. His approval meant everything to me. I hugged him. "Daddy, you're wonderful!" I said. "You solve all my problems!"

Daddy pointed to the picture on the television screen. "Isn't that your program?" he asked.

Mother started making grocery lists and reading recipe books the next day. I watched her shuffling through her cookbooks and recipe files. Her color was high and a smile played on her lips. Suddenly, it dawned on me that this was her only pleasure, and my eyes misted with pity for anyone with so little fulfillment. I looked away so she wouldn't see the emotion on my face. It was her own fault that she had nothing but kitchen activities to absorb her, but still . . .

I wandered through the week in a cloud. I went window shopping for a smashing dress to wear and finally saw The Perfect Thing in the Lion Store window. It was a yellow wool dress with a beige kick pleat. It was very simple, a classic by Anne Klein. Best of all, it had no defined waistline. My bulging stomach wouldn't show. I loved it when I tried it on and I bought it right away. I found a paisley scarf to go with it and a pair of light brown shoes. Evan Picone. I charged the whole thing to Daddy. I knew he wouldn't mind and he wouldn't let Mother mind, either.

As soon as I came home from school that Friday, I did my nails and washed my hair. I experimented with all the different hair styles I had seen in magazines. I swept it up into a pompadour like Eliza in *My Fair Lady* and then into a chignon like Anna wore for the King of Siam. I finally settled on a loose casual look like Marilyn Monroe's. I tried to hurry time by cleaning my room and sorting out my closet. I put on my favorite skirt and sweater and brushed my teeth for the tenth time. I got on the scale. No change there.

I gargled with Lavoris and then applied just enough makeup to give me back some of the color I had before I started my diet. I brushed hell out of my hair and tousled it so it would catch the light. I slopped on a lot of Arpege and came downstairs to wait for my valentine to arrive.

Mother was in the kitchen assembling her Epicurean production. She'd been cooking all week. Every night, glorious odors riveted holes in my determination to stick to my diet. But I refused to ingest more than six hundred calories a day; less if I could bear it. Every time I was tempted to sneak an extra nibble, I imagined what Michael would say if I had bulging hips and a distended belly. When he saw me, I had weighed ninety-three pounds. I was ten pounds fatter now and I had only to look at my non-existent waistline to see how much it showed.

I touched my toes and did hundreds of crunches. I walked until my legs ached. And I weighed myself every time I stopped for breath. I did not weaken. Not even once. But I was scared to death that I would. My mother was cooking my favorite dishes and I had to force myself to refuse them. It would not be easy.

I tried to think of some way to show my mother how much I appreciated all her efforts for Michael without violating my pact with myself but there *was* no other way. We never shared confidences and she didn't want to be my companion. It would be so nice if we could share a few private jokes like we did when I came home for Passover. But that closeness was never repeated. My mother didn't like me.

When I had done what I could with my appearance, I walked into the living room. Daddy was reading the news. I took his hand. "I'm so jittery," I confessed. "Do I look all right?"

Daddy looked up from his paper and nodded. "You're a knockout, honey," he said. "Why should you be nervous? That boy is probably thrilled that you like him enough to invite him to your home."

I shook my head. "You're wrong, Daddy," I said. "*I'm* the one who's lucky. I'm not good enough for a guy like Michael. I don't have any class."

Daddy patted the space next to him on the couch and I sat down next to him. "People aren't 'good enough' for one another, kitten," he said. "When two people meet, they become friends first. They talk about their interests and their goals and gradually begin to feel closer and closer until suddenly, they realize they're in love . . . and they've been in love for a long, long time. Love isn't a thunderbolt and marriage isn't an impulse. Or at least they shouldn't be. Both are needs and emotions that grow. The art of living is to let that affection happen naturally. You don't want a marriage without solid roots in respect, Susie. Don't be so impatient. You can't rush love. If you try to force a marriage, you'll be stuck with a dismal drudge of a life."

"Was it that way with you and Mother?" I asked, and I knew it wasn't.

Mother nagged him all the time. If he would have been *my* husband, I would have been gentle with him the way he was gentle with her. He treated my mother like gold and pampered her like the first crocus in spring. At least it looked that way to me. That's why Daddy's answer surprised me.

"Yes, it was, Susie," said Daddy. "And it still is. Your mother is a wonderful woman, and she's been a marvelous wife to me."

I didn't believe him for a minute. But I *was* certain that my father loved my mother so much he'd lie to protect her. My mother didn't return his devotion but that made no difference to him. My mother was fortunate that a man as wonderful as Daddy adored her, and I hoped that I would find someone half that marvelous to marry me. I sighed and stared out the window, waiting for my possible candidate to pull in the driveway. Three cigarettes later, I saw a car pull into our driveway. "Debbie, get the dog," I called. "Michael's here."

Michael! He was gorgeous; tall and more muscular than when I last saw him. His trenchcoat was unbuttoned despite the dank chill in the air, and he wore no hat. I walked over to him and held my stomach in as tight as I could. He must not see that bulge. He kissed my cheek. "Hello, Susie," he said.

He took off his coat and handed it to me. He was wearing one of those slender single breasted gray suits they wore on Madison Avenue and a thin rep tie with tiny navy and red stripes. He had a sophistication about him I had never seen before. I wondered if he could still unbend and demolish a platter of French toast in the kitchen with me at four in the morning.

I smiled and took his hand. "You remember my father, don't you, Michael?" I said.

✺ ❧

Dinner was at seven. My mother's table was a picture from *Gourmet* magazine. The centerpiece was a cascade of daffodils and baby tulips. She had polished her sterling silver candelabra for the occasion and we ate by candlelight. She set the table with her wedding crystal and china and each place had its own ashtray, butter dish and napkin in a monogrammed ring. She had decided to avoid Jewish cuisine this time. She candied a ham with brown sugar and cloves and served it with marshmallow-filled sweet potatoes and a pineapple parfait salad. She braised artichoke hearts in butter and deep fried zucchini with red peppers.

I never knew she was aware of some of these foods. She must have unearthed them from *The Joy of Cooking,* and this in itself was a great tribute to the importance of this dinner. My mother never used a recipe book except for regal occasions. She cooked according to a sixth sense that told her how much was enough of everything from pepper to yeast. She never failed, and she did not fail tonight. I had never tasted food as delicious as my mother served to Michael Rose.

And all her efforts were wasted. I was too nervous to appreciate the delicate symphony of flavors in the meal; Michael wolfed down his food as if it were dished out at a mess hall cafeteria, my sister stuffed herself with brioche and miniature French rolls slathered with butter. She looked at the clove-riddled ham and wrinkled her nose. "What do you have all over that thing?" she asked.

"I spiced it with cloves, Debbie," said my mother. "Won't you even taste it?"

Debbie stood up. "I'm going to make myself a peanut butter sandwich," she said. "And I saw some pineapple slices on the counter. I'll put some ice cream on them."

Daddy, as usual, barely tasted anything. My mother watched us all and looked down at her plate. She gripped the sides of the table and her knuckles were white. Her mouth was forced into a smile that had nothing to do with her feelings. "Would anyone like anything more before I bring in the dessert?" she asked. "It's almond torte with whipped cream filling."

"Sounds marvelous, Mrs. Talberg," said Michael. "My mother never makes such fancy desserts! You are sure some cook!"

My mother blushed. "Thank you," she said.

When we lingered over coffee, my mother decided the time was right to conduct her investigation. "Tell me about your family, Michael," she said.

"I have a wonderful family, Mrs. Talberg," said Michael. "My mom loves being a mother. She adores classical music, Susie, like you do. If it hadn't been for you, I never would have gotten through Music Appreciation, remember?"

I opened my mouth to answer, but Mother cut in. "What about your father? What does he do?" she asked.

And that was the crucial question. The one that could destroy this courtship faster than sexual solicitation. Now, she'd figure out if his family was rich enough and how old their money was.

My mother hated the nouveau riche. Perhaps, she saw too much of herself in their life styles. After all, satin covered couches with pink and magenta flowers weren't such a far cry from plastic covered arm chairs. You couldn't sit very comfortably in either.

"Dad?" Michael blushed. "My dad is a kosher butcher."

My mother folded her napkin and put it beside her empty plate. She looked at my only hope for deliverance and demolished it. "I see," she said.

Now, you did it, Michael. You really did it. You failed the interview. She has all the information she needs, now. You come from one of those camphor smelling orthodox families who walk to schul on Saturdays and really don't eat on Yom Kippur. Jean Talberg graduated from that class a long time ago. She wasn't going to permit her daughter to have anything to do with such antiquated customs and outdated beliefs. It made her look bad to her canasta group.

Mother stood up. "Susan," she said. "Debbie and I will clear the table. You entertain your guest."

Michael and I left my mother's arena and sat down in the den. We talked to Daddy until Mother and Debbie finished in the kitchen. Then, we all played canasta. It was fun and Mother was actually laughing at her bad luck in cards. "I prefer a game where I have a little control over fate," she said. "Do you play bridge, Michael?"

Michael nodded. "I love the game," he said. "I think I could very easily become an addict."

Mother nodded. "I know that feeling. Leonard and I enjoy it as well, and Susan plays a very tidy game. Perhaps we can fit in a few rubbers before you leave."

Michael smiled. "I'd love that, Mrs. Talberg," he said and he squeezed my hand under the card table.

The two of us stayed downstairs after everyone else had gone up to bed. We talked and talked and then we talked some more. His voice undulated over me like a sun washed breeze. I felt warm and glowing sitting near him and listening to the music of his conversation.

I don't think I actually heard a word he said. I was absolutely determined to find some way to get out of my mother's house. Marriage was my best hope and Michael Rose, a ripe candidate for a proposal. I wasn't going to let him go.

Michael kissed me good night. I kissed him back and then he stopped. I ached to have him hold me close forever but at the same time, I was relieved that he didn't try to go further. After all, we were in my parents' home. But was that his reason? Maybe I didn't attract him.

Michael Rose needs constant sex to reassure himself that he's a man.

Margie had told me that and I hadn't believed her. But I *had* thought he liked to make love. All men did, if they were interested in you. Well, Michael Rose obviously could control himself with me, and I didn't want to figure out why.

I kissed his cheek. "Would you like to walk through Crosby Park, tomorrow?" I asked. "The first spring flowers are trying to happen and the daffodils and forsythia are breathtaking. I'll pack a picnic basket. Okay?"

"Tomorrow night, we'll go dancing," said Michael. "I want to take you to dinner, hold you in my arms."

I felt gorged with happiness. Here I was in my own house and this beautiful boy was telling me he wanted to take me dancing. I hadn't even had to sleep with him to get the invitation. It couldn't be real. Then, I remembered what I had done. We couldn't go out tomorrow night. I had screwed the whole thing up.

"Margie, Tom, Louise and Mortie are coming over," I said. "I invited them here. And Mother planned a huge buffet."

"Margie Wiseman?" he said. "Do you think Margie will really want to see me?"

I took his hand and held it to my cheek. "Of course she will," I said. "She was delighted when I told her you were coming here. She likes you very much, Michael. She wouldn't have gone out with you for so long if she hadn't."

Michael looked doubtful. "Still . . . " he said.

"You're my guest and I want to introduce you to my friends," I said. "The only thing I regret is that we can't go out alone tomorrow night. I would love to dance with you."

Michael smiled. He took my face in his hands and kissed my lips. "I'll stay over Sunday and we'll go dancing, then, Susie. How's that?"

Oh my God. You're dreaming, Susan Talberg. This only happens to Margie or in movies. It just doesn't happen to you.

"I'll cut school on Monday," I said.

"I'll stay 'til Tuesday,"

He kissed me again. "Hold me this way forever," I said.

"Forever. I promise."

And he kissed me again.

❦ Chapter 34 ❧

I floated upstairs to bed and dreamed of paradise. The next morning, I got on the scale. Up two pounds! I hadn't eaten one fattening thing and I was becoming a blimp! I sighed and got off the scale. I was not going to let my abnormal tendency to gain weight spoil this magnificent weekend. I was *not*.

I put on a velvet hostess gown and just enough makeup to look naturally fresh. I was going to surprise Michael and cook him a divine breakfast. I would make all the things I didn't dare eat on my diet. I would share them with my brand new beloved and starve all week. He was worth it.

I decided to bake puffy cheese omelets. They were easy and very showy. I remembered some sausage patties in the freezer. I would broil them with pineapple slices on top. We'd have sugared watermelon balls to start and finish my masterpiece with those warm croissants Mother kept handy for unexpected guests. I was so wrapped up in my vision, I didn't notice the fried butter aroma floating up the stairs.

My mother was in the kitchen. She had been there for hours. She had to be to have prepared all the food that filled the kitchen counters and overflowed on the tea cart in the dining room.

She looked marvelous. Her red hair curled softly around her face, her crisp, denim housecoat shone fresh and clean. She had started a cheese soufflé and had bacon croquettes snapping and crackling in the fry pan. "I'll have blintzes and sour cream for dessert, I think," she said to me even before she said good morning. "Will you set the table and then call Michael and Daddy?"

So much for my fancy breakfast. My mother had stolen my show. I watched everyone gorge themselves on her lavish meal. I refused to eat a thing. I didn't want to give my mother the pleasure of seeing her immense buffet demolished when I had nourished such sweet dreams of giving Michael my own version of ambrosia. I smiled inside as my mother's face flooded with grief. "Nothing, Susan? Not even a blintz? You love blintzes, and I made them just for you!"

"Oh, come on, Susan," prodded Michael. "They're irresistible."

He wolfed down his second plateful smothered in sour cream and strawberry jam. Mother looked triumphant. "Well," she said. "At least *Michael* appreciates my cooking. No one else around here does."

"Oh, don't be ridiculous, Jean," said Daddy. "We all love the food you cook. I'll have another blintz, too, please."

Finally, Michael and I got out of the house and made our way to Crosby Park. It was glorious there, quiet and turning spring. The air smelled clean and I forgot my hunger for food in an eager rush to scoop up Michael's love. "You know," I said. "We've talked a lot but you've never really told me what you want out of life."

"Haven't I?" said Michael. "I thought it was obvious. I want success and I'm not afraid to go after it. I want prestige. I want people to notice me when I walk down the street and say, 'There goes the best damn insurance salesman in the state,' or the smartest businessman in town, or the hottest lover on the block. The best! Do you know what I mean?"

I did and I didn't. I wanted to be the best, too, but something about the way Michael wanted to be noticed curdled a little. "Is it that important what people say you are? Isn't it more important that *you* know how good you are?" I asked.

"Susie," he said and he put his arm around my shoulder. "Face it. You are what the world thinks you are. Just *knowing* you're good doesn't buy cars and houses and trips to the Orient. And I want those things. I want the best clothes and first row seats at the best shows in town, and I want the perfect wife to help me gain those things."

He took my hand.

Sometimes I think Michael is only buttering up people because he wants to get something from them. He's always trying to hide what he really thinks.

Margie told me that and I thought she was being really unfair. . . then. Now I had an uneasy feeling that she was right. I rested my head on Michael's shoulder. "Tell me more about that perfect wife," I said.

Michael looked at a cloud over my head. "She'll be beautiful," he said, and his voice had the same dreamy quality the prince had in that movie when he saw Sleeping Beauty. "She'll come from a good family and know all the right people. She'll entertain my clients as if they were royalty because she'll be a queen . . . my queen."

He paused and stroked my hair. "Just like you are, Susie," he said.

Well, Michael Rose was in for a very big surprise if he thought Susan Talberg was the wife of his dreams. My family did not possess one drop of blue blood and I wasn't a social person. I was too wrapped up in Susan Talberg to be entertaining to anyone.

I cleared my throat and kept my eyes riveted to the daffodils that lined our path. I better not worry about who the "right people" were and if my name was on that roster. I had a fish I was determined to catch. It was time to be

136

prudent.

"I want to get married, too," I said. "I want to make a beautiful home for someone I adore and have lots of his children. I'll work hard to make them happy and relaxed instead of tense and nervous the way I've always been."

I blushed. "I know it sounds silly, but really, all I want to do is love and not be afraid to let it show."

"I don't think it sounds silly at all, Susie," said Michael. "It sounds exactly like what my future wife would say."

And he kissed me so long and hard that I thought my knees would buckle right there in the middle of all those brave little crocuses.

As soon as we came up for air, I kissed him back.

Chapter 35

Sunday night, he proposed and I said yes. I can still taste my sweet delight. Someone really wanted me! *Me.*

All Michael Rose cares about is money and using people to get it. I think that's horrible.

You're wrong, Margie. You just *have* to be wrong, because I couldn't bear to give him up.

Monday night, we told my parents. Daddy was all smiles. "Wonderful!" he said. "I've always wanted a son."

Debbie was as happy as I was . . . almost. No one in the whole world has ever been as ecstatic as I was then. Michael had charmed my sister, and she didn't hide it. "I wish you didn't have to leave us ever," she told him. "You make everyone smile when you're here . . . Even Junior!"

Michael grinned. My happiness snapped and crackled like burning logs, and Mother threw ice on the fire.

"Isn't this a little fast?" she said. "You've only been together three days."

"But we've known each other for four years, Mrs. Talberg," said Michael. "And I've always loved Susie. I just never thought I was good enough for her."

"Liar!" I laughed. "You never noticed me. You loved Margie!"

"That's not true," said Michael. "I loved you. I thought you were too smart for me."

"I loved you, too," I said and I pressed his hand between mine. "I always will."

"It seems awfully fast to me," said my mother.

ᔆᴑ Chapter 36 ᘓᓬ

"Let's get married in the fall," said Michael. "That will give us plenty of time to find a nice place to live and plan a wedding we'll never forget."

"You don't really want a big wedding, do you?" I asked. "I'd like something simple and a super honeymoon instead."

"Sure, I want a big wedding," he said. "I want to show you off to the whole damn world. You're too marvelous to keep to myself!"

Now, how could I say no to that?

"Susie, I have the best idea," said Michael. "Prudential doesn't have a representative in Toledo. I could make a fortune if I opened an office here."

Toledo. Was I doomed to live here for the rest of my life?

"But I hate Toledo, Michael," I said. "You don't know how smothering this place can be because you only see it on its best behavior. Isn't there someplace else that needs a Prudential representative?"

Michael put his arms around me and kissed me. He tasted so sweet, I wept. I clung to his wonderful body. I held my mouth to his. I let the blanket of his sweet caresses smother the nightmare of being trapped in Toledo. It was a small price to pay for the life I wanted so badly. At least, I'd be in my own home. And Margie would be near by.

"I'll give my notice to the Board of Education this week," I said. "They'll need to know I won't be coming back."

I rested my head on his shoulder and took his hand in mine. "It will be lovely to make us a perfect home, darling. Just lovely."

Michael stiffened and withdrew his hand from mine. "Notice? Who said anything about notice?" he said. "You don't really want to quit teaching, do you, Susie? It's your *profession*. Besides, we'll need the extra income until we save up enough for a house and our babies."

A house. Babies. I'd scrub garbage cans and swab toilets for a house and babies. All right. I wouldn't tell Michael how much I hated that classroom, at least not yet. I'd figure out a way to stop work once I was married and felt safe. I snuggled closer to him and hid my face in his shoulder.

"I hadn't thought about working," I said. "But I guess you're right. I could teach until I got pregnant, anyway. But let's not wait too long to make babies, Michael. I want lots of them, don't you?"

"At least a dozen little girls just like you," said Michael.

"Well, I want a dozen Michaels," I said. "So we can't waste any time."

"Right," said Michael. "But we have to be sensible, too. I'll need to open a nice office and join the country club to make the right business connections. All that takes money. Prudential will help, but we'll need your income for at least two years, Susie."

Two years! Two years of cleaning up jam smeared faces and trying to sound interested in Dick and Jane. Two years of singing about teapots and fat little ducks. It was too much to ask. Two <u>days</u> sounded horrible enough, but two years? Michael couldn't love me and expect that kind of sacrifice.

"I don't want to wait two years for a baby," I said. "Not two whole years. Besides, I hate teaching and I want out. I thought you were earning enough to support us both. That's what you said."

Michael's face hardened and he pulled away from me. I stared at him. This wasn't the sweet, gentle boy who insisted he had dreamed about only me for four years. This was my mother in a shirt and tie. I shivered, and I listened to words I didn't want to hear.

"But I intend to be very rich, Susan," said Michael. "My parents can't finance me like Tom Hester's does him. I have to do it all myself or find someone to help me. You've had plenty of money all your life, Susie. You don't know what it's like to be poor. If you work, we can afford to live in style. Tell you what. We won't try to stop a baby and you'll work until it's born. How's that for a compromise?"

That was no concession at all; it was victory. We could wallow in spontaneous, unprotected love and hope for the consequences. That sounded very nice, indeed.

"Agreed," I said.

I paused. *Get a little, give a little, Susan.*

"We better have that big wedding you want, after all, honey. You'll need to meet the right people fast so we can support all those little Susies and Mikes. Right?"

I paused and thought for a moment. I needed to gain some extra time to make that baby before school began in the fall. "If I'm going to teach, we'd better move the wedding up to July. That gives me a month to get ready after school is over this June and lets us have a month and a half to get settled before school opens again in the fall. Will we have time for a honeymoon?"

"Sure, we will," said Michael. "We can take at least a week. Where would you like to go? New York? Bermuda? Acapulco?"

"Let's go to New York," I said. "We can get drunk on concerts and theater."

"And each other," said Michael. "Let's have a lifetime getting drunk on each other."

He looked at his watch. "I have to get started or I'll never get home. It's a long drive back to Columbus. I'll call you tonight. I love you, Susie."

"Will you be my Valentine?" I asked. "You never said you would."

"I'll be a lot more than that."

He kissed me again and then he was gone.

໑ Chapter 37 ໕

I stared after him as he drove away. In four short days, my life had turned around. It was spring. The world was in bloom and my dream life was really going to happen.

I floated into the house. Its familiar sounds and smells jolted me back into my old world again. I was in Mother's territory now where the odds were always in her corner.

I sighed and swallowed hard. I didn't look forward to the next few hours. I was petrified of her objections. I told myself they were just her *opinions*, but I treated them as if they were judgments from the Almighty.

Even though I hotly denied it, there was always a thread of logic in her disapproval. All too often, my mother's negative evaluation of my friends and my ideas turned out to be right and that was the worst part of all. I was convinced she had some macabre power to turn the pleasant things in my life sour.

"Help me get dinner, Susan," called my mother. "We'll have leftovers."

I refused to allow her to puncture my bliss. Not yet. I wanted time to fondle it and coat it with the sugar of my dreams. "In a minute, Mother," I said.

I hurried up to my room and sat on the bed. I hugged my future and wrapped it around me like an velvet blanket. Once I exposed it to my mother's critical eyes, it might shatter. I was so afraid it would dissolve into false hopes. So afraid.

I sighed and got on the scale. How much had I gained from my fattening weekend? Would contentment make me so relaxed I didn't burn up calories? One hundred and five pounds. I stared at that number as if it were obscene. I had gained two pounds on love.

I put on my shoes and walked slowly downstairs. Mother was busy in the kitchen. "Set the table, Susan," she said. "And put out the serving pieces. Will you be eating with us? I've kept some of the meat out for you. The rest is in a casserole. The vegetables should be all right. The cauliflower sauce is on the side, and I didn't put any butter on the beans. Make your own salad, will you? I did a Waldorf salad for us, with nuts and mayonnaise."

I nodded. "That'll be fine, Mother," I said. "Thank you."

I waited. I braced myself for her attack but she didn't say a word until we were all at dinner. "I miss Michael already," said Debbie. "He's so nice, Susie. You said he had a brother. Is he as much fun?"

I smiled at my sister and pretended to appreciate her. As far as I was concerned Debbie was a fat parasite, but my mother idolized her for a mysterious reason I couldn't understand. She had the proportions of a horse well on the way to becoming an elephant. Nothing my mother said or the mirror showed could keep her from shoveling in all the food she wanted.

But she *knows how to say no to food, Susan. She* tastes *what she eats.*

I felt very superior to my mother. She stuffed herself with all the food we left on our plates and complained about her weight. She couldn't control her appetite but I could. I had lost six pounds since Margie's wedding. And before I finished my diet, I would have trimmed away *sixteen* pounds that would stay off, or I would start starving myself all over again. My mother's talk about dieting was just that. Talk.

But she doesn't eat crazy like you do, Susan. She doesn't cram gallons of food down her throat and make herself throw it up. She doesn't weigh herself a hundred times a day. She gains weight in the accepted way: on food. You gain it on happiness.

"I don't think Michael is so wonderful," said my mother. "Pass your plate, Leonard. I have some beef Stroganoff for you. Wild rice?"

Here it comes. I poked around at my salad. *Oh God. Here it comes.*

"I thought he was a very nice boy, Jean," said Daddy. "Easy on the meat, honey. . . and no cauliflower."
"Just a taste," said my mother. "Give me your plate, Debbie."
No one said anything while we passed the food around. I was too afraid. Debbie and Daddy were too busy eating. For one incandescent moment, I thought the subject would disappear. But it didn't. Mother filled her own plate and began to eat. "He's trash," she said.
She chewed her meat and wiped her lips on her napkin. "He has no breeding. Pass the salt, Debbie."
"What do you mean, he has no breeding?" I said. "His family is just like ours. What's wrong with that?"
"Don't be ridiculous, Susan. Your father is a professional man. His family is lower class. That's a very big difference, believe me."

Jean thought she'd have a maid to do the dishes and she would be a fine lady, but Leonard is not the rich man she thought he'd be. Jean was never very good at watching her pennies.

My mother took a sip of water and pointed her fork at me. "That boy's father is an ignorant butcher and his mother helps him in the store," she said. "They're not our kind of people. They're just like all the nebbishes on Lagrange Street; the ones whose sons smell of borscht and gefilte fish. They wear the same clothes year after year and have never seen the inside of a movie theater. They haggle over every penny and hate the goyim. They are obnoxious."

One year we ate nothing but boiled potatoes. That was the year no one got new clothes for school and my dress was so short it didn't cover my knees. We ate like starving animals because that's what we were.

Why did she think she was better than a kosher butcher's wife? Did she go to the beauty shop to shampoo those memories out of her mind? Did she really think my father's profession freed her from that gutter that disgusted her now?

She reached for a roll and broke it in half. "You eat the other half, Debbie," she said.

She handed Debbie the roll and pulled the butter dish close to her plate. She pointed her butter knife at me. "Your wedding will be an old world kesslegarden with unshaven old men getting schickered on schnapps," she said. "You wait and see. I'll bet not one of them knows what a salad fork is, much less uses one."

I stood up. I'd heard enough. "I'm going to get some coffee," I said.

My mother reached for another roll and dipped it into the gravy on her plate. "Sit down, Susan," she said. "I haven't finished what I was saying to you."

I sat down and reached for a roll. I watched my mother eat the bread she knew she shouldn't have and I felt very strong. She talked like she was The Iron Woman, but she was weak. Look at her stuffing bread into her mouth. Tomorrow, she would complain and cry about her fat arms or her bulging waist. But she'd still sneak in tastes of cake and bits of bread all day long. I put my roll back into the bread basket and twisted the napkin in my lap. I waited.

My mother brushed the crumbs on the tablecloth into her plate. She looked up at me. "It's your life, Susan," she said. "But don't say I didn't warn you. He's coarse and his manners are unbearable. He actually wiped his hands on his jacket after dinner last night. I was nauseated. Save room for dessert, Leonard. I made a Linzer torte."

"I think you're being very hard on the boy, Jean," said Daddy. "I really like him. I like his ambition and I like the way he treats our Susie."

I smiled my thanks at him. I loosened my grip on my napkin and I could feel the muscles in my face relax. Daddy reached over and patted my hand. "Have you made any definite plans, kitten?" he asked. "We'll go along with whatever you want."

Mother's eyes narrowed. She wasn't defeated but she knew when to cease fire. "Whatever you say, Leonard. It's Susan's wedding, not mine. Aren't you going to finish your meat, Debbie? No? Then put it in the dog's dish. He loves Stroganoff. Help clear the table, Susan."

The dog waddled over to Debbie and stood with his paws on her lap panting his sour breath over the half-finished food. I rose and turned to my father. "I love him, Daddy," I said. "I'm going to marry him."

I picked up the dirty plates and took them into the kitchen. The dog raced after me, nipping at my ankles. *Little bastard! Biting bits and pieces out of me for sport!*

I stared down at Mother's darling with eyes so full of hatred, I couldn't believe he didn't expire. I kicked him with my heel and he yelped as if I had stabbed him. I scowled. I remembered *my* darling's face when I told him I didn't want to teach. I looked again at the furious dog and I shuddered. I could have sworn it was Michael snarling at me.

My mother was prejudiced against her own kind and I thought that was narrow and very small. But she was right about Michael. He would make a terrible husband for me because he was my mother all over again. I was already saddled with one opinionated bigot. Why was I so determined to live with another?

I returned to the table. I watched my family eat their cake and I drank black coffee. My mother pulled over a platter of sugared fruit and filled a sherbet glass with the mixture. She sprinkled coconut and almonds on it and added a large dollop of whipped cream. "Such a heavy meal," she said. "I thought I'd treat us to a little fresh fruit to finish it off."

She put a spoonful in her mouth and smiled. "So refreshing! Can I serve you some, Leonard?" she said.

My father shook his head. "I can't even finish my cake, Jean," he said.

My mother refilled her cup. "You don't know what you're missing," she said.

"We want to get married in July," I said. "Michael is going to open an office in Toledo, Daddy, so we'd better have a big wedding. I want him to meet some of your friends to get him started. Uncle Max might be able to send some business his way, too."

I refused to look at my mother. I knew if I did, I'd trigger another volley of criticism. I smiled at Daddy. "What do you think?" I asked.

"It's not important what I think, kitten." He folded his napkin and pushed back his chair. "It's what *you* think that counts. I'm going down to the lab for a while, Jean. I'll be back about nine."

My mother took a corn muffin from the bread basket and dunked it in the juice from her sugared fruit. "It's a shame to throw this out," she said.

She stood up and smoothed her dress. "Clean up, here, Susan," she said. "I promised Debbie I'd help her with her book report. "

She took my sister's hand and the two of them left the dining room. I did the dishes and went upstairs to call Margie.

I had been dreading this call all day. How could I tell my best friend I was going to marry her cast-off boyfriend? She'd dated him for two years. She'd probably slept with him, too. She'd certainly tried to share her life with him but he didn't meet her standards. She must have suspected that his visit to Toledo was more than a casual thing, but she never asked me about it, and I was very careful to keep Michael out of our conversations.

I forced myself to face the truth at last. I'd only been really close to this boy she didn't want for three days, and I was beginning to understand why Tom Hester won her. Michael's dreams smacked of superficiality and materialism just as she had said they did. She was right. Was my mother right, too? Was Michael trash? Was he a weak opportunist? Was <u>he</u> good enough for <u>me</u>?

Face it, Susie. It never occurred to you to ask if he measured up to your standards. All you care about is that he thought you were up to his. Be honest. He's the only one who wants you. Bobby doesn't. Ben doesn't. And you haven't had a decent date in six months.

I looked at my options and decided to ignore my common sense. If I didn't get out of this house, I would be my mother's cipher for the rest of my life. That was my only valid priority. I dialed Margie's number. "Busy?" I asked her. "You're not? Good. I have something to tell you. I'm engaged."

"I'm not surprised, Susie," said Margie. "And I'm very happy for you. The two of you sparkled together when I saw you last weekend."

I glared at the telephone. "*You* didn't want to marry Michael, Margie," I said. "Why is he good enough for *me*?"

"Everyone sees different things in people, Susie," she said. "When two people fit together, one has the qualities the other needs to become complete.

A good marriage is when you balance each other like Tom and I do. Michael didn't fill my needs and I didn't fill his. You do, I guess, and I'm happy for you."

ஐ Chapter 38 ஐ

Michael called that night and we made plans for him to come back to Toledo the next weekend. Mother telephoned his parents the next day and invited them to visit us, too. Then she invited Uncle Max, Aunt Evelyn, Uncle Harry and Aunt Sarah to meet them. "We'll have your family the next time, Leonard," she told Daddy. "I don't want to overwhelm them. Besides, Marge said she and Frank were going to Hot Springs next week. They'll be too involved to make it."

I smiled at my mother. "That sounds wonderful, Mother," I said, "if you don't think it would be too much trouble. We could just take the Roses out to a restaurant. They wouldn't mind."

"But I would, Susan," said my mother. "If you insist on going through with this thing, I intend to do it right."

I looked down at my hands and kept my mouth shut. I wanted that party because I was anxious for Aunt Evelyn to meet Michael. She was very perceptive and I believed in her opinions. As soon as I gathered up the courage, I would have to discuss my doubts with her. She would be able to tell me if my fears were real. The only trouble was that Aunt Evelyn would never hurt my feelings. If she thought I loved Michael, she would program herself to see only good things about him. It wasn't that she was dishonest . . . it was that she was very kind.

Mother began discussing wedding plans at dinner, the Tuesday night after Michael left. She proclaimed her invitation roster as if it were an established oracle. "How big is this wedding going to be, Jean?" asked my father. "Just family?"

He must have talked to her. She wasn't objecting anymore. She was planning. She loved managing shows and this one was going to be her biggest gala ever.

My mother smoothed her apron and sat down at the table. "I thought it would be a good idea to invite all those business friends of yours, Leonard," she said. "You know, the ones you meet down at the office after hours."

Her face was very flushed and I could see her hands shake when she reached for her water glass. "Now, Jean," said my father.

He put his napkin in his lap and helped himself to the platter of meat loaf and potatoes that Mother handed to him. "Whatever you want to do, dear," he said. "I imagine the Roses will have some people they'd like to invite as well.

Columbus isn't that far from here. You ought to look into reserving a block of rooms at the Park Lane or the Commodore."

"I've already thought of that, Leonard," said my mother. "That barbecue sauce is very spicy, so be careful. You said you liked it that way."

Daddy nodded. "Smells wonderful," he said. "I wonder if Michael's father plays golf? I could take him out to the club, Saturday."

"You'd better wait until you meet him before you make reservations on the course," said my mother. "He might not be the kind of person you want to introduce to our friends. Grace. . . . that's her name, isn't it, Susan?"

I nodded.

"Grace might like to meet Peggy and Blanche for lunch." said my mother. "They both keep kosher, too, so they'll have something to talk about. I'll have to buy kosher meat for the Roses when they come, so don't expect rare roast beef, Leonard. I'll probably do short ribs. Those kind of people love greasy meat."

She handed me the platter of meatloaf. I shook my head. "A little won't hurt you, Susan," she said.

"No, thank you," I said.

I sprinkled some pepper and basil on my lettuce and took a piece of Melba toast from the bread basket. I watched my sister split a Parkerhouse roll and lavish butter on it. Her fingers were shiny with butter and her round face seemed to bulge in the light from the chandelier. She reminded me of those pictures of medieval banquets where there was a gigantic platter in the middle of the table with a suckling pig on it, and everyone brandished huge drumsticks that dripped fat and gravy.

I returned the Melba toast to the basket. My mother took a tiny slice of meat from the platter. She scooped up the braised peppers and tomatoes that surrounded it and spread it across the meat. "And Peggy likes classical music," she said. "Michael said his mother enjoyed the symphony, didn't he? Although what kind of symphony they get in Columbus, Indiana is more than I can figure out. She probably listens to it on radio."

She unfolded her napkin and put it in her lap. She speared a tiny bit of meat on her fork and swallowed it. She split her baked potato and sprinkled chives on it. She spooned some of the barbecue sauce from the meat over the potato and paused. "If you do it this way, Debbie, you won't need butter," she said.

Debbie looked up from her plate and grinned. "Too late," she said. "I put the butter on *before* I put on the sour cream. I don't need barbecue sauce on it. I put that on the meatloaf."

She smiled and her face gleamed with grease and butter. "It is just yummy, Mama!" she said.

"The Roses go to concerts in Fort Wayne," I said. "Fort Wayne gets lots of wonderful things like ballet, and theater, too, and it's only forty miles away. Besides, Columbus has a chamber orchestra and a little theater group of its own. It's a very active place, Mother. It's not dead the way Toledo is."

My mother nodded toward the bowl of vegetables. "Debbie," she said. "Eat some broccoli. It's better for you than all those potatoes. You can have broccoli, can't you, Susan?"

"I can't when you put bacon bits and almonds on it, Mother," I said.

I squeezed lemon juice on my plate of lettuce and radishes. My mother sniffed and buttered a roll.

"I can't stand broccoli," said Debbie. "Please pass the sour cream. My potato is awfully dry."

"But you already have butter and sour cream on it, honey," said Mother.

Daddy looked up from his plate. "Leave her alone, Jean," he said. "I think it's good that she has a healthy appetite. She reminds me of my sister: big and beautiful."

My mother glared at him. She bit into her roll and put it on her butter plate. She took a small helping of broccoli. "Moderation," she said. "Moderation is the secret, Debbie. If you don't overdo it now, you won't have to diet the rest of your life the way I do."

Debbie nodded and scooped a heaping tablespoon of sour cream on her baked potato. "And like Susie is doing, too," she said.

Mother sniffed and shrugged her shoulders. She filled her fork with the potato mixture on her plate and paused before she put it in her mouth. "Susan doesn't need to diet, the way we do," she said. "She's just flaunting her self control."

I could feel my face getting hot. I gripped my napkin until my knuckles turned white. I clutched my fork in my hands and pushed the tines into the tablecloth. I took a deep breath. "Right, mother," I said.

My eyes burned and I swallowed an uncomfortably large lump of hurt and fury. I felt my stomach lurch and I kept my eyes focused on the lettuce leaves lying limp and dry on my plate. My mother smoothed the tablecloth in front of her and reached for a dill pickle. She put it on her butter plate. "How about some stuffed celery or deviled eggs, Leonard?" she said.

My father shook his head. "I'm just fine, Jean," he said.

Mother bit into the pickle and wiped her fingers on her napkin. "I can take his mother to Zimmerman's," she said. "That's always nice, and they serve a wonderful smoked whitefish. Maybe we can begin shopping for patterns for your silver and china, Susan. I'd like to show that woman the quality of the gifts you expect. I can just imagine what she'd select on her own: Libbey's glass and International Silverplate. That kind always does."

My father pushed away his plate. "Delicious, Jean," he said.

My mother looked at him and shook her head. "You hardly ate a thing, Leonard," she said.

She pulled his plate closer to her and picked at his leftover meatloaf.

"It's a crime to waste good food this way," she said.

She cut up a few pieces of meat and put it in her saucer. She set it on the floor and Junior rushed to her feet to lap it up. My mother took her spoon and scooped up bits of my father's leftover potatoes.

"We have to register you at Freeman's right away, Susan," she said. "July isn't very far away."

She dabbed at her mouth with her napkin and picked up the untouched deviled egg on my father's plate. Debbie reached for another potato and emptied the rest of the sour cream over it. The dog polished off the meat in his saucer. He stood up on his hind legs and put his paws on my mother's knees. My mother looked down at him and smiled. "My little man!" she said and filled the saucer with more meat.

I sipped a little water and stared at my dinner plate. It seemed so empty. A tiny portion of skinned chicken was huddled in one corner and over in the other a stalk of steamed broccoli. The food looked like two small imperfections in my mother's Lennox china.

I squeezed some lemon juice on my broccoli. I cut it with my knife and put a small piece on my fork. It looked sterile, as if it had been rescued from a hospital tray for diabetics. I returned it to my plate. I took another sip of water.

I poked my fork into the dry lump of skinned chicken breast I had allowed myself. It sat on my plate like a discarded stone and it tasted like shredded leather. I couldn't swallow it.

I pulled the platter of meatloaf and baked potatoes closer to my plate. I inhaled its onion and tomato perfume. I licked my lips and pushed it away. I took a sip of water and shredded my chicken with my knife. Now it looked like a tangled mass of white thread. I pushed it in a corner and cut into the broccoli again.

My mother finished the deviled egg and wiped her fingers on her napkin. She dipped into Daddy's potato again. She pointed her fork at me. "Do try a little of that meatloaf, Susan," she said. "I really outdid myself, if I do say so. Didn't you think so, Leonard?"

Daddy leaned back in his chair. "Anything special for dessert?" he asked.

I swallowed and twisted my napkin into a wad on my lap. I refused to look at the meatloaf again. I took a piece of Melba toast. I watched my mother finish my father's potato and start on his broccoli. I could taste the almonds and bacon as I watched her swallow. I crumbled the Melba toast into bits on my plate.

I pushed my plate away and stood up. I took it into the kitchen and scraped the uneaten food into the disposal. I brought in the coffee pot and poured some coffee. I sat down again and eyed the basket of bread next to my place. It looked as if my mother had robbed a bakery. There were three kinds of bread, a few bagels, and two kinds of rolls. I picked up a kaiser roll. It smelled as if it had just come from the oven. I hesitated. No. Absolutely NOT. I had only lost one pound last week.

Mother pushed the jar of apple butter over to me. "That tastes marvelous on a hard roll, Susan," she said. "You really ought to try it. It's not half as fattening as butter."

I put the roll back in the basket and replaced the napkin that covered it. I reached for the coffeepot and filled my cup.

"Sugar? Cream?" asked my mother.

I shook my head. I sipped my coffee and lit a cigarette. My mother took the soft roll from my father's plate and dipped it into the barbecue sauce he hadn't eaten. "I thought we'd have a big reception after the ceremony, and then a nice dinner for his family and ours at the Park Lane," she said. "If we do that, it might be nice to have a twilight ceremony. While Grace is here, we'll select the invitations, too, Susan. She can give us an idea of how many people she wants to invite. I better make a list of things for us to do. Have you discussed who will be in the ceremony with Michael, Susan?"

I wondered when my mother was going to get around to including me in my wedding plans. My Big Event was no longer mine. It was my mother's party and I'd be lucky if she even invited me. I took a deep drag on my cigarette and refilled my coffee cup. "Michael and I haven't discussed the wedding party at all," I said. "We just decided to get married the day before yesterday, for God's sake. He hasn't even given me a ring."

"Is everyone finished here?" asked my mother.

She stood up and smoothed her skirt. She picked up my father's plate and her own and carried them into the kitchen. "I never should have eaten that last piece of bread," she said.

I heard the plates rattling as she scraped them clean. "Susan," she called. "Start putting away the meatloaf and vegetables. Is anyone in the mood for apple pie?"

"I am," said Debbie. "With ice cream?"

Mother turned to me as I walked into the kitchen. "Cut her a slice, will you, Susan?" she said. "I have some telephoning to do. I hope Helen can work this weekend."

Once again, I realized how barren my mother's life really was. She tended a house none of us cared about and planned elaborate meals none of us wanted to eat. She went shopping with Aunt Evelyn for clothes she would never wear, and talked about those clothes and her newest recipes once a week with her canasta group.

She had wanted more than that. I recalled Aunt Evelyn's words and my eyes filled with tears for this woman so angered and disappointed with life that cooking was the only activity that could make her happy.

Marriage to your father wasn't what Jean expected it to be. She thought they would get dressed up every night and go to fancy parties just like they did before they were married. She thought she'd have a maid to do the dishes and she would be a fine lady, but life didn't turn out quite that way. When she had you, she realized that all her pretty dreams would never happen. She was locked into her home with a child to take care of, and there wasn't enough money to hire anyone to help her out. She never expected to work as hard as she did those first few years. I think that's what made her so bitter.

That was why she objected to Michael Rose. She knew he would give me the same empty marriage my father had given her.

❧ Chapter 39 ☙

Now that my engagement was official, my days were packed with preparations for married life. I taught all day, endured silent, angry shopping expe-
ditions with my mother, and talked to Michael every night on the telephone.
In between all the bustle, I managed to weigh myself several times each day
and create intricate myths of what my life would be like in just a few teeny
months. I dined on dry lettuce and dreams, washed down with black coffee.
And as I drank, I imagined the day I would be brewing coffee in my own little kitchen with a geranium on the window sill and Michael shaving in the
bathroom.

That first week of my engagement was such a whoosh of activity, I could-
n't believe Friday happened so fast. Friday meant Michael. Now, I could hug
him once more and feel the reassurance of his arms around me.

My vague doubts had festered for seven days. Every time I shut my eyes,
I heard my mother's indictment: *"He's trash, Susan. Trash."*

I would try desperately to rekindle the warmth of my beloved's arms
around me. I concentrated on that picture of Susan Rose in her own home
with no Mother in the kitchen to dynamite her dreams. But still, deep down
inside me, a tiny voice insisted, *"She's right, Susan. Your mother is always
right."*

Now, it was Friday and my dark shadows would vanish. I would see how
silly they were once I looked into my Michael's sweet eyes.

I spent Thursday night washing my hair and doing my nails. I weighed
myself over and over but I couldn't force that disgusting scale down one single notch. Worry! I was bloated with worry.

It just wasn't fair.

Friday. Michael pulled into our driveway. The dog charged at the door, a
flash of snarling, furious fur bouncing up to the screen and tearing his way out
to the porch. Debbie ran after him and chased him into the backyard. Mother
ignored Junior's wild yelps and Debbie's shrill cries. She walked to the door
and opened it as if she were the queen of England greeting her subjects.

I could feel drops of perspiration gather under my arms even though it was
a bleak forty degrees outside and chunks of gray snow still clung to the curb.
My hands were moist and my stomach was bouncing like an aerated tennis
ball. I felt like I was clamped in a mangle.

I looked at my mother. She was dressed in a simple, light blue shirt dress, her hair brushed into loose curls around her face. She had been cooking all week. She drove around with me on all my errands every day when I came home from school and she still found time to keep our house in its usual immaculate condition. She had also managed to attend her weekly book review club Tuesday morning. It was her turn to give the review. She had chosen Michener's *Hawaii*.

She found time Wednesday to take Aunt Evelyn shopping for a new dress and bought herself another of her crazy hats. This one was green straw and it had a huge satin rose on the brim that cascaded over the side. She looked very fresh and spring like when she put it on like a Renoir lady dressed for a garden party.

Thursday, she had taken Debbie to her dancing lesson and done her regular volunteer work at The Red Cross. She and Aunt Evelyn had been at Darlington House all this morning serving the old ladies lunch. My mother couldn't have been home more than an hour. In that hour, she had tidied the house, fed the dog, finished her dinner preparations, bathed and changed clothes. She looked as if she had just gotten up from a nap and had a refreshing massage before her maid dressed her.

My mother put on her company face and smiled at her guests. She held out her hand. "You're Grace," she said to the tall, mountain of a woman at Michael's side.

Grace Rose was dressed in a bulky brown suit that reeked of Tabu and mothballs. Her feet were so swollen they bulged out of her shoes. One stocking had a runner in it. Her gray hair was beauty shop blue sprayed into parallel waves around her face. The red lipstick smeared on her lips sliced across her face like a raw wound. I could see my mother shudder.

I never realized how young and pretty my mother was until I saw her next to that huge lump of a woman that was to be my mother-in-law. My mother looked like one of those pictures of efficient housewives in *Good Housekeeping*, the ones who did five thousand things in a day and still managed to be relaxed and smiling when they served their husbands cocktails before dinner.

Mrs. Rose looked like the before picture in a Weight Watchers' ad.

"I'm so happy you and David could come," said my mother. "Leonard should be home any minute. Is the dog in the yard, Debbie?"

My sister nodded. Her face was dangerously red, and she was out of breath from her wild chase through all the neighbors' yards to catch Junior. She gulped for air and wheezed a few times. Then she smiled and held out her hand to Mrs. Rose. "How do you do," she gasped.

"What's wrong with you, Susan?" said my mother. "Don't just stand there.

Take the Roses' coats. Michael, we'll put your parents in the room you had last time. You can take Susan's room. She'll sleep with Debbie."

Michael nodded and put his arm around my shoulder. He gave me a hug and I felt renewed. I put my arm around his waist and hugged him back. I couldn't remember what I was worried about. I sighed like a cuddled kitten.

"Sounds fine to me, Mrs. Talberg," said Michael. "I'll go out and get the bags."

Michael's father looked just like Michael but much shorter. He was very thin and he had a beautiful smile. His white teeth sparkled like a keyboard in his ruddy face. Little as he was, his arms were very muscular and his hands were huge. I pitied the doomed chickens he butchered every Friday for his Jewish balaboustas to roast. Those poor little birds didn't stand a chance.

Mr. Rose didn't say much at all. Maybe that was because Grace didn't give him a chance. She sounded like a non-stop machine gun without a silencer. A continual hemorrhage of words gushed from her bright red mouth. "It was such a lovely drive," she bellowed. "We stopped at Kentucky Fried Chicken for lunch. It was delicious!"

Mr. Rose nodded. "And then we saw this irresistible gift shop!" thundered Mrs. Rose. "I made Michael pull over right away! They had Almond Roca. It's been years since I've tasted Almond Roca, and this is the real McCoy. I bought you a few pounds, Mrs. Talberg. I thought you'd like something a little out of the ordinary to serve all your company."

She handed my mother a very large pink canister of candy. My mother smiled and held the present with her fingertips as if it contained TNT. "Yes," she said. "How sweet of you to think of me. Here, Susan. Put this in a candy dish."

She smoothed her hair and turned to Mr. Rose. "Let me hang up your coat, David," she said.

"I made short ribs for dinner," she said to Grace. "I hope you like it."

"Lovely," bellowed Grace. "But would you mind drying the meat between some paper towels? David can't eat fat...or salt. I hope you didn't salt it."

My mother had a heavy hand with all seasonings. That's why her cooking was so marvelous. She was not going to admit that everything she cooked wallowed in fat and salt and additives that caused every disease known to man. Let David Rose have his heart attack when he got home. She was not going to let these schnooks from Columbus, Indiana spoil her dinner. "Don't worry about it," she lied. "I never salt meat. It makes it stringy. Why don't you go upstairs and freshen up? There's plenty of time before dinner. Leonard won't be home for another half hour."

Grace ignored my mother. She put her arms around me. Her voice resonated like Ethel Merman in rehearsal. "You're Susan," she cried. "Welcome into our family. I've always wanted a daughter."

And she smothered me in a fog of Tabu and soft bosom.

As I tried to fight my way up for air, my sister said, "Isn't that nice? Daddy said he always wanted a son. And Susie has always wanted to be married. So I guess everyone's happy. Even me, because I always wanted a great brother-in-law and I'm getting the best one in the whole world."

Grace laughed. "Of course everyone's happy about this wedding. Why wouldn't we be?" she roared. "Come upstairs with me, Susan. I want to know you better."

I loved her because she wanted to love me. She was a big, blowzy woman and her perfume smothered me, but I didn't care. She was human and vulnerable. I could imagine her being afraid of mice or crying in movies. I'll bet she never screamed at Michael when he spilled his milk or did something stupid. Her mouth wouldn't make harsh words. It was too gentle. I looked into her eyes and I saw a softness that made me feel warm all over. I took her hand and I smiled.

I'd never had a mother to hug or one who wrapped me in approval the way this woman did. She didn't even know me and she accepted me just because her Michael loved me. She was a giant-sized, coarse Aunt Evelyn and I was thrilled. If the whole world were filled with people like my aunt and Michael's mother, what a sweet, comfortable place it would be. We wouldn't need to reach for heaven; we'd be living in it.

Grace Rose and I chattered warm nothings for a while. "I'll bet you're exhausted after such a long drive," I said.

She shook her head. "Not at all," she said. "My Michael is a wonderful driver. Have you been in a car with him?"

"Not for any length of time," I said. "At Michigan, we always walked everywhere and when he was here last weekend, the farthest we went was the park. Let me get you some fresh towels."

Mrs. Rose sat me down beside her on the bed. "Not just yet, honey," she said.

She opened her overnight case and pulled out a red satin peignoir and a flannel nightgown. A tiny jewelry box was nestled between her hairbrush and a bottle of Spray Net. She opened it and I gasped. The prettiest diamond brooch I had ever seen was sitting in a nest of black velvet. The stones were small and they twinkled with light. The setting was delicate gold filigree, fine as a crystallized spider's web. It was feminine and understated.

Grace Rose smiled and gave me a hug. "It's so lovely," I breathed.

She laughed and she actually pinched my cheek. I felt like Molly Goldberg had just crashed through the television screen into our guest bedroom. "I want you to have this now as an engagement present. It goes with your ring. That's been in our family for years, too. David's father brought it here from Poland. It was his grandmother's. She gave it to him before she was murdered in one of the pogroms.

"It's just beautiful," I said. "Are you sure you want me to have it? It looks awfully valuable."

I swallowed a surge of triumph. My mother would love this jewelry, but it was mine.

David Rose walked into the room. He must have heard our conversation because he smiled and said, "Nothing is valuable unless it's used. That pin has been sitting in our safe deposit box for over twenty years. Wear it and enjoy it. That's all the thanks we need."

I loved him instantly. He radiated goodness. How could I resist? I couldn't wait to see the ring. And I couldn't wait to hug my Michael again. I hadn't even had a chance to say a proper hello with all the madcap activity of his arrival and the dog's hysterical cacophony of yelps and snaps. I walked out of their room just as Michael came up the stairs with their luggage. We grabbed a quick kiss in the hall. "I didn't think Friday would ever get here," he said. "Let's escape after dinner. I have a surprise for you."

The ring. Oh dear Lord. I was going to get my ring. My left hand ached for it. I longed to see the twinkle of a diamond on my finger. Then I'd know that all this wasn't another of my foolish dreams. It was real, real as the beautiful human being I clung to now. I inhaled the tweedy smell of his suit, the fresh lemon of his aftershave. "Tonight is all we have so we'd better make the most of it," I said. "I have to spend tomorrow afternoon with the mothers and tomorrow night, my mother invited her sister and brother over. Just wait till you meet my Aunt Evelyn and Uncle Max. They're still lovebirds and they've been married twenty years. I hope we still see each other through golden lenses after that long."

"How can we help it?" said Michael. "Every time I talk to you, I find something else to love. It'll just get better and better every year for us."

"Promise?" I said.

"Promise."

"Uncle Max can do a lot for you," I said. "He's a very important lawyer in Toledo. So be nice."

You're learning, Susan. Say what he wants to hear. He won't give a damn that your Aunt Evelyn gave you the only warmth you knew as a child. He won't care that Uncle Harry is a practical joker that loads our freezer with exotic ice cream. But he'll grab at the chance to meet Uncle Max and get on his good side. Is that the kind of priority you want in the man you marry?

"When am I not nice?" Michael asked.

"Never," I said. "Kiss me again. Quick. I need a little fuel to go downstairs and help my mother."

And that was our weekend: an endless procession of relatives, endless talk about endless plans. Michael and I had no time alone together at all. He slipped the ring to me after dinner just before Aunt Evelyn and Uncle Max surprised us with a visit. I was too tense to be properly excited, and I think Michael was a little hurt. "Don't you like it?" he asked. "I wanted to get you something new, but my mother insisted you have this. It's been in the family forever."

I kissed him. "Oh, honey, I'm thrilled," I said. "I'll cherish it because it's from you. It's just that I'm concerned about all that mess in the kitchen. If I don't help my mother clean things up I won't hear the end of it from her. And when she's angry with me, my life is hell. Kiss me once more and let me get downstairs to that kitchen. You go in the living room and get to know my aunt and uncle. I warn you, you're in for a treat. They're the best people I know."

What I didn't tell him was that I didn't want to leave Grace at the mercy of my mother. She hadn't had a chance to sink her fangs into that innocent, well-meaning woman during dinner. She was too busy trying to avoid leftovers and urging second and third helpings on her stuffed guests.

Grace Rose was a lower class Jew. She had no savoir faire and that was something my mother could not forgive. I wanted to be there to ward off my mother's attack. I sailed downstairs: Susan Galahad to the rescue.

I needn't have worried. My mother was a gracious hostess and if there was some condescension in her manner, only I noticed it. I cringed when she handed Grace a dish of the Almond Roca she had brought us and said, "Of course, *we* stay away from things like this. I'm very health conscious. I wouldn't want my children to suffer from tooth decay and obesity because of my neglect. Do have some candy, Grace. I'd hate to see it go to waste."

Grace smiled and took one of the foil wrapped candies. She handed another to my mother. "Just this once," she said. "It's delicious."

The Roses left Sunday afternoon in a flurry of kisses, hugs and promises that I would visit them in Columbus the next weekend. Michael said he would call when he got home and then they were gone. Mother didn't say anything even then. She waited until we were all together at dinner.

"Well, what did you think of them?" I asked.

"They're *your* in-laws, Susan," she said. "Take some turkey. It's not fattening."

She filled my plate with fat-encrusted turkey bits and pieces that had been floating in gravy. "I'll just have dry white meat, Mother," I said. "Please don't make this diet harder on me than it already is."

"I'm not making it harder, Susan. There isn't any white meat left. The company ate it all. I'll give this to Debbie and you can scramble an egg if you like."

I got up to go into the kitchen. "That's just what I'll do," I said.

When I returned to the table with my dry salad and two hard boiled eggs, my sister had taken my filled plate and added some cauliflower in tomato sauce and a big mountain of sweet potatoes. "Here's some extra gravy for those potatoes, Debbie," said my mother. "Would you like some, Leonard?"

Daddy shook his head. Mother put her napkin in her lap and took a few pieces of turkey from the broth in the platter. She scooped up a small helping of cauliflower and took a kaiser roll from the breadbasket. She split it and dipped it in the turkey gravy. "Thank God, they'll be your family, not mine," she said. "Did you see their manners? That man pushed his vegetables on his fork with his knife! I couldn't believe it."

"So did Grandpa Martin," I said. "And he always tucked his napkin in his collar, too."

My mother flushed and pointed her fork at me. "My father came over to this country in his thirties," said my mother. "His manners were those of the Polish intelligentsia. My uncle Mordecai entertained nobility in his home."

She reached for the casserole of sweet potatoes and then pushed it away. She cut a piece of turkey and I could see her hand quiver as she put it in her mouth.

"Maybe David Rose was born in the old country, too," I said. "Anyway, what difference does it make how people eat? It's what they are that matters. I think Michael's parents are the sweetest people I've met in a very long time."

I squeezed lemon juice on my lettuce and sliced my eggs in half. I sprinkled pepper on them and speared them with my fork. "Susan," said my mother. "Will that be enough to eat? You know, you really shouldn't get any thinner. You have hollow eyes and a terrible skin color."

"This is plenty," I said. "What else didn't you like about my in-laws?"

My stomach knotted up and the food on my plate repelled me. I pushed the dish away and lit a cigarette. My mother frowned. "*We* haven't finished eating, Susan," she said.

I stubbed out my cigarette and took a sip of water. "What was wrong with them, Mother?" I said.

"Are you blind? Did you see the schmata that woman had on? It looked like a Sears Roebuck special. I'll bet she's never been inside a decent fashion salon."

"What difference does that make?" I retorted. "She's good and kind. She reminded me of Aunt Evelyn. She's Michael's friend, just like Mrs. Wiseman is with Margie. I think that's wonderful."

"And I suppose it's wrong to be just a mother?"

My mother pulled the bowl of cauliflower closer to her plate and spooned some of the sauce on her turkey. The tone of her voice was the same she used when she snapped at my father. She looked at me with so much disgust that I flinched. "I don't want to fight with you, Mother," I said. "Don't dig into me."

I tried to pour some coffee into my cup, but my hands were shaking. I put the pot down. My mother reached for a roll and buttered it. She waved it at me as she talked. "Who's digging into you, Susan? I was simply voicing an opinion. And wait until I tell your Aunt Evelyn that you thought that mountainous woman was like her! How on earth can you compare my educated, cultured sister to such a loudmouthed excuse for a human being?"

She didn't wait for me to respond. She barely took a breath before she continued. "I hope you know what you're doing, Susan. Those people aren't in our class at all. They have very different ideas about life. I can't imagine a daughter of mine being comfortable with them. They probably don't know what an art exhibit is and the only theater they see is what's on Playhouse 90. I can just picture how she dresses when she drags that little butcher of hers to the Indianapolis Symphony. I have latkes, Leonard. Save room."

Daddy blunted her words. "Jean," he said. "You know what we discussed. They're Susie's family now and that's that. Did you two decide how big your wedding party would be, kitten?"

"Not yet, Daddy," I said and my eyes sparkled with my love for him. "We had no time alone this weekend. I'll talk to him about it when he calls, tonight."

I poured my coffee and took Daddy's cup. "Let me fill that for you," I said.

I put my hands on his shoulders and rubbed my face against his cheek. "You're a prince," I whispered.

"Thanks, kitten," said Daddy.

He pushed his plate away. "I'm stuffed," he said.

My mother looked at his plate and frowned. "You didn't eat a thing, Leonard," she said. "I thought you liked sweet potato pie. I used nutmeg and brown sugar this time."

My father nodded. "I do, Jean. But I've had enough."

He sipped his coffee. Debbie reached for the casserole of tomato pudding and took two large helpings. "I love this stuff," she said.

My mother smiled. "It's the Tally Ho recipe," she said.

She picked at Daddy's leftover potatoes. I sipped my coffee and lit another cigarette. "I'm going to Columbus next Friday," I said. "Michael and I can talk about wedding details then. It's the only time I'll be able to visit there and meet the rest of Michael's family. Everyone here has been after me to schedule parties. And next week, Margie and I are going apartment hunting."

My mother stood up and smoothed her skirt. She slammed her napkin on the table and picked up my father's plate and hers. "I warn you, Susan, I disapprove of this whole thing. That boy is cheap. His parents are nobodies, and you hardly knew him before you accepted his proposal. Don't fool yourself, Susan. He saw our house and thought you had money. He thinks your father can set him up in business. That's the only reason he proposed."

I pulled at the napkin in my lap until I heard it tear. I reached for my coffee cup. It was empty. I took a drag on my cigarette, but it had gone out in the ashtray. I tried to re-light it, but my hands were shaking so much the match went out. "That's not true," I said. "The trouble with you is that you don't think anyone can love me. Well, you're wrong. Aunt Evelyn loves me. Daddy loves me and so does Michael. It's only you who hates me, only you."

My mother chewed her pancake and slid another on her plate. "These are wonderful," she said. "Very crisp. You really should try one, Leonard."

My father shook his head. "Is there more coffee in that pot?" he asked.

My mother took the half-finished roll on my father's bread and butter dish and broke it in two. She dipped it into the gravy on the serving platter. She held it in her hand and pointed it at me. "What about Margie?" she asked. "Why didn't *she* hang on to him? Why did she dump him for Tom Hester? I'll tell you why. Because she's smart enough to see right through him. You're so anxious to get out of this house, you refuse to use your head, Susan. You're making a big mistake, young lady, and you're going to have to live with it the rest of your life. Clear the table, please. I have chocolate pie for dessert."

"Why do you spoil every good thing that ever happens to me?" I screamed. "What pleasure do you get out of spreading your venom over me? Can't you let me have anything, ever?"

She stood up and gripped the edge of the table. "Don't you raise your voice to me, Susan Talberg. I will not tolerate that kind of talk. You can give your father and Debbie dessert. I don't want any."

She turned and walked out of the room with the dog at her heels.

Daddy pushed his chair away from the table. "I'll talk to her, kitten. She's pretty upset."

The telephone rang. "I'll get it," said Debbie. "It's probably Ellen. We're

162

drilling each other for the history midterm tomorrow."

There I was in the dining room, surrounded by platters of turkey and cold potato pancakes. The sweet potatoes were in a bowl crusted with baked marshmallows. They smelled like a candy shop ready to open its doors. That damned tomato pudding actually beckoned to me with its glistening bread cubes. A plate of challah was still on the table next to the uncut chocolate pie my mother baked just to make me miserable. *Everything* she did made me miserable.

I put my head down on the table and I sobbed. I just despised her.

I loathed her because once again, she was right. How could Michael Rose love me? He didn't even know me. And I didn't know him.

Well, it was too late now. I had to select my silver and china patterns next week. There were parties scheduled every weekend in May and relatives were calling to set dates to entertain me. I had to find a wedding dress and furnish an apartment. I needed to shop for a trousseau, and I had to do it all with that viper who called herself my mother.

Don't think, Susan. Clear the table. You'll just get into trouble if you think.

I picked at the turkey left on the platter.

You'll get the life you deserve, now, Susan. You are worthless and only vermin can love you.

I packed that turkey down my throat so fast my eyes bulged and I was sure my ribs would crack.

Go ahead, Susan, cry. Is there anything in the world that you don't cry about? You wept because no one asked you to marry him. And now you're upset because someone did. You are a fool, Susan Talberg. A fool.

I jammed sweet potatoes, marshmallows, latkes and pickles down my throat as if I were loading an assembly line. I didn't bother to chew the mass of food packed in my mouth. I swallowed it whole and I hated myself. I emptied every platter. I scooped up that chocolate pie in my hands and drank melted ice cream from the carton on the table. I gobbled up the crumbs on the tablecloth. I gasped and sniffled and moaned. I didn't see that food; I didn't see those dirty plates. I saw my mother pointing her finger at me.

"That boy is cheap; his parents are nobodies."
Right you are, Mother. A nobody is the only somebody who would marry

me. I'll get fucked by a nobody and have little nobodies instead of babies and Oh my God why can't I just die?

I staggered out of the dining room into the bathroom.

Okay, Susan. You know this routine. You've done it a hundred times. Vomit. Shit. Vomit again. Boil the smell of overindulgence out of your skin and try to sleep. Your stomach will throb. And your heart? Face it, Susan.

YOUR HEART IS DEAD.

❧ Chapter 40 ❧

Mother and I went shopping for my trousseau together. I cannot look back on those weeks without blushing at my callous behavior. Mama devoted hours of her time to take me to her favorite shops and share her pleasure wandering through elegance. When we entered Moseley's Bed and Bath, her eyes glistened with enchantment like a child discovering an enormous Christmas tree. She paused before an arrangement of ivory sheets and towels monogrammed in brown. "Oh, Susan!" she whispered. "Isn't this lovely?"

She held up a washcloth and pressed it against her face. "Like velvet!" she exclaimed. "Imagine washing your face with something this soft!"

She paused and ran her hands over the percale sheets as gently as if they were alive. "My sister and I slept in the same bed when we lived at home and we only had one sheet to cover the mattress. Mama washed it by hand in the kitchen sink where she did all our laundry. She wrung it out with her hands and I helped her hang it outside. If it was windy or cold, the wet material flapped against our ankles and often dragged on the ground before the two of us managed to pin it on the line to dry. We brought it in that night, dry or not. . . . because it was the only one we had."

She looked at me with solemn eyes and for a moment, I saw how vulnerable she was, how innocent. "It was so stiff from the soap Mama couldn't rinse out that it scratched my legs like thorns," she said. "Evelyn and I used to huddle together and try to keep our legs covered with our nighties so it wouldn't scrape us."

She returned her attention to the silken sheets on the display table. "What do you think of these, Susan?" she said. "I think they would make up very nicely on your bed. Ivory is especially effective against a blue coverlet."

I turned away. "I like white," I said. "It looks cleaner to me."

Jean wants you to have all the things she never had, Aunt Evelyn had told me that long ago day in her kitchen. What she doesn't understand is that you don't want those things. You have other ideas . . modern ones that she doesn't really appreciate.

Mama had dreamed of finery such as this when she prepared for her marriage to my father. She thought I would want the rococo elegance in my home that she could never own, but I had different tastes. I hurried her from display to display and didn't hide my impatience with her. "I hate fancy things," I said. "Let's go, Mother. It's getting late."

Michael and I did our apartment hunting together, and it was the most fun we had together that heady, wonderful spring. We found a spacious two bedroom flat in one of the best neighborhoods in town; not too far from Margie and Tom. . . and very far from my parents' home. Our building had a doorman and a marble foyer. Michael loved that. "I've always wanted to live in a place like this," said Michael. "It has real class. Won't my clients be impressed when the doorman announces them before they take the elevator up to our place?"

When we opened the door of our very own flat, I felt the same thrill I had as a child when I played house. Michael and I wandered from living room to kitchen and into the master bedroom, each of us seeing different furniture used in different ways. I saw a big plush double bed; Michael saw twins. "I am a restless sleeper," he explained.

"I love to cuddle," I said.

"Even while you're sleeping?" asked Michael.

"*Especially* while I'm sleeping," I said.

We walked into the spare bedroom. "This will be the baby's room," I said.

"Not at first," said Michael. "You're going to teach for two or three years until we're on our feet financially, remember?"

That's what you think, Buster. I'm getting pregnant if I have to make you screw me twenty times a day. Two or three years? Don't make me laugh.

I had a gut instinct that if I didn't have my babies fast, I wouldn't have a husband to have those babies with. The minute Michael realized all my horrible faults, the ones my mother told me about so often, he wouldn't be able to stand me. I needed to get pregnant before that happened. "You promised we wouldn't stop a baby from coming, Michael," I said and I held my breath.

What if he said, "It's either me or a baby right away?"

What would I do then?

But he didn't. "Let's start the room out as a den," he said. "Then, when you're pregnant, we can remodel it."

"I hate to spend your money for nothing," I said. "We won't have much time to use a den, Michael. It isn't that hard to make a baby. And won't it be fun trying?"

I smiled at him and remembered Bobby Mosten. It would be marvelous to lose myself in that sea of sensation again. I couldn't understand why Michael hadn't tried to go further than the intensive petting we had done on the couch

166

in my parents' den. I hoped it was because he was afraid Debbie would walk in on us or Junior would start barking. Or maybe his reticence was out of respect for me. But he hadn't respected Margie. She told me so. He had *desired* Margie.

"It won't be my money we're spending when we decorate this place," he said. "We'll have to use your savings for that, honey. I'm spending every cent I have for my office."

What was it that Margie said when I scolded her for choosing Tom and his money instead of poor Michael Rose? "If you think I'm materialistic, you should hear Michael Rose. All he cares about is money and using people to get it. I think that's disgusting."

I hear you, Margie. I hear you, but it's too late now. It isn't me that Michael Rose loves. It's my Daddy's money. Or maybe it's anybody's money, as long as it isn't his.

I looked now at this man who was so inadequate for my best friend and knew he was inadequate, period. No wonder he hadn't tried to sleep with me. It wasn't Susan Talberg's body that attracted him. It was her bank account. Michael took me in his arms and I squelched the sharp words that might finish my marriage before it began. Instead, I snuggled close and breathed the heavy wool fragrance of his coat. I shut my eyes and replayed life with Mother since I had graduated from Michigan. I rubbed my face in the rough male texture of that coat and I knew. I couldn't give up my passport out. I wasn't going to let money or my paranoid suspicion send me back to my mother.

I looked up at him and gave him my best Doris Day smile. "Maybe Daddy can help with the apartment, too," I said. "You're right, honey. Our home has to be nice if you're going to entertain clients there. Besides, I want us to live beautifully, too. I think it's very important."

Michael held me closer and I couldn't see his face. But I could feel his body relax. He'd won. He'd gotten his dream without footing the bill. But what about *my* dream? Was my daddy going to have to pay for it? Or would I just not get it at all?

"Don't you want to help choose our furniture?" I asked.

"I'll love anything you decide," said Michael. "As long as it doesn't look cheap or secondhand the way our house does. Mother has a bunch of junk she accumulated from her own parents and my aunts and uncles. She's never redecorated the place since I can remember."

"But I loved your home, Michael. It was comfortable. You could relax there."

"It smelled of dog and stale cigar smoke," said Michael. "It was dirty and looked so shabby, I hated to bring anyone home to visit. I was ashamed you had to see it after I'd seen what a beautiful place you live in."

"Beautiful? Our house is beautiful? My God, Michael, it's just like a show-room in a decorator's studio. I always feel like I should dress and put on fresh make-up before I walk into that rigid, immaculate living room of ours. No one would dream of smudging an ashtray or putting his feet up on the couch the way we did at your house.

"Our home will be completely different, I hope. We'll have flowers on the window sill, real logs in the fireplace and a great big, plushy bed."

I kissed him before he had a chance to bring up that twin bed idea again. I buried my face in his shoulder and tried desperately to recapture the magic that was vanishing from us the more we talked, the more we saw what we really were.

✍ Chapter 41 ଓ

Then Margie gave us a dinner dance at the country club. She invited all the young couples who mattered and Michael was delighted. "I'll bet I get one hundred clients out of this party," he told me as we drove to the club.

"Do you think it's in good taste to drum up business at a party like this, honey?" I asked.

"I won't drum up business, Susie. I'll just make friends. Don't you trust me?"

"Of course I do, Michael," I said, but I didn't. How could I? He talked like a vulgar con man.

"Why can't you just enjoy the people you meet instead of always thinking of what you can get from them?"

"That's unfair, Susan," he said. "What's wrong with seeing potential in people? I wouldn't be a good insurance salesman if I couldn't spot the people who can afford my policies, and convince them they need what I sell."

I didn't like the steel edge to his voice. I'd heard that sharp, slicing tone all my life. It was the one my mother used when she wanted to show me who was in control.

As soon as we arrived at the club, Michael disappeared. I was swept into a sea of welcomes and forgot all about him and my ever-growing doubts. Margie came up to me and kissed my cheek. "You look beautiful, Susie, but so thin," she said. "How much weight have you lost?"

"I was down to ninety this morning," I said. "I know it's a little low, but with all this rich food around, I like to have a few pounds to play with."

"But you never eat anything, Susie," Margie said. "Every party we've been to this week, you've just pushed the food around and drunk black coffee."

I remembered sticks of butter and scoops of ice cream floating down my throat in a sea of hot fudge. I remembered ribs of beef and an endless procession of blintzes marching into my mouth. "You should see me when I get home," I said. "I eat plenty."

And I saw myself crouched over the toilet, blobs of pie and chunks of bread-coated meat pouring out of my mouth. I shuddered. "More than enough," I added.

"Well, just don't lose any more weight. It's unhealthy to get so skinny," said Margie. "Where's Michael? It's time to sit down at the head table."

"I don't know," I said. "Maybe he's selling insurance policies in the men's room."

Margie grinned. "He was always a go-getter. He seemed so shy in school, but after a while, I got the feeling he was like a silent mouse ready to pounce on his victim. Isn't that silly? Oh, look. There he is at the bar."

I saw Michael. I saw Elaine Bloom. And I died inside. The two weren't touching. They were only talking. But something about them was too close, too intimate like a visible electric current. Was it the way they were standing together? The way their eyes met? No. It was the harmony of their bodies together. They looked like two parts of a puzzle that only needed to move one inch closer to lock in place.

Elaine Bloom was a tall, slender willow, cold as ice. Her splash of dark hair framed arctic eyes and alabaster skin. Her lips were painted red and full. She had a vixen's face, as disturbing as it was beautiful. She ran away when she was eighteen and returned to Toledo only last year. Everyone said she had a baby and Uncle Max took care of finding it a home, just like he did for the Goldman girl.

If the rumors were true, she sure didn't show it. I would have given my life for a stomach as flat as hers. I wondered if *she* ever gorged on food? Was her soul tearing her to pieces the way mine was? I doubted it. Her ego was well fed. She was a model now at Lamark's Specialties. She went to all the classiest places in town with every rich bachelor who lived within a radius of one hundred miles of Toledo.

She and I were never close. I was a bookworm, a classical music nut, and I didn't make friends easily. I was encased in my own world and only emerged for Margie and my Aunt Evelyn. Period. I walked over to Michael and Elaine. *Keep it light, Susan. You don't know anything yet. You just suspect. You just feel. And that's not enough.*

I glanced in a mirror and I saw my mother's face when my father told her she was beautiful. Her eyes were cold and her body so stiff it looked starched. "Do I measure up to your late night floozies, Leonard?" she'd say.

I continued toward my fiancé and touched his arm. "Hey, you two, break it up," I said. "It's time for Michael to escort the bride-to-be to dinner."

Michael jumped as if I had clashed cymbals in his ear and then he flushed red as a stop light. "Susie!" he said.

"You *were* involved, weren't you?" I said. "Can you continue the conversation after dinner? I don't think Elaine is at our table."

After we were seated, Michael turned to me. "Elaine is looking for a job, Susie," he said. "She doesn't have much insurance background but she could learn. And she'd be a knockout in my front office."

I looked at Elaine. Her hair swirled around her ivory skin and cold, dark eyes like a storm cloud. When she bent over her shrimp cocktail, she reminded me of Picasso's 'The Crow Lady.' She was an evil sprite, a harbinger of my own disaster. I knew it as surely as I knew that my fiancé was planning to give her a lot more than dictation when he got her alone in his office. "She certainly would," I said.

All during dinner, I listened to Michael's talk about money (other people's); he talked about betting on the horses (you could win a fortune if you got lucky); and he talked about people he'd met (that man over there distributes Coca Cola. He must be a walking treasury).

I watched my gorgeous prince diminish into a slimy frog. He drank too much, he smoked until he shrouded us all in a thick blue haze. His voice was so loud, I thought he'd stop traffic on Hill Avenue. After dinner, we danced. He held me close and I should have been in heaven but I wasn't. The pungent, sour alcohol smell of him made me sick. When Daddy cut in on us it was like a whiff of fresh, clean limes. "How about giving me my kitten for a while, Michael?" he asked. "I don't have much longer before she's yours."

Michael squeezed me tight. "But not for long, Dad," he said. "I'll come and get her after this set is over."

Oh, it felt good to move to the music in Daddy's arms. The band played Stardust and I almost wept. The stardust had left my eyes and it was too late. My wedding was less than three weeks away and I didn't even *like* the guy I was going to marry.

If I felt that way now, how would I feel next year? And the next? My future would be linked to a social-climbing, money-hungry man. I clutched at my father's shoulder and looked up at him. "Daddy," I asked. "Does love sometimes fade and then come back between two people, sort of like the tide does?"

"Sure, it does, honey. Lots of days go by when I don't feel any particular way about Mother at all. I just live with her. But don't ever try to take her away from me. She's part of me and I'm empty without her. Pretty soon, Michael will be part of you, too."

He stopped dancing and cupped my face in his hands. "These weeks before your marriage are the hardest you'll ever live through, kitten. You and Michael are both in the spotlight too much to relax and be yourselves."

But every time Michael was himself, I loved him less. I couldn't tell Daddy that. He'd just laugh at my suspicions. But I knew I was right.

My father swirled me around and I looked out into the balcony. Michael was there. I saw him in a flash as we turned. He was dancing with Elaine. I recognized the shimmer of her velvet gown. Why was he holding her so close? Were they kissing? They disappeared into the star speckled night too swiftly for me to tell.

That night, Michael and I had our first real fight. It was ice cold and very short. Our words were brittle icicles that pierced any pretense that remained in our decayed relationship. After the party, we had some coffee in the kitchen with Mother and Daddy. As soon as they went upstairs, I pounced.

"I saw you, tonight," I said.

"Saw me?" said Michael. "What do you mean, 'saw me'?"

"You were kissing Elaine Bloom on the balcony," I hissed. "Is that the way you interview women for a job?"

"Susie, you're ridiculous. I danced with Elaine to be polite. I didn't kiss her. I don't love her. I love you."

"I saw you," I said.

I stood up and left the room.

ഇ Chapter 42 ൚

Michael and I didn't say much to each other the next day. I left him to Daddy and their talk about Toledo's elite and golf course techniques. I remembered all the advice I refused to hear and I knew Margie was right. Michael was too wrapped up in himself to love anyone. Mother was right, too. He was trash. He was using me and my family to climb his social ladder.

And I was right. . . not about Michael, but about myself. I was right and it made me sick. No one could ever love me. I wasn't good enough. Because if Michael really loved me, he wouldn't see Elaine Bloom. He'd only see me.

Michael left late Sunday night. His kiss goodbye was like acid on my mouth. I welcomed his absence and wished next Friday would never come.

I said nothing to my family until Thursday night. Daddy was reading the newspaper in the den. Mother was mending. Debbie was watching television. I took a deep breath. Goodbye, dream. Goodbye, love. Hello, hell.

"I want to call it off," I said.

"Call what off?" asked Daddy.

Mother held her needle up to the light. She threaded it carefully and began to sew the hem on Debbie's skirt.

"The wedding. I want to call the wedding off."

That'll stop her. Now, she'll put her sewing down and pay attention to me.

Silently, swiftly, her needle darted in and out of the bright red material.

Debbie turned off the television set. The melodrama in the den was far more exciting than Dragnet. Daddy put down his paper.

"Susie," he said, gently. "Come sit beside me."

I sat down and let the tears flow. I was ashamed of my haste. I had grabbed at Michael's proposal like a lifeboat speeding by my sinking ship. And now I was sorry and very frightened. Had I waited too long to stop the events that had cascaded through my life since I sent that desperate valentine? Was it only four months ago? It seemed like a lifetime, a lifetime scaling a shimmering glass mountain, only to have it shatter just before I reached the top.

I told Daddy what I'd seen. I told him what I felt. Debbie gasped, and Mother sewed. And I? I wept for my shattered dream. It was all gone now, my sweet life to be. All gone.

"Susie," Daddy said. "These are last-minute doubts, that's all. Everyone has them. I did. Mother did. Didn't you, Jean?"

My mother pulled her needle out of the red material. She knotted and cut the thread. Then, she unfolded the blouse on the table next to her chair. She spread it across her lap and started to mend the shoulder. She held her needle up to the light and threaded it again.

"What about all your presents?" asked Debbie. "What about your apartment? I've told all my friends I was going to wear a gorgeous dress in your wedding. You can't *do* this to me!"

She stamped her foot and left the room, her face flushed with anger.

"Don't make any decision yet, Susie," said my father. "You're too upset. I'm calling Rabbi Falberg. Promise me you'll talk to him, first."

I tried to keep my voice steady. I tried to sound sensible; logical; sane. "What's there to talk about?" I asked. "It's over. I don't love him. He doesn't love me. I'm lucky to find out before the ceremony."

And then I waited. I waited for Daddy to say something to save me, something to patch up my shattered glass mountain and give me back my pretty dream.

But he didn't. The rabbi did.

❧ ❧

I'd always loved Rabbi Falberg. He was a quiet, gentle man, and I trusted him. Daddy and I went to see him in his study the next afternoon and I told him the whole story.

"Susan," he said. "I've heard this hundreds of times. You're having last-minute doubts. You're seeing things that didn't happen, making tragedies out of chimeras because you're afraid. Your wedding is two weeks away and I expect to launch you and your Michael on a lifetime of contentment just as you have planned.

"If you back out now, you're letting your fears conquer the common sense you used to make your decision. And once fear gets the upper hand, it controls us. Believe in me, Susan. If you do not marry this boy, you'll never have the courage to marry anyone, ever again."

I believed in him but I knew he was wrong. I didn't use common sense when I decided to marry Michael Rose. I grabbed the first chance I had to escape my mother. It took me four months before I dared allow myself to admit the cost of that escape. I didn't love Michael Rose. I only loved love. Now this gentle, wise rabbi was telling me I risked living forever in the Talberg jail if I didn't marry Michael. I'd never be brave enough to try again. I refused to take that risk. Any marriage was better than none and any home was better than my mother's. Maybe if I had enough babies, I'd be too busy to notice my husband.

Maybe.

Daddy and I drove home in silence. I had no options anymore. I felt beaten and very tired.

"Feel better, kitten?" asked my father.

"I guess so, Daddy," I said. "We'd better go inside. Michael will be here any minute."

ஐ Chapter 43 ଔ

The weekend with Michael did nothing to erase my desolation. We rushed from one party to the next with no time to talk, no time to repair the rift that widened every minute we were together. Daddy fawned over his future son-in-law and I thought it was nauseating. But that was nothing compared to the way Michael ogled every eligible girl in town. He never just said hello. He put an arm around each soft shoulder and that arm strayed down her back to rest casually on her well-padded hips.

He didn't bother to hide his admiration for Elaine Bloom. He danced with her whenever he could. He insisted she join us at the head table. "Elaine is going to be my private secretary," he announced proudly at Louise and Mortie's Ice Cream Social, Friday night.

Elaine gleamed triumphant, and everyone congratulated her. Margie gave me a funny look, but we had no time to talk. . . not yet.

It was at Aunt Evelyn's dinner that my fairy tale exploded.

This party was just family; no Elaine Bloom lurking in dark corners for Michael to pinch and fondle. Instead, my husband-to-be concentrated on winning my Uncle Max. I watched as my fiancé put his hand on my uncle's arm and started talking so fast his lips looked like a study in perpetual motion. Uncle Max's eyes wandered around the room. He straightened his tie. He shuffled from one foot to another, and Michael's mouth didn't stop moving.

When I saw him take out a notebook and begin jotting down the answers my uncle gave him, I hurried to the rescue. He was asking Max for names to contact as I came over to them. I took Michael's arm. "Honey, can't this all wait for another time?" I asked. "Uncle Max should be greeting his guests and so should you."

Uncle Max smiled at me and moved away from Michael too quickly to hide his relief. "Susan's right, Michael," he said. "After you've settled down a little, you can come to my office and we can talk again."

Michael pushed me away and stood up, too. "Well, maybe after dinner, I can ask your advice about a few matters I need to settle right now," he said. "Would you mind?"

"Of course he'd mind," I said. "Uncle Max is our host. He always tends bar at Aunt Evelyn's parties. You can ask him your questions when we get back from our honeymoon."

Michael said nothing, not then. But on the way home, he blew up. His voice was even and controlled, but rage thundered beneath his words. "You keep out of my business, Susan," he hissed. "I don't want you ever to walk up to me and take over the way you did with Max, tonight. Your uncle was giving me valuable information and you interrupted me. Now, God only knows how long it will be before I get him in a private conversation like that."

I moved to my side of the car and faced my fiancé, my back against the window. He looked like an angry child who hadn't managed to pin the tail on his donkey. I pulled the gloves off my hands and rolled them into a ball. My eyes narrowed and I could feel a torrent of disgust sweep over me. "It's rude to isolate a host from his guests, but you're too selfish to figure that out, aren't you, Michael?" I said.

I hated myself for the quaver in my voice. I looked down at my hands. They gripped the wadded gloves as if they were hand grenades. I shoved them in my pocket. Michael glared at the road ahead. I lit a cigarette. "My Uncle Max is always a wonderful help to Aunt Evelyn when they entertain, but you didn't give him a chance, tonight," I said. "Aunt Evelyn had to do everything herself."

Michael stopped at a red light. He switched on the radio. The Big Band sound exploded into the tense atmosphere in the car. I switched the radio off and inhaled my cigarette. "Did you ever think it might have been nice to talk to one of my relatives who *couldn't* help you out? They might have enjoyed getting to know you, too. What was wrong with my cute Uncle Harry or Uncle Frank? You never bothered to say two words to them. All you did was flirt with Lois or Sally, I couldn't tell which."

I inhaled my cigarette until it singed my fingers. I stubbed it into the ashtray and lit another. My throat felt raw and my stomach hurt. Michael pulled into our driveway and stopped the car. He turned off the ignition and got out of the automobile. I waited for him to open the door for me as he always did. He walked straight to our front door and let himself in. I grabbed my purse and followed him into the house. We each marched upstairs without a word.

I walked into my bedroom and weighed myself. I had gained a pound. This time, I knew what was making me fat. It was fury. Fury at my stupidity; rage at the idiot I was tied to for the rest of my life. I wanted to evaporate, and instead I was ballooning into a mountain of flesh, huge and uncontrollable, just like the wedding farce I was planning.

The next morning, we met at the breakfast table. I hadn't slept all night. I had huge dark smudges under my eyes and I felt like an arthritic old maid. Michael didn't even nod to me when I sat down at the table. He looked refreshed. His face had that wonderful clean-scrubbed look that had made me love him not so very long ago. He exuded aftershave and good will. He sat down at the table and put his napkin in his lap. "Everything smells wonderful!" he said. "I can't wait to dig in!"

My mother handed him a plate with three waffles dripping in butter. "Waffles!" he said to my mother. "You're spoiling me, Mother Talberg. And I love it."

My mother smiled. "Syrup?" she said.

I couldn't even swallow my black coffee. The sight of Michael Rose with his artificial smile turned my stomach. He was a self assured, grasping . . . animal . . . yes, animal. That's what he was.

I watched bites of sausage follow the waffles down his throat. I saw the grease on his lips and the way his Adam's apple bobbed as he swallowed food I hadn't tasted since the day I had tried to squeeze into a size twelve skirt.

"How about another waffle, Michael?" said my mother.

"I'll have one, Mama," said Debbie.

My mother beamed. "And coffee?" she asked Michael.

Michael nodded. He finished his breakfast, kissed my sister and my mother. He shook my father's hand. "Well, goodbye," he said. "I'll see you next week."

He picked up his suitcase, threw his coat over his arm and walked out the door.

He hadn't even looked at me.

I stood at the window after he left. I stared at his car backing down our drive, and I tried to cope with the feelings churning inside me. I was happy he was gone; I was sick because I knew he'd be back; and I was desolate because I couldn't stop the events that would destroy my life. I had tried, but no one would listen. I looked out that window for a long, long time.

I left the living room and walked down the hall to the den. Mother was talking on the telephone to Aunt Evelyn. She didn't hear me come in. I paused before walking into the room. My mother was crying. I couldn't believe my ears.

I had never considered my mother a human being with emotions like other people's. She seemed so cold and aloof; it always surprised me that she did human things like go to the bathroom or burp. I knew she'd never put up with the emotional roller coasters I rode through life. She'd dispose of anyone who dared try to block her like dirty wastepaper. And here she was being vulnerable. Over what?

I remained outside the door and listened. I had to be mistaken. My iron willed mother would never break down.

"My God, Evelyn, tell me what to do!" she sobbed. "I see my daughter letting herself in for exactly the kind of hell I've lived through for twenty years, and I can't do a thing to stop her. Leonard won't even talk to me about it. I don't know why I'm surprised at that. He won't talk to me about anything. Just runs out of the house to go to the lab, he says and comes home reeking of liquor and someone else's perfume.

"And Susan's Michael is just like Leonard. Exactly. Would you believe he actually made a pass at Sarah? She was so shocked, she almost dropped her hors d'oeuvre. Then, after dinner, he was dancing hip to hip with Sally or Lois, I can never tell which. It was revolting.

"What do you mean, can't I warn Susan? I tried to tell her when she got engaged, but she paid no attention. I saw what a fake he was and told her so. All she did was get angry and push away that delicious banquet I cooked especially for her. Besides, what good will my speaking out do? The wedding is a week away, for God's sake.

"The real tragedy is that Susan sees now that I was right, Evelyn. She tried to break it off last week, but Leonard and the rabbi talked her into going through with it. And I'm ashamed to say I did nothing. I know it sounds unnatural to you, Evelyn, but I'll be thrilled to have Susan out of the house. She has never brought me one shred of pleasure. She has rejected me since the day I brought her home from the hospital. She was an unpleasant child right from the beginning and she has turned into an obnoxious adult.

"She hates me and doesn't bother to hide it. I can't figure out what I've done to make that child treat me like a pile of garbage. I have always been a good mother to her, Evelyn, and you know how difficult she makes things for me. She doesn't know the meaning of appreciation.

"No, Evelyn. You're wrong. The only thing she's trying to do is drive me crazy. No matter what I do, it's never enough for her. I cook her favorite food; I try to make this a lovely home for her and what do I get? 'No thank you, Mother. I don't want to bring anyone over here. It's not comfortable in your living room.'

"My living room that I decorated so she'd have a home she could be proud of instead of the shabby conglomeration of Goodwill furniture we had when we were kids.

"Or she says, 'No thank you, Mother. I'm on a diet.'

And there goes the chocolate cake I spent all morning making or the chicken I roasted and stuffed just for her. Then, when I'm not looking and can't have the pleasure of seeing her enjoy my efforts, she eats everything in sight.

"And that's another thing, Evelyn. Have you looked at her lately? She's so skinny she looks like a candidate for Save the Hungry. When I tell her she seems a little pale or thin, she just snaps, 'Well, I don't want to be a bloated pillow like my sister or too fat to wear last year's blouse like you are.'

179

"And she's right. Debbie is too fat and so am I. Susan was the only one of us with a decent figure before she traded in food for rabbit feed and caffeine. No wonder she does that strange eating at night, stuffing herself with everything in the icebox. She starves herself for weeks until she can barely move. Then, she lets down the barrier and can't control herself. One night I came downstairs and I saw her rummaging through the garbage, eating leftover crusts of buttered rye bread and bits of corned beef. You can't tell me that's normal, Evelyn.

"Why didn't I say anything? What could I say? She'd spit in my face if I tried to criticize her.

"Leonard? Notice? You've got to be kidding. He doesn't notice anything around here, not me, not Debbie, not even Susan, although she practically kisses his feet. I don't want to be there when she sees just what kind of weak, vacillating idiot her father really is. And I don't want to be there when she realizes he's a carbon copy of that boob she's going to marry.

"Listen, Evelyn, I'd better hang up. She'll be in here any minute and I don't want to let her see me cry this way. You've been such an angel. You listen to me . . . and I know you listen to Susan, too. At least she has you to talk to. God knows, she can't talk to me."

My mother hung up the telephone and put her head in her arms. Her sobs tore at me like claws gripping my flesh. So that was it. I had always known she thought my darling Daddy wasn't so darling after all. But I never realized how awful living with him was for her. She said he was an irresponsible playboy just like Michael was. I had heard her hints and innuendoes, but they never meant anything to me. I thought they were just words. Now, I was convinced that she really believed my father cheated on her.

She had been trying to hide this from us all these years. And that was nothing compared to the hell she must have been going through to keep up appearances and maintain a stable home for the two of us.

For the first time in my life, I saw Jean Talberg as a woman, with all the problems and tortures that a woman faces, and I wanted to rush into that room and hug her. I wanted to cradle that crying bundle of misery in my arms and say, "It's okay, Mom. It's okay. You tried so hard and I never understood. I thought you wanted to hurt me, but you were only trying to save me from the hell you've suffered. "

But I couldn't. I couldn't break down the wall we'd built between us for over twenty years. I had been that woman's whipping post for twenty-two years. She manipulated me like a pawn on her chessboard to soothe her wounded ego. She blamed me for being a cranky baby, and I was certain that most of that resentment had nothing to do with my behavior. When I arrived, she lost her freedom, and she still hasn't forgiven me. That was neurotic. My mother was a Hitler and I hated her.

I wanted to believe she was wrong about Daddy. But then I remembered how little he was home and how late he returned from those visits to the lab and I wondered. I saw him fawning over Michael and protecting him from my attacks. Was he some kind of hypocrite who lacked the guts to take a stand?

He oozed sugar with Mother. I'd heard him. And he comforted me. He tried to make each of us believe he was really on our side and only pacifying the other. Now, he was doing the same thing with Michael and me. No. It couldn't be. And yet . . .

I had to admit Daddy was never around to help her when she needed him. As soon as he came home, he lost himself in the newspaper or went out in the yard to practice hitting golf balls. She attempted to be both parents to us and she couldn't do it.

It was too much to absorb right now. Right now, I had to figure out a way to keep my mother from realizing that I had listened to every word she said. It would have felt really good to humiliate my mother; but I couldn't do such a cruel thing to that broken woman crying in the other room.

I tiptoed back into the living room and slammed the door. "Do you need any help in the kitchen, Mother?" I shouted. "If not, I'm going over to Margie's."

Mother's voice was under control now. She was her usual chunk of granite. "All right, Susan. But be home by five. I want to take the dog for a walk and I have some errands to do before my canasta group. You'll have to make dinner tonight. It'll be good practice for you."

❧ Chapter 44 ❧

July 1, 1956: My Wedding Day. It was so hot the pavement sizzled. I felt sticky and sick to my stomach. I had been riding a relentless merry-go-round of black coffee and cigarettes punctuated with wild gorging in the dark hours when my terror squelched my resolve to see this marriage through. I had weighed myself so many times the rubber footrest on the scale was curled and ragged around the edges.

The scale had inched down to eighty-nine pounds, and I was thrilled. I could really gorge on my wedding feast. Mother and I had planned all my favorites for dinner, and I intended to eat every single thing. There would be shrimp and fillet mignon wrapped in bacon. We were having baked potatoes soaked in sour cream and vegetables laced with butter and almonds. Oh my God. It seemed an eternity since I had enjoyed any of those things. My mouth watered at the thought of that supper. It was only when I realized that the tab for this dinner was a lifetime of Michael Rose, that I felt ill.

Margie was my maid of honor. She looked like a daffodil in frothy yellow lace. Debbie and Louise wore ice blue dresses and carried daisy nosegays in their arms. I wore white. "I feel like a fraud," I told Margie.

"You and ninety per cent of the women sitting in that Temple," said Margie. "For God's sake, Susie. What do you want to wear? Red?"

The Temple was a garden of baby's breath and stephanotis. Michael waited for me at the altar with his brother Brad at his side. The rabbi stood in front of him, smiling and nodding at me. Neither of us realized then how his words to me that day in his study would destroy so much of my life. *If you don't marry this boy, Susan, you probably will never have the courage to marry anyone. Trust me. I know.*

Mother, Grace and David took their places. The organ exploded in thunderous chords and my daddy took my arm. We walked together down that endless aisle, and I walked alone up to the altar. I felt as if I had stepped into the hangman's chamber. I took my place beside Michael and held his arm. He looked down at me and smiled but I didn't smile back. I couldn't. My eyes were filled with tears.

Fifteen minutes and it was over. Michael kissed me, stomped on the wine glass and we ran up the aisle, our wedding rings flashing in the candlelight.

I loved it all. I loved the kisses and the congratulations. I loved the silly rituals and I adored being the center of attention. But I couldn't blot out my mother's ominous countermelody. It haunted me, still.

He doesn't love you, Susan. Don't fool yourself. Don't fool yourself. He loves your money. He wants your father's business connections. Don't fool yourself. . .

Well, I wasn't fooling myself. I was doing far worse. I knew my mother was right, and still I was going ahead with this farce I called a marriage.

Elaine came through the reception line. She took both Michael's hands in hers. "I'll meet you in the office, August first," she said to my husband.

She kissed him full on the lips for what I thought was forever. When she came up for air, she pulled Michael's handkerchief out of his breast pocket and dabbed at his lips. She refolded the hankie, tucked it back into his pocket and smoothed her hair. She ignored me. I stared at her, my eyes cold as ice and she looked through me as though I didn't exist. Then, she was swept away by others waiting to congratulate us.

I could feel humiliation color my face. I gripped my bouquet as if it were an iron club. I wanted to smash it into my husband's self satisfied face. He'd hired her. He'd hired her just like he'd threatened to do. Even after I made such a dramatic scene when we were at Margie's ice cream social. He didn't listen. He didn't care.

Michael put his hand on my arm. "Excuse me a minute, Susie," he said.

Before I had a chance to ask where he was going, he followed Elaine Bloom into the crowd and he, too, disappeared. I turned to my father but there was no time to appeal to anyone. My guests were congratulating me and my vanished groom.

I didn't see my husband until we all met at the Park Lane at seven-thirty. Daddy drove my family and the bridesmaids to the hotel. The Rose family was in another car. No one asked where Michael was. I'm sure Margie and my mother guessed, but why didn't Daddy say something? If mother was right, he envied my husband his double conquest in one day.

The dinner was elegant and I ignored my diet, just like I shut my eyes to Elaine Bloom and Michael; just like I erased my mother's words. I blotted it all out and wallowed in my fragile dream world. I ate and ate and ate some more. And when I ate, I felt nothing, no fear, no regrets. I was submerged in sauces and flavors I hadn't tasted since Margie's wedding.

I danced and flirted with everyone there. I felt very glamorous and very full of food. Uncle Harry took me in his arms and we swirled to a Viennese waltz. "You're light as a feather, Mrs. Rose," said my darling Uncle and I laughed.

"Those tutti fruiti tropical parfaits of yours make marvelous fuel, Uncle

Harry," I said.

I danced with my sweet father-in-law, too. He held me in his arms and I could feel his goodness. Perhaps Michael would mellow into another David Rose. Perhaps. I closed my eyes and saw the steel in my husband's eyes when he told me he had hired Elaine Bloom. The man I saw would never become a David Rose.

Michael and I cut the cake and I ate again. My color was high and I felt supercharged with energy. I wanted to talk and laugh and soak myself up in this, my Big Event. I knew there would never be another. And I also knew it would be the last happy moment I would have for years and years to come.

Michael drank. He drank and he danced with his secretary. He drank and he smiled at me when the photographer asked us to pose. He held me close when we danced the first dance together. But he looked over my head as we danced and nodded to Mr. Weiner, president of Toledo's largest bank. He waved to Mr. Freid, the largest property owner in town, and he positively leered at Lois or Sally. I couldn't tell which.

I didn't want the night to end, but the clock crept on and I knew it was time for Michael and I to drive away into our married life together. Everyone gathered at the foot of the stairs in the hotel lobby. I paused at the landing and threw my bouquet.

Debbie caught it. She was thrilled, but I wasn't. Mother loved her best, and she got it all: private schools, fashion clothes and love. And now, she caught my bouquet. She'll get her marriage, have her babies and bask in the golden cloud of approval that protected her all her life.

I ran upstairs and changed into my going-away suit. Margie was there to help me dress. I looked into her kind eyes, and my own filled with all the tears I had refused to shed during this endless masquerade that was my wedding. "You were right," I sobbed. "Oh, why wouldn't I listen?"

Margie put her arms around me. "You're just nervous, Susie," she said. "I was a wreck too after my wedding. I was sure I had married Frankenstein instead of Tom Hestor. Now stop crying or your eyes will be all red when the photographer takes your picture."

I sniffled and unbuttoned my gown. I laid it on the bed and smoothed the signs of wear away. Its satin bodice gleamed in the lamplight and the skirt was so full it covered the bed. "I loved wearing that dress," I said to Margie.

I folded my veil and put it across the pillows. It had been my mother's veil and her mother's before her. It was yellowed with age. It had adorned two very unhappy women. I wondered if my grandmother too had found tragedy instead of contentment after she wore it down the aisle.

"You looked like a beautiful princess today," said Margie. "Now, hurry up and change clothes. Everyone's waiting."

I put on my suit and perched a hat with a red feather on my head. "Ready?" asked Margie.

"Ready," I said.

I took one last look at my wedding dress and hung it in the closet. I caressed its satin folds. It was history, now.

At least, I could hang on to that: a lavish, opulent memory of My Day.

Michael was waiting in the lobby. We ran out the revolving door in a shower of rice and kisses. Mother took my hand. I had a momentary feeling she sympathized with me. But that feeling vanished as soon as I remembered her words to Aunt Evelyn, that day I heard a Jean Talberg I never knew before. *I know it sounds unnatural to you, Evelyn, but I'll be thrilled to have Susan out of the house.*

She saw the disaster that lay ahead and she was glad. I looked at her, but I didn't smile. I could be a glacier, too.

"Everything will be fine, Susan," she said.

Grace put her arms around me and buried me in her enormous bosom. "Have a lovely life, darling," she said.

I looked at the goodness in her face, and I wondered if she really knew her son as I did. I hugged her and smiled. Of course she didn't know. She saw her children glossed with love. They were royalty and I wasn't going to spoil her illusion. "I'm a very lucky woman, Mother Rose," I said. "I'll take good care of your son. I promise."

Her eyes filled and I felt like the winner of the Hypocrite of the Year Award.

Daddy kissed me goodbye. "You see, kitten. Everything is working out just fine. If you'd listened to those blue devils of yours, none of this would have happened. Now, relax and enjoy tonight. We'll see you tomorrow."

I looked at my father's smiling face but I didn't see him. I saw my mother's Satan and I wondered if he were mine as well.

Part IV: 1956 ~ 1958

❧ Chapter 45 ❧

When we entered our hotel room, Michael took my hand. "I have something to tell you, Mrs. Rose," he said.

He leaned down to kiss me but I turned away from him. I knew what was coming. He wanted a divorce. Thank God. I looked into his eyes and forced a neutral expression on my face. I was not going to let him know how relieved I was. "Yes?" I said.

Michael put his arm around my shoulder and led me to the bed. "I canceled our reservations to New York," he said. "I had an opportunity to meet with the big man at Monroe Construction. He's interested in a group policy and I couldn't postpone it. I knew you'd understand."

I shook him away like an unwanted shawl. I unpinned my hat and put it on the bureau. "Then we won't have a honeymoon," I said and I peered in the mirror to see if I looked as haggard as I felt.

He put his hands on my shoulders and turned me around. "Of course we will, darling," he said. "We'll have it in our very own little home!"

He kissed me and it took all my willpower not to slap his face. "I've ordered a late supper, honey," he said. "Why don't you get into some comfortable clothes? The meal will be here any minute."

I unbuttoned my suit jacket. "I'm not hungry," I said. "You can cancel the order."

That is how my marriage began. The only bright spot in my future was the prospect of making a baby. My single sexual encounter was the best memory I had of the past two years. I thought sex was sex. If you loved it, you would enjoy it with anyone. Well, I was very wrong. Sex with Bobby Mosten was a very different experience than the one I had with my husband. Our mating was a dry collision of muscle and bone. Nothing more.

Michael never even noticed that I wasn't a virgin that first night. He was too preoccupied proving he was a man. But he didn't convince me. He was more like a child rushing to devour his ice cream before it melted. As soon as he entered me, he had an orgasm and it was over.

Just like that.

He insisted we try again, but it was no use. He never bothered to kiss me. He didn't touch me or tell me he cared. He just dropped his pants and spread my legs. I was barely in position before he entered me. I was dry and tight, but he didn't care. He pushed himself inside me and the next thing I knew, he had rolled over, his sex limp between his legs, his face relaxed and at peace. I wasn't Susan to him. I wasn't his wife. I was a vagina.

Every night after that, I cringed at the contest that loomed ahead as my sex-starved husband assaulted my body. He treated me like a new tool for masturbation and I felt used. I was humiliated and terribly disappointed.

At first, I was determined to respond to him. I thought it was my fault that I had no orgasm. I tried to find some bit of pleasure in our union, but he was so quick to come, so fast to slumber that I barely had time to slip off my nightie before our loving was over. After the first few nights, I didn't bother to try anymore. He was hurting me and I hated it. My desire was dead and so was any pretense of love. The Susan Talberg who ached for sex had disappeared. Susan Rose was a cold, unresponsive piece of glass.

It was just as well we didn't have a honeymoon with only ourselves to face. In Toledo, we were swept into a river of activity so busy neither of us noticed that we didn't love each other. We didn't have time to realize we weren't even friends.

School started less than two months after the wedding. I barely had time to get used to the Mrs. in front of my name before I was trying to dream up units for second graders I couldn't control.

I was as inadequate in the classroom as I was in my marriage and I dieted to punish myself for my failures. I watched the scale dwindle; eighty-six, eighty-five, eighty-four. I knew, now, who my blue devils were. They were the Daddy who didn't protect me and the Michael who married his money. My mother was right about both of them, and I hated her even more for her perception. She was my enemy. She had seen my tragedy coming and was enjoying it like the black comedy it was.

She hadn't stopped her barrage of disparaging remarks, and they felt like acid each time she spoke. "It's ten in the morning, Susan. Do you mean to tell me you haven't finished your housework, yet?"

"Molly Heffner saw you at Krogers' yesterday and called me last night. She thought you looked sick and she was right. You are pale as a sheet. Haven't you ever heard of make-up, Susan?"

I hung up the telephone and pushed away the dry salad I had made for lunch. It looked as dead as I felt and I was too fat, anyway.

When Michael stayed late at the office and returned smelling like he had fallen into a rose garden, I ignored him. I cut out more calories from dinner and called my mother to torture myself. "I'm broiling whitefish for dinner tomorrow night, Mother," I'd say. "Can you think of a nice vegetable dish to set it off?"

"Grilled tomatoes," said my mother. "Use lots of butter and breadcrumbs, Susan. You might boil some new potatoes and make a Roquefort dressing for them. Add lots of fresh parsley for color, Susan. Food should appeal to the eyes as much as the palate."

When it came to cooking and keeping house, my mother was an artist and she loved to give suggestions even to me. I followed her advice and gave the best dinner parties of the young country club set.

"How do you do it, Susie?" said Margie.

She and Tom had come over for dinner and bridge. I had baked my own brioche to go with candied veal pot roast and did mint parfaits and oatmeal crisps (baked from scratch, of course) for dessert. "It's nothing really," I said.

"What do you mean, 'Nothing'? Poor Tom lived on hamburger and pizzas-to-go the whole first year we were married. I still won't attempt anything more complicated than roast chicken."

I looked at my darling friend. She never said a word about Michael, but I knew she sensed our relationship had died before it ever began. She'd been to bed with him. Was he as cold and demanding with her? How could she stand him for two years?

If I had paid attention to her, I would have known exactly what to expect from my husband. I ignored her words because I didn't want to tarnish my image of sweet, mistreated Michael Rose.

Believe me, Michael's only interests are making money and making me. He needs constant sex to reassure himself that he's a man.

She told me that right after we wrote Michael his "Dear John" letter. I thought she was rationalizing her heartless rejection of the nicest, sweetest boy I knew. But I didn't know him at all. Margie did, and she escaped him as fast as she could. Smart Margie. Stupid Susan.

Margie understood me and my silence told her all she needed to tell her how wise her own decision had been. The two of us discussed everything but my marriage. When Michael and I were with the Hestors, Michael gave stock market predictions to Tom while Margie and I giggled and gossiped. "The Dow Jones was at 520 today," said Michael to Tom. "And inflation is almost 3%. When will it stop?"

"Have you tried substituting Carnation milk for cream in your casserole recipes?" I said to Margie. "It's just delicious and costs half as much."

Margie and I talked about bubble skirts, whiskey-flavored toothpaste and "Wake Up, Little Susie." We giggled over Tom's cute habits, Margie's disastrous meals and my wild classroom. But we never discussed Michael.

We never discussed how skinny I was, either. I was gaunt as a ghost on Halloween, but I couldn't stop dieting. I looked in the mirror as my flesh melted away and I didn't see the hollow cheekbones, the antique white flesh. My stomach, distended from so much roughage and gallons of coffee, stuck out from my hip bones like the bellies of starving children and I called that fat. I touched my toes, I twisted from left to right and I cut out more calories and still it grew. My head told me it was bloat not flesh, but I ignored it. I was convinced that I gained weight on air.

I hated to get up in the morning because of Michael's insatiable desire to ejaculate inside me; I loathed going to bed at night. I began to hope he really *was* schtupping Elaine Bloom. She'd have to be quicker than mercury to manage any pleasure from my husband's brand of instant intercourse.

I had finally stopped dreaming about food. I dreamed of good sex, instead. Every night after I endured my husband's dry thrusts inside me, I closed my eyes and opened my arms to Gary Cooper. He clasped me in his arms just the way he had embraced Audrey Hepburn in *Love in the Afternoon*. We walked through daffodils in the park, I in my flowing white dress, my straw hat in my hand and he in an open shirt and soft gray slacks. We smiled at a little bird twittering in a dogwood tree and had sex in the grass behind a sheltered copse.

My dreams were so real that I was sure Michael would see my bruised mouth and the love bites on my neck. But as soon as I opened my eyes, I was jolted into cold reality as my husband mounted me for his morning calisthenics.

I lay beneath him, limp and bored. I planned menus while he ground into my body and when he had a climax, I moaned too. That was usually when I figured out what to serve for dessert the next day. It was always some magnificent pastry I wouldn't touch.

❧ ❧

Life hurtled us from one day into another. Monday, Michael went to B'nai B'rith; I had Sisterhood. Tuesday, bridge with the Hestors. Wednesday, my book club. Thursday, symphony, or sometimes a play. Friday at Mother's. Saturday, we went out or I entertained and Sunday, my parents came for dinner.

I baked my own bread and prepared elaborate, gourmet meals to show my mother two could play her game. She made brisket and cold slaw; I did stuffed flank steak and escalloped corn with a wine glaze. She roasted chicken and a potato kugel; I stuffed Cornish hens with wild rice and served asparagus creole.

Her food tasted like heaven on a plate. That's what Michael said and I remembered very well how good it was. I can't tell you how my meals tasted. I never ate them and Michael barely touched them either. He was a disinterested eater at my table; at Mother's, he shoveled food into his gullet like an elephant who had just returned from a safari.

The next year was a montage of pain, endurance and starvation for me. I was hungry for the life I thought I would have when I married Michael, and I kept my thoughts focused on the food I refused to eat instead of the love I neither gave nor received. I hardly noticed that a year had vanished and summer was here again.

Margie was pregnant. I was excited for her and jealous too. I endured the humiliation of Michael's instant orgasms but nothing ever happened to me. My periods had stopped when I broke ninety pounds, but my temperature chart had a definite curve. I knew I was ovulating and I also knew I wasn't conceiving a thing.

So I dieted some more. The more I dieted, the more elaborate my dinners for Michael became. I remember one night when I prepared a potato and cheese casserole, lamb chops with mint sauce, asparagus Hollandaise and pineapple whip salad. I served homemade angel food cake with Uncle Harry's double rich fudge coconut ice cream and brandied cherries for his dessert.

I watched him pick at his food while I dutifully ate lettuce with a sliver of tomato and shredded carrot. When he finished his lamb chops, I chewed the bone. Then I drank coffee while he took a few disinterested bites of the dessert I adored.

He pushed away his plate and stretched. He looked at his watch. "It's seven-thirty!" he said. "I'd better hurry. I have an appointment with a client at eight."

He grabbed his coat and disappeared. I scraped his almost-filled plates into the sink. I ached to lick my fingers when they touched those cheesy potatoes. I shut my eyes and relived the taste of Hollandaise sauce on asparagus. My stomach convulsed and I lit a cigarette. I inhaled it and put it in the ashtray next to the sink. I looked at the cherry sauce that had congealed into a candied canopy over his cake and ice cream. I paused.

I grabbed the plate and scraped it clean. I pushed all the food down the disposal and turned the machine on. "Better down the drain than in my stomach," I told myself.

I felt like I had just won a war.

The scale descended further and I was elated. Eighty-four, eighty-three, eighty-two. Every morning and every night, I watched Michael eat while I drank black coffee and smoked an endless chain of cigarettes. Eighty-one, eighty, seventy-nine. The pounds dropped more slowly now.

I was tired. I taught all day. I cleaned, cooked, did laundry and played hostess all evening. Late at night, before Michael came home and I dropped off to sleep, I wrote my sweet mother-in-law. I told her how happy I was and how her son had impressed everyone in Toledo. I didn't mention that the sight of my husband made me sick or that he was so rude to my relatives that they refused to invite him into their homes. I didn't discuss his evening adventures or the perfumes I detected on his collars and his jackets. I told her we both missed her and asked when she and David could drive down to see us. Then I sealed the letter and wondered what I would do if Michael's parents really did visit our frigid love nest.

I reached for a stamp and put the letter on the hall table ready to mail. I was far too hungry to worry about it. They were Michael's parents and if they did visit, they would be his problem, thank God. Not mine.

➣ Chapter 46 ⋐

You learn to cope using your parents' weapons, and I battered myself the same way my mother did. But I went farther. She only dieted. I starved. When I created exotic meals, I saw my mother and I muttered to myself, "You see? You're not so great. I can make soufflés so light they float, and a quiche that gives your taste buds a high."

I cleaned house for my mother, too. I scrubbed the bathroom floor every morning before I left for school, cleaned the tile and polished the chrome. As I rubbed and scoured, I heard my mother's voice:

"You're a dirty pig, Susan. No one is as filthy as you are; dirty underwear left in the bathroom; make-up spotting the bowl! You are disgusting!"

And I answered as I worked in my own apartment. "Come, look, Mother. Hospital clean. My whole house is hospital clean."

And it was. It sparkled. I washed windows and polished the furniture every week. Tired as I was when I came home from school, I managed to vacuum and dust everything before I plunged into poached trout garnished with pickled beets for Michael's dinner. Creme brulee for dessert: lovely and light; something my mother never tried.

On Sundays, she walked into the home I created and never said one word about my immaculate house, my unusual and provocative meals, or my wasted life. She walked into my living room and tidied my coffee table or polished my silver before she would use it. She wasn't letting me think I could better her with my fancy recipes and elaborate table settings. She knew how unhappy I was and she was satisfied at last. I was the one who insisted on marrying Michael. I had asked for this life, and she knew better than anyone what hell it was to live it.

Teaching was torture for me. Oh, don't get me wrong. I loved the children and wished every one of them were mine. As the months went by and I still wasn't pregnant, I pretended my students were my very own babies. We sang a lot, took nature walks and played lovely games. And they loved me to pieces. They hugged me hello and cried when I dismissed them at the end of the day.

But they didn't learn a thing. They were my substitutes for the family I wasn't creating with a man I loathed. My classroom was chaos; my bulletin board a hodgepodge. The principal dropped in on me a little too often and I was a bundle of anxiety. What if I lost this job just like I was losing my husband? Just like I lost my daddy?

I could feel my nerves squeeze my self-confidence into pulp and I restricted even more food from my diet. I weighed myself at least three times a day and each time I got on the scale, I readjusted the pointer to the exact center of zero and tried desperately to move it down from the number it had said the time before. I stood on the edge; I moved the scale from the rug; I made sure the floor was absolutely level. And very slowly, like a glacier creeping down a mountain, the scale co-operated. I weighed seventy-eight, then seventy-seven and then it stalled.

I skipped lunch because it was an unnecessary meal. I used the time to grade papers and decorate my classroom. I stayed after school long hours planning elaborate projects to infuse mathematics into each child's blood and drill geography into his brain cells. I devised clever art projects to charm the children into opening their minds to their environment. We drew a huge map of the neighborhood with trees and parks and even street lamps. Everyone found their own street and painted in their homes. "My house is white with blue shutters," said Stevie Liner. "And it's right next door to Miltie's Market. Can I draw that, too?"

I nodded. Andrea Benson pulled at my skirt. "How do you make bricks?" she asked. "Our house is red brick and it has a white door. The mailbox is on the corner. I'll put that in, too. Where is a blue crayon?"

I looked with pride at my thirty babies on their hands and knees intent on creating an accurate picture of their community. The principal chose that moment to walk into my classroom. I pointed to my intent boys and girls. "That's geography!" I told him, triumphantly.

He examined our map and then he looked up at me and smiled. "Mrs. Rose," he said. "*That's* learning!"

I felt charged with success.

But what could I do to boost my drooping marriage? I thought about that for a long time and at last, I hit on the perfect answer: A party. That's it! Michael would love a party with lots of potential clients on the invitation list. And I would get to show off my cooking skills and play happy wife to my friends. I decided to give an open house for Christmas. It would be our second holiday together, and I wanted to make it a festival. I'd start with a dinner for our good friends and then invite masses of Toledo society for drinks later.

When I told Michael my idea, he was thrilled with it, especially when I suggested we include Toledo's cream of the young married set.

We were sitting in my not yet baby's room. It was Wednesday. I was getting ready for book club and Michael had a committee meeting for the Temple Brotherhood, he said. I sat on the arm of his chair as he read the paper and I thought out loud. "We'll have the really special people for dinner, first. Margie and Tom, of course; Louise and Mortie too, if they don't take that cruise they were talking about. Oh, and I don't want to forget Ben and Carol Weiss. *(Damn her. She got him. Why couldn't I?)* Judy and Elliot Samuelson would be nice, too. I see her a lot at book club, and isn't he on the finance committee with you at B'nai B'rith?"

Michael nodded. "Don't forget Beth and Jerry Klein," he said.

"Why Beth and Jerry Klein?" I asked. "We hardly know them."

"Didn't I tell you?" said Michael. "I sold them a policy a few months ago and they've introduced me to several business and family friends that bought, too, because Beth and Jerry recommended me."

"No, you haven't said a word," I said. "Who are all these new people? I've introduced you to everyone they'd know. Beth and Jerry have lived in Toledo all their lives and we were all in school together. They belong to our temple and neither have a very big family."

Michael folded his newspaper carefully and stood up. "They are people from out of town," he said. "Bigwigs in the main office at Peat Marwick. No one you'd know, honey, except George Samuel. He and his wife each bought a huge policy and then George introduced me to Herman Lord, the new vice president at First National. I sold him a policy, too."

"Goodness," I said. "That's a lot of policies. You'll be in the million dollar roundtable if you keep that up. And maybe I can stop working."

His face hardened. He gripped the back of his chair and his eyes bored into me. "Don't start that again, Susan. You know our agreement. When you're pregnant, you can stop."

I stood up and faced him. My hands were shaking, but I was determined my voice would be steady. I reached for a cigarette. I heard Mr. Odesky open the door of his apartment down the hall. One of his children shouted, "It's Daddy!" and I closed my eyes to the vision of little Normie Odesky rushing into her father's arms. She was a pudgy bundle of happiness with golden curls. Every time I gave her a hug, I wept because she wasn't mine. I took a deep breath. "Maybe I'm not pregnant because I'm all worn out from the sixteen million things I have to do," I told my husband.

Or maybe it's because you never give me time to relax and let your sperm in when you mount me every morning like a hired floosie.

194

Michael turned away from me and walked toward the closet. I inhaled my cigarette and brushed an imaginary bug from my sleeve. I would not lose control. I would not.

"You're worn out because you're so damn skinny," said Michael. "Why the hell do you diet when you look like a blade of wilted grass? How much do you weigh now? Fifty?"

I gripped the arm of the chair and my nails bit into the upholstery. I closed my eyes and saw the number on the scale that morning. It wasn't fifty, but it was getting there. I took out a cigarette and waved it at him. "Don't be ridiculous," I said. "I diet so I won't get fat like my sister. My whole family has a tendency to put on weight. If I even look at a brownie, I put on five pounds."

"You don't make sense," said Michael. "You've been too thin ever since college and lately you look emaciated. You could pose for one of those posters exposing world hunger."

Now it was my turn to get my coat. I crushed the unlit cigarette in an ashtray and turned my face away from him. I didn't want him to see my flushed cheeks or the rage in my eyes. "I could not," I said. "I'm at a good weight. I have more energy now than I ever had when I was a fat horse."

I pushed past him and grabbed my coat. It fell from the hanger and I reached down to get it. I stared at the polished toes of my husband's shoes and wished a sudden fire would leap up and dissolve him. I stood up and twisted to get my arms into the sleeves of my wrap. Michael made no move to help me.

He put on his own coat and he laughed. I looked at his smiling face and I wanted to reach out and tear the lips from his face. I looked in the mirror and smoothed my hair. The face I saw was expressionless and cold. It was my mother.

"Oh, come on, Susie," said Michael. "Just when were you a fat horse? Tell me that. Just when?"

I opened my purse and took out another cigarette. I struck a match but it went out. I tried again but this time my hands shook so much the match fell, unlit, to the floor. I looked at my husband and I despised him. "Right before you asked me to marry you," I retorted. "I weighed one hundred and three pounds and it took me forever and six months to lose that weight. I could never go through that kind of torture again."

"And what do you call the dry salad and black coffee you live on now? A banquet? I call it starvation."

I struck another match. "I am not starving," I said. "I eat carefully, that's all."

I looked at the clock. The match burned my finger and I blew it out.

"I have to leave, now. We're discussing *East of Eden* tonight. It was a marvelous book and I don't want to be late."

The conversation was getting far too uncomfortable and I wanted to close it. I weighed seventy-seven pounds and still counted every calorie I ate. I knew all too well what would happen if I touched forbidden food like cake. One taste would inflame me. I'd finish the whole thing and then continue an inevitable, agonizing journey through every edible object I could find in the kitchen. I'd finish my orgy kneeling in front of the toilet, my fingers down my throat.

And that must not happen. It must not.

You're like an alcoholic, I told myself. *Once you touch food, you can't stop.*

Well, I *could* stop when all I ate was dry lettuce and shredded carrots. I could stop when I only cooked enough skinned chicken or lean beef for one meal. It was leftovers that tortured me. The smell of the food mingled with my longing. I ached to eat. . . just as I ached for love.

Michael and I had been married almost two years, and he had never seen me binge. I never did it while he was home. It was those times when Michael stayed downtown and I faced his uneaten meal and my own sour suspicions that I fell apart. It was on those nightmare nights when I knew the husband I hated was all Toledo's gigolo and I was the fool people snickered at. . . or worse, the one they pitied.

That was when I ate. I ate my dinner, then Michael's. I nibbled at the leftover roast from yesterday, the loaf of bread I'd baked that morning before school. Down it all went. An avalanche of butter, peanuts, sour cream and chocolate pudding; the candy I put out for our bridge game Tuesday, the uncooked gingerbread I was going to bake that night. I tossed down noodle pudding, pickles and sweet rolls, cake, casseroles and pretzels, ending it all in a paroxysm of pain.

I spent the night hollow eyed, staring at the ceiling. My guilt was so tangible, I could feel it wrapping itself around my throat like an angry snake.

The next week, I fasted. I smoked until my fingers were yellow. I gulped black coffee and staggered through my days in a paralyzing mist of hunger and caffeine. Why did I do it? I didn't know. I was too ashamed to ask anyone about it, too frightened and far too sick.

I weighed seventy-six pounds.

❧ Chapter 47 ❧

The day after Christmas, we got our statement from American Express: I couldn't believe it. $3500, and not one charge slip had my signature.

We had opened our account with them last September, and I had never seen their bill before. Michael usually picked up the mail when he came home to change for his evening appointments about four-thirty. He took the statements down to the office. "Elaine can pay these," he told me. "I like to keep our tax records in one place."

I never came home from school until after five. I always stayed in my classroom to clean up some of the clutter and mark the children's papers. When I left the school, I did my errands before I came home. I picked up the cleaning, did my shopping or browsed in the library.

But this was my vacation. For the first time in three months, I was home when the postman delivered our letters. I heard the mail drop in the slot and hurried to get it. I opened the envelope from American Express and looked at those receipts. Most of the charges were from prestige restaurants. There were several receipts from the Holiday Inn on the way to Cleveland. Each was for one room, always for one night, with room service and bar bills that stunned me.

So that's where he takes them, I thought. *That's why he hasn't kissed me in over three months. He's all sexed out with his perfumed ladies. I'll just bet Beth Klein is his latest. That's why he wanted her at the party.*

Damn him. Damn, damn, damn. Well, now I had proof: tangible signatures on two dozen American Express slips. Now, I'd make Michael admit what he's been doing.

I paused and looked again at the bill in my hand. I imagined my triumph when I blasted holes in the fabric of lies he had woven. I saw him defenseless and beaten. What would he do, then? Would he walk out on me?

For one silver moment, I saw my life without Michael Rose and I felt peace. Let him walk out. He hadn't given me a marriage and I wanted him for nothing else.

I lit a cigarette and shuffled through the charge slips again. I had never spent the night in any room as elaborate as those in that new Holiday Inn. I'd heard that they had wet bars and sunken tubs, complimentary drinks and morning coffee. *I wonder if he ordered satin sheets?* I thought.

I had tried to be a good wife to Michael Rose. I consented to live in Toledo with him. I gave up my honeymoon and I slaved at a thankless job to feed his taste for elegance. Yes, I had sacrificed. What had he given up? I clutched that American Express statement in my hand like a magic weapon. *This is the last time you kick me, Michael Rose,* I thought. *The last time. Now its my turn. I'm kicking back.*

I inhaled cigarette smoke like a predatory dragon and I watched that front door. I heard his foot on the stair and I stiffened. The doorknob turned and I pounced. "Look at this," I screeched.

"Look at what?" he said.

I waved the American Express bill at him. "One night stands at Holiday Inns. Bills from The Commodore and Cuisine Elegànce. $3500 to satisfy your sex drive. What's your excuse this time?"

"Calm down, Susan," he said.

He pushed me out of his way and walked to the closet. I seethed as I watched him hang up his coat. And I calmed down a little. . . just a little. I walked into the kitchen and turned down the oven. I had a leg of lamb roasting for dinner. Margie and Tom would be here by seven. I had too much to do to fuss with infidelity right now.

I started the water for the green beans and whipped the cream for my lemon parfaits. I put out vegetables for the salad and marched back into the den to pull the pin on my hand grenade. "Well?" I said.

Michael was reading the paper. He looked up and smiled. "Susie, I've told you time and time again how expensive it is to entertain clients."

"Entertain clients? At the Holiday Inn sixty miles out of town? What do you have to do to sell a policy? Service their wives? Is that how you got Beth Klein to give you all those leads? You're no insurance salesman. You're a stud. And if my experience means anything, not a very good one. I'm surprised you get any return customers with your lightning technique."

It happened so fast. He stood up and slapped my face. I could taste the blood trickling down my chin. I gasped and struggled to release his grip on my arm.

"I've had enough of you," he said. "Always prying, always suspecting me. Always getting yourself in a righteous little wad over nothing at all. I've worked hard to make a name for myself in this town, and all you've done is nag and complain. You're a lead weight to me, Susan and I won't let you drag me down any more."

He threw me against the wall. I crumbled to the floor. He picked me up by my collar and banged my head on the door molding again and again until I thought it would snap. "Get on with your fancy dinner for your prissy friends and shut up," he said. "What time are they coming?"

The couch and the lamp melted into a wild circle of light and blue tweed. My tears stung like angry wasps as they coursed through the cuts on my cheek and my torn mouth. I wept more from humiliation than pain. I was too stunned to feel anything but the urgency to get myself together before Margie and Tom walked in the door.

I stood up and wiped my mouth. I took a deep breath. I needed time to think, time to plan my escape from this twisted personality I had lived with for almost two years.

Just a minute, Susie. Whose personality was twisted, yours or his?

Well, I didn't have time to figure that one out now. Not yet. Seven o'clock was almost here and I had to clean me up before I could approach all those tomatoes and carrots waiting to be sliced.

My voice sounded like it was coming from Jean Talberg. "We'll discuss this later, Michael," I said. "Please get the den in order while I wash up. I'll set the table and toss the salad as soon as I stop this bleeding. The canapés are all ready and so is the dip. Margie and Tom will be here in less than half an hour."

I blotted the blood on my face with my apron. "You haven't heard the end of this, you know," I said. "My father will kill you when he hears what you've done to me."

"Oh, no, he won't," said Michael. "He'll wish he'd had the courage to do the same thing to your mother. Face it, Susan. Your father is a wimp. Your mother is the man of that house."

"Don't be ridiculous," I said. "You don't know what you're talking about."

But I knew he wasn't ridiculous at all. He was right.

❧ Chapter 48 ❧

As soon as Margie came in, she noticed my cut lip and the slowly blackening bruises around my eye. "My God, Susie! What happened? Did you fall?"

I gripped her hand and searched my mind for an answer. Michael put his arm around my shoulder and I pulled away. He ignored me and smiled at our guests. "She slipped on the ice," he said. "I've told her time and time again to watch those stairs when it snows. But you know Susie. Always in a hurry, always carrying packages. Here, let me take your coat."

Did he really think my best friend would swallow that one?

But she did or at least she pretended she did. "Where did you fall?" she asked. "Most of the snow and ice has melted from our last storm."

"Right out here on our drive," said Michael. "I keep meaning to speak to the janitor about it. He never gets the place shoveled clean."

"Oh, I see," said Margie. She handed him her coat. "Come on, Susie. Let me help you get dinner on the table."

I still don't know how I managed the next hour. Bette Davis couldn't have done a better job. Neither could Jean Talberg. I was a gracious hostess, and a caring wife. I put the platter of meat and roast potatoes in front of my husband. "You carve the lamb, Michael," I said. "I'll serve the beans. Margie? Would you care for garlic bread?"

I watched them all eat the meal I had created while I pushed a few cabbage shreds around on my salad plate. I listened to Tom and Michael discuss the new shopping center on Central Avenue. "It might be a good place to open a branch office," he said. "Everyone's moving out of downtown into the suburbs, these days."

I told Margie anecdotes about the children at school. "We have a rabbit," I said. "I let it out of the cage every morning and Kenny Roberts follows it around with a dustpan to catch its droppings. I wonder what he tells his mother when she asks him what he learned at school today?"

We laughed. The silverware scraped against the plates. The grandfather clock in our study chimed the hour. Someone turned on their stereo in the flat next door. Margie finished her meat and wiped her lips on her napkin. Tom reached for his water glass but it was empty. I picked up the pitcher and took his glass. "Let me," I said.

"Thank you," he said.

"Anyone for seconds?" I asked.

Michael pushed his plate away. "Not for me," he said. "I'm stuffed."

I looked at his filled plate. The meat was barely touched; the string beans remained just where I had put them. The gravy had congealed around his roast potato. "But you haven't eaten anything!" I said, and I gasped.

How did Jean Talberg get into this conversation?

"It was delicious, Susie," said Margie.

I smiled and stood up. "I'll bring in dessert," I said.

Margie and I didn't have time to talk until we were washing the dishes. "Your poor eye, Susie," she crooned. "Put some ice on it, tonight. You've got to learn to be more careful when you run up those stairs. Does it hurt very much?"

Why didn't I tell her? Why didn't I say, "Margie, my bastard of a husband just beat the living hell out of me?"

In those days, no one spoke of wife abuse. I didn't know it existed, and I thought I was the only one in the world whose husband mutilated her when she stood up for herself. I imagined what Margie would think if she knew what Michael had done to me: "I always knew he was no good," she'd think. "Thank God I figured him out in time."

No, I wasn't going to let her know that her castoff lover was a wife beater. Besides, I *had* goaded him to do it. In almost two years, he'd never touched me before. I attacked him the minute he walked in the door. Maybe I had it coming.

If it happens again, I'll tell Daddy. He'll know what to do. After all, I'm his daughter. He wouldn't let anyone hurt me. Would he?

I wasn't very sure about that. Well, I had to get help from someone, and I certainly couldn't expect any sympathy from my mother. She would be certain that I got what I deserved. She was probably busy thanking whoever she prayed to that I was out of her house. No. I would have to tell Daddy.

But only if it happens again.

I forced my swollen lips into a smile and I gave Margie my 'honest to God' look. "It just throbs a little," I said. "I'd almost forgotten about it until you mentioned it. Come on, Margie. We'd better get back in there. The boys want to play bridge."

"Yes," said Margie. 'It's already nine and we don't want to be out too late. I promised the baby sitter we'd be home by midnight."

I swallowed a large lump of envy. She had her baby and had loved conceiving him. I hated the act and the man who did it to me. I had prostituted myself just to have a baby like hers and after two years, where was it? It was still in my someday category. That's where it was, along with those other things everyone else took for granted like a faithful husband and a family who cared.

I untied my apron and hung it on the door. "How is the baby?" I asked. "Still cutting teeth?"

Margie nodded. "Yes, poor thing. He's so uncomfortable. But he's such a darling, Susie. Come over tomorrow after you've cleaned up and help me give him a bath."

"I'd love to," I said. "But I can't stay long. I've got to get ready for our party, Saturday night."

"Susie," laughed Margie as we walked back to the den. "I've never seen anyone like you! Your affair isn't until Saturday and this is only Thursday. You've had everything baked and frozen for at least a week and you made all your place cards last weekend. Why can't you ease up a little?"

"Well, it's the biggest crowd we've had here all at once since we got married and I want to do it right," I said. "Mother's Helen is coming to help me serve and clean up but I'm doing all the cooking. I have the brioche to bake yet and the pies. I've made some marvelous hors d'oeuvres, too. My freezer is bursting!"

"Have you ever thought of ordering a couple trays from David's Delicatessen and enjoying your party?" asked Margie. "You slave in the kitchen for days. You decorate with fresh flowers and place cards as if you were entertaining the Queen of England. What fun is that for you?"

"It keeps me out of trouble," I said. "Cut the cards, Tom, and I'll deal."

Michael and I didn't speak to each other during the game and we were all four so absorbed in playing that I began to think the appetizer Michael gave me before dinner was a mirage. Only my throbbing head and swollen mouth reminded me that it was real. But then Tom ignited a new stick of dynamite. "Did you get the announcement about the fraternity spring alumni weekend?" he asked.

"It just came the other day," said Michael. "I sent in the money for us, today. Are you going, too?"

I put down my cards and stared at him. He was absorbed in sorting his hand. I picked up my cards again and forced my voice to remain even. "You sent in the reservation?" I asked. "You didn't tell *me* about it. Since when are our social activities unilateral decisions? Don't I have anything to say about what we do?"

Margie and Tom were silent. The room was still. I heard nothing but my angry heart pounding against my ribs. I picked up my cards and began to sort my hand.

Michael kept his eyes on his cards. His face was blank. "All right," he said. "I'll ask you. Do you want to go to the fraternity spring reunion?"

"No," I said. "I don't want to go. Unlike you, I've outgrown college. I don't need to put on my bobby socks and run around getting drunk at juvenile house parties. I don't want to spend hundreds of dollars for dinners I can't eat with people I don't respect. And I don't want to see you with your hands in every ripe pair of panties that sachets by."

He threw his drink at me.

I could smell the Jack Daniels as it trickled down my forehead and burned the cuts on my face. The glass shattered on my skull. Bits of glass and ice cascaded down my neck in a waterfall of blood and whisky. I was too stunned to move.

Margie stood up. "I've seen enough," she said. "You get out of here right now, Michael Rose, or I'll call the police. Susie didn't fall on any ice, did she? There wasn't one shred of ice on your driveway or steps when we got here. You gave her that black eye and cut mouth. "

"I'm not moving," said Michael. "This is my home. You get out. You're nothing but a meddling do-gooder. You can't push *me* around."

Tom took a step toward him. "Stop," said Margie. "Just call the police, honey. Wife beating is frowned on in official circles."

She turned to me. "My poor Susie," she said. "Come with me and I'll help you clean up."

❧ Chapter 49 ❧

I don't know what I would have done that night without Margie and Tom. I sat huddled on my chair drenched in whisky and pain. I could not utter one single coherent sentence. Margie led me into the bathroom and took off my dripping clothes. She wrapped me in a towel while she ran the water in the tub. Then, she forced me into the steaming bath. She called my doctor and sent Tom out to get some Sominex so I could sleep. Then she tucked me into bed.

I pushed her away and sat up. I was choked with fear. "Where's Michael?" I asked. "Where did he go? As soon as you leave, he'll hit me again. I know he will."

"It's all right, Susie. Everything's all right. Tom got him out of here, and I'm staying with you tonight. Tom called your father and he'll have someone here to change the locks tomorrow morning. Debbie will spend the day with you. Don't be afraid, honey. Just try to sleep."

I lay in bed and fought down the waves of terror that choked me. I clung to Margie's hands and stared at the ceiling. As soon as Tom returned, Margie gave me a sleeping pill. "Shut your eyes, Susie," she said. "Give the medicine a chance to work."

She turned off the light and left the room. I tossed and scrunched the covers into a wrinkled mass and I dreamed I heard Margie talking to Tom.

"Susie brings all this on herself," she said. "She hasn't learned that life is gray, not black and white. She does everything in such wild, erratic extremes. She was about five pounds too heavy for a size six skirt over two years ago, and she's been starving herself into a toothpick ever since. She didn't have a proposal of marriage the first six months out of college, and she grabbed the first male animal she could get."

"And that's just what she got," said Tom. "An animal. Listen, Margie, he doesn't just cheat at marriage. He cheats at cards at the club, at golf on the course, at everything. He's nothing but a crook. Everyone in Toledo knows he's been robbing Susie's family of capital to set himself up and spending it on poker or fancy ladies. No one can stand him. Why the hell doesn't Susie leave him?"

"Oh Tom!" said Margie. "Haven't you figured my Susie out? She's a masochist. She enjoys flagellating herself after she deliberately puts herself in impossible situations. She insists her mother is a monster, and I agree Mrs.

Talberg isn't exactly sugar and spice. But if Susie hates her so much, why does she call her all the time and expose herself to her mother's barbs and taunts? Why doesn't she stay away and live her own life? It's almost as if she wants her mother to criticize her so Susie can feel injured. Poor Susie! She's created her own hell and now she thinks she's stuck in it. All she has to do is walk away. That's all. But I don't think she really wants to stop her pain. I think she enjoys it."

"That's sick," said Tom.

Sick. I'm sick. My own best friend thinks I'm a crazy. What was worse, I agreed with her. I tossed and turned and winced as the pillow slip rubbed against the bruises on my face. I tried to wake up from my nightmare, but I couldn't surface. I wasn't even sure it *was* a nightmare.

And then I stopped thinking at all. The sleeping pill sent me deep into the lowest shelf of slumber, a dreamless bliss where pain is forgotten and peace blankets the aches of life.

❧ Chapter 50 ❧

Why did morning have to come? Why couldn't I always be cushioned in the drugged calm of that black night? Michael didn't matter. Food didn't matter. I was lost in a sweet pool of peace until noon the next day.

But when I surfaced, everything felt even worse. I replayed the night before in my head and I was afraid to open my eyes. I turned my face into my pillow and I groaned. I felt a hand on my forehead and I opened my eyes.

Debbie was standing by the side of the bed. "Are you up, Susie?" she asked. "I thought I heard you. I have some orange juice for you, and the coffee's ready. How about some toast to go with it?"

I was still in a fog of drugged sleep. "Where's Margie? Where's Michael?" I asked.

I staggered out of bed to go to the bathroom. I looked in the mirror and saw a battered hag. Both eyes were black and I had a huge diagonal cut on my forehead. My lip was bruised and swollen. Angry, purple cuts and bruises stained my face and neck. I sank to the floor, a huddled ball of despair.

Debbie found me there. She knelt down beside me and put her arms around me. "It's all right, Susie. It's all right," she said. "Daddy's coming over tonight to take you home. We've changed all the locks on the doors here and Daddy swore out a peace bond for you. Michael can't hurt you again."

The control of my life was slipping out of my hands and I was too weak and tired to snatch it back. I let Debbie sponge my face and put me in bed. She brought me a tray with coffee, juice and cinnamon toast and sat down beside me while I ate. I drank a little of the juice and pushed the toast idly around the plate. I held the warm coffee cup in both hands and stared into space trying to make some sense of all that had happened to me.

"You'll feel better if you eat, Susie," Debbie said. "I never realized how skinny you are until today. You're light as a rag doll. I'll bet you don't weigh seventy pounds."

"I'll weigh a hundred and seventy if I eat this toast," I said. "Just coffee will be plenty."

"Not even juice?"

Debbie's eyes were warm velvet globes of concern. They filled with tears. "I promised Mother I'd take care of you, but you won't let me. Please eat something or you'll die."

She put her arms around me and cradled my throbbing head against her

206

warmth. I wrapped myself in the comfort of her soft, scented bosom and my own embittered self pity. How safe and gentle to be loved this way. But this sanctuary, like all the harbors I had sought, was a mirage. . . only a mirage.

I squeezed my eyes shut tight and tried to come to grips with reality. I couldn't stay here in my sister's arms. I had to get out of bed and get dressed. I had to combat the new threat that was facing me. The cold, granite disapproval in my mother's castle waited to trap me within its walls once again. I couldn't go back home with Daddy. I just couldn't.

I couldn't bear the humiliation of walking through that door. The dog would snarl and bite at my shoes. My sister would chase after him and my father would sit down with the evening paper. My mother would be in the kitchen. She'd never bother to greet me. She'd just call, "Hurry up, Susan. I want you to set the table. You have to earn your keep here, you know. I'm not your servant."

No. I couldn't face that again.

But I did go home. I was too frightened to stay in that apartment all alone. I felt like a defeated war veteran who couldn't survive his war. My mind was numb and my will power was gone. I barely stammered a protest when Daddy came and bundled me, half asleep, out of my apartment.

I looked at the closed door with its mezuzah tacked on the molding. I heard Normie Odesky laughing in the next apartment and smelled the pungent odors of dinners being started. Mrs. Dougherty was doing another stew. Its cabbage and garlic aroma filled the hall. I leaned my head against the door. Inside our apartment, I heard the clock strike three. I felt as though I was watching my own funeral. This was the home I had made. And now it was gone.

"I've packed enough clothes for a couple nights, Susie," said Debbie. "Margie was over this afternoon. She called everyone to tell them the party was canceled. You'll have a whole week to recuperate before school starts again."

I turned my tear-stained face to look at my father and my sister. They could never understand what I was giving up. I clenched my teeth and forced my voice to remain even. "What about Michael?" I whispered. "What about my beautiful home? Oh my God, Daddy. What's going to happen to me?"

My father put his arms around me and held me against him. He stroked my head. "Go ahead and cry, kitten," he said. "Let it all out."

He was no longer the incompetent Leonard Talberg my mother had exposed to me. Once again, he was my daddy, the only one in the world who acted like he cared if I lived or died. I groped for his hand and clung to it. "Everything will work out, kitten," he said. "Just give it time. Come home, now. We'll talk when you're rested. I'll help you into the car. Okay?"

✖ Chapter 51 ✖

I awoke in my old bed in my old room. My head throbbed and my body felt like a sack of nails. I forced myself to sit up. The same white dotted swiss curtains framed a view I had seen every morning when I opened my eyes for over twenty years. The cherry tree was bare now and frosted with snow. I could see the Kaplans' antenna wires and the pine tree that shielded their home from ours. The chipped paint on my window sill was still there and that stain on the wallpaper when I spilled a glass of Coca Cola and the liquid splashed against it.

My suitcase had been unpacked and the robe from my trousseau lay across the foot of the bed. It was champagne lace and looked strangely out of place on my folded chintz bedspread. I smelled my mother's cooking. She was baking something. . . something I would have to face and refuse. Our silent battle of wills had begun.

I forced myself to get out of bed to go to the bathroom. I got on the scale. Seventy-five pounds. I hadn't eaten in over thirty-six hours and all I lost was a few ounces. I stepped off the scale and readjusted the marker to the exact center of the zero. I got back on the scale. Seventy-five. I sighed and looked in the mirror.

My eyes were black and I didn't recognize the twisted, bruised face that stared back at me. It was hollow eyed and vaguely familiar. Where had I seen an image like that? Then I remembered. My face looked exactly like the faces I saw in the movie newsreels of the liberated prisoners in Auschwitz. I turned away from the mirror and got on the scale again.

Seventy-five.

I walked slowly back to bed and lit a cigarette. The doorbell rang and the dog roared. Mother had turned on the stereo. Maria Callas was singing *Un Bel Di* from *Madame Butterfly*. I could hear Junior's shrieks obliterate the poignant harmonies of the song Butterfly sang as she waited for her Pinkerton. I squeezed my tears back into my eyes. There would be no Bel Di for me for a very long time.

I smelled the cooking odors that had always inflamed me but I felt nothing now. I shut my eyes and pretended those familiar sounds had disappeared. For just a tiny while more, I wanted to pretend I wasn't in my mother's house. I wanted to imagine I still lived in my own little apartment, the one I had created all by myself. I shut my eyes again and the next time I opened them, it

208

was dark.

Debbie brought me some soup and a grilled cheese sandwich for dinner but I couldn't eat. "That soup has globs of fat floating in it, Debbie," I said. "And Mother drenched this sandwich with melted butter. I don't eat greasy food."

"Try, Susie," said Debbie. "Just try. Would you like me to bring you some cottage cheese, instead?"

I shook my head. I pushed the food away and took two more Sominex. I pulled the covers up over my head. The night blurred and people seemed to wander in and out of my dreams. I remember Margie standing near me stroking my head. Debbie came into the room several times and Daddy sat beside me for a long time and held my hand.

I didn't see Mother until I finally got out of bed and came downstairs the next day.

It was Saturday, the last night of Chanuka. Mother and Debbie were wrapping Chanuka gifts. "Good morning," I said. "Any coffee?"

My mother looked up from the chaos of ribbon and tinsel on the dining room table. "You're up at last, Susan," she said. "Do you feel better?"

I refused to dignify that one with an answer. "I'll get some coffee," I said. "Has anyone heard from Michael?"

Debbie started to speak, but Mother put her hand on my sister's arm. "He called your father last night," said my mother.

She tied a ribbon around a long box and knotted it. "Put your finger there to hold it tight, Debbie," she said. "And I'll make the bow."

"What did he say?" I asked.

I braced myself against the wall as if I expected her words to lacerate my flesh. What more did Michael Rose want to do to destroy me?

My mother walked over to me and put her arms around me. I was too shocked to move.

"Susan," she said and her voice was the one she used with Debbie. I had never heard those tones directed at me. "I know you won't believe me," she said. "You and I have crossed the line where we can exchange understanding words. But I do realize what a nightmare this is for you. No one but you can save yourself from drowning. Michael is coming over tonight. Your father and I thought . . . hoped . . . you'd be up to dealing with him."

I sat down at the table and buried my head in the crumpled tissue paper and paper draydles. "I can't do it," I said. "I can't hold myself together, anymore. I'm too tired."

Debbie held the dog in her arms and stared at me with grief-stricken eyes. Her tears ran down her plump cheeks and soaked into his bristled coat.

"Oh, Debbie," I said and my tears joined hers.

"Crying is not going to help, Susan," said my mother and she put a consoling hand on my arm.

Where was that understanding when I needed it? Now, her words meant nothing to me. I knew very well that her only regret was that I had returned to her home. I had heard her tell Aunt Evelyn how much she longed to be rid of me. She couldn't fool me, now. I pulled away from her.

She flushed and started wrapping another package. Her voice was colder now. She sounded like the mother I knew once more. "You might as well know Michael wants to stay, Susan," she said. "Your father thinks you should give him another chance."

"Daddy does?" I couldn't believe it. "Daddy doesn't care that my husband beat the hell out of me? He doesn't care that Michael has laid every rich dowager and frustrated young matron in this town? You're lying."

My mother cut a piece of gold paper to fit the box she had filled. She didn't look at me. "Ask him yourself when he comes home," she said.

She folded the ends of the paper and taped them in place. She looked up at me and her mouth was a hard, straight line. Her eyes were narrowed and her voice very firm. "I told your father I never want to see Michael Rose again. He is trash and I don't waste my time on garbage. I told you from the beginning that he was no good and now you see that I was right."

She cut some ribbon and twisted it into a bow. She looked up at me once again and I saw tears in her eyes. She really did understand and she hurt for me. For me! I watched her expression soften and my stern mother vanished. I saw the Jean Talberg Aunt Evelyn showed me in her photograph album. This woman had felt the same pain and was trying to show me how she survived.

"It's not too late for you to do something about this, Susan," she said. "People get the lives they ask life to give. Try asking life to deal you a better hand. Margie will help. So will your sister. And so will I, if you'll let me."

She paused. Then she walked into the kitchen. "I've kept the coffee hot and I'll make you some eggs and bacon if you like. You haven't had anything to eat in almost three days. You'll need something to fortify you for tonight."

"Just diet toast, if you have any," I said. "And thank you, Mother."

I needed time to think; time to sort this all out. I knew only one thing. I was through with Michael Rose. No marriage was better than marriage to him. I realized that now. But what next?

I was twenty-three years old and I'd never be twenty-three again. I had thrown away almost two years of the only life I had trying to make a guy I don't love, love me, trying to have a baby he didn't want, trying to be a perfect person in an imperfect world. I drugged myself with caffeine and nicotine and I was hungry all the time. I didn't understand why I was doing such terrible things to my body, and I was too frightened to try to find out.

The minutes ticked away one by one. I chewed at my diet toast and it tasted like gravel. I drank some coffee, but it hurt the rawness in my throat. I lit a cigarette and walked over to the window.

Our living room window looked out on the park I played in when I was a child. I used to hide behind those snow-frosted trees when all the neighborhood kids played tag. I remembered the day Mary Kaplan and I found some old keys and went over to the empty house on the other side of the park. We tried every single key on that ring, but we couldn't open the door. We were locked out.

I had been locked out of every door I wanted to enter ever since. I never had the right key. I lit another cigarette and watched Mother and Debbie wrap Chanuka gifts. Debbie put two bottles of perfume on the table. "Let's give the 'Evening in Paris' to Sally," she said. "She's the one who likes exotic things. She always wears black sheaths and lots of jewelry."

My mother shook her head. "No," she said. "That's Lois. I bought the 'Heaven Sent' for Sally. She's the one who loves the outdoors and fresh wholesome things. Isn't that right, Susan?"

I shook my head. "I don't know," I said. "They look exactly alike to me."

Debbie laughed. "Let's put both of the bottles in one box and write 'Lois and Sally' on the package," she said.

They both laughed and I tried to laugh too but it hurt my lip. I looked at my mother and Debbie as they sorted out gifts together. The light from the window played on Debbie's dark curls and cast its soft glow on my mother's face. The two of them were absorbed in cutting paper and twisting ribbons. My mother measured and Debbie cut. They didn't need any words between them. They looked so close . . . so family.

I lit another cigarette and walked back to the bay window. I sat down on the couch and the dog jumped up beside me. I stiffened and waited for his snarl.

He crawled into my lap and licked my hand. He knew. Junior knew. I stroked his head and sniffled a little. Maybe he wasn't all that bad, after all. I wiped my eyes on my sleeve and buried my face in his fur. He felt warm and caring and I needed that. "You're a love," I whispered to him. "A real love."

He licked my hand and snuggled closer to me. My breathing settled down and I looked out the window once more. The world was still a giant Christmas card filled with tall trees and twinkling lights. Maybe, somewhere there was a gift tucked in all that snow for me. The trouble was I had no more energy left to search for it.

Finally, Daddy came home. We all sat down to dinner. "Michael will be here at seven, kitten," he said. "Don't make a hasty decision. Hear what he has to say first."

Mother wasn't lying. I thought Daddy would want to murder Michael for what he'd done to me. But no. My father wanted someone to listen to his smutty stories. He was more interested in keeping his partner on the golf course than he was in protecting his own daughter from physical harm.

I looked at him and this time, I stopped willing myself to deny what I saw. He was Michael Rose all over again. He said he spent his evenings at his lab making glasses so others could see their world. But he refused to see his own. He ignored our turmoil: Mother's, mine, Debbie's. He never was around long enough for me to see him as he really was. My eyes filled with tears for Jean Talberg. She, too, had married disappointment instead of a man.

No wonder she hated me. I had made no secret of my preference. Daddy was perfection; she was the load of bricks that dragged us all through the mud. I wondered how I would treat a daughter who thought I was a witch.

What was happening to my life's certainties? My fairytale marriage had become a thankless slavery. My gentle father was really weak and blind to everyone's needs but his own drive to be the "good guy." My evil mother was nothing but a frustrated woman trying to make the best of her empty marriage. This woman I thought was strong as iron was too weak to walk out of her hell, and look what happened to her. She was a warped, sour human being who got her only pleasure from sniping at my father and forcing all of us to eat food she was afraid to touch.

I took a deep breath and gripped the table. I was not going to let a thing like that happen to me. I had taken all I was going to from Michael Rose.

I refused to allow myself to be as weak as my mother. I was strong enough to walk out of this marriage and take my chances on my own. "Daddy," I said and I tried to choose my words as carefully as I could. "In the year and a half we've been married, Michael has had affairs with three women I can name and God only knows how many I don't know about. And now, he's begun to beat me when I object to the money I earn being spent on his amours. Do you really think he could say anything that would make me want to live with him again?"

My father split a roll and buttered it. He held it in his hand and smiled at me. "Now, Susan," he said. "You don't *know* he's been sleeping with other women. He's an insurance salesman. He has to entertain his clients to sell his policies."

I gripped my fork as if it were a weapon. I speared a leaf of lettuce and heard the tines grate against the plate. I kept my voice low and tried to hide my disgust. "Does he have to sleep with them in a Holiday Inn sixty miles out of town?" I hissed. "Does he have to kiss them until their lipstick rubs his face raw? He comes home every night reeking of strange perfumes. I pick up the telephone when they call, and hear them hang up when they hear my voice."

My mother and Debbie watched us as we spoke. Their heads moved back and forth as if they were in the bleachers of a tennis match. I still had the ball and I wasn't going to serve it to my father. Not yet. "Two days ago, I finally saw our American Express bill with all the receipts from the Holiday Inn and a few from The Ambassador even farther away from town," I said. "No one takes a client to dinner at that Holiday Inn when we have one right in Toledo. And The Ambassador doesn't even have a restaurant."

My father put his roll down and took a drink of water. "You'd never make much of a lawyer, Susie," he said. "You can't create a case on filmy evidence like that. You didn't *see* Michael with one of those women. You are only guessing. Marriage is too serious a commitment to break on supposition. People have to work hard at a relationship, Susie. Don't run out before you've given it every chance you can."

My face flushed and I slammed my fork down on the table. "I'm not imagining a thing, Daddy," I said. "What I was imagining is that I could make a success of a marriage with a person I neither love nor respect."

My mother sat back in her chair. She nodded and folded her hands in her lap. "I tried to warn you before your marriage, Susan," she said. "I told you Michael Rose was no good. I told you he only wanted our money and your father's business connections. But you wouldn't listen. And now you're paying for it. Did it ever occur to you that you brought this all on yourself?"

That's what Margie said in my dream. Was she right? Was I a masochist? Was I sick? I felt lost and uncertain and very frightened.

Mother got up from the table. "Debbie, give these bones to Junior. Susan, please clear the table. You're not a guest here, you know."

Her voice softened and she put her hand on my arm. "This is your home, Susan. Always remember that. This is your home."

My eyes filled. I didn't want this home. I wanted . . . that was the trouble. I was so numb, I didn't know *what* I wanted. I sighed and picked up the platters from the table.

ഔ Chapter 52 ര

At seven o'clock, the bell rang. The dog snarled and charged at the door. For once, I didn't resent his rage. I was glad he hated Michael as much as I did. When Daddy opened the door, Junior grabbed my husband's pant leg. "Stop that!" Michael shouted. Debbie ran into the room and snatched the dog. I could hear Michael's trousers rip as she pulled the hysterical animal away from him, and I smiled. "Serves you right," I thought. "Now you know how it feels to be attacked."

"Did he get you?" asked Daddy as he hurried into the room.

"Just a few scratches," said Michael. "Don't worry about it. Hello, Susan."

I examined my fingernails. I smoothed my skirt and let my eyes wander around the room until it rested on my husband's face.

He looked rested. He bore no evidence of the hell he had perpetrated two nights before. He took off his coat and folded it over a chair. He was dressed in a business suit and his hair had that tousled little boy look I loved. It was hard to believe that this was the man who had cut my lip and blackened my eyes. He looked so sweet. . . so All American.

I lit a cigarette and moved to stand beside Debbie. My father smiled and put his arm around Michael's shoulder. I turned away and inhaled my cigarette.

"Sit down, son, sit down," said Daddy. "Would you like some pie and coffee?"

"That sounds good," said Michael. "Will it be too much trouble?"

"Not at all," said Daddy. "Come into the dining room. Jean has the coffee made for all of us. Come on, kitten. You'll join us for coffee, won't you?"

I followed them into the dining room and then went into the kitchen to help mother. Debbie put the dog in the backyard and came back with iodine and a bandage for Michael's leg. The dog had clawed angry red stripes around his ankle and his pant leg hung like confetti. His socks were spotted with blood.

"My God, that looks terrible," said my sister. "Does it hurt?"

Michael grinned. "The iodine you're putting on it hurts lots more than the scratches. I think I'll survive."

Debbie sloshed on more iodine. Did I see her smile? No. I must have been mistaken.

My husband didn't flinch. He patted Debbie's head. "Thanks a lot, honey," he said.

214

My goodness, but we're being tactful tonight. When Michael wanted to be charming, he was gallant as a knight. I put my fingers to my swollen eye to be sure he really had hit me. And I watched the scene in our dining room unfold like a Chekov play.

My mother may not have liked Michael, but she couldn't resist the opportunity to entertain. She served apple pie with huge slabs of cheddar cheese from a fluted silver pie holder. She filled her pewter coffee server with coffee and served it with real cream in a chilled pitcher. The table was set with her Lennox china cups and saucers and the centerpiece was a brass menorah surrounded with pine branches and holly. She even put out little trays of after dinner mints. "Would you prefer ice cream with your pie?" she asked Michael as she sat down at the table.

"No thanks, Mother," he said. "This cheese is fine."

He accepted the dessert from my mother and looked directly at me for the first time since he had entered the house. "Aren't you having any pie, Susan?" he asked.

I didn't bother to answer that one. I looked down at the steaming brown liquid in my cup and twisted the napkin in my lap. I lit a cigarette.

Daddy handed Mother his plate and she filled it with pie. "Thank you, Jean," he said. "It looks wonderful."

My mother nodded. She cut a small slice of pie and handed it to Debbie. Debbie handed it back. "I'd like some cheddar cheese on it, please," she said. "And ice cream."

Daddy tucked his napkin in his lap and leaned back in his chair. "Well," he said. "What have you got to say for yourself, Michael? Are you ready to talk this out with Susan and see if the two of you can get patched up again?"

Michael took a bite of pie. "You outdid yourself, Mother," he said. "This is the best apple pie I've had in a long time."

My mother filled a saucer with bits of pie and a scoop of ice cream. She put it on the floor at her feet. Junior galloped to the plate and slurped up the food. My mother smiled and stroked his head. "That's my little man," she crooned.

"How did he get into the house" I asked.

"I let him in, Susan," said my mother. "He gets chilled if he is outside too long."

Michael smiled at Daddy. "We talked about all this on the telephone, Dad," he said. "Marriage is too big a commitment to abandon because of a little difference over a college spring weekend. I don't know about Susan, but I'd like to forget the whole thing and just start again."

I gripped my coffee cup and watched my father. *Well, Daddy. Say some-*

thing. Tell your son-in-law that giving your daughter a black eye and a bunch of bruises is a pretty extreme reaction to a "little difference."

Daddy took a bite of his pie and nodded to me. "Susan?" he said.

I twisted my napkin and wound it around my fingers. I bit my lip until I tasted blood. My mother bent her head and picked out some apples from between the crust of her apple pie. I could see her hands tremble. Debbie stopped eating. The ice cream on her plate soaked into her pie while my sister waited, wide-eyed, for someone to answer Michael.

No one said a thing.

Finally, my mother spoke. She put down her fork and touched her lips with her napkin. Her eyes were cold and her mouth barely moved as she spoke. "We were very upset at your behavior the other night, Michael," she said. "My daughters have never seen that kind of violence in this house. No matter how angry Leonard is, he wouldn't dream of laying a hand on any of us. We can't understand what would make a person lose control of himself the way you obviously did when you struck Susan."

Michael blushed. I couldn't believe it. He actually had the good grace to be embarrassed. I sipped my coffee and it tasted like cold brake fluid. I refilled the cup.

"I guess I did overreact, Mother," said Michael. "I'm really sorry. I probably had too much to drink and I lost control. I certainly never intend to let such a thing happen again."

He turned to me. He reached out his hand to touch my arm. I drew away and lit a cigarette. I stared at him out of swollen eyes. The match flickered in my fingers and went out. I put the cigarette down and waited.

"I love you, Susan," Michael said. "And I don't want to walk out on our marriage. I've made a lot of good friends in Toledo. I like it here, and I don't want to leave."

I looked down at my hands. I had clutched the coffee cup so hard, it cracked apart. The boiling coffee poured through my fingers to the tablecloth. Mother got up immediately and handed me some napkins to sop up the liquid. "I wish you'd be more careful, Susan," she snapped. "This was the tablecloth your father and I bought in Bermuda. It was hand painted."

Sorry, Mother. Sorry, I spoiled your tablecloth. But you see, I'm trying to gather the courage to tell your hypocrite of a son-in-law to go fuck himself.

I struggled to keep my voice level. My words felt like tasteless paste oozing out of my mouth. "Do you really think I want you to leave because of one quarrel, Michael?" I said. "I want you out of my life because we're no good

216

as a couple. You know it as well as I do. If you didn't love the money and the women you make in Toledo, you'd want nothing to do with me. I'm just your front of respectability so you can make your fortune and play the lover. Well, no more. You've given me nothing I wanted in this marriage. Nothing. I expected a loyal, loving husband. I wanted babies. What I got was an inadequate idiot who doesn't know how to love anyone but himself. You are determined to work me to death to pay your bills and beat me when I have the gall to complain. Well, that's not what I have in mind for the rest of my life. I've got dreams I want to make come true, and you're not in them. Now get out. I never want to see you again."

My father's pie fork clattered to the floor. His face paled. "Susan!" he said. "Do you call that being reasonable?"

Michael stood up. His face twisted into the familiar one that had attacked me during our bitter life together. "Forget it, Dad," he said. "She doesn't know what reasonable is. She's crazy. Look how thin she is and she diets all the time. She has wild tantrums accusing me of ridiculous sexual escapades, but she hasn't let me sleep with her in six months. Just where does she think this baby she wants will come from? Cloud nine?"

I stood up. Then I gripped the table and sat down again. I reached for a cigarette and took a deep breath. I refused to allow myself to scream. I absolutely refused. "Not let you sleep with me?" I said. "You're a liar, Michael Rose and you know it. I've let you maul and grind into me night after night whenever you're not too tired from screwing Beth Klein or Elaine Bloom. And just what do you call your morning assaults on my body? Calisthenics? I've let you force your way into my body over and over again and it hasn't gotten me one thing. Not even sweet words."

I struck a match and it went out. I tried again. My voice was beginning to screech and I could feel tears in my eyes. I looked at my mother. She was watching me, willing me not to break down. I inhaled on my cigarette and then I smashed it out in the ashtray. When I finally spoke my voice was hard as a diamond and just as clear.

I was Jean Talberg's daughter, after all. I knew how to talk to scum. "The first time I heard you say that you loved me since the day we were engaged was tonight at this table," I said. "You don't fool me, Michael Rose. You don't want me for anything but the financing my family gives you. If I can't have a husband who cares about me, I don't want any at all. Now get out before I throw up. You make me sick."

Michael stood up and I felt as if all my words had rolled off him without so much as soaking his jacket. He smiled the same triumphant smile he always gave me when he beat me at cards. "Okay, Susan," he said. "If that's what you want, it's all right with me. Give me the key to the apartment. I'll pack up and be out of there by tomorrow. My lawyer will contact you as soon as I get back to Columbus."

Daddy looked at me. His face was gray with disappointment. "Susan," he said.

I shook my head. "I know what I'm saying, Daddy," I snapped. "I don't want him anymore."

"Hooray," said Debbie.

"Deborah Ann!" said my mother.

Did I see her smile?

Daddy sighed and handed Michael the key to our apartment. "I'm sorry, son," he said. "I hate to see everything disintegrate this way. You don't have to leave town, you know. You could stay here if you wanted."

"I don't think so, Dad," said Michael. "Tom and Margie have been doing a lot of talking, and so has your daughter. My business career is too smudged with their accusations. Everyone in Toledo thinks I'm a hot-pants wife beater out to despoil all the virgins in town. I could never sell a policy here again. I'll go back to Columbus and pick up where I left off. I still have some good solid contacts there. And my family is there, too. I'd like to go back home and catch my breath. These past couple years have been a nightmare for me. Susan isn't easy to live with."

He turned to me. "You know, Susan. I should be angry with you, but instead, I pity you. You're a sick woman. In all the time we've been married, we've never talked about anything but food and babies and my sex life. There's a whole world out there that you don't even know exists. Inflation is up and they stoned the vice president in Caracas. Alaska was admitted into the union and people are talking about finally getting a man to the moon.

"All you care about is how many calories you can stuff into me and take away from yourself. Nobody starves themselves the way you do. You eat crazy and you have wild delusions. You imagine I'm doing all kinds of things I never do, and I can't convince you it's all in that nutty head of yours. You need help."

"Get out of here," I hissed. "That's the only help I need right now. Get out of here and let me get on with my life."

He walked to the door and Daddy handed him his coat. Suddenly, the room was filled with a cloud of leaping, roaring dog. Junior tore through the hall, fangs gleaming. Michael raced out the door and slammed it. The dog tore at the screen, tearing huge gaps out of it and scratching the molding raw.

Daddy was furious. "Who let him in here?" he roared.

"I did," said Debbie.

๑ Chapter 53 ๑

What now?

I had nothing to fight for anymore. I walked into the dining room and began to clear away the dishes. "Get that soggy tablecloth off the table right away, Susan," said my mother. "I don't know what possessed you to break your coffee cup that way. It was my Medallion pattern and I'm sick about it. That design was a limited edition. The cup is irreplaceable. I only hope the coffee didn't destroy the lacquer on the table."

I nodded. I carried the coffee service into the kitchen and then took in the empty plates and the leftover pie. I put the mints and the flowers on the serving cart and rolled up the tablecloth to put in the hamper. "I want to soak that in lemon juice," said my mother. "Coffee stains can be very stubborn."

She took the cloth from me and examined the finish on the table. "Look at that!" she said. "The varnish is eaten away. I'll have to call Mr. Davies in the morning to see if he can fix it. Why are you so careless, Susan? Did you destroy all *your* nice things this way, too?"

I thought of the way I had cleaned and polished our apartment. I remembered the hours I had spent shining silver and ironing tablecloths for the home I never had, for a marriage that wasn't real. I filled my mother's sink with soapy water and began to wash the dishes.

My mother took off her apron and hung it on a hook behind the basement door. She smoothed her skirt and walked over to the bread box. She opened it and pulled out a slice of rye bread. She spread a little jam on it and bit into it. She put it down on the edge of the sink and wiped her fingers. Then she turned to me. "You know, Susan," she said. "You created the situation you're in. You rushed into this marriage helter skelter. I knew right from the start that boy wasn't right for you. Michael Rose is not in our class."

She picked up the piece of bread and finished it. I watched the tidy way she chewed. I saw her teeth masticate the bread just as her voice masticated me. I saw her throat constrict as she swallowed. There was no joy on her face, but then there never was. The only emotions I ever saw in my mother's expression were those of disgust and superiority. I had always envied her beauty, but tonight I thought she was the ugliest human being on earth.

She brushed crumbs from the counter and opened the bread box once again. She looked inside and closed it. She took a dish with half a grapefruit in it and spooned out a section. She watched me put the dishes in the dishwasher for a few moments and then she said, "Michael Rose has the morals of an animal. When you reach into the gutter to snatch a husband, you can't expect to be treated like a princess. You might as well face facts, Susan. This mess is as much your fault as his."

I rubbed caked pie and cheese from the plates and scoured encrusted sugar from the cups. My eyes misted but I refused to let her see me cry. She'd had all the victory I was going to give her.

I turned my face away from hers. I bit my bruised lip until it bled. My mother ate another section of her grapefruit and wiped her fingers on a paper towel.

Then the telephone rang. Debbie came into the kitchen. "It's for you, Susie," she said. "It's Uncle Max. I told him you were busy, but he said it was important."

"You didn't tell him about Michael, did you?" said my mother. "I want to break it to Evelyn, first. She's going to be terribly upset."

"I didn't say a word," said Debbie. "Hurry, Susan. He's waiting."

I dried my hands on my apron and went into the den. "Hi, Uncle Max," I said. "What's up?"

That sounded pretty casual. Maybe he wouldn't hear the tears in my voice. Maybe he wouldn't notice that my life had crashed a few hours ago and I was still in little pieces.

"Susie!" said my uncle. "Oh, Susie, do I have wonderful news for you!"

"Good," I said. "I could use some wonderful news right now."

"One of my clients just had a baby and it's up for adoption. I told her I could find a marvelous home for the baby. . . it's a little boy, by the way, and healthy as an 8 pound horse. Anyway, she said to call you. I know how much you want a child, and I thought you and Michael might like to start your family with this precious little boy."

I sat down. I looked around me at the familiar bookcases and television set in my mother's den. Her sewing basket was beside her chair and there was a big bare spot in the rug where Junior had gnawed his way through the pile. Babies and love nests were only wishes for me. They could never be reality. Not anymore. "Who was the mother?" I asked. "Elaine Bloom? Beth Klein?"

"What are you talking about?" said Uncle Max. "What do I have to do with those women? The mother of this child isn't anyone you'd know. Anyhow, what do you say? The sooner I can place this baby, the better for the little boy and his mother."

I took a deep breath and tried not to screech into the receiver. "What do I say, Uncle Max? I say, `Thanks but no thanks'. You see, I just threw Michael out of my life and I don't have a home for that little baby anymore. What a shame you didn't call a few days ago. You might have given me a future."

And I hung up. I didn't wait to hear what he had to say. I didn't want to face questions impossible to answer. I couldn't take any more iodine on my wounds.

I returned to the kitchen. Mother was wiping the counter. "What did Uncle Max want?" she asked.

And then I broke down. "He had a baby for us. A little boy."

I sat down at the kitchen table and I sobbed. My mother had the good grace to leave me alone. She picked up her dish of grapefruit and paused at the kitchen door. "Shut off the lights when you come upstairs, Susan," she said.

I dried my tears and filled the tea kettle. I put it on the stove and turned on the flame. I walked over to the counter and cut a piece of pie.

One piece can't hurt me. Nothing can hurt me again. Eat Susan. Eat and fill the empty hole inside you, the space where your heart used to be.

Oh, look! Cheese! You just love cheese. How about more pie? LOTS more pie. Hurry, Susan. You are bleeding and you need to pack your wounds with food, lovely, sweet-smelling, delicious, wonderful, delightful food.

The water in the teakettle whistled. I poured some in a cup with instant coffee. I gulped it down to rinse out the sweet slimy feel of apple pie sliding down a throat raw with cigarettes and shouted words.

MY GOD! THAT'S HOT! Get some ice cream, Susan! Quick! You need something smooth and cool to make the burn go away. Vanilla ice cream! LOTS OF VANILLA ICE CREAM!. Scoop it out of that carton and into your mouth. More, Susan. More, more more until your throat is numb at last and your whole damn body is dead. Pie! Ice Cream! FOOD! Yum, yum, yum!

I opened the freezer again. My hands were coated with lemon custard, meringue and ice cream. My fingers stuck to the handle as I pulled the door open. I peered inside.

Look at that! Uncle Harry's newest flavor! Huckleberry Ice! And there! Bavarian Choco-lime! Goodness, but that stuff is COLD! Your teeth will fall out if you don't put something warm in that mouth of yours. How about nice warm bagel? . . . a lovely, toasted bagel with apple butter and jam and honey and peanut butter and cream cheese. Oh dear! There's no room in your mouth, Susan. Swallow faster! Swallow more! Gulp down everything in your mother's freezer! That will make her so happy! She just loves your appetite,

Susan. The trouble is that she doesn't love you.

Bits of cheese dribbled into the neck of my blouse. I was breathing as if I had just run a race but still I forced food down my throat. I chewed; I swallowed; I belched; I ate some more. I crammed bagels, broccoli, chicken, potatoes, challah, dill pickles, macaroni and cheese down my throat faster than falling leaves on a windy day. My thoughts were drowned in a sea of food.

Goodbye, Michael Rose. Farewell, Mother. You don't exist. Not anymore. All I know is the pain in my stomach and this terrible emptiness I cannot fill.

Choco-lime ice covered my blouse. It smeared across my face and dripped down my arm. Bits of macaroni dropped inside my shoe. They squished against my ankle as I staggered from counter to refrigerator to the sink and back.

*Woosh! There goes Daddy! Uncle Max and that little baby are gone, gone, gone. I have found cold brisket and potatoes. I don't need anything but these frozen brownies anymore. Oh, look. Do I see **blintzes?***

When I stuffed that frozen food into my mouth, I tasted grief that wouldn't stop. Would I explode with food and still keep eating?

My mother walked into the room. "What are you doing, Susan?"

She folded her arms and her mouth was straight and hard as railroad tracks. She looked at the empty pie plate and the dripping cartons of ice cream. Her eyes traveled to the open freezer and my stained blouse. The chocolate had run down my chin and dripped on my bodice. My face was smeared with dark smudges of chicken grease. The coffee cup was rimmed with ice cream and my hands were sticky with fudge.

My mother's face was an iron mask. Her voice slashed into me like a dagger. "You're sick, Susan," she said. "I've read about people like you, and you're sick."

She gestured at the shambles I had made of her kitchen. She nodded toward the emptied refrigerator, the crumb filled tablecloth and the littered counter. Her eyes probed into me and I shivered as she spoke. "Do you think I don't know what you do? Do you think I come down to my kitchen and see the counters empty, open my refrigerator and see it ravaged of food and have no idea what's happened?

"You gorge yourself until you can't move and then you force yourself to throw up, don't you? You starve yourself for weeks on end and when your body is so hungry it screams for nourishment, you pour food down your throat like you were stuffing a dead pigeon. You've done this again and again in my kitchen. God only knows how many times you've done the same thing in your own apartment. What are you trying to do to yourself, Susan?"

I gripped the back of the kitchen chair. I stared at her and felt my heart thunder against my aching ribs and the food swell and roll inside me. I had no idea what made me eat this way and I was terrified. I could feel my eyes fill and I looked down. The tears dropped on my knuckles. My mother's voice rolled over me in bruising waves. I struggled to control the scream rising in my throat. Why wouldn't she stop? Why did she insist on kicking me when I had already crumbled into a thousand fragments?

My mother smoothed her hair and folded her hands. She looked like a judge pronouncing the final verdict. Her voice was laced with derision. "That kind of eating is absurd," she said. "And it's repulsive. Look at yourself. You're stained with overindulgence. It makes me sick to look at you."

I saw the revulsion on her face and my shoulders slumped. My stomach felt like it would explode. It throbbed so violently, I bit my tongue to keep from screaming. My mother folded her arms close to her body as if she felt a chill.

"You need professional help, Susan," she said. "Your father and I can't do a thing for you. Not anymore. It's too late. Why don't you talk to Dr. Harder? He's the one who helped Betty Samuels when her husband left her. I'm sure he'll be most sympathetic."

I stared at her through a haze of pain. I didn't bother to conceal my hatred. She was vile. She was like a predatory animal teasing her prey before the kill. I shuddered at the sight of her.

I looked at her ice cold face and I matched my tones to hers. "Are you calling me a crazy, Mother?" I asked. "Do you want to send me off to a loony bin, now? What will you tell your friends? Susan had a nervous breakdown? Well, I'm not insane. . . I'm just me. And me is exactly what I don't want to be."

The tears started again. My mother turned her back and walked to the door. "I'm sorry for you, Susan," she said. "But if you don't want to help yourself, don't expect anyone to do it for you. We all have our own lives to lead. Please clean up this mess before you come upstairs."

And she walked out.

I picked up all the dishes and put them into boiling dishwater. I cleaned them carefully, wiped the counters and swept the floor. Then I opened the refrigerator again. I stood at the door and used both hands to stuff butter, olives, pickles and apple butter down my throat. Apricot juice splashed on my shoes, mayonnaise dribbled down my chin.

My throat was raw and my knees buckled. I gripped the counter and tried to shut the refrigerator door. My fingers slipped and the emptied catsup bottle slid from my hand. It shattered across the linoleum and splatted its contents like red blood on my shoes. I grabbed a fresh towel and blotted up the liquid. Then I wiped my hands on my skirt and tried to grip the broom tight enough to sweep the floor once more.

I staggered upstairs. I crouched over the toilet and forced myself to throw up again and again and again. I stood up and got on the scale. Eighty-one.

Eighty one!

I groped my way to the medicine cabinet and found the bottle of Nembutals the doctor had given me. I tore off the plastic top and I swallowed the rest of the pills.

"Now it's over," I said. "It's finally over."

I lay down on the bathroom floor and waited to die.

✂ Chapter 54 ✂

I floated in a mist between sleeping and waking. I heard strange voices like twittering birds. I frowned but I couldn't separate one song from the other. I felt myself carried someplace and then I had a nightmare. Someone stuck a pipe down my throat and all the horrible food came pouring out. I gagged and gasped and hated the pain. But I was relieved, too. The calories were gone. Now, I wouldn't get fat.

I tried to sink deeper into my sweet silver fog but someone kept pulling me out. Why did I have to walk this way? My feet felt like warm butter. My arms were spaghetti. But the arms around me were like tight ropes that propelled me back and forth. "So tired," I muttered. "So awfully tired. Let me lie down. Please, let me lie down."

"You can't lie down, honey. Not yet."

Who was that? I smelled starch and hospital disinfectant. Where was I? I remembered the cold sheen of the bathroom tile. I remembered those pills. Is this what being dead is like? Is it cold and white in heaven? Do the angels swab the clouds with Lysol? Doesn't God let you sleep?

I shook my head and opened my eyes. "That's a good girl," said that brisk voice. "Open your eyes and let me see what color they are, honey. Come on. Let's walk some more. When you can do this all by yourself, I'll get you some breakfast. Doesn't that sound good?"

I shook my head and tried to pull away from the arms that held me. "Please leave me alone. I need to die. I took the pills so I could die."

Then, I heard more voices. "Very common in cases like this, Mrs. Talberg. She'll be all right. I doubt if she'll try it again. If she'd really wanted to commit suicide, she wouldn't have sprawled on the bathroom floor where she knew you'd find her. She would have gone somewhere less conspicuous, a basement, outside, even her own room wouldn't have been so obvious."

The warm mist was clouding my brain again, but my mother's voice pierced it with the precision of a laser beam. "Just like Susan," she said. "She makes a big production out of everything. All she wants is pity. And frankly, she gets too much of that from herself."

And then Daddy's voice. "Now, Jean . . ." he said.

Pacifying, soothing, understanding . . . whom? I didn't want to hear Daddy's voice. I didn't want to think about what he had become to me. No. I have to hurry back into my safe velvet cloud.

"Come on, honey."

There's that shrill, strange tone, again. The one attached to those iron arms wrapped around my shoulders. "Let's walk once more to the door and back. That's a good girl. Pretty soon, I'll get you some nice, cold orange juice. Won't that be nice?"

I smelled antiseptic and face powder. I opened my eyes for a moment and was blinded by a huge expanse of white. I pushed to free myself but it was no use. I was exhausted. Didn't this voice know how terribly tired I was? "Don't want to eat," I muttered. "Don't want to get fat. Let me sleep. Oh please, please, please."

I shut my eyes and all the voices disappeared. Those arms forced me back and forth and I was conscious of doors opening and closing until I heard that first voice again; the strange one I didn't recognize. "It's a blessing you found her so quickly, Mrs. Talberg," said that other voice. "Thin as she is, she wouldn't have lasted much longer if we hadn't pumped her stomach right away. You saved her life."

So, it was Mother who did it. It was Mother who wouldn't let me escape. Why couldn't she leave me alone? Why couldn't she let me leave this black life of mine? "Let me lie down. I can't stand up anymore."

"Jean, you are so harsh with her."

Daddy's voice, again. . . .the voice I used to trust. Who is he making up to, now? I tried to concentrate but his words faded in and out of my mind. He didn't sound conciliatory at all. He sounded angry. "It makes me sick to hear you talk about her the way you do," he said. "She has had the worst week I can imagine. She deserves all the pity we can give her. What kind of future does she have now? Tell me that?"

And then I heard Aunt Evelyn's voice. "Oh, Jean!" she said. "I came as soon as I heard. How is she?"

"You shouldn't have bothered, Evelyn," said my mother. "This is just another one of Susan's dramatic productions. She wanted an extra dose of self pity so she took just enough pills to scare Leonard. She'll be just fine and back to her old tricks in no time."

"Jean," said Aunt Evelyn and I had never heard such anger in her voice before. "How can you be so insensitive? This divorce isn't Susan's fault and you know it. Michael Rose had us all fooled, didn't he, Leonard?"

I heard Daddy's voice rumble something and my mother's voice cut in. "I always said . . . "

"I know only too well what you always said, Jean," said Aunt Evelyn. "You never let Susan enjoy one thing she earned. You've made it a career to belittle her and poor Susie had begun to believe you. No wonder she tried to kill herself."

I smelled Aunt Evelyn's sweet perfume and felt her cheek rub against mine. She stroked my head and held my hand and she spoke again. This time I heard no anger in her voice. She was choked with tears. "Your own daughter, Jean! Mama would be so ashamed of you. I've never heard you say one kind word to your Susan. Not one kind word. You've never given this child a chance, Jean. You refuse to see what a sweet little person she is. All you ever saw was the time she absorbed that you could have used being a social butterfly."

I felt Aunt Evelyn's kiss and then I heard my Mother's angry voice again. "I've heard enough," she said and I heard a door slam.

"You know Jean and her temper, Evelyn," said my father. "She'll come around."

Aunt Evelyn rested her cheek against mine. "Will she, Leonard?" she said. "After all these years, do you really think she will? She hasn't forgiven you for not being a millionaire. Do you actually think she'll ever manage to blame herself for her empty life? God knows why you've stuck to her all these years, but you have no right to expect your Susie to suffer one more minute for something she couldn't help. I am disgusted with both of you."

She kissed me and stroked my head. "Live, Susie," she said. "Live for *me*, sweetheart. I couldn't bear to lose you."

For the first time in my life, I hear tears in my father's voice. "You're right, Evelyn," he said. "And maybe I'm a masochist. I love my wife in spite of what she does to us all. I was wrong to make Susie accept that kind of punishment. Terribly, terribly wrong."

"Let's see you walk to the door all by yourself, honey," said that brisk voice again. "Can you do it? Then, I'll put you back in bed. Okay?"

And so I walked. I heard the sharp staccato of my mother's heels and Daddy's voice once more. "You're back, Jean," he said.

I forced myself to open my eyes. I let that nurse lead me back into the arena where my mother always won. There she was: My Conqueror.

She stood at the foot of my bed talking to a man I'd never seen. Daddy came up to the bed and smiled. "Hi, kitten," he said. "You've had quite a night, haven't you? Well, you're safe, now. Pretty soon, we'll take you home and everything will be all right."

Home? What home? You're wrong, Daddy. Everything won't *be all right. Nothing can ever be right for me in my mother's home.*

"Susan, this is Dr. Harder," said my mother. "We called him after we got you to the hospital. He'd like to talk to you."

"Go away," I said to the fat man leaning over my bed. "I don't want to see you. I'm not crazy. I don't need fat little men telling me how to think. Go away."

And I turned my face into the pillow.

"She's very confused right now, Mrs. Talberg," said the man. "I think my presence frightens her. Let me say goodbye for now. If she decides she's ready for therapy, you have my number. I'll be only too happy to help. I've worked with anorectics before and I think I understand their problems. I must warn you, though; unless she seeks my advice herself, you'll be wasting my time and your money. She has to want to get well very badly or we won't make any progress at all."

The nurse came in with orange juice, coffee and toast. I pushed aside the juice and took the warm coffee cup in my hand. My mouth was dry and I felt very cold. I stared at the man by my bed. He was bald and had the clearest blue eyes I had ever seen. "I don't want your help," I said. "I want to sleep."

හ Chapter 55 ශ

Once more, I returned to my mother's house and I couldn't bear to be me. I wasn't even good enough to kill myself. I was no better than Michael. I was scum.

Margie came to visit. She took my hand and held it to her cheek. "I know, Susie," she said and her eyes glistened with tears for me. "I know."

But she didn't know at all. She had a gentle, loyal husband. She had a precious baby. She didn't face an eternity of teaching other people's children and living in another woman's home.

I smiled and gave her a hug. "Well, this is one way to get out of teaching for a few days," I said. "How's Eric?"

She told me, and I wished I'd had the wisdom to hide under the bed after I took those pills. My mother's medicine cabinet was empty now. There would be no escape for me there anymore.

When I was strong enough, I had to sort out everything in the apartment. I had to tear apart the little castle I had tried to mold into heaven. Slowly, in a mist of stifled tears, I crammed the remnants of my marriage into big, brown cartons. I packed all the things that belonged to Michael, and Uncle Harry sent them back to Columbus, Indiana. I packed up the china, the silver, the books and records that were mine. Then Uncle Max and Daddy held a rummage sale and banked the money for me.

It felt like I was viewing the holocaust of my dreams. The home I had tried so hard to create was nothing but blank walls and empty windows now. Its tables were covered with unwanted linens, vases, even a breakfast set from Aunt Evelyn. . . all those things that were supposed to give my marriage a bright start. My Queen Anne dining set stood like an orphan against the wall. It was flanked by the high backed chairs that Michael and I sat on when we acted out a marriage neither of us wanted. And there was the bridge set where everything ended for me.

Two years of my life were on the auction block. There was not enough money in the world to compensate for my loss. The furniture, the linens, the lovely props I had chosen for my beautiful dream were all for sale. Like that dream, they were mine no more.

When it was over, I sat in the family room of my mother's home and I knitted. That's what I did to keep from tearing myself apart. I made afghans. I did a pink and white one for Margie, a blue tweed for Aunt Evelyn, a cable stitch

229

throw for Daddy's office. I knitted and knitted and knitted some more. I couldn't read. I couldn't think.

I taught by rote, exactly the same lessons I had used the year before. I let the children scream and fight. When the noise was so loud it penetrated my consciousness, I took them out for recess.

The principal called me into his office and gave me notice that March. He was a tall man with a smile for everyone. This time, his smile concealed teeth of iron. I wasn't fooled by the way he put his arms around my shoulders. I wasn't teaching in that classroom and we both knew it.

"We're awfully sorry, Mrs. Rose, but we can't renew your contract," he said. "Your work has simply not been the caliber that we demand in this school. I know you've had a great many personal problems this year, but I refuse to allow the children to suffer because of your unhappiness. Perhaps you need a year or two to get your life in working order before you're ready to teach and guide children."

I nodded and turned to leave. He reached for my hand. "Goodbye, Mrs. Rose," he said.

I pulled my hand away and left his office. Someone else had caught on to me. I wasn't good enough to teach, either. My career, like my marriage was over. And I was better off without either of them. I returned to my mother's house and picked up my knitting needles.

My mother put down her sewing and watched me. I felt her gaze and I bent closer to the wool. I didn't want to look at her. I didn't want her to see that once more, she had triumphed.

"Susan," she said. "Can't you do anything but sit there? You've been mooning around the house for over three months. Do you think you can expect your father and me to support you forever?"

I looked up at her. I met her eyes and then I looked down at the yarn once more. She was right. I had to earn a living. But how? I had no talents. I had no skills. I couldn't think of a thing I wanted to do but knit.

"What kind of job can I get?" I asked. "My only training is in education and I can't do that anymore."

My knitting needles clashed together as I speared the elusive yarn. I looked down and picked up the stitches I had dropped.

My mother folded the nightgown she had mended and picked up one of Daddy's socks. She inserted a darning egg and threaded her needle. Her mouth was pursed with disapproval. "You should have thought of that when you were being so careless and slipshod in your classroom. Jobs aren't that easy to get these days," she continued. "You lost a wonderful opportunity, Susan. Now you'll have to look elsewhere to support yourself."

"Yes, Mother," I said.

I slipped four stitches onto my cable holder and knit four from the needle. The yarn was the only thing that was real to me. I had no idea what kind of life I wanted.

I only knew I didn't want to get fat. But why?

I was a skeleton. I weighed seventy-two pounds and the scale was creeping downward slowly as a sleepy turtle, but downward just the same. Was this another way to commit suicide? Slow, careful starvation? I didn't know. I didn't even think about it. I knit.

And then the dog ran away. My mother was frantic. "You did it," she screamed at me. "You left the gate open in the backyard and now my baby is gone."

I looked at her twisted face and I struggled with the smile that flickered across my lips. Her eyes were filled with tears and her face was flushed. She gripped at the dishtowel in her hand and twisted it into a whip. She ran to the window and looked out, and then she buried her face in the towel. "What's the use?" she moaned. "He isn't there."

She turned to me again. Her voice was low and thick with tears. "You!" she hissed.

She was talking about an animal, for God's sake. You would have thought she was keening for the prince regent. I looked at her torment and it was my turn to be hard as glass. I spoke quietly and didn't hide my scorn. "I didn't do it." I said. "I never go into the backyard."

"You are lying, Susan Talberg," sobbed my mother. "You did it. You've always hated me and this is your way of getting back at me. Taking away the one thing I love."

What kind of woman was this person I called Mother? What kind of human being could love an animal more than her husband, more than her own children? *She's insane,* I thought.

I paused and saw myself knitting away my life. I saw myself at the table, my skeletal arms pushing away food, my hollow eyes burning with longing for a piece of meat. I watched myself take off all my clothes, hold my breath and step on the scale every morning, every evening, every time I felt attacked.

Yes. We deserve each other, Mother. We're both mad.

My mother stormed out of the room to call the Humane Society. I knit until Daddy came home.

She was waiting for him at the front door. Words poured from her mouth like acid. "Susan let Junior loose, Leonard," she said. "And she did it on purpose."

My father looked at her angry face and he put his hand on her shoulder. "Now, Jean . . . " he said.

My mother didn't even hear him. She pushed him away. Her words catapulted against him like frozen hail. "I've had enough of her, Leonard," she hissed. "You'll have to get rid of her. I won't tolerate her in my house any more."

My mother's words shot across the room like machine gun fire. I was defenseless against them. I bowed my head and knit.

My father walked into the den and my mother marched behind him. He still had his hat on and held his brief case in his hand. He wasn't smiling now, and there was anger in his voice. "Calm down, Jean," he said. "You don't know what you're saying."

He put his case down next to the desk and reached for my mother's arm. She snatched it away. "I know exactly what I am saying," she said. "Susan is a terrible influence on Debbie and you know it, Leonard. All she does is sit and stare into space while she starves herself to death. I am warning you, Leonard. I don't want her in this house."

My father walked over to me and put his hands on my shoulders. I could feel his love warm me but I knew he couldn't save me. He was as much Mother's victim as I was. I looked at the wool on my needles. I had knit the same stitch over and over again.

"Jean, you're talking nonsense," he said and he stroked my bent head. "Susie is our daughter and this is her home. She is welcome here and she is loved. She's going nowhere until she gets settled in her own mind. She'll find direction, I know she will."

He turned my face up and looked into my eyes. My knitting needles moved but I couldn't spear the stitch. My hands shook and I thought I would faint. I looked down at the beige yarn between my fingers and I twisted it around the needle. It was no use. I couldn't pull the yarn through the loop.

I put the afghan down in my lap and reached for a cigarette. How could she talk about me as if I were as insensate as an ornament on her coffee table? How could she?

Daddy stroked my head. He still had his coat on and I could smell the outdoors in his embrace. He kissed me and reached for my hand. "You'll be all right, kitten," he said. "Don't pay any attention to your mother. She's just upset."

He leaned down and kissed the top of my head. "We all make mistakes, kitten. Every one of us. The trick is to learn to forgive ourselves and get on with life."

232

I looked up at him and my eyes filled with tears. I had no life and there were no more pills in my mother's medicine cabinet. I picked up my knitting needles again.

My mother started to cry. "The Humane Society lady said he'll probably come back, but she doesn't know my Junior. He's never been out of the yard, before. Oh, Leonard! What if he gets run over? What if he *dies*?"

She was ridiculous. That dog had terrorized the neighborhood. He even bit Debbie when she fed him. "It'll be the best thing that ever happened to us," I muttered.

"I heard that, Susan," said my mother. "I think you're being horrible. But I'm not surprised. You're never very sweet to have around."

She flounced out of the room. I had never seen her lose control of her emotions that way, except that time on the telephone with my Aunt Evelyn. When Debbie got hurt or had disappointments, she was caring and kind, but she didn't fall apart. My catastrophes seemed to strengthen her. But let her lose her little man-eating dog and her world crumbled at her feet.

Well, I guess we all have our little quirks. All I had to do was look in the mirror at my hollowed eyes and gaunt, sunken cheeks to know I wasn't all there. And Daddy? He ran away to his lab and his ladies to escape *his* reality. Debbie was the only one that seemed to hold together. But give her time. A few more years in this bedlam and she'd unravel, too.

We all sat through dinner barely speaking. I picked at some dry lettuce and lit a cigarette. I waited for the others to finish my mother's roast chicken. Her eyes were red from crying. Every time she heard a bark, she ran to the door and called, "Junior? Angel? Are you there?"

After dinner, Debbie went out to look for the dog, and Daddy drove Mother around the neighborhood to find him. I cleared the table and washed the dishes. I looked at the chicken, sitting on the platter, all but uneaten. I walked over to it and grabbed hold of the leg.

Then I stopped. I could feel myself sinking into the same quicksand that had drowned me so many times before. But this time, I didn't want to drown. I didn't want to eat that chicken leg. I was tired of the hurt, tired of the vomiting, tired of the emptiness afterwards.

Would I attack the dog's food next or ransack the garbage? I didn't know. I only knew I was allowing myself to be controlled by an evil force I didn't understand. If I ate that chicken leg, I would start the whole cycle again.

Did I really want to pour all the energy I had into a battle to resist food? Did I want to be like my mother? Empty and cold? The only thing that touched her heart was a dog. What kind of person was that?

I remembered Jean Talberg. Not the mother I hated, but the girl I saw laughing and joking in Aunt Evelyn's photo album. . . . the sensitive, feeling woman I heard crying to Aunt Evelyn. Did I want my agony to harden into cruelty the way hers had? Did I want to be so wrapped up in my own tragedy that I froze out the rest of the world? There were a lot of nice people out there but I would never find them if I devoted all my energy to digestive gymnastics. What's the use of having life if you don't try to live it?

NO! I must not touch that chicken leg. I MUST NOT.

I covered the chicken leg with waxed paper and put it in the refrigerator.

I remembered all my dreams. I remembered that once I had wanted to be a writer. Once I had wanted to study English Literature. Once I had wanted to do something besides starve myself. Well, I had my priorities upside down. Before I could function in this world, I had to make Susan Rose a happy person. I had to learn to like her. Then I could worry about leading a good life. Now, all I was good for was knitting afghans and eating up my mother's leftovers.

And that wasn't enough.

What was it Mother said? People get the lives they ask life to give them. If I was going to save myself from rotting in my own hell, only I could do it.

Well, she's right. I hate to admit it, but she's right. And I'm through asking life to give me a lot of garbage. I want it to give me a rainbow so I can find my pot of gold.

I squared my shoulders. I don't need to take the abuse I've dished out for myself. I've had enough.

I walked to the telephone. I picked up Mother's address book and found the number I sought. I dialed it and let it ring. "Is this Dr. Harder's office?" I asked. "This is the answering service? Fine. Can you tell him I called? My name is Susan Talberg and I need help. Oh my God, do I need help."

Susan's Vernacular

Baleboosteh   An excellent, praiseworthy homemaker, totally involved in home and family.

Blintzes   An irresistible pancake filled with cottage cheese, fried in butter and served drenched with sour cream and other delights such as jam, cinnamon or honey.

Borscht   A cold beet soup served with a big blob of sour cream.

Brisket   A greasy pot roast smothered in garlic, diverse herbs, seasonings, onions, garlic, and carrots and surrounded by browned potatoes. It is made from the same cut of beef as corned beef.

Bubbe   Grandmother.

Challah   A braided loaf of bread, yellow with eggs and butter, glazed with egg white and usually served at the Sabbath meal on Friday nights in Jewish households. Real baleboostehs bake the challah for the Sabbath.

Chanukah   The Feast of Lights, a Jewish holiday celebrated near Christmas and often used by Reformed Jews as a substitute for Christmas for their children.

Charoseth   A mixture of chopped nuts, apples, cinnamon and wine that represents the clay from which the Israelites made bricks while in slavery.

Chozzer   A glutton.

Cheder   Hebrew school.

Daven   The act of praying in Hebrew, usually chanted rather than spoken.

Draydl   A four-sided top used in a Chanuka game.

Fartootst   All worn out; discombobulated.

Farpootzed   Overdressed; in bad taste.

Gefilte fish   A fish ball made of chopped whitefish, eggs and onions. It is served in the jelly that is formed while it is cooked and topped with horseradish, usually homemade and very hot.

Goyim   People who are not Jewish.

Hadassah   The Women's Zionist Organization of America; it has branches throughout the country and has become a Jewish club where women meet to arrange good works, aid to Israel and social functions.

Haggadah   The prayer book read at the seder that contains the Passover ceremony.

Kesslegarten	A ghetto of poorly educated, uncultured, undisciplined Jews.
Kosher	Literally, clean; foods that meet the rigid standards of Orthodox dietary laws.
Kugel	A tantalizing casserole of grated potatoes, onions, eggs and seasonings baked in schmaltz or Crisco until the crust is an inch thick and the cholesterol level in the thousands.
Latkes	The same combination fried as pancakes and traditionally served with sugar or jam at Chanukah. It is humanly impossible to eat only one latke.
Mazel	Luck.
Matzoh	Unleavened bread that is eaten at Passover.
Mechaieh	A pleasure, exquisite joy such as when a child is exceptionally good to his mother or becomes a violinist.
Meidele	A young girl.
Mezuzah	An oblong container affixed to the right of the front door-jamb of a Jewish home. It contains a rolled up parchment on which is written verses from Deuteronomy and begins "Hear, Oh Israel, the Lord our God, the Lord is one."
Nebbish	A jerk; a Sad Sack.
Pesach	Passover, Jewish holiday commemorating the Jews' exodus from Egypt.
Pushke	The small, blue tin box that is kept in a Jewish home. The women put small change in it and donate the money to an Israeli charity. In our house, it was used to plant trees in Israel.
Sabbath	The Jewish Sabbath is from Friday at sundown to Saturday at sundown.
Schlep	(adj.) Drag or haul.
Schlep	(noun) A dope, a slowpoke.
Schlub	A gauche, insensitive person; a yokel.
Schmaltz	Rendered chicken fat; used to flavor casseroles and even as a spread for sandwiches.
Schmata	A rag; an old dress unfit to be seen in public.
Schnook	A fool; an idiot.
Schtupp	To fuck in the coarsest sense of the word; literally, to shove it in.
Schul	A synagogue; a Jewish house of worship.
Seder	(pronounced say-der) The combination dinner and religious service that initiates Passover, the holiday celebrating the Jews' exodus from Egypt.

Shabbes	The Jewish Sabbath from Friday at sundown to Saturday at sundown.
Shayner	Beautiful.
Shochet	The authorized slaughterer of kosher meat. He is supervised by a rabbi.
The Sisterhood	The woman's organization composed of the members of a particular temple or synagogue. It is a local group; Hadassah is its international counterpart.
Torah	The first five books of the Bible; the entire body of Jewish faith, morality, ethics, social thought and culture.
Trayf	Not kosher.
Tsedrayt	Wacky; demented.
Yahrtzeit candle	A small glass of paraffin with a wick that burns twenty-four hours. Jews light this candle on the anniversary of a loved one's death.
Yarmulke	A small caplet worn by religious Jewish men.
Yiddish	The language of the Jews of Eastern Europe.
Yom Kippur	Day of Atonement, the holiest of all Jewish holidays where Jews fast for twenty-four hours and absolve themselves of their sins committed in the past year.
Zayde	Grandfather; an old man.